REBEL BRIDE

ELIZABETH MOSS

sourcebooks
casablanca

Published by Sourcebooks Casablanca, an imprint of Sourcebooks, Inc.
P.O. Box 4410, Naperville, Illinois 60567-4410
(630) 961-3900
Fax: (630) 961-2168
www.sourcebooks.com

Originally published in 2014 in Great Britain by Hodder & Stoughton, an
imprint of Hachette UK.

Library of Congress Cataloging-in-Publication Data

Moss, Elizabeth (Novelist)
  Rebel bride / Elizabeth Moss.
      pages ; cm
  (trade paper : alk. paper) 1. Great Britain—History—Henry VIII, 1509-
1547—Fiction. I. Title.
  PR6112.A497R43 2015
  823'.92--dc23

2015031432

Printed and bound in the United States of America.
VP 10 9 8 7 6 5 4 3 2 1

To His Rebellious Mistress

I thought thee devil-sent: to love dishonestly.
For once my love was lust, I do confess.
My mind was not by vows, but carnally
Devour'd, my rebel love, my sweet temptress.
Now more than ever am I drawn to thee
To spend my passions on thy nakedness
And revel in our sin, if sin it be
To yield to love and love's hot lustfulness.
My prison walls have given me the key
To chains that bound me to this cold address
That lust I named, and now call ardency,
Yearning for its consummation more, not less:
I love thee now more true, rebelliously,
Than ever I did love when I was free.

—Hugh Beaufort, 1536

Prologue

Lord Wolf's estate, Yorkshire, England, March 1536

THE AFTERNOON WAS UNSEASONABLY warm for March, a too-bright sun glinting on Susannah's long, fair tresses as she rode ahead of Hugh Beaufort, making for her new brother-in-law's hall. From time to time she swayed delicately in her sidesaddle, turning to smile back at him. And Hugh, having steeled himself to resist her country beauty, found himself staring back like a fool, his breath strangled in his throat.

Again, he reminded himself that she was but eighteen years of age and not a prize he could ever hope to seize.

Susannah glanced back at him again, an inviting look in her eyes. Her simple gown had fallen off one shoulder, the pale skin beneath reddening slowly in the sunshine. Her mouth was a little wide to be considered attractive in court circles, and she was too forward in her manners. But he could not help imagining what it would feel like to slip his tongue between those generous lips, and feel her squirm beneath him, urging him to lose control.

"Is the hall far from here, sir?" she asked, though she had been born only a few miles from this spot and must surely know the land better than him. "I swear, I am grown so hot under this sun, I can scarcely breathe."

By the rood, the young virgin was teasing him.

His body stiffened with desire, his response almost painful. It was only through an act of painstaking mental discipline that he resisted the lure of her body and did not ride forward, dragging her from the horse. He recalled how Wolf's hawk had come plummeting out of the blue sky earlier that morning, snatching at its meat with vicious talons, and knew the same hunger drove him too. Like talons from above, driving down. A whistling sound, then thwack: she would be under him.

Though perhaps Susannah was the hawk here, and he the hapless prey. How to tell the difference?

"Another half hour's ride, by my count," Hugh managed huskily. He pointed ahead, hoping the girl would stop gazing wide-eyed at him and follow the line of his arm instead. "Over that way, beyond the woods there."

Why in God's name had he ever agreed to escort this headstrong wench back to Lord Wolf's home?

The colossal stupidity of his offer. "My lord, if you permit it, I would be happy to ride back to the hall with Mistress Susannah," he had suggested back at Wolf's hunting lodge. For Susannah had asked to return to the hall, not wishing to explore the old hunting lodge with her sister, and Lord Wolf had glanced at him meaningfully. So he, like a fool, had leaped in to smooth over the awkward moment.

Wolf might be a soldier, one of the king's top commanders, but he was also a newly married man and wished to be alone with his bride.

"You may then show the lodge to your lady," Hugh had offered lightly, for he and Lord Wolf had been friends some years now, "and return home in your own time."

Hugh grimaced, jabbing compulsively at his reins as he remembered his naive suggestion. He had spoken with genuinely good intentions, unaware of how Susannah's smile would weaken his resolve once they were alone together on the ride. Never one to lose his head over a pretty face, he had thought himself safe from the lusts that beset other young men of the court.

But now, riding alone with Susannah in this broad, empty Yorkshire landscape, no other person in sight for miles, the temptation to take what she was offering—even unawares—was powerful indeed.

He had met maids like her before, of course. Girls fresh come to court and too innocent to know how strongly a man might be moved by a smile and a sidelong glance. And he had broken a few maidenheads in his youth, and enjoyed them too, for he was no saint.

But Susannah was no ripe apricot he could pluck from the bough and taste at his whim, the juice running down his chin. She was the daughter of Sir John Tyrell, a respectable landowner, and one of the oldest knights of King Henry's court. She was also now the sister-in-law of Lord Wolf, by all accounts one of the most powerful men in the kingdom these days, and close to the king.

To seduce a girl like Susannah would result in a forced marriage. And he had little to offer the daughter of a landed gentleman besides his current usefulness to the king. So he might end up in the Tower of London instead, for debauching a respectable virgin without the means or the ability to make her father due recompense.

This was all Wolf's fault, he thought bitterly.

Lord Wolf had suggested to him before their ride out to the lodge that he would be grateful for a little time alone with his new bride.

"Eloise needs to see me away from the hall," Wolf had explained quietly as they mounted their horses outside the sunlit hall. "But it has been hard to separate her from her younger sister these past few days. I know you are my guest here, Hugh, but you would be doing me a kindness if you could spirit Susannah away from Eloise today. Just an hour might suffice."

Hugh had looked at his friend with raised brows, tempted though he was by the idea of spending time alone with the pretty Susannah.

"Is that quite wise, my lord?" he had queried. "The girl is not easy to manage. And she is all but betrothed to Sir William Hanney, for you know Sir John is intent on giving her as a bride to his old friend from the campaigns."

"Oh, I trust you not to sully her innocence," Wolf had replied with a laugh, then swung up into the saddle.

Hugh had smiled. "As you wish, my lord."

He had been flattered at the time by that unquestioning trust. Now though, it seemed grossly misplaced. For the more distance he put between himself and the remote hunting lodge where they had left Wolf and his new wife, the more tempted he was to become improperly intimate with Eloise's fair sister.

Which would hardly please her father, nor her prospective bridegroom, the elderly Sir William Hanney.

They passed through a bank of trees, then found the ground sloping away. As they descended, he could no longer see Wolf Hall in the distance, but kept his eye on a large rocky outcrop on the other side of the valley, for he felt sure they had passed that on the ride out that morning.

The ground became rough and waterlogged in the valley bottom, tussocks of thick grass and reeds barring the narrow track. He rode with one hand on his sword hilt, for he did not know the countryside in that part of Yorkshire, but knew the inhabitants were not always friendly. On their journey north from the court, a small party of armed raiders had set upon their cavalcade and might have killed them if it had not been for Wolf's military training and the courage of his men.

This was Wolf's land though, of course, and Hugh did not expect to be attacked. But it was in his nature to be cautious.

A few paces ahead of him, Susannah glanced over her shoulder in that same inviting way, smoothing back her rather wild fair hair. He set his jaw hard, and wondered if the foolish girl had any idea how much he was tempted to despoil her.

Suddenly she gave a startled cry, snatching up her reins as her mare stumbled and almost fell. "A rabbit hole!"

He spurred his mount forward at once, and reined to a halt beside her. The mare limped on a few paces and he followed, frowning, for the animal seemed in distress.

"What is it, mistress? Is your mount hurt?"

"Oh, poor Lady," Susannah exclaimed, and jumped down easily from her sidesaddle without even waiting to be helped. "It is my fault; I was not watching where I was going."

Shaking out her crumpled skirts, she turned to examine the mare's fetlock, running a hand down it experimentally. The chestnut mare whinnied, dragging on the reins, and Susannah straightened, soothing the frightened beast with a gentle pat on her neck.

"I think Lady has a slight sprain. To be safe, I should not ride her back to the hall but must walk." She sighed. "What a nuisance. It's not far on horseback, but it will take ages on foot. And we have not yet crossed the river. My gown will be soaked."

"Nonsense," Hugh said shortly.

He dismounted and bent to examine the mare's fetlock himself. Sure enough, the unfortunate beast did appear to have suffered a strain through putting its hoof into a rabbit hole. He was surprised by Susannah's knowledge, and could not hide it. Most gentlewomen of his acquaintance did not have the first idea how to care for an animal.

"Well, you are right; it does appear to be strained. But as for walking, there is no need for such drastic measures. You will have to sit up before me, that is all," he told her, then saw her smile and the slight flush that entered her cheeks, and cursed himself for a fool.

"Though it might be better, over such rough terrain, for you to ride and me to lead the horse," he added.

Her blue eyes teased his. "Oh, it is not so difficult a journey from here, sir; I promise you."

"I thought you did not know this path."

"I have remembered it now." Susannah shook her head when he came to set her on his horse, a sudden merry defiance in her face. "There is no need for you to walk, good sir. You will ruin your fine courtly hose amongst these briars. Besides, I cannot sit that saddle. It is not fit for me."

The wench was mocking him. *You will ruin your fine courtly hose.* Why, he was wearing nothing but what was fashionable in the southern reaches. Thrown off balance by her laughter, Hugh struggled to keep his patience, unaccustomed to being mocked by young women.

Especially a young woman with eyes as blue as the sky in summer.

"And why not, pray?"

"That saddle has no hook for a lady. I cannot sit astride like a man, sir. It would not be seemly."

She was making fun of him, Hugh was sure of it now. *Not seemly?* He could not imagine any gently bred lady less concerned about seemliness than this one. "Then you must sit sidesaddle and…grip the horse's mane, mistress. That should suffice to steady you."

Impatiently, he put his hands to her waist, meaning to hoist her up onto his horse. But her arms came about his neck at the same time, dragging his head inexorably down to hers. He saw a bright flash—her blue eyes, dancing with mischief—then suddenly her mouth was on his, kissing him.

Afterward, Hugh could not have said for sure how it happened. One moment he was still in control, fully intending to push the saucy girl away and chastise her for such forwardness. The next moment his control had snapped, and he was kissing her back like a starving man.

Susannah might be inexperienced, an innocent virgin, but her lips felt like fire on his, impossibly hot. Reason fled on a wave of hunger, and Hugh jerked her close, abruptly needing to feel her whole body against his.

Her soft lips parted on a gasp of surprise, or perhaps fear.

At once, his tongue stroked inside her mouth, reveling in her taste, sweet as summer berries, intoxicating as wine on this hot afternoon.

God's blood, he chided himself, he should not be kissing her like this. He was one of the king's advisors, and he had been entrusted with Susannah's safety and well-being by Lord Wolf less than an hour ago. Yet here he was, breaking his word as a gentleman and a courtier, and taking shameless advantage of an innocent virgin.

"Hugh," she murmured against his mouth. Her hands slipped down his back and cupped his buttocks, pulling him harder into her.

Hugh was astonished by such wanton lustiness even as his cock hardened ferociously. Virgin she almost certainly was, but not as innocent as he had assumed.

To take such a firebrand into his bed…

He imagined what Sir John would say, receiving back a despoiled daughter. And his friend, Lord Wolf, who had handed the girl into his care. It had seemed a small thing at the time, accepting her charge. A short ride back to the hall across easy terrain. Instead, her horse had gone lame, she was burning up in his arms, and he had little doubt that in a few moments more he could have his way with her willing body.

Common sense finally reasserted itself.

"No," he exclaimed, dragging his mouth from hers.

Hugh expected words of accusation and reproach from the maiden, perhaps even a slapped cheek. And he fully deserved such affronts. Yet there was only a soft sigh from Susannah, who looked up at him dreamily, her eyes half-closed, her cheeks flushed.

"N-no, sir?"

"No," he repeated, more firmly this time. His hands tightened about her slender waist. "You will mount and I will lead the horse.

You are promised to Sir William Hanney. And I have sworn to escort you back to the hall unscathed, which I fully intend to do."

Frustratingly, Susannah seemed unmoved by this declaration. Her hands continued to cup his buttocks, squeezing them shamelessly. "But what if I should have no objections to being scathed?" she demanded, and tilted her head to one side like a little sparrow, watching him, curious to hear his response. "Would you change your mind, sir?"

His jaw clenched. "Get on the horse, Susannah."

"Or what?"

"Or I shall put you across my knee."

Her blue eyes flashed at that threat. "You like to hit women, do you?"

"I should very much like to discipline you," he said tightly, struggling to ignore the growing heat in his groin as he imagined this fair-haired termagant bent over his knee, her skirts raised. "This is not how a gentlewoman behaves, Susannah. You need a good spanking."

"Now you sound like my father," she said drily.

Susannah released his buttocks, but only so her hands could trail round to the front. He drew in a hiss of angry breath at her touch, then carefully reached down and seized both her wrists, holding her still.

"Have you no shame, girl?"

Her eyes widened as she took in his terse expression, seeming to grasp for the first time that he was serious. "I thought…" Her voice faltered. "You do not want me?"

Too late, he saw the wounded look in her eyes and was surprised. The girl had seemed wanton in her forwardness, and his response had met her head-on. Yet his refusal had stung, it seemed.

Or perhaps not.

She stepped back, her face cold. "Forgive me, sir. I misunderstood your purpose in escorting me."

There had been a sharp, almost accusatory note in her voice. Offended, he was unyielding in his reply. "My only purpose, as you put it, was to assist Lord Wolf."

She looked down, swallowing, and Hugh caught a glimpse of vulnerability in her eyes, a hurt that left him feeling as though he were in the wrong. That he was a churl, not only for having rejected her generous offer, but having done so in a most villainous manner.

"Lord Wolf," he continued more carefully, "wished to show his bride the lodge. You preferred to return to the hall. It was clear you could not return unaccompanied. I offered my escort for his lordship's sake, so his visit to the lodge need not be cut short." He weighed each word so as not to cause her further affront, but saw from her expression that it was to no avail. He had spurned the girl, and could not be lower in her eyes. He added pointedly, "Not so I might seduce you."

"Yet you did not push me away when first I set my lips on yours."

He could not deny it. "I am a man."

"As I can see."

Hugh noted her head toss and withering glance with the first stirrings of irritation. He had been right to think her pride stung by his rejection. Now she would make him suffer for it.

"Perhaps now you will mount," he said shortly, his gaze narrowed on her averted profile, "and allow me to lead the horses back to the hall? The afternoon grows long. We have wasted enough time on this…misunderstanding."

"Very well, sir. But I do not need your help to mount." Susannah glanced about herself. Her cheeks were flushed, her eyes overbright, but she seemed unrepentant. "I can stand on that rock if you would be good enough to lead the horse to me."

Against his will, Hugh's anger rose to meet hers. His hands closed about her waist, his gaze holding hers. Without a word he lifted her, hoisting her effortlessly toward the saddle.

Susannah did not struggle, light as a bird in his arms, but stared back at him, her lips slightly parted, darkly pink from where he had kissed them.

For a second she was in flight, poised above him, looking down. Dazzled by the sun, he had an impression of a fragile, tiny-boned creature, a lady of fairyland who he had caught unawares, her presence so fleeting she might vanish at any moment, disappearing back into his bewildered imagination.

Then she was seated on the horse, twining her fingers in the coarse mane, and he took a step back, breathing hard.

"Susannah," he began uncertainly, but she lifted a hand as though to silence him.

"You are right. We have wasted too long here." Her wild blue gaze lowered to his face and devoured him, like the fairy creature he had just thought her. For a moment he was torn with lust for her again, thrown off balance by that stare. But it seemed he had read her awry, for as their eyes met she looked away, suddenly dignified. "I wish to return to Wolf Hall at once, if you please."

With that, she kicked his horse and the animal walked briskly forward in response, leaving him standing like a fool, staring after her.

"Wait!"

Muttering an oath under his breath, Hugh gathered up her mare's fallen reins and strode after her, leading the lame horse up the steepening track. He looked at her corn-gold hair, which fell so invitingly to her waist, and cursed his friendship with Wolf. For what had struck him as an entertainment when he first met Eloise's younger sister, a game to while away a few dull months in the north of England, now felt like a serious misjudgment on his part.

This maiden was dangerous, he thought. He had come north on the king's business, not to seek a wife. God's blood, he was ill-fitted for marriage, unwilling to share his bed for longer than a night, even with a mistress.

On arrival, Hugh had intended to keep himself aloof from the locals, to visit the holy priories hereabouts and discreetly communicate their worth to King Henry on his return south. Nonetheless, Eloise's fair sister had caught his eye at their wedding feast, and Susannah herself had not been slow to return his smiles.

Foolishly, he had not discouraged the girl's interest. Hugh had thought a kiss or two behind her father's back would keep them both satisfied. But if he was not careful, he would soon be up to his neck in a flirtation that could cost him his freedom—and his hard-won place at court.

When he finally caught up with her and seized the reins, leading both horses back toward the hall, Susannah said nothing for the next few miles but sat very straight on his horse, swaying gently with the motion.

Perhaps she was no longer angry with him.

"Master Beaufort, will you stay on in the north for my marriage to Sir William Hanney?" she asked abruptly as the hall came in sight. "Our wedding had been set for this autumn. But my father says I may have to marry him sooner, for Sir William is an old man and his health is ailing."

Disturbed by the vision of her impending nuptials, Hugh could not at first reply. The bile rose in his gorge at the thought of this fair young maiden in an old man's bed. It should not be allowed, he thought furiously, his nails biting into his palms. That she should be forced to submit herself…

"Sir?" she prompted him softly, and he had the impression that she was well aware of his disgust.

"I must return to court within the month."

"Oh." She sounded disappointed. Even a little lost. "So soon?"

He did not trust himself to look back at her, to meet that fierce blue gaze again. For she would surely know what he was thinking, and his weakness could be no help to her in the coming months.

If Susannah Tyrell was to marry Sir William Hanney, she ought to resign herself to that fate as soon as possible, not waste her time on dreams of younger men.

"If I were to run away," she whispered as though to herself, "I might be spared that marriage."

He said flatly, "You would be found and returned to your father."

"Not if I was in the company of another man."

His jaw tightened. "A daydream. You have some unfortunate man in mind for this escapade?"

There was a long pause. "You."

"God's blood."

Briefly, his eyes closed. Even more briefly Hugh knew himself tempted by her suggestion. Run away with Susannah. Despoil her innocence at his leisure in some private place. Ruin her for marriage. Enjoy her hot kisses and her slender body writhing beneath him. The things he would teach her…

His cock hardened.

Then he thought of King Henry's anger, and his standing at court, and the all-but-empty purse at his side, and disabused himself of that insane notion at once.

God protect me from respectable young virgins, he prayed fervently. For their ruination shall also be mine.

"It would never happen, Susannah. I have nothing to offer your father as a prospective son-in-law. No money. No property. Not even a title." He spoke coolly, for it was nothing but the truth. "I am a younger son. I must accept bouge of court from His Majesty, and cannot afford to keep a wife by my side."

"Then I shall be your mistress."

"Enough!"

His mistress indeed. As if a country virgin could understand what such a life would entail: the disgrace of it, the cold looks from other women, the lewd advances she would face from other courtiers. Yet if it were not for her father's justified anger, Susannah Tyrell would make a good mistress, warm and willing in his bed, and he knew it.

Desire coiled inside him again like a serpent. Wolf Hall might be in sight, but the temptation to pull this sorceress from his horse and make love to her on the sunlit grass was almost overwhelming.

Hugh looked at her and saw the hope in her face. He knew he must be cruel and crush any girlish affection for him still lingering in her heart. The thought of this young firebrand married to her ancient suitor and pining away for Hugh every night was too much to bear. He knew what punishments she might face as a young bride who would not submit.

Better for Susannah that she should hate Hugh and accept her husband instead. Not risk a nightly beating for refusal.

"I will return to court and you will marry Sir William as your father intends." He shrugged, trying to sound careless. "It is for the best anyway. I could never marry a girl whose virginity I cannot trust. If you have thrown yourself at me, perhaps other men have tasted your lips too. No, when I marry, it will be to a demure and innocent maiden. Not a headstrong wanton who cannot keep her hands off me."

She said nothing, but when he glanced back at her as they approached the hall, Hugh felt his breath catch at the contempt in her eyes.

Better the girl should hate me, he reminded himself, than disobey her father's wishes and be punished for it. But he knew himself unsettled by the look of betrayal in those fierce blue eyes. And when he lay in bed that night, remembering how she had kissed him with such naked desire, another voice whispered in his heart that he was a fool and a coward, and deserved a beating himself for not stealing Susannah away while he could.

One

SUSANNAH SAT AT THE open window in the late afternoon sunshine, plaiting her hair and staring down into the yard below. There always seemed to be noise and bustle at her father's manor house, for it stood on the southern edge of the village and was a farm too. On fine spring days like this the high walls of the yard echoed to the noisy squawks of fowl and the grunts of young black piglets rooting in the dirt. Her fingers worked slowly, twining her hair into a plait, for she was bored of Yorkshire and bored of her father's house, so confined she might as well be dead.

A piglet ran squealing across the yard on short stubby trotters and she watched it sullenly. A place farther removed from the elegant pleasures of court she could not imagine.

Her old nurse, Morag, appeared below at the back door, shooing two of the younger kitchen maids outside. The silly girls stood giggling and nudging each other, making laps with their stained aprons into which she poured a few handfuls of feed for the chickens. Then Morag disappeared inside, closing the door, and the two maids began to scoop feed out of their aprons, scattering it and kicking away the eager chickens.

It was such a warm afternoon, Susannah thought, it might almost be summer. She watched three laborers in old-fashioned smocks cross the yard, heading for the meadowlands beyond. Their coarse hats drooped across their foreheads against the sun. One of the men called out a lazy greeting to Tom Hobarth as he came panting through the yard. The massive old porter was carrying a dusty hod of red bricks, balanced over one shoulder, his load bound for the back of the kitchens, where the wall was being extended to make way for a newfangled oven.

Her plait had gone badly awry, Susannah realized, and tugged at it impatiently, struggling to untwine the thick golden strands.

Five days.

That was how long it had been since Hugh Beaufort had departed for the court, accompanying her sister and Lord Wolf on horseback. By all accounts it was a long and tiring journey from Yorkshire to the southern reaches where the court lay that spring, but five days would probably suffice. Eloise and Wolf should be there by now, discreetly housed in some comfortable apartment near the king, with silken bedspreads and the best French wine on their table. Hugh might lodge with some other gentleman, or perhaps he had a chamber of his own, for he was high in King Henry's favor by all accounts.

Hugh Beaufort would never think of her now. He had royal business to attend to, his books and accounts. Eloise would not miss her either. For how could she? No doubt there would be hunting during the day, then dancing and feasting in the evenings, the courtiers dressed in their costly finery and waited on by liveried servants as they attended the king and queen.

"Oh, why could you not have taken me with you to court, Eloise?" she demanded of the air, then wrinkled up her nose at the stink from below her window. "This place is a prison…and full of squealing piglets!"

Giving up on the plait, which hung half-untwined over one shoulder like a fraying yellow bell rope, Susannah jumped up and went to the door.

"Morag?"

But her old nurse did not answer her call.

Leaning over the landing rail, Susannah peered down into the darkened stairwell, calling out "Morag!" again.

Nothing stirred in the unlit hallway. All the servants were too busy with their chores to heed her, she thought bitterly, and listened to the clatter of pots from the kitchen, the hoarse shouts of the cook that meant preparations for supper were already underway.

Besides, she was no longer important. Her father would see her married off to Sir William Hanney soon, and then her life would be over, if it was not over already. She supposed that at least once she was married she would have a personal maid to change her gowns and fashion her hair as befitted a married lady. Until then, she must learn to plait her own wayward tresses and not call for Morag every time like a child.

Sighing, Susannah wandered along the dark hallway. The floorboards creaked, but she knew where to step to avoid the noise. It was odd to think she would soon be mistress of her own house, perhaps never to return here to the manor, the home where she had grown up without a mother, only Morag and her sister, Eloise, to guide her.

The door to Eloise's old bedchamber was ajar. She went inside and stood staring about at the chaos: emptied clothes chests, lids thrown open, a poorly stitched cloth sweet bag of dried rose petals split, its contents strewn across the floor, the mattress stripped of its linens, even the window shutters fastened tight against the sunshine.

The disused bedchamber smelled musty, for the fire had not been lit in weeks. Susannah ran a finger along the dusty bedpost. She had not realized how much she would miss having her older sister back at home. She had barely thought of her while Eloise was at court, after all. But perhaps seeing her again, and hearing all her tales of court life, had made Susannah all the more acutely aware of how narrow and confined her life was in Yorkshire. And how she might suffer once she too was married. Not just in her everyday life but at night, in her marriage bed.

Sir William Hanney was no Lord Wolf, that was for sure. She would never start the day as she had seen her married sister do, with flushed cheeks and coyly downcast eyes…

A sudden loud creaking above her head made her stiffen.

What on earth?

She stared up at the ceiling beams, frowning.

Only the longest-serving female servants had bedchambers in the attic. And she had thought them all at their chores this afternoon. Yet the creaking continued overhead, strangely rhythmic. Then a sharp cry split the silence. A high female cry, abruptly hushed as though cut off in mid-breath.

Immediately following the cry, Susannah heard the threatening rumble of a man's voice in the attic chamber above.

Her eyes widened.

The kitchen maids and younger house servants slept in the kitchens, and the seamstress and housekeeper lodged together in the front attic. Only Morag's smaller chamber was above this part of the manor house.

Was her old nurse in trouble? Had she been attacked by one of the men? Perhaps her father's chamberman, for Renford could be a surly brute when he had taken too much ale.

Horrified, Susannah ran along the landing to the heavy door that hid the servants' stairs. It creaked open noisily, and she gathered her skirts, staring up into glimmering darkness, for the door at the top was also shut. She had not been up into the attic quarters for several years, for her father was strict about keeping the family apart from the servants.

There was no time to call for assistance. If some villain was hurting Morag, and all the other servants were busy elsewhere…

Ducking her head for the low ceiling, Susannah ran breathlessly up the stairs. "Morag?" she called, emerging on the attic landing.

The dark space was narrow and unadorned, the floorboards warped and split, yet clean-swept. She recalled playing here once as a girl, in the forbidden place, and screaming at some house beetle that had come scuttling out of a knot in the wainscot, large and black as a polished chess piece. How her father had scolded her afterward, seeming to appear out of nowhere, red-faced, his temper up like a spring wind.

Some terrible premonition came to her. Her gown snagged on a nail in the wall as she hurried along; she swore under her breath, tugging it loose so the material tore.

"Morag, where are you?"

At that moment, the door to Morag's attic chamber flew open. She straightened, staring hard, and met her father's furious glare.

"How dare you come up into the servants' quarters, Susannah? This is no fit place for you." Her father seized her by the arm and shook her like a rag doll. "Get you back down the stairs to your chamber at once, and if I do not put my horse whip about your sides, it will only be out of regard for your tender sex."

His face was flushed, his breathing erratic. It was impossible to miss that his shirt and doublet were not fastened as they should be, his silver hair disheveled, his hose askew.

"But Father, I heard…"

"I said, get you back to your chamber!" His hand flashed out like a magpie wing, dark in her eyes, bringing a flash of white as it met her cheek. She went sprawling back and Sir John stepped over her, tall in his rage. "And don't bother coming down to supper. There will be no place set for you tonight, girl. I will teach you not to meddle in what does not concern you."

Fastening his doublet, her father lurched to the end of the landing and shouldered his way through the narrow doorway. Susannah groped blindly up the wall and stood listening as he slammed downstairs. Her hand was at her cheek, her mouth gaping.

"Let me see that," Morag offered gently from the doorway behind her.

Susannah turned, blinking back her tears. It was hard to speak without her voice wavering. "I don't understand," she began, then looked at her old nurse more closely.

Morag wore nothing but her shift dress, and stood barefoot on the floorboards, showing her thick ankles and swollen feet without shame. Her long graying hair had been unpinned; it hung loose about her shoulders. And there was a strange, wild look in her eyes. When Susannah glanced past her into the narrow attic chamber, she saw the pins scattered across the floor, and Morag's demure white cap and workaday gown lying in a heap beside the unmade bed.

Truth hit her violently. "You and my father were...are..." She could not finish, but stammered something incoherent, willing Morag to deny it. Make it into a jest. Any response would do. She willed it fervently but Morag stood silent. "Oh sweet Lord, no."

Morag held her gaze steadily. "Do not judge me, Susannah." She brushed Susannah's hot cheek with the back of her hand. She was trembling. "That is only for God to do."

"I do not judge you." Susannah caught her hand, squeezing it gently. A wave of sympathy flooded her. Swiftly followed by horror. "Morag, does my father force you to...couple with him?"

Morag lowered her gaze, her flush deepening. "It did feel like that at first," she admitted. "Sir John is master here, and I have been his servant since I was little better than a child. There was never any thought in my head to refuse him. But it is many years now since he first..." She stopped, and a defiant look crept into her face. "I have no complaint against Sir John. We give each other comfort."

"Comfort?" Susannah's voice was high.

"After your mother died..." Morag drew a sharp breath. "Your father could never have wed me: my station is too far beneath his. But we had an understanding."

"Oh, Morag."

"You will not speak of this to the other servants, will you? Some of them have guessed, but we try to be discreet." Morag bit her lip. "I had forgot you were returned from Wolf Hall. Else we would have found some other place to—"

"No more, I beg of you!" Susannah exclaimed, and clapped her hands on her ears.

Morag looked at her sorrowfully. "Forgive me, little one. You are still so young. I would not have had you discover such a thing before you were even wed yourself. You will not understand this now, but men have…needs. Your mother has been dead these many years, and although your father chose not to remarry, yet he is still a man."

Her mind flew back, horrified, to the conversation with Hugh Beaufort. I am a man, he had said, as if that alone explained his desire. Not that she was a woman and desirable. But that he was a man.

She backed away when her old nurse would have embraced her. "All these years, you and my father have been lovers."

"I know it is a sin, but it is not so terrible," Morag tried to re-assure her, following as Susannah stumbled down to her chamber. "Susannah, wait. This was not a choice I made willingly. Once you are wed to Sir William, you will see how it is, and…and forgive me."

Susannah shut herself in her chamber, and leaned against the door, breathing hard.

"Please, Susannah, let me in."

"Go away," she cried, and would not open the door. Her cheek ached. Why must her father have such a heavy hand? "I need to be alone."

"Allow me to bring you some supper up on a tray. You cannot sit in your chamber and starve, child."

"I am not a child anymore. And yes, I can."

Morag sighed, speaking more softly through the door. "You are right. Sometimes I forget you are no longer my little one. Well, let me bring you a bowl of stew at least."

"No, I shall fast like a nun, and come to no harm through it. Besides, you risk a whipping yourself if you go against my father, and I will not have you punished for my fault."

When Morag had finally given up and gone down to the kitchen, Susannah sat down at the open window, tearing once again at her wayward plait. She thought of her father. His doublet unfastened, hose askew. His cold fury. Morag's sharp cry above her head.

Once you are wed to Sir William, you will see how it is.

Her fingers trembled.

The rustic smell of the animals in the yard below was suddenly unbearable. She slammed the shutters across, enclosing herself in welcome darkness.

Hugh Beaufort had rejected her because she was too rustic in her ways, a girl with clumsy manners and the rough burr of Yorkshire in her voice. And who could blame him for returning to the court with Lord Wolf and Eloise after their summons, back to a more elegant and civilized way of life? What a fool she had been to think any courtier would want a simple girl like her, that he might save her from the marriage her father had arranged to the vile old Sir William. Master Beaufort, every inch the king's man, like Lord Wolf himself, must have laughed himself sick at her advances, and thought himself lucky to be offered a chance to escape without having to slap her down openly.

On that ride back, she had thrown herself at him without any shame. Yet Hugh had not even bothered to seduce her for the sake of his entertainment. And why would he? She was a country clod whose father rutted with her nurse and put his daughters' maidenheads up for sale like young breeding sows at a village fair.

A knife hung at her belt for cutting thread and meat at table. She fingered it. Why not?

How furious old Sir William would be, pulling away her veil after the wedding ceremony to find not the long golden tresses he so admired, but the shorn locks beneath of a rebellious bride. Indeed, if he heard Susannah had cut all her hair off, the elderly knight might drop his suit for her hand and turn his attention to some more obedient young virgin instead.

Stone-faced, Susannah unsheathed the blade and set it to her thick, fair plait and began to saw away at her hair, just above the shoulder.

To be a woman is to be weak, she thought fiercely. I will not be weak.

The blade was a little blunt though, and would not cut easily. A few golden strands came away in her hand and she stared down at them, suddenly shaken by the enormity of what she was doing. She recalled how Hugh Beaufort had stroked her long fair hair as they kissed, looking at her afterward with undisguised lust.

Hugh would never look at her that way again, she realized, chagrined. Not once she had hair short as a boy's.

While she had no desire to trap her head in the marriage noose—even for such a handsome, green-eyed courtier as Master Hugh Beaufort—she did not wish to remain a virgin all her life. And only a nun would willingly part with her tresses.

Putting down her knife, she rummaged for a box of pins and began pinning up her golden plait instead, coiling it high, so that it did not even touch the nape of her neck.

She had a plan.

To her relief, dusk arrived with no further visitations from either Morag or her father. Susannah heard the supper bell being rung out in the yard, followed by feet on the stairs, loud voices in the hall, then silence. During this quiet time, she drew together a few things, emptied the coins from her jewelry box, then crept into her sister's old room for ink and a quill, and a piece of spare parchment.

By candlelight she sat and penned a few terse lines, which nonetheless took nearly an hour to compose.

She waited until she was sure Morag was not bringing her up a supper tray, then crept out of her chamber and listened. She could hear the servants at dinner below, the muffled hubbub of their conversation, yet no sound from her father's dining room.

But then he would be dining alone tonight.

She slipped down into the hall, expecting at any moment to be discovered and chided. But all was quiet. The door to the linen store stood closed but not locked. She opened the door and groped about in the dark, eventually locating first an empty old linen sack, then a pair of loose men's trousers and a coarse smock shirt in the chest reserved for men servants.

Breathlessly, she hurried back up to her room with this treasure. She dragged off her night rail and donned male attire instead, and then examined herself critically in the candlelight. She was tall for a girl, but the trousers still had to be doubled over at the hem. The smock shirt drowned her, but at least it hid her breasts convincingly.

About two hours after sundown her father came stumbling drunkenly up the stairs and slammed into his chamber, further down the landing. Soon afterward the dogs were chased out into the yard below, then the bolts were drawn across, and the manor house quietened toward bedtime.

Susannah opened the shutters quietly, then sat watching as the chief groom finished his check of the stables and climbed the ladder to his quarters in the hay loft, his closed lantern the only light permitted to be kindled there for risk of fire.

Once she saw his candle extinguished, she snuffed out her own, then left her chamber for the last time, having to avoid each creaking floorboard from memory as she crept to the stairs.

Susannah heard her father turn over heavily in bed, his door only a few feet away, his snores interrupted as though he had just woken up.

Her heart beat painfully.

The darkness itself seemed to thicken as she waited, every sense alert, until she heard her father begin to snore again. Still terrified of discovery, she negotiated the ancient stairs, freezing at every tiny sound, her meager bundle of possessions thrown over one shoulder in the linen sack.

Pausing in the hall, she stole a pair of boots from the store room, leaving her own thin-soled slippers in their place, then took a patched and hooded old cloak and cap of her father's from his private closet. The cloak dragged behind her with every step, far too long, and she could not see anything with the hood up. But the cap was a surprisingly good fit, though it sat awkwardly on her coiled plait. So she pushed the hood back and wore the cap instead. At least they were so old it was unlikely anyone would miss them. Not for a few days, at least.

She made her way out through the narrow pantry window, for the main entrance was kept bolted at night and the potmen slept in the kitchen door passage. Although the window was narrow, she had climbed through it a few times as a child. But that was before her hips had grown, she thought ruefully, eyeing the impossible opening in the wall.

Tossing her pack out first, Susannah struggled to squeeze through the stone-framed window; she finally tumbled out and down a steep slope into what had once been a moat. She rolled helplessly all the way down, higgledy-piggledy; fetched up by her pack at the bottom, and lay there staring backward, panting and terrified that someone might have heard her precipitous descent.

A dog barked somewhere, then fell silent. The house was upside down, a dark looming edifice without lights. Above it, black and faintly starlit, the night sky wheeled.

She stared up into blackness, suddenly dizzy, and turning her head fixed her gaze on the quarter moon instead, waxing gently as it rose.

Her father's old cap had fallen off.

On hands and knees, she retrieved the cap, then stumbled along the track toward the courtyard gate. Her father kept deer in the old moat; several raised their heads as she passed, then quietly continued cropping the dewy night grasses.

A hound was sleeping across the entrance to the stable block. He whined and wagged his tail in a perplexed manner at her approach, as though inquiring why she was out of bed at such a late hour. She crouched and fussed over him for a moment, then stepped over him and unlatched the stable door as noiselessly as she could.

Above her head she heard the chief groom and his stable boy snoring. Only the horses stirred, watching as she led out her favorite sorrel mare, a tidy jennet named Mirabella. Hoping the sound of Mirabella's hooves would be muffled on the tight-packed earth of the stable yard, Susannah paused only to steal a saddle and tack. She almost reached for the cumbersome sidesaddle before she remembered she was dressed as a boy.

She hurriedly adjusted the broad girth straps, fitted the iron bit, then looped the reins about the horse's head, and was suddenly grateful for having watched this done a hundred times. Else she might have stood here all night trying to understand the workings of the saddle straps.

Just as she was finishing, the mare whinnied questioningly, no doubt nervous at the thought of a moonlit ride.

"Hush, girl," she whispered in the mare's cocked ear, then tugged on the bridle, turning the agitated animal toward the mounting post. "Another minute, we will be on the road and free."

Then Susannah froze in horror. The horse shifted, tossing her head restlessly. For both had heard the unmistakable sound of a bolt being drawn back on the kitchen door.

Who would be coming out into the yard in the middle of the night? Unless she been missed already. Perhaps the horse neighing had woken one of the servants who slept each night on the kitchen floor.

Climbing the mounting post, she dragged herself up into the saddle with no attempt at dignity. It felt clumsy and unfamiliar to be seated astride, but there was no time to adjust. For in the doorway to the kitchen stood Renford, her father's servant, holding up a lantern to survey the dark yard. His head turned toward her and Mirabella, then he raised a shout, alerting the grooms.

"Hey there, thief!" He began to run toward her, the lantern swinging violently. "Stop boy, get down off that horse. You'll hang for this!"

Renford thought her a thief. Which she was, of course. Though not the way he assumed.

Dragging Mirabella's head round, she kicked her rather hard in the ribs and felt the jennet mare leap forward. No doubt she was startled by the angry shouts, for she responded with eagerness, heading straight for the muddy track away from the manor house, riding toward the village. Behind them Susannah heard shouts but did not dare look back, bent low over the mare's neck, her fingers tangled in the mane for safety.

"Quick as the wind, Mirabella!" she urged her mount, though the moon had slipped behind a cloud and the way ahead was black.

Despite the darkness they soon came to the head of the track where the road led either north toward Thirsk, where her old aunt lived, or south toward London and the king's court.

She had not thought this far ahead, Susannah realized with a start, pulling the horse up while she considered both directions. To own the truth, she had not truly believed she would get this far.

Behind her, thudding hooves and coarse shouts broke the

stillness of the night. Renford or one of the grooms had mounted and was coming in pursuit. Perhaps more than one man.

If she was discovered like this, dressed as a boy on a stolen horse, she would be utterly disgraced. Her father would give her a whipping, and he had a hard hand when his anger was roused. Her marriage to Sir William would be hastened, not called off. Her fists clenched at the injustice. The hypocrisy. All these years she had thought him pining for her dead mother. But Sir John had been content with Morag's obedience, and felt no need to shackle himself to a wife of his own station, who might nag him or demand an expensive bride-gift.

No, why should Sir John marry when he could take his pleasure in Morag's bed with no cost to himself? He had no care for his daughters' unhappiness in marriage though, so long as they were matched according to his will.

Well, she would not marry that dotard Sir William. Not for all the gold in the king's coffers. Let the two old men stew over her flight. She would ride for London and the court, and once there…

She was already turning Mirabella's head toward the south when the wicked idea stole into her head, unbidden. She would find Hugh Beaufort at court and seduce him. Make that big, green-eyed courtier want her, and lose his careful control, and be sorry he had ever rejected her. Though not so she could marry Hugh and give herself into his keeping, as Eloise had done with Wolf.

Marriage was not for her, not if marriage was what she had seen from her father's example, where a wife was a possession and not meant for love. She disdained to accept what a man would not offer willingly but which must be gained through seductive wiles and feigned obedience. Besides, what kind of freedom was it that consisted of merely passing herself from one man's power to another, from father to husband?

No, she would become Hugh's mistress, if he would have her,

until they tired of each other. Then her choices would be her own, not enforced by law. And it was an old custom for mistresses to be tolerated at court, or so she had heard. Even lusty King Henry had taken his pick of his courtiers' wives, with none daring to say him nay: it was whispered as many as a dozen of his bastards were running about the court under other men's names, only one or two acknowledged as his own.

For a short while, at least, she could lie in Master Beaufort's bed without a stitch on her body and let him make love to her as his mistress. Flaunt her wantonness before the court, as other women had done before her, as the queen herself was accused of having done.

And bring her father much-deserved ruination.

Two

HE WAS HUGE. A god. Thick fair hair, green eyes, shoulders that could ram doors, and almost foreign with that elegant southern drawl that made her shiver. Somehow he had found her in the forest, appearing out of nowhere in the cool dawn light. Susannah was staring up at him as he lowered her to the earth, then put his mouth to hers. She moaned a little, but did not push him away. His breath was warm and sweet, his tongue licking, licking…

"Faugh!" she exclaimed, her head suddenly jerking up as she realized it was not the seductive Hugh Beaufort who was licking her face but a small black and white terrier.

A dog?

She forced herself awake.

It was indeed dawn, she realized, the misty air cool enough to raise gooseflesh on her arms and the back of her neck. She was half-sitting, half-lying, wrapped awkwardly in her father's cloak under a tree in a small stretch of woodland. Her body was stiff as an old woman's. A toadstool had sprouted near her face during the night, pale and unpleasantly fleshy, and beneath it a fat-bellied cob spider was crawling across a gossamer thread.

And she could taste dog on her lips, she thought, grimly wiping her mouth with the back of her hand.

Above her the new budded leaves shone, unfurling in hope of sunlight to come. The wood was still and quiet about her, a light wind barely stirring the branches.

The dog had run away at her exclamation, but now turned,

barking defiantly and wagging his tail at the same time, apparently oblivious to the contradiction.

"Shoo!" she told the dog, and scrambled to her feet, picking leaves and dirt from her hair before reaching down for her cap. It must have tumbled off while she was sleeping.

The terrier barked a few more times, then trotted away through the wood. She watched him, a little concerned to see a dog out here on its own. She hoped there were no homesteads nearby. He had not looked like a wild dog. But perhaps the poor thing was lost.

"I must look a sight," she muttered, bending to tidy her rumpled clothing. The too-long sleeves of her rough smock slipped down over her hands; she pushed them up, folding back the stiff cuffs, then stretched and yawned.

She had stopped riding last night when the moon finally disappeared behind thick cloud and the road became too dangerous to negotiate. Knowing her father's men might pass along the road in the morning, hunting for her, she had ridden roughly half a mile into the woods before finding this sheltered spot. A bank protected from the wind, a row of ancient beech trees, and a stream rushing nearby.

Exhausted, she had sought out the stream in the darkness, both her and Mirabella gulping down the chill water with gratitude. Then she had tied her mount to a thorn bush, dragged off the mare's saddle, and crawled up to sleep under her cloak.

Now though she was thirsty again, starving too, badly needed to relieve herself, and…where was Mirabella?

The little hollow between trees where she had secured Mirabella last night was empty.

Gathering up her cloak and riding gloves in a panic, she began to walk toward the stream, whistling and calling her horse, "Mirabella? Mirabella?"

Susannah reached the fast-flowing stream, but there was no sign of the jennet mare. She had been there at some point since last night though; the shallow edges of the stream were muddied with hoof prints, several feet away from where they had drunk in the darkness. The opposite bank was rocky, constantly splashed with water from the race of swirling water beside it. There was no way to tell where Mirabella had gone next.

She stood on the mossed bank, staring up and down the stream. The dawn mist was beginning to rise; a warmth on her back suggested a fine day ahead. To be out here alone with no horse, no way of escape from her pursuers, no way to reach London except on foot, which could take her ten days or more…

Without Mirabella, she might as well return home.

A shout made her spin around, horrified. An old man with a rough handcart, struggling through the woods, had seen her.

"Hey there!" he called out in a thick northern accent, dropping the long wooden spars of the handcart and stopping to stare. His beard was long and grizzled, yet he wore some manner of faded and torn blue livery, as though he had once served some local dignitary. "You, boy!"

Susannah backed away, shaking her head in mute denial, and tripped over a large rock. She went sprawling, tried to right herself, and somehow landed on her knees in the stream. The cold water was a shock. Struggling forward she crawled out of the swift-flowing water and back up the bank, dripping miserably. The old man was still staring; he called after her hoarsely as she ran back to where she had left her pack. She scrabbled to gather her possessions, hooking Mirabella's saddle over her arm, then stood a moment, panting, unsure what to do, which way to go.

Where in God's name was her horse? She could not simply leave the woods without her. The mare was her only hope of escape from her father. Perhaps she could hide and come back later, when the old man had gone, and try to hunt down the feckless Mirabella.

"Hey!" The old man had limped after her. He stood at the top of the slope, staring down at her. He looked ancient. His small dark eyes fixed hers, then his arm lifted and he pointed behind her through the gnarled trunks of trees. "That your mare, boy? Best catch her before she strays further…"

She turned her head slowly.

Mirabella stood in a small clearing not a hundred feet away, grazing quietly on a patch of coarse grass. Her reins were trailing after her, and dangling from them was a prickly thorn branch. She must have dragged herself free during the night, or perhaps as light began to dawn, and trotted away in search of fresh grass.

"Mirabella!" she breathed. Then nodded to the old man, touching her cap, remembering to speak thickly, like a stable boy. "Thank you, sir. Thank you kindly."

She rode slowly for the rest of that day, picking her way south through the woods alongside the road, and saw no one else after the old man. Her hunger grew as the afternoon progressed and by dusk, she was beginning to devise ever more cunning and outlandish methods of trapping rabbits and roasting them over a fire.

All she had was the knife at her belt. How could she trap a rabbit with that? Perhaps if she were to dig a pit and lay brushwood over it…

So her thoughts went on, wearily, and her belly rumbled. But she had left Yorkshire behind. Soon it would be safe to venture onto the main road again, for her father's men would not search so far south.

"Why did I not think to bring proper provisions for the journey?" she asked Mirabella, halting for the night in a quiet spot at the wooded, sloping edge of a meadow. A stream ran through the woodlands a short distance away, and if it rained, they could always move deeper under the trees. "I'm famished!"

The horse tossed her head and whinnied as though in reply. No doubt she was wondering when her nightly feed was coming. But there would be nothing but grass again for her.

Susannah slipped down from the saddle, her buttocks and thighs aching from the unaccustomed exercise, and leaned her head against Mirabella's warm flanks. Then she patted the mare's reddish-brown neck and began unfastening her girth straps.

"I wonder what Father thought when he found I was not in my chamber. Nothing good, I expect."

Once the saddle was off, she tore up several handfuls of meadow grass and used it to rub down the mare's sweating back. This was a job that took the groom a few moments back at the manor house. She was weary though, and her arms ached, so even this simple act seemed to take ages.

"He must have been very angry."

Mirabella turned her head, nudging her as though for a treat.

"Forgive me, I have nothing for you," she told the mare, stroking her long neck. "Maybe tomorrow I will be able to stop at a farmstead and buy some oats for you."

She thought of the letter she had left for Morag. Yes, her father would have been very angry. But the longer she was missing, the less likely it was that he would attempt to force her into marriage with Sir William Hanney. For she knew in her heart that she could not remain forever on the road, nor live always estranged from her family. At some point she would have to give up the struggle to survive alone, and then she would be caught and taken back to Yorkshire.

Her disguise as a boy was thin indeed. Under cover of darkness she might pass, but not in broad daylight. And a girl alone in these wild northern parts was a rape waiting to happen. She knew that, and dreaded the possibility. For she would not yield easily.

It had been dark for some hours when she woke suddenly, hearing the crack of a twig underfoot. Her eyes snapped open but the night was cloudy, the moon obscured, and she could see nothing but black shapes like tree trunks. Perhaps it had been Mirabella, pulling on her tether. Then she saw shifting movement in the darkness, and the gleam of eyes.

Men, watching her!

Before she could move, she was seized and dragged to her feet. Her cloak fell away, her cap too, though thankfully her hair was still pinned tight to her head.

"What's this? A boy lying out here alone in the forest?" Foul breath was coughed into her face and she recoiled, but could not get free. She could not see her attacker properly, but knew from his smell that he was a common man, perhaps even a vagabond, one of those beggars who was whipped from town to town. Her heart sank, for such a man would have no qualms in killing her and taking her possessions. Indeed, his very next words confirmed that fear. "That sorrel mare is too fine for the likes of you, boy. Where did you steal her from? No, don't bother to struggle. I shall spit you on my dagger before you even find yours, and take your horse for my own."

"She is not stolen, sirrah; she is mine by right!" Susannah exclaimed. "Your breath stinks foully. Let me go!"

He shook her violently, so that her teeth ached in her head. "My breath stinks? Why, you little runt, I'll make an end of you right here."

"You can try!"

She stamped on his feet as hard as she could. Her attacker hopped backward with a howl of pain, and she ducked under his flailing arm. But she had not run more than a few paces before a second man caught her round the waist and spun her to the earth.

"No you don't, my young cock. You're caught!"

Fighting wildly, she was nonetheless no match for his strength and height, and soon found her arms pinned to the dirt above her head. Both men had hold of her now. She kicked out, and caught one of them in the groin by sheer luck. With a curse, the first man dropped to his knees beside her, and she felt the cold steel of his dagger at her throat.

Let it be quick, she thought suddenly, staring up at their dark faces and hating them. Better a quick death than rape and long servitude to such men as these. For if they discovered her sex…

"Hold a moment," the second man muttered. She groaned in furious shame as he groped her breasts through the smock shirt. "I thought as much. This is no boy, Ralph."

"What?"

The dagger was withdrawn. Without any regard for her modesty, the man called Ralph drew off his gloves and thrust his hand between her legs, feeling her in the crudest, most intimate fashion while he stared up and down her struggling body.

"Get your hands off me!" she spat.

But Ralph's expression grew leering, his touch more invasive, rubbing directly at the entrance to her body. "You're right, Kit. Our luck has changed. We've caught ourselves a hen, not a cock." He spat on the earth beside her head. "Only question now is what to do with her?"

His companion pushed her smock shirt up to her neck and Susannah froze, suddenly terrified. Both men stared silently at her breasts, pale in the darkness.

"Holy Mother of God, she's a beauty." Ralph released her to fumble with his codpiece instead. His voice was suddenly hoarse. "And I thought we'd only get one mount out of this night's work. Hold her down for me."

The one he had called Kit was grinning too. He was a big man and held her effortlessly, for though she was tall for a girl, she was too slender to have much strength against a man of his size.

"Cowards!"

Kit merely laughed, leaning across her bare chest, his rough clothing scraping her nipples, his fetid breath in her face.

"If I didn't know you'd sink your teeth in it," he whispered in her ear, "I'd gag your mouth with my cock, girl. Now be silent and take what's coming to you. If you don't struggle, we won't have to hurt you too bad." He looked down, watching avidly as Ralph tugged her hose down to reveal her naked thighs and what lay between them. "You might even enjoy it."

A dirty finger pushed inside her and she yelped, kicking out wildly. Ralph swore and slapped her hard about the face.

"You want pain, you shall have it."

"Wait, wait!" she cried. "Please wait and hear me out... I have more worth to you as a virgin!"

Ralph spat again, his tone disbelieving. "You are no virgin. You are some thieving slut who's run away with her master's horse, and I shall have my pleasure of you."

"No, truly. I am the daughter of Sir John Tyrell. I...I have run away from home. That is my own horse, Mirabella." Her voice strengthened when she saw both men hesitate, staring down at her through the murky dark. "It is the truth, I swear it. There will be a reward for my safe return. But only as a virgin. I...I am betrothed to Sir William Hanney. He will pay nothing if you take my honor."

Kit had already released her arms. He crouched back on his heels, his eyes narrowed on her face. But Ralph was still poised to take her maidenhead, kneeling lustfully above her, and she could see he would need further persuading.

"If this is true," he demanded thickly, "why sleep out here in the forest, so far from home?"

"I told you, I ran away."

"This is nonsense." But he drew back, no longer kneeling between her thighs. "Why run away from home if you have all this wealth? You said you are betrothed to this Sir…Sir William, whatever his name was. So why risk death by coming out here alone?"

"Because I do not wish to be his bride, of course." She sat up, pulling down her smock shirt and dragging up her hose to cover her bare nethers. To her relief, neither man tried to stop her. She added breathlessly, "Because he is an old man, and I…I am in love with someone else."

"Lies!"

Kit stayed Ralph's hand when he would have struck her again. "Hold your hand," he said urgently. "If what the girl says is true, Sir Francis can send word to this father of hers, maybe get a reward for catching his runaway daughter. But if we rape her, it's my guess he will pay nothing."

"Very well," Ralph agreed hoarsely. "We'll wait and see what the master thinks. But the little slut will serve me first if her tale proves false."

Kit shook his head, busy unlooping Mirabella's reins, which she'd wrapped about a tree trunk the night before. "You know better than that, Ralph. Whoever she may be, this girl has been gently raised. She is no meat of ours. We should leave her to Sir Francis."

Listening to this exchange, Susannah felt a surge of hope and did not protest when they mounted her on Mirabella, handed up her belongings, and began to lead her deeper into the woods.

Sir Francis seemed to be the name of their master. If she was indeed to be taken to a gentleman of honor, knighted by King Henry, her case could not be as bad as she had assumed when these two first sprang on her out of the night. Yet she was still uneasy at heart. What kind of knight would employ these wretched and villainous rapists to do his bidding?

Susannah checked that her dagger was still hidden in her boot, but left it there. She had a suspicion she might need it later, with Sir Francis.

Day was dawning by the time they approached the squat, unkempt farmstead that was Sir Francis's manor house. She eyed the place with misgiving. A knight lived here? It looked as though three or four old buildings had been cobbled together to make one new dwelling. A thin gray smoke was rising from the central chimney as they rode into the small, filthy courtyard; Ralph instantly called for a stablehand, an old man who emerged yawning sleepily up at them and scratching the fleas in his beard.

On their approach they were greeted with barking from the slinking dogs in the yard, who then ran about the legs of the horses, snarling viciously. Mirabella reared up in protest at this rough treatment, almost unseating Susannah, so that Kit had to take his whip to the hounds.

Once the dogs had been subdued, Susannah was helped to dismount, none too gently. She found herself surrounded by a crowd of chickens, mangy and ill-fed, pecking disconsolately at her boots.

"Come on," Ralph growled, seizing her by the arm. He dragged her through a low doorway. The hall was dark and stank unpleasantly of cabbage. "Sir Francis!" He saw a slatternly looking women peering through a narrow doorway. "You there, is our master still abed?"

"Aye," she muttered, her pale eyes fixed on Susannah.

"Get upstairs and rouse him, then. Tell him I have brought him a gift."

"Rouse the master?" She spat contemptuously on the floor, which was dusty with ancient, befouled rushes. Like the two men, she had a thick burr to her voice, common to country folk in the north. "He'd have me whipped for impertinence. The master is never up before ten, as well you know. Who's the boy?"

"Never you mind." Kit's bulk, behind her in the hallway, blocked the light and Ralph thrust her roughly toward him. "Here, Kit, look after our prize. I'll wake Sir Francis. He'll know what to do with her."

With that, Ralph took the dark stairs two at a time and disappeared along the landing.

"Her?" The woman echoed, staring at her again through narrowed eyes.

"This one's no boy." With a crude gesture, Kit squeezed Susannah's breast, ignoring her furious protest. "See?"

The woman's eyes gleamed. "Ah, that'll put the master in a better temper at last. A new whore for his bed. Where did you find her?"

"In the woods. A runaway, by the looks of it."

A roar from upstairs silenced them both. Their heads turned as Ralph stumbled down the stairs backward, his hands held out in a gesture of conciliation.

Above him a tall figure was descending, wrapped in a cloak.

"Now, good Sir Francis," Ralph was saying, his tone placatory, "don't fret yourself over an early awakening. I would not lie to you, master. I have brought you good sport. We found a fugitive girl in boys' weeds out in the woods, passing fair to look upon…and gently reared too, I'll swear to it." He pointed down at Susannah. "See?"

The man in the cloak stopped, looking down at her, and Susannah had her first glimpse of his face.

Handsome, dissolute, cruel, his look was fierce, his gray eyes hooded, boring into hers as though intent on some great evil. She was suddenly frightened, for she could see at once that although Sir Francis might be a knight of the realm, he was no gentleman. And there was no one here to protect her from his greed.

No one but herself.

Three

"Sir, my name is Susannah Tyrell."

Susannah moved to the foot of the stairs to greet this man as an equal, and was surprised when her voice did not shake.

"My father, Sir John Tyrell, will be glad to hear of your hospitality to his daughter. I can give you his direction so you may send him word at once that you have found me."

"Found you?" His brows had risen steeply at her first address. But now, coming to stand before her, he looked her up and down with undisguised lust in his face. "Rather it seems you have found me, Susannah Tyrell. You were trespassing in my woods, according to my man Ralph." He was watching her. Trying to gauge her reaction. She would not give him the satisfaction of seeing her afraid. "Which makes you a criminal and mine to punish under the law."

"It was never my intention to trespass on your land. I was out riding and took a wrong turn in the woods." A wild story came into her head and she followed it blithely, her words growing in confidence. "I kept riding, you see, hoping to hit the right track again. But I became lost in the forest. It grew dark and I did not know how to return to the road. So I lay down under a tree…" Her voice tailed off before his mocking laughter. "What? What amuses you, sir?"

"A young lady permitted to go out riding alone, in these northern woods, in such mannish attire? Come, girl, you are a runaway. No doubt you are fleeing some cruelty of your father's; I am not a fool."

Sir Francis smiled when, confused and embarrassed, she looked away. "Wanted you to marry where you did not love, is that it? An old story, yet it still goes on. Tyrell... I know the name."

She waited while he frowned, studying her.

"I remember now. I saw old Tyrell at court once or twice when I was younger. But his land lies a good day's ride north of here. Sure, you have strayed a long way." Sir Francis knocked off her cap, then deliberately plucked the pins from her hair one by one until the heavy fair locks fell tumbling about her shoulders. She gritted her teeth, wishing she had cut her hair short as she had originally planned. Short as a boy's. Then he would not have found her comely. "Never fear, my sweet runaway, I shall not send you back to your father. Or not until you and I have become better acquainted."

"Sir?"

He ignored her chilly tone, looking over her shoulder at Ralph. "You did well to wake me. Find one of the maid servants and have her make up a bedchamber for Mistress Tyrell. And let food be prepared for our guest. The lady looks half-starved, and we cannot have that."

He paused, and she heard regret in his voice. "It is unfortunate, but I cannot keep you company this evening at supper. Nor for the next few days. I have business to attend to in Doncaster and must lay my head elsewhere for a while. On my return we shall discuss how you should be punished for your trespass. Punished or rewarded. I shall allow you to choose which word will best suit our time together."

She dared to meet his gaze directly, and shivered at the look in his handsome face. His gray eyes showed his desire, stripping her body in shameless fashion, and yet were cold at the same time. Sir Francis felt the same urge to despoil her as his men had in the forest. Yet many courtiers of King Henry's court, as she knew from her sister Eloise's account, had learned to disguise their carnal appetites under the veneer of chivalry. He was polite, yet he too wanted her maidenhead.

Sir Francis would make a formidable opponent. She wondered how long she would have to remain his prisoner until she found an opportunity to steal Mirabella and escape.

But if this villain dared lay hands on her body… God's wounds, Sir Francis would know her dagger more intimately than he would ever know her, she swore silently.

—⁓—

Held prisoner in a meager chamber that smelled of damp, with a fire that smoked relentlessly, she spent much of her time at her casement. It was narrow and unshuttered, letting in the cold light at dawn, but at least it allowed her to see the comings and goings of the household.

She watched with interest when Sir Francis rode out, and remained by the window for hours that first day and evening, studying every creature that passed below in the filthy courtyard. But when several days had passed and he did not come back, she took to lying on her bed in the daytime, wondering what Hugh Beaufort would do if he knew where she was being held, and her probable fate on the knight's return. Twice a day a servant would bring her a platter of cold meats and bread, with fresh or stewed fruit, and a small tankard of ale.

She waited behind the door one time, and then leaped on the servant and struck her with a stout cushion from her bed. But after running wildly down the stairs she was soon overpowered by his men and brought back. After that, the servants were more wary when entering her room.

But now that Susannah knew how many of Sir Francis's men seemed to inhabit the place, she did not attempt to escape again. What chance would she have of getting to the door with so many eyes on her? It seemed a hopeless situation, so she turned her mind instead to ways of sweetly persuading Sir Francis to let her go unharmed.

Though in truth she would rather kick her captor in the groin than smile and flatter him.

Once, she was allowed out into the gardens of the ramshackle manor, under Ralph's close guardianship. Walking in the fresh air, Susannah took discreet note of the low wall around the herb garden, and the forest beyond it, and which windows looked down upon the gardens from her floor. Then, on the fifth day of her incarceration she was permitted to wash herself from head to toe, then encouraged to dress herself in a lavish red gown one of the hard-faced maids produced after her ablutions.

"Why should I wear this?" she asked the girl, examining the low-cut bodice with displeasure.

The maid looked at her slyly. "Sir Francis has come home. He brought that gown for you, and wishes you to wear it when he dines with you tonight. Sir Francis was very particular on that point."

She stared. "I did not hear your master return."

"He came back late last night. No doubt you were asleep."

She did not like the scarlet gown and almost refused to wear it. But after nearly a sennight's wearing, the coarse cloth of her boy's attire smelled none too pleasant and at least the gown was clean. The red bodice was tight-fitting, almost obscenely so, and the skirt cut immodestly close to her hips. There were no sleeves, but a thin white shawl had been provided and this she wore instead to cover her bare arms, wishing her breasts were not quite so prominent.

No cap was given her, so she combed out her fair hair and let it hang down her back. Then she sat on her bed and waited.

Less than an hour had passed before she heard the sound of approaching horses. She hurried to the window, and stared down in disbelief as a small band of horsemen rode into the courtyard, the chickens scattering before them, dogs barking fiercely. Then she recognized the livery as that of Lord Wolf, her new brother, and her heart leaped.

There at the front, quite unmistakable, was Hugh Beaufort. With his powerful build and thatch of fair hair under his feathered cap, there was no doubt that it was the king's clerk.

"He has come, he has come!" She pinched herself and the vision did not fade. Hugh Beaufort at the head of Lord Wolf's men, riding to her rescue. "But how did he know where to find me?"

At that moment, as though sensing her gaze on him, Hugh looked up. She raised her hand in a greeting and drew breath to call his name, but was suddenly seized from behind and thrown unceremoniously down across the bed.

Her jailor had returned.

"How dare you!" she exclaimed, staring up at Sir Francis. "Those men below were sent by my father. They have come for me; you can no longer hold me here against my will."

"Can I not?"

Sir Francis knelt above her, grabbing her wrists and pressing her easily down into the feather mattress. She struggled, slapping and clawing at his hands, desperate to get back to the window.

The knight half-smiled as he gazed down at her in the tight gown, his eyes gleaming, as though enjoying the way she writhed and fought against him.

"Hush, girl." She tried to scream, but his hand clamped heavily across her mouth. "Friends of yours, are they? I saw the horsemen from my chamber and knew you might be excited by their presence. But never fear; no visitor can spoil our reunion tonight. These men will not stay long. I've sent Ralph down with orders to deny you ever came here."

She made a furious noise behind his hand.

"I had thought to ask your father for a discreet ransom, in exchange for your safe return to him. But you know my identity, and besides, you have been under my roof so long your reputation will be ruined. You will be no use to your father now."

His smile chilled her. "So I have hit upon a better plan. I shall use you myself, then apply to your father for your hand in marriage. You are not lowborn, and your body pleases me, so the match would be a fair one. And I need someone to make this manor habitable again, for I am almost never at home these days and the place is all but a ruin. If I take you to wife, it will save me the expense of employing a steward to put the place to rights." He slid his hand down her body, ignoring her struggles. "You can keep my bed warm here while I am at court, and give me an heir or two."

He seemed unperturbed by the muffled noises of disgust she made at this suggestion, merely bending his head to nuzzle at her breast.

She tried not to think what the villain was doing, instead straining to hear what was happening below in the courtyard. How came Hugh Beaufort to be here instead of her father? For she could think of no other reason why the king's clerk should have arrived, accompanied by a band of Lord Wolf's men, except that he was searching for her, house to house, in the area. She wondered if her father had been taken ill on her departure; guessed he must have searched the immediate vicinity for her, then sent word to Lord Wolf and her sister at court that she was missing.

And Wolf had sent his friend Hugh to find her.

Voices echoed below. That was Hugh speaking, she would know his deep voice anywhere. Then the sound of another man replying. Calmly denying. Ralph, she was sure of it.

Panic flooded her. Surely Hugh would not take the word of such a villainous servant and simply ride away? Something must have led him here, some clue to her whereabouts. Perhaps one of the other servants had talked too loosely of her presence in the house, and a rumor had begun. A rumor Hugh had heard and pursued.

If Hugh Beaufort and his men were to ride away now, leaving her in this villain's power, she would have no choice but to kill or wound Sir Francis, and escape on her own. But how?

Sir Francis laughed, seeming to read her thoughts as he straightened, looking down at her determined expression. "Considering mutiny already? We are not even properly acquainted yet, let alone wed. Though as I suspected, you make a pretty girl." He fondled her breast in the grotesquely tight-fitting bodice. "This gown becomes you well. But you would look better in the flesh, as God made you."

She shuddered, held captive against his long body.

"Ah no, you need not tremble at the thought of what comes next." His breath was warm on her neck. "I am not without skill as a lover, and my physician assures me I do not have the pox. Of course, once we are married and you are safely with child, Ralph and Kit will expect their share of your charms. It is by such generosity that I keep my men loyal, for this poor estate earns little enough for my coffers." He kissed her throat, moving down to the soft skin above her breasts. "Strive to obey, keep yourself clean, and you will soon earn your place in my household."

She could hear no more voices from below. Then one of the horses whinnied, and there was a sound of restless hooves, turning about. Were they leaving? If only she could reach the window and call out to him, Hugh might hear and insist on searching the house.

Perhaps if she were to fool Sir Francis into thinking her resigned to an enforced marriage between them…

The plan took shape inside her head. She pulled up her knee, the movement slow and seductive, as though acquiescing to his caresses at last; then she abruptly kicked out at him.

Her foot collided with his knee, and Sir Francis cried out sharply. His arm loosened, and his hand on her mouth went slack. Then she bit down hard on his fingers and his hand jerked back, escaping her teeth.

Sir Francis roared with fury as she rolled away, no doubt guessing her intention, and made a grab for her.

But Susannah was already on her feet, running to the narrow casement.

She was too late, she realized in horror, but nonetheless shouted, "Hugh! I'm up here, Hugh! Master Beaufort, come back, for the love of God!" even as the small band of horsemen rode at a smart trot out of the courtyard, harnesses jingling, dust rising in their wake, hooves thudding noisily on the dry earth.

Soon they were out of sight. It was the moment of her defeat, and she knew it. There was no chance even the last horseman could have heard her shouts.

"Now those fools have gone, I may go about my business in peace," Sir Francis said in a furious voice, and began to unbuckle his belt. "First of which is a hard belting in revenge for that little show of temper. Second will be the taking of your maidenhead. Third, you will learn to entertain my men and enjoy your new whoredom."

Susannah swore under her breath. How stupid she was! She had forgotten her weapon. She ran at once to her discarded boots and drew out the little dagger she had concealed there.

He came toward her, belt in hand, smiling grimly.

"Do not think you will take me so easily," she warned him, teeth bared, up against the wall. "I will make sure you bleed before I do."

Sir Francis stopped and looked at her, clearly weighing up the amount of damage she could do him with the little belt dagger. Then he shrugged and limped back to the door. "Kicking and biting are not the acts of a lady, my dear. But it matters little. Your savior has gone, and you will soon come to heel once you grasp that he will not be coming back."

"I hate you," she told him loudly. "You are foul, and the very thought of you in my bed makes me retch. You may ruin me but I shall fight you all the way, and never agree to marry you."

He smiled lightly at these insults, as though undisturbed by her vehemence. "I would curb that shrewish tongue of yours by occupying your mouth to a better purpose. But first I must speak to my men about securing the manor against further visitors. Later we shall dine together in comfort downstairs. I will send a maid servant to attend and prepare you. After supper, I promise that you will mend your manners and learn to please your new master." He locked the door after him, threatening her through the thick oak of the door. "Or else feel the bite of my whip, Mistress Tyrell."

Susannah stood a moment after he had gone, head bowed. She could no longer hear the horsemen. Hugh had gone. And taken her last hope of rescue with him.

She stripped off the hateful gown, threw it onto the floor, and dragged her hose and smock shirt back on instead, not caring if the coarse fabric chafed her skin. Finding her discarded belt, with its small leather pouch, she fastened it about her waist, then sat on the edge of the bed and waited for the servant to attend her.

It was not long before she heard the door being unlocked. The woman, entering with a heavy pitcher of steaming water, paused on the threshold and stared at her male attire in surprise.

"Mistress?"

Susannah grimaced. "Forgive me."

With a blow that sent the pitcher flying, hot water splashing everywhere, she knocked the woman to the floor and escaped her prison room, dragging the door shut behind her.

As she had hoped, the large iron key was still in the lock.

Susannah turned the rusty key, managing to lock the door just as the startled serving woman reached it, then ran along the landing. The woman started shouting and banging on the door, her voice shrill. It would not be long before one of the knight's men came to investigate.

But Susannah had not wasted the short time she had spent waiting. Since there was little hope of escape if she went downstairs, she had determined to find a window large enough to climb through, then try jumping down. On first being taken to the chamber, she had noticed a door standing open at the end of the landing, and a large window beyond.

Sure enough the door was open again. Warily pushing inside, she found a chamber cluttered with storage chests, the whole place musty with disuse, a rack of last year's herbs still hanging from the ceiling, dried but unused.

Closing the door, she ran for the window. To her relief it was both unglazed and unshuttered, perhaps to air the damp room, and overlooked the quiet herb gardens, where it was unlikely she would be seen descending.

Dusk was already gathering, the sky dark with the threat of coming rain. Even as she swung her leg over the sill and began to let herself down from the window, Susannah felt the first heavy drops of rain on her head. She had neither cloak nor cap, and her arms were bare. But she did not care if she was caught out in a rainstorm; all that mattered was that she escaped this vile house before Sir Francis took his pleasure of her.

It was a long drop to the weed-thick sandy path that ran around the house. Susannah lay facedown for a moment, winded by the fall, before stumbling to her feet and looking up.

Inside the house, she could hear booted feet running up the stairs, then shouts as they discovered her flight.

"Mirabella," she muttered, staring about the overgrown herb garden, undecided what to do next. She was not sure in which direction lay the stables. She did not wish to leave poor Mirabella behind, yet there was no time to rescue her mare without risking capture.

Already there were shouts round the front of the manor house, men being sent out to hunt for her in the thickening dusk.

It was no use; Mirabella was lost to her.

Clumsy in the too-large boots she had taken from her father's house, she stumbled through the wilderness that had once been a herb garden. There was a red brick wall ahead. She dragged herself over it and tumbled into knee-high rough grass at the edge of woodland; the sky glowered above the trees, rusting as the sun fell into shadow. She heard dogs barking and guessed that Sir Francis had loosed them in pursuit.

If she could not put some distance between herself and the manor, she would be brought down like a fox by a baying pack of hounds.

Running in earnest, she made for the shelter of the tree line and plunged in without looking back. It was already dark in the woods, the air thick with dusk, the light uncertain. She tripped more than once over the uneven ground, but hurried to her feet again each time, determined to escape the manor house and her cruel jailor. She did not stop running until she had forded a broad woodland stream, taking care to splash downstream a few hundred yards before crossing to the opposite bank. By the time she clambered up, her hose were sodden and her smock shirt muddied. But she knew running through the water even that short distance might obscure her scent, slowing the hounds who were tracking her.

With no track to follow, and glimmering darkness all around her, Susannah came to an unsteady halt. She bent over, trying to get her breath back, then straightened, checking over her shoulder. She could see nothing but black trunk after trunk, merging together as night fell in the forest.

Had she lost her pursuers?

She listened, hearing only the nearby stream rushing over stones, and felt suddenly tearful. What now? Again she wished Hugh had insisted on searching the house. But then she could not guess at why he had been there in the first place, nor imagine what information had led him to Sir Francis. This was all her fault, anyway. If she had not run away from home…

Pointless to think such things. She could not undo the past. Equally she could not go back, only forward.

So on she trudged in the dark, refusing to feel sorry for herself, her face stony. Her chances of traveling all the way down south to the king's court seemed remote, though not impossible. She had lost her money, her few possessions, and most pressingly her horse.

"Poor Mirabella." She closed her eyes briefly. "I hope they treat you well. Vile thieves!"

She was no great walker, and had no means to buy food and drink to sustain herself along the way. Not unless she worked for it, which would mean less time for travel. No, without Mirabella—for whom she grieved—she could not hope to reach the court for several weeks, by which time everyone in Yorkshire would think her dead or lost forever to her family. Certainly there would be no man who believed her still a virgin and untouched.

And Hugh Beaufort would never wish to ally himself with such an outcast, for he was a king's man and too aware of his office, and his good reputation. He would not even take her on as his mistress. Not once her honor was so badly sullied.

Susannah did not dare consider what lay ahead for her now. She must hope for the best, regardless. For if she gave in to despair, she might as well turn back and take Sir Francis's offer.

An owl out on its nightly hunt for mice gave a haunting, tremulous cry, somewhere to her left amongst the trees, and she stopped to listen.

She stiffened, for now that she was standing still she could hear something new in the evening quiet, the soft thunder of horses' hooves in the distance. Susannah could see nothing but tree trunks in the murky dark, but she guessed the road from York to London must lie ahead, for no man could ride that swiftly on a forest track.

Should she run forward and beg for help, or hide herself in case it was her enemy?

Then at her back she heard the high yelping of hounds, and her skin prickled in horror.

Sir Francis, still on her track!

Heading instinctively for the swift-moving horsemen, Susannah flailed through thick undergrowth and after a brief struggle emerged on the road. It was a broad track illuminated by moonlight, surely the main road south that she had been seeking. Flushed and breathless, she blundered into the path of the oncoming riders, hands and face scratched by thorns, loose hair disheveled, no doubt the very image of a madwoman.

"Stop!" she cried out, casting up her hands. It was folly, but she could only pray the men would see her in the moonlight and not ride over her. "For the love of God, I bid you halt!"

Seeing her at the last moment, the front rider gave a muffled curse and wrenched his horse sideways. The following riders scattered in disarray. Too exhausted to move, she stood and stared, one arm thrown up before her face, and wondered how much it would hurt to be ridden down like a dog in the road.

The horse reared up, whinnying furiously, its hooves lashing out and just missing her head.

"Sweet Jesu, you little fool, I could have killed you." The rider was suddenly out of the saddle and before her, seizing her by the shoulders, his face in shadow. She might not be able to see his expression, but his voice was grim. "So I have found you at last, Mistress Tyrell."

It was Hugh Beaufort.

Four

He had found her at last!

Hugh's first reaction on seeing Susannah Tyrell in the middle of the dark track, dressed in men's clothing as her father's messenger had said, had been relief. Intense, overwhelming relief, so that he almost sagged in the saddle, relaxing the reins that had wrenched the horse aside from hurting her. Yet almost in the same instant, he felt anger at her reckless stupidity in running away from home, and his heart had begun to thud.

Slipping from the horse's back, he had seized her by the shoulders, roundly cursing the girl for a fool even as he wished desperately to kiss her. Her face seemed to pale in the moonlight at his exclamation of fury. She did not pull away as he had expected though, her wide blue eyes fixed on his.

"What do you have to say for yourself, girl?" he finished, shaking her, filled with impatience.

He had imagined a dearer meeting than this, with Susannah sleeping rough in some field and looking up at his arrival, golden hair tousled, soft cheeks flushed, pleased to see her rescuer. But instead she seemed almost grieved by this encounter, her gaze turning back the way she had come, though indeed she was hot-cheeked and be-draggled in her boyish attire, more urchin than lady.

"Dogs…" she panted, pointing behind her at the thick woods. "He has loosed his dogs… They are almost upon us."

An abrupt and insane jealousy ate at him, and he released her. He took a step back, fists clenched by his sides.

"He?"

"My…captor."

His mind flashed back to the nearest dwelling where they had stopped to inquire of her. A rundown manor house, partially in ruin, the door answered by a surly, ill-favored servant who had sworn his master was away at court and there had been no stranger seen in those parts, neither boy nor girl according to Hugh's painstaking description. What a fool he had been, riding up to the manor with a band of Wolf's men at his back and assuming he would meet with truth at such a godforsaken place.

Had Susannah been hidden away from his sight there? Perhaps in some upper room, her hands tied, her mouth gagged…

Fury gripped him.

Now that he thought of it, the sour-faced knave had seemed most impatient to direct him back to the road. Too impatient for an honest man, he had offered no refreshment although they had ridden hard that day, calling at every dwelling and barn they passed, and asked no further particulars of the missing lady unlike every other household they had checked.

He knew a sudden violent desire to break that fellow's neck. And his master's.

"You have been held prisoner nearby?"

She nodded, still panting. "The manor house… You stopped… I saw you… But…you rode away."

"Forgive me, I did not know."

A simple hanging would not be good enough for the master. To assuage Susannah's honor, there would need to be some personal combat between them. He wanted the satisfaction of watching his own blade penetrate this villain's foul heart.

"The blackguard's name?"

"Sir Francis," she managed huskily, but shook her head when he pressed her. "Indeed I know no more. Please, make haste, for pity's sake! The dogs!"

Even as she spoke, a rangy hound broke cover from the east and came their way, baying in a bloodthirsty manner as it lurched out of the trees, followed by another thin dog, its ribs showing, then a third, then a fourth and fifth. Behind the hounds of hell came horses, and on their backs, hooded men. The front rider shouted a hoarse order to his men, heading directly for Susannah and Hugh.

"At arms!" Hugh called to Lord Wolf's men, then turned to seize his horse, acutely aware of their vulnerability on foot while the enemy was mounted.

In that moment, Susannah broke away, as though poised to run again, shouting defiance at the man almost upon them, her eyes fierce.

"Susannah, no!" Hugh cried out, reaching for her, but it was too late.

The horse darted between them.

Laughing wildly, the rider grabbed up Susannah and threw her over the front of his saddle like a sack of bones. Golden hair flopping down, his captive shrieked and struggled uselessly as the man set spurs to his mount and sped on into the dark woods on the west side of the track.

Cursing, Hugh flung himself up into the saddle and dragged his horse around to follow the leader.

He had no choice but to follow alone, for his own men were engaged in furious hand-to-hand battles with the other hooded riders, or busy kicking away the vicious hounds attacking their mounts. Nonetheless he called out to Fletcher, his second in command, ordering him to "Follow when you can," then urged his horse into the woods.

Hugh could see nothing at first in the woods, riding blindly in the best direction he could guess. He reined in once he was far enough away from the track, listening instead for the telltale beat of hooves. He heard it at once, a faint rhythmic thudding, heading southwest, and turned his horse that way. A moment later he caught a woman's scream, and spurred his horse faster, disregarding the thick dark of leaves overhead which admitted little moonlight.

Damn him!

Thin branches whipped at his face as Hugh rode, bent over the horse's neck. If he had hurt Susannah, he would make this Sir Francis suffer, whoever he might be. Certainly the name was not known to him from court, but perhaps Sir Francis was some disgraced knight who rarely showed his face in the king's presence. It was well known that many northern barons and knights still clung to the old Roman faith, worshipping in secret at each other's houses while outwardly accepting the king's edicts.

This was no doubt a man of that ilk, some clandestine Catholic who could not shake his liking for the Roman Mass. Perhaps he even plotted the king's downfall, here in the north of England, far enough from court for his intrigues and schemes to go unnoticed.

He tried not to consider what he would do if her captor had despoiled Susannah. He had kept her prisoner, that was clear. But for what purpose? Would this Sir Francis have dared rape a gently born maiden, even one whom he might have come across dressed as a boy?

He loosened his sword in its sheath. Retribution would follow swiftly if the villain had taken Susannah against her will, here and tonight, even if Hugh should by rights seek proper justice for such an outrage. Out here in the wild northern woods, with no witness but the moon, what did it matter how retribution was achieved?

Grimly, Hugh caught a sudden shadow ahead, fleeing through the trees, and rode behind as silently as he could.

With a shock he realized it was Susannah. Somehow she must have kicked free of her captor's saddle. At her back, cursing as he reached down to grab her and kept missing, rode Sir Francis, hood thrown back to reveal a thin-boned face, fierce eyes glaring.

"Come back, whore!" Sir Francis snarled, leaning precariously out of the saddle. "You will not escape me, nor tell your tale to those men of your father's. This nonsense merely draws out your suffering."

He almost seized her that time, but Susannah twisted away, darting sideways in the dark and nearly dragging him from the horse.

His voice rose in fury. "I would have married you like a respectable woman. But if you do not give yourself up to me freely, I'll wring your neck when I've finished and cast you aside like a dead pigeon."

Hugh drew his sword, spurring forward. "Leave your threats and face me, sirrah! I shall prove that lady's honor on my sword."

The man dragged his horse about, his eyes narrowing at the gleam of a weapon in the dark. "What's this? Poor fool, to draw your sword on a knight. You serve her father, no doubt." He drew his own sword. "Are you content to die for her, peasant?"

"It is you who will die. Have at you, miscreant!"

Their swords clashed, and sparks flew in the murky air, white and blue. Hugh felt the shock down his arm and fell back slightly, turning his startled horse round in a circle, for the animal was unaccustomed to combat. Like his master, Hugh thought drily. But he did not go far, urging his gelding forward once more. Their swords met again in the darkness. This time their blades grated together, Sir Francis pressing hard, controlling his mount with an iron will, and Hugh was nearly pushed from his horse.

He fell back again, wondering whether to dismount and fight on foot, for he was not used to swordplay on horseback. Another stroke and his opponent's sword caught his horse, slicing his neck so that the blood flowed freely and the terrified animal reared up.

With a muffled oath, Hugh shortened the reins, fighting to keep his horse under control, for he could feel the wounded animal was ready to bolt with him.

Seeing his sudden weakness, his enemy closed in with raised sword, and Hugh was forced to parry a series of energetic blows, his bloodied horse dancing beneath him.

"Your champion wearies fast," Sir Francis sneered, looking across at Susannah as he turned for another attack.

"He will kill you nonetheless," she replied sharply, her back against a tree as she watched the fight.

Will I?

Hugh glanced briefly down at her, wishing he could be so certain of the outcome, and saw her pale face in the thin strips of moonlight falling down between the trees. Pale but composed, she stared back at him, her fierce gaze willing him to end it. The lack of fear in her eyes worried him. It was almost as though she had seen too much, that she would never be afraid again. What had this man done to Susannah since she had left her father's home, less than two days' ride north of this place? Was she in truth despoiled?

Rage seized him. Hugh whirled his horse, catching the knight off guard. His blow glanced off Sir Francis's left shoulder, wrapped in its thick cloak, yet he felt the blade bite as it passed.

He had done some damage there at least.

Sir Francis hissed, a grimace on his shadowed face. Nonetheless he continued to fight, wheeling his horse about and parrying Hugh's blows as though unhurt. His own blows were defensive though, no longer attacking. Then he fell back slightly, beginning to give ground. He dropped his reins, the sheen of sweat visible on his forehead. It was clear that his strength was waning.

Hugh saw an opening, and spurred forward, thrusting deep. Turning aside too late, Sir Francis took Hugh's blade in his right side and cried out, cursing and dropping his sword. A moment later the knight slumped in the saddle, half-fainting over his mount's neck.

The scared horse whinnied and turned abruptly, heading for home, his wounded master still clutching at his neck.

Neither spoke as they listened to horse and rider receding in the distance. The moon had disappeared behind a cloud and the forest was dark. The air seemed thick and tense, almost warm. Hugh shifted uncomfortably in the saddle; a drop of sweat ran down his back under his heavy riding tunic. His chest was tight, as though he could not draw breath properly.

Hugh looked down at his sword and saw blood on the blade. Carefully, he wiped it clean on his saddle cloth, then sheathed the weapon.

He slithered down from his horse, and left the animal trembling with fear, his head down, neck bloodied. "Susannah?" He held out his hand to her. "Are you hurt?"

"Are you hurt?" she echoed back at him.

"He never got near me."

Susannah stared, then began to laugh, almost wildly. "I will survive. I did not think to see you again."

"I'm sorry. If we could have found you sooner…"

He took her bare hands in his and turned them over. Thin scratches, some still bleeding. From the forest, he guessed. She had a long cut on her cheek too, not deep.

But what of her other hurts? Those he could not see?

"My fault," she muttered.

"This is perhaps not the moment to be apportioning blame. I am merely glad to have you safe at last."

"You came to find me," she stated, as though she had never doubted he would rescue her.

Hugh smiled grimly. He felt her blue gaze on his face, yet could not meet her eyes. What was wrong with him? "Your father has been searching for you ever since you went missing. I was sent by Lord Wolf to aid in the hunt." He paused. "You gave your sister a terrible shock, running away from home."

"I could no longer remain there."

"Evidently." He unfastened his cloak and set it about her shoulders, seeing how she was shivering. "That was Sir Francis, I take it?"

She nodded.

"Knight or not, he will pay for your rape."

Her eyes met his then, through the darkness. Her voice was suddenly awkward. "He did not… That is, Sir Francis intended to put me beyond any other man's claim, but some business in Doncaster kept him from my chamber until tonight. I feared he would force me. But then you arrived and…I am untouched still."

He could not help but be relieved at her account of events, and the innocence in her face that had first attracted him. The thought of Susannah Tyrell in another man's arms left him sick.

Relief made him reckless. "Thank the Lord for that mercy, at least." He lifted one of her hands to his lips and kissed her cool skin. "Indeed, it is the best news I have heard since first learning you were no longer safe under your father's roof."

She mumbled something he did not catch, then added, "Sir Francis kept me restrained in my chamber, else I would have run away sooner."

"No, the fault is mine. I accepted that villainous servant's word when I should have insisted on searching the house."

She stared about herself, as though only now becoming aware of the darkness and silence of the woods around them. For the first time Hugh realized how far they had ridden from the road. Though he was no longer sure which way the road lay. Glancing up, he found the night sky cloudy and starless. So he could not even navigate by the stars.

Perhaps he could track their hoof prints back to the road…if it were not so dark.

One large raindrop fell onto her cheek. She wiped it away, frowning. "Where is this place? We must not stay here. Sir Francis may come back, and next time he will not be alone."

"Yes," he agreed, his skin prickling, "we must rejoin Lord Wolf's men. There is a storm coming."

"Is Lord Wolf here too? And my sister, Eloise?"

Hugh had forgotten how large her eyes were, and so blue, even in this darkness, that he felt transfixed, staring into them. Had she always been so beautiful? Or was it merely the thought of her loss that had brought Susannah Tyrell into his mind so often these past few days?

Belatedly he registered her eager questions. "Your sister was required to remain at court over this terrible business of the queen, the infamous charges that have been brought against her. Lord Wolf stayed with his bride, and asked me to find you…and bring you back to court."

Hugh expected her to look happy, for he remembered how much Susannah had resented being left behind when Eloise rode south. Instead she merely nodded, gazing over his shoulder.

"Sir, where is your horse?"

Turning, he searched the shadowy trees in every direction, but could see no sign of his mount. Then he recalled its bloodied neck, how the animal had trembled with fright during his struggle with Sir Francis, and could have kicked himself for failing to soothe and secure the unfortunate creature before tending to Susannah. No doubt his gelding was lost in the depths of this wild forest now, having fled the scene of its wounding in search of some quieter place.

"Mother of God," he muttered.

Now they were both on foot in enemy territory, with dogs and riders abroad intent on doing them harm.

And it was raining…

She was looking at him, her expression unreadable. Waiting for instruction, perhaps. Or thinking him a fool.

Hugh hesitated. This was not the rescue he had envisaged when he set out from court to find her. But he must not compound his stupidity in allowing the frightened horse to stray by failing to keep them safe from Sir Francis and his villainous servants.

"Well, so we have no horse. We must seek shelter for the night and hope Lord Wolf's men catch up with us before first light. You look too tired to walk back in search of them, and indeed I am unsure which way lies the road." The raindrops were falling more quickly now. He glanced up at the night sky between the trees, feeling it weigh down upon him, dark and oppressive. "Besides, the rain grows heavier with every minute. No good will be done by you getting wet, mistress."

"Susannah," she muttered, correcting him.

He deliberately did not look at her. "Mistress," he repeated doggedly, and gestured her to walk before him. To use her Christian name instead of her title could only lead to the kind of intimacy he knew she sought from him, but which must be avoided if he was not to prove himself an even greater villain than the unknightly Sir Francis.

For he had murmured the name "Susannah" to himself a hundred times since their first meeting, and each time it had been said with his cock in his fist, imagining the golden-haired beauty naked in his bed.

They headed deeper into the forest, walking some ten minutes under the increasing pitter-patter of rain before Hugh found a likely spot. He halted beside a low sloping bank, below which three trees grew entwined together, which in the dark he guessed to be two birch trees and a stout, heavy-girthed beech: their lower branches had crisscrossed, forming a natural shelf that could be used to support a roof.

"Wait, this looks like a good place." He glanced about, frowning. "You had best gather ferns; I'll cut branches to make a shelter. That way at least we'll keep the rain off our heads."

Raising her brows in a haughty fashion, Susannah looked back at him. "Gather ferns?"

"Unless you would rather sleep on the bare soil tonight?" The rain had begun to fall in earnest in the last few minutes. He wiped the wet from his forehead and glared at her. "If you do not make haste, Mistress Disdain, the ferns will be wet through and of no use. And it is not as though your finery will be ruined by stooping to labor."

Her mouth tightened mutinously as his gaze moved speakingly over her boy's attire. Yet to his surprise she did not bother to argue. Turning her back on him instead, Susannah started to root amongst the dark undergrowth, hunting for the feathery growth of new ferns.

Hugh hung on his heel a moment, watching as she searched, unable to drag his gaze away. There was something disturbing about the sight of her in men's hose, her slender thighs outlined, her shapely bottom on show each time she bent over.

His cock stiffened to wood, and suddenly he doubted the wisdom of sharing this shelter with her.

To lie beside Susannah Tyrell all night and lay not a finger on her would be exquisite torture for any man. But for him, one who had tasted the sweetness of her mouth and knew how swiftly physical desire could flare between them, it would be nigh impossible.

Yet the girl must sleep after her long ordeal, and he must keep guard—and not forget the honor due to her as the daughter of a gentleman.

Unsheathing his belt dagger, Hugh also turned his back and set to work cutting down the longest, leafiest branches he could find. His work was hampered by darkness and rain, but eventually he had made a good heap of branches, dense with new green foliage and unfurling buds. Some he laid carefully across the lower branches of the close-growing trees, weaving them together until he had constructed a frame of sorts, broad and high enough to accommodate them both for a night. The rest he arranged in a fence-like fashion about the trunks, leaning them in and binding them to the upper branches with ivy creepers wrenched from a nearby ancient oak. Within a short time they had a shelter, rough and spiny, but good enough to keep the weather out for a few hours at least.

He glanced about for Susannah after a while, but she had vanished, no doubt retiring to perform her female ablutions in peace. He too did what was necessary, and as he was coming back from the bushes, found her arranging several armfuls of ferns on the patch of bare earth beneath his shelter.

By then the rain was falling heavily, and a wind had risen. He felt the tension of a storm in the air and tugged the branches tighter, hoping to keep out the worst of the weather for a few hours at least.

Susannah straightened, a little out of breath, lifting a troubled gaze to his. Her hair was damp, fine golden tendrils clinging to her wet forehead and cheeks.

"Will that be enough ferns, do you think?" she asked, wiping dirty hands on her smock shirt as she stepped back to consider their handiwork.

Unbidden, his gaze strayed to her chest. The boyish garment might drown her body, but it did little to disguise her breasts from one who knew what was hidden there, that intriguing rise of flesh nothing short of carnal temptation.

His temper stirred at the knowledge that the villainous Sir Francis might have seen her nude, might even have touched her…

"Sir?"

Hugh blinked. Had he been staring at her like a dolt? His jaw tightened at his own foolishness. "It will have to do," he said shortly, and sheathed his dagger.

In God's name, he must conquer this lust. Her reputation might already be lost, but he would not compound that disgrace by taking her virginity. He had promised Lord Wolf that he would find and protect Susannah. Not ravage the girl himself as soon as she was in his power. And her reputation might still be saved if this little adventure could be kept quiet.

Against his will, Hugh's gaze returned to her smock shirt, hanging wet and awry now, then the muddied hose that clung to her long legs. Legs that might soon be wrapped around him in passion if he was prepared to break all his rules of conduct.

Violently, deep inside, desire struck at him with almost uncontrollable force. The need to know this woman, to see her naked beneath him, to hear her cry out in pleasure as he entered her. He shoved that vision back down inside, cursing himself for a fool, but his desire would not be so easily banished. Thoughts crowded in on him, crude as any schoolboy's at the sight of a comely woman, and he struggled against them in vain.

Her damp hair blew back in the rising wind. The trees rustled around them and she turned, looking up at the dark sky with wide eyes. He watched, acutely aware of her scent, sharply feminine, stirring his arousal again even as he sought to quell it.

By the rood, he wanted her. He needed her. He was on fire for her. And no amount of gentlemanly restraint would be enough to stop him if he once allowed their mouths to meet again.

"Come, the storm grows wild. You will be soaked to the skin if we stay out in this rain much longer." His voice sounded hoarse to his ears. It was the voice of desperation, of a man lusting after a forbidden prize; not a king's man, a respectable clerk of the court. "Let us go inside."

What would she think if she knew how ardently her protector wished to despoil her?

His smile was savage. No doubt she would strip off those damp boyish clothes and invite him to seduce her, just as she had tried on their ride that afternoon in Yorkshire. For he had guessed by her flight how keenly Susannah wished to avoid her arranged marriage to Sir William—and how better to do that than by losing her honor to another man?

So now he must spend the night lying beside Susannah Tyrell without touching her delicious body. That was his duty; he knew it as he knew his own name.

The trouble was, like a hawk in a blue sky, he was no longer sure he could resist the whistling call of her lure.

Five

At his words, Susannah knew she was lost.

His green eyes had narrowed on her face, guarded by short dark lashes, yet curiously heated, every glance giving away the lust he felt for her. Was Hugh Beaufort aware of her desire for him? Yet how could he not be, when she had never succeeded in concealing it from him?

With a start, she realized that she was breathing hard, just as though she had been running, not gathering ferns in the rain. Her heart was thudding and she could feel heat in her face.

She had to control this madness. Or lose his respect. To borrow a revealing gown from her sister and seduce him at court was one thing. To throw herself at his head at their very next meeting—here in the murky forest, with the rain pelting down—would make her look desperate and foolish. For even though she could see how much this man wanted her, could hear the lust thickening in his voice, Hugh Beaufort had made it plain at their last meeting how little he was interested in her beyond a desirable body. If he rejected her advances—again—she would have to spend the night beside him in embarrassment and horror.

Seemingly oblivious to her reluctance, Hugh set a hand to the small of her back and steered Susannah inside their makeshift shelter.

"No, you go in first," he muttered when she tried to refuse. "I must pull the branches across to keep out the worst of the weather."

His large male hand seemed to burn into her skin even through the cloak he had given her to wear. Briefly, dangerously, she wondered how it would feel to have that same hand on her bare skin, holding and stroking her, then found she could not dismiss the thought. Her desire for him was like a splinter in her flesh, working deeper with every step.

"Mind your head," he told her as she scrambled inside, then knocked off his own cap when he stooped to follow her. He grimaced, pushing a hand through his damp hair, but did not replace the cap. Instead he crouched to drag a screen of leafy branches across the narrow entrance. "Best make yourself comfortable. We may have to stay here until dawn."

Hugh was a shadowy figure in the darkening shelter, so close now she could touch him just by reaching out her hand. In God's name, how would they manage to pass the night together in this tiny space without being tempted into making love? Though would it be such a dreadful thing if they both gave in to the urging of their bodies?

Watching him, Susannah allowed herself to imagine the forbidden act. Her cheeks flushed with heat and she sighed, eager for him to teach her everything he knew about love.

She did not care that they were not married. Indeed, she was glad, fiercely glad, that she was unwed. Some might call it sin, yet how could something so easy and natural be sinful?

A wild laugh rose inside her and she struggled to suppress it. Not content with questioning her father's authority, she was now questioning God's.

Dropping onto the bed of ferns she had gathered, Susannah unfastened the wet cloak and pulled it from her shoulders. "Is it entirely wise for us to remain hidden?" She draped the cloak over one of the jutting branches behind her, hoping it might dry off during the night. "Will your men not come to find us soon?"

"Lord Wolf's men," he corrected her. "And no, for we cannot be sure they are not wounded or lost themselves. They were fighting fiercely when I rode after you and Sir Francis. Besides, it will soon be too dark for them to mount a search party through unknown terrain. They are unlikely to look for us now until first light at the earliest."

Hugh frowned, settling beside her on the bed of ferns. He was kneeling up, his arms folded across his chest; she could feel his disapproval like a tangible thing. "Why did you remove the cloak? I gave it to you because you were shivering. You will be cold without it."

His proximity nearly undid her. Her hands longed to reach for him, to feel again his hardness and maleness against her own body.

"I am not cold," she whispered, and her eyes sought his through the darkness. "Besides, it was too wet to wear."

"Then you were right to remove it," he said grudgingly, watching her. "There is an oat biscuit in my pocket from when I broke my fast today. Are you hungry, mistress?"

She hesitated, then answered daringly, "Not for food."

His face stiffened, his body tensing. For a second she thought he would take her in his arms. Only he did not. His eyes widened on her face though, and she did not look away, holding his gaze through the gloom of their little shelter.

Desire beat between them. Yet she must not touch him. He had rejected her once already, and her heart still hurt from that humiliation. She wanted to know his hands on her, to become his lover, to ruin herself in his arms. But she must not show her need for him, nor give him the chance to hurt her again.

This time he must be the one to make the first move.

Hugh Beaufort drew a deep breath, then let it out slowly, perhaps considering how to respond to her comment without falling into the trap of asking what she meant. Or perhaps he was deciding it would be better to pretend not to have understood her.

Rain trickled coldly down her neck from above. She gasped, twisting to look up, but it was growing too dark to see. "The shelter… It's leaking."

"Hold still." He reached up to shift one of the leafy branches a touch to the left, closing the gap above her head, but then did not draw back his hand. His voice grew husky. "There, it's fixed."

He was too close. She could not bear it. Briefly she closed her eyes. It might be drier out of the rainstorm, but this makeshift shelter might yet prove more dangerous than the weather outside. The small dark space smelled sweetly of leaves and ferns, as heady as any wine. And it was such an intimate place, forcing them to sit so close together…

She risked a swift glance in his direction; shadows played on his face, dark stubble on his chin, his clear green gaze watching her. There was turmoil in those eyes, the tension in his body telling her without words how close he was to snapping the thread on his self-control.

Hugh Beaufort was tempted, there was no doubt of it. But he seemed on edge too.

"You must forgive me for having brought you here, Master Beaufort. Since leaving my father's house, I seem to have caused you much difficulty," she admitted, watching him from under her lashes. "You, my sister, Lord Wolf… It was never my intention to be so much trouble to you all."

His mouth twisted. "I do not like to contradict a lady, Mistress Tyrell, but I suspect you had every intention of causing as much trouble and alarm as possible."

"No indeed," she began hurriedly, meaning to explain in part how she had come to leave her father's house, but he interrupted her.

"For shame, Susannah!" Hugh leaned close in the darkness, his voice suddenly harsh, attacking her. "Let us be honest with each other at least. You are a very thorn in my flesh. If I did not know it to be impossible, I would say you had engineered this enforced intimacy between us tonight. How else is it possible that we have been stranded together like this? To have run out of the forest at precisely the moment I came riding by and cast yourself under my horse's hooves, with that villain only moments behind you, so forcing me to chase after you and defend your honor, seems fortuitous indeed."

She breathed faster, taken aback by his anger. "What are you saying, sir?"

"I'm saying that if it was any other woman, I would call it fate and accept God's will in this matter. But with you, it feels less like chance and more like…careful planning."

"You cannot mean that."

"Can I not?" His voice sounded almost slurred, as though he were drunk, yet she guessed it was not drink, but strong emotion that drove him to make such cruel accusations. "You ran away from home and your father's protection without considering how such recklessness might affect those you love, what the cost of your disobedience might be at such a time. Even now your sister is at court under suspicion of collusion with the queen; if found guilty, she could face the executioner. I wished to be there, to support her and Lord Wolf, and lend my aid if I could." His voice tore at her. "Instead I had to leave court, to ride north and find you, risking much in the process."

"I did not ask you to come in search of me!"

"I am not just talking of myself, Mistress Tyrell." They were so close now, shoulder to shoulder in the dark, narrow space. It would be night soon. Rain ticked loudly on the makeshift roof of branches, then a rising wind shook their pitiful shelter as the storm swept in around them. "Those men back there, Lord Wolf's retinue… They were attacked by Sir Francis and his mob. Some of them may lie dead or wounded from that skirmish. Now do you see how your willfulness may have cost lives?"

He was twisting everything about the wrong way, making her seem the guilty one, when in truth it was her father who was guilty for having betrayed her trust, and Sir Francis for having incarcerated her, meaning to rape her at his leisure. And all Hugh Beaufort could do was blame her for being…what, female and unmarried?

She stared back at him, shocked by the vehemence in his voice, and could not find the right words to say.

Hugh dragged off his riding gloves and cast them aside. "Now it falls to me to do what your father, Sir John, seemingly could not," he said thickly. "To tame you and break you to bridle."

A red tide of temper blurred her vision at this final insult. What, was she no better than an animal, to be treated with so little regard for her feelings and station in life?

Instinctively she moved, meaning to slap his face. He must have caught the gesture, even in the dark of their shelter, for he seized her wrist and drew her toward him instead.

"Let me go!" she exclaimed.

"Not yet," Hugh told her huskily, and jerked her forward over his knees like a prize of war. "There is a time for all things, even for a woman to be chastised. Tonight I have been granted an opportunity to teach you how a man responds to being teased, and to having a woman risk his life with her reckless behavior. I do not wish to hurt you, far from it. But I cannot allow this opportunity to pass me by."

Teased? Chastised?

She lay stunned, facedown across his lap. What in God's name did he mean?

Then his hand came down hard on her bottom and she gasped, realizing too late what he intended.

"What are you doing?"

"Forgive me, Susannah," he said grimly, one arm hooked round her waist, holding her in place across his knees, "but in truth, you have brought this chastisement on yourself."

His hand fell again a second later, flat-palmed and stinging, just hard enough to leave her bottom smarting even through her rough clothing. She had thought he spoke in jest, or to frighten her with words. But it seemed Hugh Beaufort was in earnest; the king's clerk intended to spank her, and soundly too.

And why? To punish her for teasing him with smiles? For running away from an arranged marriage? Fury flooded through her at this injustice. How dare he treat her like this? Only her father had ever chastised her before, with his hand or his riding crop, when she had disobeyed him as a girl.

What gave Hugh Beaufort the right to stand in for her father?

Struggling and kicking her heels, she cried out, "No, stop!" but her tormenter neither stopped nor let her up from his knee.

"This is for making eyes and flirting at your sister's wedding feast, even though you knew yourself promised to another man."

His hand slapped her bottom in response to every accusation, making her jerk and hiss with indignation.

"This is for attempting to seduce me when we rode back together from Lord Wolf's hunting lodge. This is for risking good men's lives by fleeing your father's house and riding alone through such dangerous country. And this...this is for being damn impossible to resist..."

His voice grew more charged as he spanked her, again and again, until at last Hugh tumbled her over on his lap, staring down into her flushed face, framed with wild wet hair.

"Dear God, what am I doing?"

Susannah could not reply, too shaken by his chastisement, her body aching. She drew a furious breath, determined to tell this cruel brute exactly what he had been doing and how much she hated him for it. But the words of hate would not come.

His spanking ought to have hurt her. Instead it had driven her higher and higher into a state of physical excitement. Now it felt as though she were floating above his lap, no longer connected to the earth, or to anything. Her thighs trembled, and between them, a moist pleasure bloomed. Suddenly she longed for something she had never experienced before: penetration.

Abruptly, Hugh Beaufort bent his head, lifting her toward him at the same time.

"So beautiful," he said thickly.

Their mouths met, and she forgot everything. Everything except how desperately she wanted him.

She had thought Hugh would take her mouth cruelly, that his kisses would be an extension of the stinging punishment he had just meted out to her bottom. Instead the king's clerk kissed her with passion, his mouth slanting firm against hers.

His hands closed possessively about her waist, holding her tight, and she closed her eyes, willing him not to let go. There was no anger or resentment in his kiss, only an urgent desire that Susannah understood perfectly well, for she felt it too.

"Susannah," he muttered against her mouth, then brushed down her throat in a row of hot, fiery kisses before returning to her mouth.

She pressed herself against him as they kissed, grasping his shoulders, so broad, so powerful, then felt her way up to the back of his strong neck. His tongue pushed between her lips, parting them. She sighed as his tongue slipped inside her mouth, her own tongue stroking against his, remembering how wildly they had kissed that afternoon in Yorkshire.

That day they had been out in the open air, under the sun on the rough York moorland, where anyone might have seen them together.

Now though they were alone, enclosed in this dark womb of a shelter, with no one to see them or insist they call a halt. She suddenly knew, with an internal jolt like a punch to her stomach, that Hugh Beaufort was going to take her tonight, to make her his mistress.

She gave a muffled groan against the tongue exploring her mouth. She wanted him. And she did not care what it would mean to be his. Even if it brought her ruin.

"Yes," Hugh murmured, as though she had spoken, and she felt cool air on her flesh as he dragged the smock shirt over her head.

It must be too dark in the shelter for him to see her clearly, she thought. Yet when he reached out, Hugh found her unerringly. His finger flicked across one nipple and she moaned again, oddly enjoying the way he tormented her. He flicked it again and her nipple tautened, her whole breast growing ripe and heavy, eager to be touched and discovered.

Without a word, Hugh bent his head and dragged her nipple into his mouth, sucking hard.

Breathless, Susannah cried out incoherently, her head falling back in wonder and delight. His lips tightened about her nipple, licking furiously over the whorled ridges as they swelled inside his mouth. Her body arched toward his, eager to show her willingness. She wanted more, needed more, yet did not know how to tell him.

It seemed Hugh understood, however, for he laid her gently on the floor of the shelter, kneeling over her in the darkness. She sighed, lying there with her breasts exposed, feeling no shame at her nakedness but only a marvelous rightness. Under the muddied hose, her core was already melting with anticipation.

She could not read his expression, but heard the harsh tear of his breathing and guessed he must be as aroused as she was. He cupped her breast and squeezed, playing with her flesh. Then lowered his head to her nipple again, this time seizing a goodly mouthful of breast too, and suckling hard there, as though to milk her with his lips.

"Hugh," she managed, and led his other hand to her untouched breast. Hungrily, he moved his mouth from one nipple to the other, then back again, squeezing and fondling both her breasts as he sucked. He was not gentle. But she did not want kindness. His driving possessiveness, his male aggression, that was what she needed and what he was offering her. "Please… Oh yes, please."

He lifted his head, looking down at her. His eyes glinted with lust. "It's good? You like to be touched there?"

"Yes, sir."

He made a harsh noise under his breath, and his voice deepened. "I like it when you call me sir, Susannah."

"Then I shall always call you sir."

He took her mouth again, and their tongues mated this time. Every inch of his body was pressed against hers so she could feel his arousal, his hard cock pulsing. She raised her hips toward it, saying his name silently, begging him with her body for completion. It was like every dream she had had where Hugh made love to her, except the reality was better.

Gasping, he sat up and unsheathed the dagger at his belt. Slowly, watching her through the darkness, he laid the dagger to one side— no doubt where he could easily find it again if they were attacked.

He removed his boots and his doublet, then began to pull down his tight hose, wearing nothing at the end but his unfastened shirt. She watched him, fascinated by the thick swinging cock that sprang free between his thighs. Her mouth grew dry at the sight of it, and she panted softly, her heart suddenly racing. For although she was a virgin, her body's instincts were already beginning to take over.

Then he laid hold of her hose at the waist, pulled them firmly down to her knees, and thence to her feet, and off.

Naked, she lay beneath his stare, moist and ready. And knew that she had always been ready for this.

Six

"Yes," she whispered as Hugh trailed a long finger from her breasts to her belly, then lower still, seeking the natural split between her legs, the place where life was meant to issue forth…as well as enter. "Yes, I need it… Need you. Just a little lower…"

His finger found her.

She cried out in surprise, even though she had been expecting it. Her hands clutched the ferns she had thrown down for their bed, crushing their delicate fronds. Her head throbbed with blood as though she would faint. She wanted to beg him to stop teasing, to take her and have done with it. Yet her body tingled pleasurably; it seemed to want more curious exploration, more of his strange meticulous passion.

"Sweetest Susannah." His finger traced her hidden lips, stroking up and down in a slow, insistent way that made her toes curl and her body ache. Then he pressed inside, invading her virgin body, and she stiffened beneath him. His voice shook. "I meant to resist your beauty. To hold you at arm's length. But you have conquered me. You have destroyed me."

"Only to make you afresh."

He took her hand, placing it on his shaft. "To imprison me." He drew her hand up and down his cock, showing her how to pleasure him. "That's it. Slow and steady."

She followed his instruction. His cock hardened beneath her fingers, and he drew a sharp breath, watching as she stroked him.

"You have a sure touch," he murmured, "for a virgin."

She focused on his cock, his long shaft, veined and boldly erect, the big head glistening as she stroked her thumb across it. Good clean strokes, she told herself, massaging him firmly, enjoying the way he jerked and pulsed in her hand. Something about his hardness loosened her belly, her core melting at the sight and feel of such arousal. His scent was irresistible too, strong and masculine, making her body weak with longing. Yet her head still worked, mulling over what had been said, despite the desire churned up inside by his kisses.

So Hugh thought she wished to imprison him by yielding her virginity to him? He meant marriage, no doubt. Then why not simply spurn her, choose not to lie with her? Hugh Beaufort was a man of good family, a courtier, a servant of the king, and free to make his own choices. He did not have to be conquered and destroyed, as he put it.

She was a woman. As such, her father would make all the choices for her while she stayed under his roof and accepted his rule. Then her husband would tell her what to say, what to do, which gowns to wear, how to behave in public and in the bedroom. Even if she lived outside such ties, having lost her honor, some man would make her his mistress, and then she would dance to his tune instead. Either that or shut herself up in a nunnery for the rest of her days, and wither there, cold and unloved, never again knowing the touch of a man.

He was a man. That meant his choices were still all open to him, that he could choose for himself how to live, and who to love.

She did not understand Hugh Beaufort. She did not understand why he should be so angry with her for leaving home. Nor why he desired her when he clearly disapproved of her ways. It could not simply be his physical needs, she thought. There must be other women he could turn to for relief: a mistress, a paid whore, a courtly lady whose husband did not care whose bed she shared.

Yet instead of those women, he wanted to kiss *her*, Susannah Tyrell, to take *her* virginity, to be inside *her*.

Susannah smiled, aware for the first time that she had power over this man, power of a sort she had never before experienced.

Instinctively she bent her head to take his cock in her mouth, eager to learn how it would feel and taste there.

"Sweet Jesu!"

Hugh sounded shocked. Yet he made no move to stop her. Indeed he encouraged her. His hand tangled in her damp hair, tugging as she pursed her lips, then drew them slowly down his shaft as far as she could manage.

It was a struggle not to gag on his length, but she did her best, wishing to please him as he had pleased her with his caresses. Then she straightened, drawing her mouth up again, leaving his broad shaft gleaming with her spit.

"Again," Hugh muttered, guiding her head down, "again."

He tasted good and clean. Strong and ready. Susannah reveled in the smooth glide of his flesh between her lips; there was indeed power in this exchange, she thought, and was glad she had escaped from Sir Francis before he could make her perform such lewd acts with him. That would have been more than she could have borne. With Hugh though, this act did not feel lewd, but potent and heady.

The world shrank to his cock in her mouth, the patter of rain on wet leaves above them, the small sounds of pleasure she found herself making in the back of her throat.

His need became her need. Her nipples stiffened as she sucked; her core was soon slick with excitement.

"Enough," he muttered, almost harsh in the way he spoke to her.

Susannah fell back, balancing on her heels, looking up at him. Naked, she felt so vulnerable, utterly open to this man, yet knew herself to be safe with him. Tonight at least he would not hurt her. She was innocence and he was experience: coming together they would set this damp shelter alight, a blaze in the darkness that would be seen for miles.

But afterward… What would happen afterward?

Damn afterward, she told herself, closing her mind to the voice inside her head that spoke of wickedness and carnal knowledge and untold punishments for sin.

She did not have to trust Hugh Beaufort forever, she reminded herself. Only for tonight.

I will never be a wife, she insisted to herself, and in that instant was determined to make her own prophecy come true. Wives were dull and respectable creatures who sat at home, and sewed samplers, and raised their husbands' children, and died in the dutiful throes of childbirth. She would never accept such a fate.

"Better a whore than a wife," she said out loud.

He kissed her fiercely. "You are neither tonight. You are love itself. Sweet, intoxicating, and irresistible."

"Am I?"

She wanted to believe him. Only sometimes she still felt a few steps away from being a child. Uncertain what to do or say, fearing to displease him with her ignorance. Then heat would catch at her and bring her back to life, a woman and no longer a child, aware of her body, gauging her physical needs as a man would.

She cupped her breasts, weighing them, enjoying their heaviness in her hands, and saw his gaze narrow.

"You are so very beautiful," he whispered deeply.

She smiled at the compliment, then touched him instead, slowly, unsure. Ran her fingers down his strong neck. Played along his shoulder and down his powerful chest. Hugh Beaufort was beautiful too, she thought. With his shirt open, she could see—and feel—his nipples. She ran around one with the tip of her finger, and felt the dusky skin stiffen, growing swiftly erect.

She heard his breath catch, then he captured her hand in his, stilling its caress even as he pressed it against his chest.

"Take me," she whispered.

With her free hand Susannah continued to stroke slowly down his flat belly, then paused; she knew what lay below his waist, for she had tasted him there. Could still taste him, in fact. A ravening hunger filled her, immense, building to a storm in her veins.

She ran her tongue along her lips, wetting them. "Please, Hugh. It's time."

He moved above her, but hesitated there, poised to take her. "You would lose your honor with me?" he asked, his voice hoarse, shaking. "I have struck you tonight. I have chastised you. I am no gentle lover. Susannah, you are sure this is what you want?"

She had never felt so sure of anything in her life, Susannah thought. It was like being drunk though, this sensation. As on a feast day when she had supped too much wine, her head felt too light, her breath high up in her chest, and everything off-balance.

"Do it," she urged him, parting her thighs in blatant invitation.

His eyes met hers through the darkness, testing her resolve. His hands slid down the inside of each thigh at once, all the way to the melting heat at her core. Hot hands, cold thighs, racing her heart.

His breath came warm on her thighs, the fair mass of his head descending. "First, this."

Susannah moaned; his kisses tingled on the delicate skin of her inner thighs where no man had ever caressed her, let alone kissed. She had not even known that a man would wish to kiss a woman there. But she was not unwilling. Far from it. Let him but taste her, and she feared her whole world would shift and topple, the stars would tumble into darkness and her breath stop.

Hugh's head bent. His lips brushed her sex, gently tracing her mons veneris; then he cupped that fleshy mound, groaning under his breath. She whispered his name, and suddenly his mouth was right there, sipping at her slit, the moist cleft, like it was nectar.

She could not bear it!

"Sweet Jesu," she groaned.

Heat bubbled within, and something deeper, more alien and disturbing. The secret power she had sensed before seemed to draw near again, as though it knew her name and was intent on possessing her soul. She became frightened, even though she knew it to be ridiculous.

Still the power stormed at her and Susannah cried out, gripping his hair, dragging him nearer even as she pushed him away, suddenly lost, no longer sure what she wanted.

"Let me know you," he managed persuasively, fighting against her strength. His voice was husky, coming from deep in his throat. "Let me in, Susannah."

When she moaned but did not refuse him, his lips grew bolder, slanting over the heart of her heat, the slick core of her being.

He sucked at her flesh, and her thighs jerked in violent response.

"No!" she sobbed, but he was not listening.

Hugh sucked at her again, settling into a steady, pulsing rhythm. She lay beneath him, jerking, crying out, gripping his fair head. His lips clamped over her flesh, silent and relentless in his drive to destroy her, and her body began to shake. It was too much. Too much, too much. She did not think she could survive such intimacy. She would die…

"Hugh!" she moaned, twisting under him. "Oh God…Hugh!"

Susannah shuddered, and her whole body seemed to burst apart from the inside, like a seam splitting under tension.

For a moment she thought that she was dying, that Hugh Beaufort had killed her. Yet somehow she was unable to prevent her hips from pressing up hard against him, her voice crying out huskily, urging him to finish her. At the same time, an agonizing pleasure lanced through her, radiating out from her belly in the most delicious way to every inch of her body, and she convulsed, tensed beneath him, lost in the moment.

Her hands still clenched in his hair, she felt herself come down from the heights of pleasure, but slowly, her body trembling.

"What...what did you do to me?"

His laughter rumbled about the small dark space. "Nothing you will not do for me soon enough. If you wish to?"

"Yes," she managed, though she felt too shaken even to release him. "Yes please. Only show me how."

Hugh kissed his way up her belly and back to her breasts, teasing her nipples with his clever tongue. She was so intent on his caresses, she did not notice how he positioned himself between her thighs until it was too late, he was already there, his organ large against the virgin opening to her body.

His cock felt hot and tense, and larger than ever before, and she was suddenly fearful. What if he could not fit? What if he tore her in his passion?

"Hush," he murmured, seeming to sense her trepidation, and his hands smoothed down her thighs, keeping her wide for him. "I have you safe."

Her fingers still tangled in his hair, she drew him close and kissed his mouth, taking his lips hotly, her tongue thrusting inside, eager for him to feel her desire, to know how much she wanted this. Their tongues clashed, playing violently, every stab and thrust loosening the knot in her belly, making her slick and pliable, ready for his entry.

She drew back, gasping for air. "You taste of me," she said wonderingly.

Hugh bowed his head against her shoulder, groaning. He nudged the broad head of his cock inside, and she gasped, beginning to tremble again. He seemed to pause, as though checking she was not afraid, then pushed on. His progress felt inexorable now, his organ stretching her sex, entering her at last, the increasing sensation of fullness unfamiliar.

Susannah muttered "Now!" in his ear, and Hugh made a compulsive noise under his breath, then thrust hard inside, embedding himself fully between her thighs.

"Yes!" she cried as he took her virginity, wildly excited that the long-awaited moment was finally at hand.

Her first time was not as she had expected though. She had tensed at his entry, steeling herself for pain, yet there was almost none to be felt. No pain when he first entered her. No pain when he tore her maidenhead. And only the slightest twinge of discomfort as Hugh began to thrust, taking his weight on his hands, his head raised now, watching her, their gazes locked hotly together.

Yet she had been a virgin. She had never lain with a man before in her life. How was it possible not to feel pain at her deflowering?

"Susannah," he managed hoarsely, searching her face as though afraid he had been too forceful. "What is it? Did I hurt you?"

"It's good, it's good," she reassured him, and wrapped her thighs instinctively about his back, urging him deeper.

His eyes closed briefly at this assurance. Then Hugh let his head tilt back, the veins standing out on his neck, his whole body working as he thrust hard and fast. It was as though he had been holding himself in check the whole time they had been kissing, and could now race as he desired, taking his pleasure.

Susannah had always thought, secretly imagining a man and a woman together, that the woman would lie passive while the man ploughed her body like a furrow in a field. But to lie still while Hugh made love to her was impossible. A deeper impulse took hold of her, and she moved with him, raising her hips for each thrust, her hands grasping the broad expanse of his shoulders, his open shirt, damp with sweat.

Hugh grunted as her legs tightened about him, and thrust deeper, stroking his cock inside her slick body.

Hugh looked down at her for a long moment, his green eyes hooded, oddly unfamiliar, glittering with lust. "You like this? You like me inside you?"

"Yes!"

"I want to make you my slave, Susannah. My concubine. Keep you beneath me forever." His voice was unsteady. "Is it wrong for me to feel like that?"

"Perhaps."

Susannah licked her lips though, more than a little excited by the idea of being this man's slave, *his concubine*, and saw his eyes flash, as though that tiny movement alone could provoke desire in him.

Hugh bent his head to kiss her, and their tongues slid hotly together, warring, competing with each other. His cock thickened and pulsed, fitting inside her so snugly now her sex had to stretch to accommodate his girth. Now it felt like pain. But a pain she had never known before, more stark pleasure than pain, her body twisting exquisitely on an invisible rack.

His cock was so long inside her it was hitting bottom with each thrust. She must have made some inadvertent noise, for suddenly his hands slid beneath her buttocks, raising her; the angle of his entry altered so that he was no longer hurting her. Now the depth was perfect: his thrusts were straight, fast, plummeting blows that drove her deeper and deeper into some kind of furious sexual frenzy.

She caught her lower lip between her teeth and bit down, muffling the moan that was rising within her. It felt so good!

"Let it possess you," he commanded her, frowning. "Stop holding back."

But Susannah could not. She fought against his order, suddenly scared of the powerful surge cresting in her body. What if she were to scream? Or thrash about like a madwoman?

Above their shelter, the wind howled, snatching at the branches he had woven so patiently together for a roof. She imagined them being wrenched away, their heaving bodies exposed to the storm's power, the shirt plastered to his back under lashing rain. It would be fitting, she thought wildly. For another few minutes would see the storm inside her smash through the tattered barriers of her self-control and leave her helpless.

He was holding her off the ground now, shortening his thrusts as he strained for completion, their hips locked together. His shirt swung open as he thrust, falling loose from his shoulders. Hugh Beaufort no longer looked like a courtier and the king's clerk, she thought, staring up at him. Now he looked dangerous, forced to the very edges of what was permissible; a man who had broken so many rules there was no going back to his old, careful way of life.

One hand stroking down the dark expanse of his chest, Susannah reveled in the heat of his skin, the erratic beat of his heart. She guessed from his labored breathing that Hugh was not far off the end, and wished secretly that it could last a little longer, that she could experience again that intense pleasure of his tongue on her sex.

So her eyes widened in surprise when Hugh felt between their bodies, expertly locating the slick nub of flesh aching there, and rubbed back and forth across it with his thumb.

The rough callouses on his thumb seemed to bring her to a peak more swiftly even than his thrusting cock.

"No!" It was too much; she could not bear his touch there, in so intimate a place. Not when her whole body was falling apart. "Please, Hugh, I can't…I can't take it!"

But his gaze captured hers, and she felt herself burn up slowly from the inside under that authoritative stare, like a twist of paper held to the fire.

"Now, Susannah," he said thickly, his thumb rubbing and pressing her flesh mercilessly. "Come now!"

With a high feverish cry, she tensed against him, thighs clamped tight about his back, her nails raking down his chest.

"Hugh!"

She came swiftly to her peak after that, head thrown back, her mouth open, sobbing in sheer wonder at the pleasure firecracking through her body. To her amazement, she felt the narrow passage of her sex pulse in violent spasms about his cock, dragging him in deeper as she came, squeezing down hard on his cock as though willing him to come with her.

A quiet groan told her he was not unmoved by those strong muscular contractions. A second later, while she was still shuddering with pleasure, Hugh thrust suddenly deep, burying his head in her shoulder as he too reached his peak. With a shout of pleasure, he surged ferociously inside her, their bodies as one.

As he lay there in her arms, panting into the darkness as though he had just run across three fields, Susannah felt a slow, warm, spreading sensation between her thighs which could only be, she reasoned, the release of his seed.

The wind continued to shake their makeshift shelter for some time, and she felt rain dripping from the branches above. But a sweet drowsiness filled her, and she nestled into his covering body, letting sleep take her wherever it would.

"Susannah." The voice was quiet but insistent. "Susannah, wake up. I can hear horses."

A moment later Hugh was gone.

Susannah blinked, sitting up in a daze and picking leaves from her long, unbound hair. She was naked. That shocked her for one horrifying instant. Then she remembered the events of the night before, and heat glowed in her cheeks.

Not shame. She no longer thought herself capable of

shame—and besides, why should she be ashamed of following her heart?

No, the heat in her cheeks was a mixture of excitement and girlish pleasure. For last night she had entered an astonishing new world where she was no longer a virgin, and the secret ways of men and women in the bedchamber had been stripped of their mystery. It was almost like having peeked round the frustrating rood screen at church to find God Himself at the altar, winking at her.

She had lain with a man last night. Nothing would ever be the same again.

Abruptly she heard a noise outside the shelter, and her mind flickered back, revisiting Hugh's words.

I can hear horses.

With unsteady hands, she reached for her discarded clothes. The shelter beneath the trees was still largely intact, but there were gaps where the storm had ripped away a branch or two during the night. She dressed hurriedly, realizing that her nudity might be spied through one of the thin, leafy gaps between branches.

She could hear Hugh's voice now, clear and strong, carrying through the forest. He sounded pleased rather than angry, and seemed to be asking more questions than he was answering.

Staring through the wet leaves, she was relieved to see that it was not Sir Francis who had arrived, but Lord Wolf's men. She recognized their livery and badges, and in a flash went from relief to consternation. To be discovered in such disarray, with a man not her husband…

Gathering her wits, Susannah crawled out of the makeshift shelter and stood, head held high, tidying her hair.

She swung Hugh's cloak around her shoulders to hide her rough clothes beneath. Let Wolf's men think what they would. She would not betray even with a sideways glance what had passed between her and Hugh Beaufort last night.

Hugh came, leading a horse for her. "Wolf's men routed those thugs last night with a good fight, by all accounts. Thankfully we took a few of their mounts as booty, so none will have to share a saddle."

His expression revealed nothing as he waited for her response. When none came, he frowned, his sharp green gaze searching her face. "I have told the men it would be best if we quit this area at once and ride south, for the court. Are you ready?"

Susannah nodded, not meeting his eyes, and allowed him to help her to mount the dappled gray mare, setting her foot in his cupped hands.

"There is no sidesaddle," he explained awkwardly.

"No matter."

He heaved her up into the saddle, then bent his head, unnecessarily checking the girth straps. There was a dark color in his cheeks. "Susannah," he began, but she shortened the horse's reins and turned the animal away a few paces.

"There is nothing to say," she told him.

As she glanced back, she caught a swift flash of anger in his eyes and was surprised. She had thought he would prefer to forget last night's events. Certainly she had no desire to dwell on them. Not before this rough company, at least.

"Then let me at least give you this," he muttered, and dragged off his riding gloves. She saw the glint of his ring as he drew it off his finger and followed, handing it up to her. "I want you to keep this. Not as a promise but as a gift." He saw her hesitation, and his face hardened. "Please."

She stared, meeting his eyes. She knew how hard it was for her to beg for what she wanted. How much harder must it be for a man like Hugh Beaufort?

"Thank you," she said huskily, and took the ring, weighing it in her hand. It was a heavy gold ring, set with a small ruby that flashed as she turned it over, too big for her finger. Carefully she pushed it inside her belt pouch and dragged the drawstring shut.

Not as a promise, but as a gift.

"It will be my token until we can speak privately," he told her shortly, then gave an abrupt nod before she could argue, effectively dismissing the subject.

Susannah stiffened, for she knew what that meant. Until he could ask her to marry him because they had slept together last night. Anger and despair flared inside her. To marry a man out of a sense of duty and honor seemed to her as empty and cold as any marriage arranged between strangers for the sake of an heir. She knew her answer already. But she could guess how he would take it.

Well, let him try to get her alone on the road to court. He would find it harder than he thought.

She watched in frustration as Hugh strode back to his horse, a stout black horse with a single white star on its forehead. He swung up into the saddle and raised his gloved hand to the others who rode with them.

"For the south, and King Henry's court!"

Seven

SUSANNAH HAD NEVER BEEN more than a day's ride south of Yorkshire, and had certainly never seen a royal palace before. So when they joined the dusty track beside the River Thames and the flagged towers at Greenwich came into view, rising stately above the treetops, she found herself staring at the huge turreted palace like a country yokel, her mouth open. It did seem a home fit for a king. And all his court too, she reminded herself. Fine lords and ladies, and their servants, and their servants' servants, and the grooms, and the potmen and the drabs who worked in the kitchen stews. Many hundreds cramped together, she had been told, and by Eloise's account the royal residences never smelled too sweet after a few months' occupation.

Yet now she could see for herself how vast the place was, she thought it a wonder the king could ever find his bedchamber for it must be a rabbit warren of chambers and corridors inside.

She lifted her face to the sunshine, smiling up at the blue sky. This was a happier end to her adventure than she had dreamed possible after Sir Francis had dared to incarcerate her in his foul country manor.

Ahead lay court, and its countless marvels. And what a fine day it was to be entering Greenwich. The river ran broad and glittering in the sunshine, cutting a swathe through meadow grasses that seemed so much greener and more lush than those in the north. Birds sang in the hedgerows and the bright air hummed with insects. It was hard to imagine, on such a glorious day, that Queen Anne had been arrested for treason and lay not far along this shining river in the Tower of London, awaiting trial.

Hugh spurred his horse alongside hers. He had been speaking to one of Lord Wolf's men, and she could see from his face that he was concerned.

"Mistress Tyrell," he began, for since that night in the forest he had only ever addressed her formally, and had kept far away from her chamber whenever they lodged at roadside inns, "I have been thinking."

"Oh dear."

Hugh's face stiffened, but he continued calmly enough, "It will not do for you to be seen entering the royal court in men's attire. I wish you had allowed me to find a gown for you. And a sidesaddle. Then you could have arrived at court with proper ceremony. As it is, we shall have to draw as little attention to your presence as possible." He surveyed her for a moment, his lips tight. "I shall tell the steward that you are my page boy. If you draw your hood forward, and keep your face and hair hidden until we are safely inside, we may yet avoid a scandal."

"And these men?"

"They are loyal to Wolf, and therefore to you, as his bride's sister. Besides, they are not fools. They know how heavily their master's wrath would fall on them if any man blabbed."

She looked at him coolly. "You are cross with me, Master Beaufort. I do not know why."

"On the contrary, I think you have a very good idea why."

"Because I would not bend to your will by dressing myself in some ill-fitting gown borrowed from a tavern wench?"

"The landlady of the Rising Sunne might not have shared your taste in gowns," Hugh remarked tersely, "but at least she wore one!"

Her brows rose at his sharp tone, which she matched with her reply. "I am happy in shirt and hose, sir," she told him airily. "I need nothing more to cover my modesty."

"Is that so?"

She watched as Hugh jabbed accidentally at his horse's mouth, sending the poor animal jerking sideways. He shortened the reins, trying to correct its course, and swore when the horse reared up, nearly throwing him from the saddle. By the time he had his confused mount under control again, his face was slightly flushed, his mouth a straight line.

"You are beyond willful, Mistress Tyrell," he growled. "I am no longer surprised that you ran away from home, for your father must have been forever punishing you for one thing or another. Though not harshly enough, it seems. If you were my daughter, I would be inclined to whip some better sense into you."

Susannah's gaze narrowed on his face. "Yes, clearly that is your answer to every woman who dares to gainsay you. To bring out the whip or the ducking stool."

"That is unjust!"

Her gaze warred furiously with his. "Is it? I seem to recall your hand being put to good use on my behind a few nights ago, in the hope of teaching me obedience."

"Little good that did." He glared back at her, giving no indication that he regretted having spanked her that night. He looked weary, his eyes slightly bloodshot, chin dark with stubble. They had ridden hard these past few days, Hugh constantly pushing the pace, as though he could not bear to be on the road a moment longer than necessary. Now his riding boots and clothes were stained with road dust, and his patience seemed to be running out. "And keep your voice down: the men are staring."

"Let them stare. I threw my good name away when I left the protection of my father's house, as well you know. There seems little point in hoping to retrieve it now."

"This is nonsense," he muttered angrily, then swore under his breath, for they were approaching the outskirts of the palace and it was becoming harder to ride two abreast.

Susannah looked about herself with interest, for the busiest place she had ever been was York on a market day. But this was nothing like York. Dwellings had been erected in a haphazard fashion along the approach to Greenwich Palace, their high-built fronts overhanging the route, and the track was narrow and increasingly crowded with traders. She saw ragged young children playing a ball game in the dust, and others paddling in the sunlit river beyond the road, and listened wistfully to their laughter. Further along, the road suddenly broadened out to accommodate all the provisions wagons and other travelers like themselves coming in and out of the royal estate.

On the approach to the royal parkland, three filthy old sailors in rags came limping alongside the horses, their caps held out for alms, crying in cracked voices that they had each lost a limb in "the king's service." Even as she stared down at them in pity, two burly liveried men with whips charged through the crowds, threatening to throw them in the stocks as beggars.

The sailors turned and fled at the sight of their whips, surprisingly nimble on their feet for cripples, and Susannah watched them go in astonishment.

The palace gates suddenly loomed ahead. Hugh drew closer in the crowd, their knees brushing as they rode. He seemed distracted. "We have not had a chance to speak privately since Wolf's men caught up with us in the forest. Yet there are things which must be said." He looked at her intently. "Might I beg five minutes alone with you before I take you to see Lord Wolf and the Lady Eloise?"

Susannah narrowed her eyes, searching his face. Some instinct warned her against speaking privately with him. For she knew he was troubled over what they had done together. But she was not. And now she had cast aside her reputation, she would be damned if she would be forced to marry where there was neither love nor mutual respect.

"No," she decided at last.

"No?"

"There is nothing that needs to be said, sir. What's done is done. So I would prefer it if you would escort me directly to my sister's chamber."

He stared at her, and she could almost hear his teeth grinding together. "You are the most infuriating, troublesome—"

"Yes, yes," she agreed blithely, interrupting him, "and oh, for a whip to lay about my sides like one of these shiftless beggars. But hey ho, it is not to be. This is who I am, Master Beaufort, and I shall not change my colors for all your wishing. You must like it or lump it, as we say in Yorkshire."

Hugh said nothing to this sally, but rode ahead with a grim expression to speak with the sergeant at arms on the palace gates.

Moments later the small troop was ushered through, dust rising in their wake as they trotted gently under a stone archway and into a sunlit courtyard overlooked by many glittering windows. Susannah had never seen such an astonishing sight and sat her horse in wonder, craning her neck to see how high the buildings rose until she felt quite dizzy.

Hugh helped her dismount, his face tight with impatience. "Susannah," he said in her ear, "it was one thing for you to eschew my company on the journey south, and refuse to sit at table with me. I know ladies must have their revenge on men they feel have wronged them in some way, though what I did to offend you is still uncertain in my mind. But you must be made to see sense in the matter of our future. Five minutes' privy speech with me. That is all I ask. Then I shall take you to the Lady Eloise and say no more on the subject."

She looked at him speculatively. They had lain together for one night, yes. But that was no reason to enter into a rigidly binding agreement to remain bedfellows forever without love on both sides. And the sooner he knew her mind, the better.

Besides, Hugh Beaufort was tiresome enough to keep pressing her for an answer until he had been heard and refused. To hear him out now would save them both trouble.

And she had accepted his ring in the forest as a token. Indeed, it still sat heavy in her belt pouch, from where she had taken it out once or twice when alone, trying it on each of her fingers in turn. But only out of curiosity. Not because she harbored some secret wish to be Mistress Beaufort, wife to the king's clerk.

"Oh, very well." She saw a flash of triumph in his green eyes, and shook her head warningly. "Five minutes. Though it will do no good, sir. So you may wipe that smirk off your face."

He gave orders to the weary men who were dismounting around them, then inclined his head to her.

"Follow me then." Hugh Beaufort tapped a riding crop impatiently against his dust-stained thigh as he waited for her to say farewell to her horse, for Susannah had grown fond of the dappled gray who had carried her so swiftly and faithfully over the past few days. "And once we are inside the palace, for God's sake keep your hood up, your head down, and speak to no one. These are dangerous times at court. Lord Wolf will flay my skin from my back if I bring further shame on his family name by letting anyone see you in that guise."

—⁓—

Hugh led her to his quarters, seeing the surprise on her face as he ushered her inside and barred the door against intruders. His room was no doubt smaller than she had expected for the king's clerk, little better than a bare cell with stone flags, one narrow window, and grim stone walls dominated by a large wooden cross hanging opposite the bed. But he hoped there were signs that he was not a mere servant: a row of calf-bound volumes with gilt-tooled spines stood neatly on the desk, and the place had been kept clean and swept during his absence, the grate set with logs and kindling against his return. A fur-lined cloak hung draped over a screen in the corner, and a dark chest stood under the window, his initials carved elaborately into the wood.

Indications of his status at court had never mattered much to him. But now, looking about his chilly, unwelcoming quarters, Hugh knew he needed to change his ways or resign himself to a monk-like existence for the rest of his days. For women liked to be kept by their husbands, and kept well. So he must make more of an effort to seem wealthy, even if he could not quite manage the ostentation of a jeweled cap or thread of gold on his sleeves.

Susannah stood silent as he strode across the chamber, threw his dusty saddle bags across the simple wooden cot that served as his bed, then turned to face her.

"Sir," she began, but did not have a chance to finish, for Hugh took her in his arms at once and slanted his mouth hungrily across hers. Her hood fell back and his fingers tangled hungrily in her long fair hair, pulling her nearer.

Hugh had not intended to kiss her.

He had told himself to remain calm and aloof, to speak to her of necessity and custom, persuade her that they must be married if only to protect his friend's wife, Lady Wolf, from further embarrassment over her runaway sister. Instead, he had taken one look at Susannah Tyrell standing in his privy chamber, the two of them alone together at last, and a convenient bed not a few feet away, and all his careful intentions had fallen away. Now here he was, holding her close, consumed by the most savage sexual need he could ever remember feeling.

The long ride must have infected his brain, he thought, then could think no more, for her hands came up to cup his face, and she leaned into him, eagerly returning his kiss.

Desire surged through him as her lips parted and his tongue met hers, bringing him swiftly, almost painfully erect. He kissed her deeply, savoring the sweetness of her mouth. His hands dropped to her waist, drawing her even closer, once more thrown by the feel of a woman's slender body in boy's clothing. It was both unnatural and exciting at the same moment, for he knew how tightly outlined her thighs and shapely bottom were in hose. What man could resist the lure of such a display?

He felt her breasts press against him, and remembered how they tasted in his mouth, the delicious upward tilt of her nipples, so tantalizing…

"Susannah, we must marry," he said huskily, pulling back to stare into that delightfully innocent blue gaze. Her eyes flashed, growing defensive at once, and he hurried to make her see sense, stumbling over his words. "We have been more than private together, Susannah. There may be…consequences. God forbid I should leave you with child, unmarried as you are. Or that you should marry Sir William Hanney with another man's babe in your belly."

Hugh drew a sharp breath, surprised by how sick with fury he felt on hearing those words from his own mouth.

He had known all along that she was betrothed to another man. There was no reason for him to feel so thrown off balance at voicing that possibility.

"Lord Wolf would never permit such an outrage against his family, so it is best we marry—and quickly," he finished.

Surely she must now understand how things had changed between them? The intimacies they had shared, however secret, made it imperative that she should marry him.

Hugh could see no other way forward if her family was to retain their honor. For although he had assured Susannah of the loyalty of Lord Wolf's men, in fact he knew it would only take a few loose words at court to condemn her as a whore—for leaving her home unaccompanied, for having been Sir Francis's unwilling guest for several days, for spending a night in the forest alone with Hugh himself, and for wearing such indecent clothes, unfit for a woman.

But Susannah was already pulling away from him, shaking her head. "No," she replied flatly, seeming to exclude any chance that she could change her mind.

Hugh closed his eyes briefly on a wave of frustration. Why must she be so stubborn? He counted silently to ten before asking lightly, "Your reason?"

"I would have thought my reason was clear to any but a fool. I do not wish to marry you just to ensure honor is satisfied. And you most certainly do not wish to marry me."

He felt a muscle jerk in his jaw. Did he wish to marry her? He did not know the answer to that, though he could answer with complete honesty, if she chose to ask the question, that he felt it was his duty to do so.

"I take it you now intend to marry Sir William Hanney after all? It was my belief you ran away from your father's house in order to avoid being forced into that unhappy alliance."

"Oh no," Susannah sharply corrected him. "I do not wish to marry Sir William. Nor any man, indeed."

"I see."

She arched her delicate brows. "I doubt it."

"I hope you will explain this surprising wish to remain celibate for the rest of your life. Though it is too late, I fear," he said drily, "for you to devote your virginity to the church."

She flushed.

"Come now, Susannah," he murmured, watching her downcast face. "Is it such a terrible prospect, consenting to be my wife? I am not wealthy, it's true. Sir William would give you a more comfortable life than I could offer, for my wage as the king's clerk is barely enough to keep me, let alone a wife as well."

"As if I care *that* for wealth!" she exclaimed, snapping her fingers.

"I am no old man either," he continued doggedly, trying to ignore her outburst as he pieced together his argument, careful as a lawyer, while remaining oddly unsure himself of his motives. But one thing was certain. He drew her close again, tightening his arm about her waist in a meaningful fashion. "With me as your husband, your bed would never be cold."

Her lashes lifted at that. Her eyes met his, a warm shining blue that left him breathless. "Oh, I know that, at least."

At least.

What had she meant by that? So there were objections in her mind…but what were they? Her gaze examined him openly, almost greedily, and she did not pull away but let him hold her with an intimacy that would have been shocking for a virgin. It was not that she did not desire him, clearly. And his need for her was becoming urgent.

Still he kept his hunger on a leash. This was a conversation they must have without being distracted by the tension singing between them.

"So what holds you back from an acceptance then?" he pondered aloud, watching her. "You fear your father's wrath, perhaps, at taking a husband not of his choosing?"

She laughed at that possibility, raising her brows again, and Hugh frowned. Frustration churned inside him, and not merely because of the unrelenting ache between his legs.

"You must forgive me, Susannah, but I do not understand you." He stepped back, releasing her. "You have no wish to be married to Sir William, you do not fear your father, and there is no doubt in your mind that I would make you a good husband. So why refuse me?"

She sighed, and reached out, placing her hand on his chest. Those intelligent eyes flashed up to engage his again, and he felt a shuddering jar through his body as though she had struck him.

"Hugh, I thank you kindly for your offer. But I have no wish to take a husband for myself. I am too much of a wayward spirit, or so my sister has always told me. And she is right. I could not tolerate any husband, whether he be young or old, poor or wealthy."

He was incredulous. "You will never marry?"

"Not without love to sweeten the cup, no." Even as the flat terms of her rejection left him frowning, her flirtatious smile made him suck his breath in harshly. Her hand still lay warm on his chest, a suggestive reminder of how intimately they knew each other now. "But that does not mean I wish to join the sisterhood and dedicate myself to Christ instead. Alas, I was not cut out for life in a nunnery."

His gaze fixed on her mouth, so luscious and sweet. "That I cannot deny."

"Yet I have begun to think I would not enjoy the life of a pampered mistress either. For I would still be under some man's power. No, I rather prefer to wend my own way."

What she was saying became suddenly clear to him. Turmoil filled his heart as he realized the fantasy she had constructed for herself.

Hugh shook his head, anxious for her safety. "Susannah, no. It is not possible for a woman to live independent of a man. Not without an income of your own, and I know that you have none. You must be serious and listen to me. No, don't make that face. How would you support yourself except in the company of a wealthy man?" He swallowed, hating himself for destroying her hope of freedom but knowing it must be done if she was to survive. "And no man's interest lasts forever. You would be passed from man to man, then abandoned to your fate once you were with child."

Her eyes shone, looking up at him. Were those tears?

"I see." Her voice was calm, level, yet it accused him all the same. "You are calling me a whore."

"No, never," he said swiftly. "But others will. And I would not see you treated badly. Not when I can prevent it."

Susannah turned away, and although Hugh wished to take her in his arms again, to reassure her in some way, he did not follow but stood uncertain. However much he might want her, she did not want him. Or not in terms that he could understand and accept.

He had been raised by a simple man with simple needs, and had learned the ways of the world accordingly. To his mind, a wife was a wife, a mistress a mistress, and there could be no third type of woman in a man's life, except for a whore. And he would never treat Susannah Tyrell so insultingly.

Reaching the unshuttered window, she looked down toward the river. A slight wind ruffled her fair hair.

He watched her averted face, and his need for her grew stronger than ever, perhaps because she had refused him. There was no more piquant sauce to a man's desire, the king had told him once, than the word "No" on a woman's lips.

Was he simply stung because Susannah Tyrell had spent the night in his arms, then rejected his offer of marriage out of hand? If so, the fit would soon pass. Tomorrow, or next week, or maybe next month, he would have forgotten this insane desire to possess her body again. He would see her in passing at court, and think her a mere curiosity, a beautiful woman who would not marry when asked, though she might lie down willingly enough with a man.

The sudden thought of Susannah in another man's bed hit him. For a few seconds he could not breathe, his chest tight, both fists clenched by his side. She could not, would not…

Yet what else did the future hold for a woman alone?

His jaw tightened. Susannah might not be his responsibility now they had reached the court. But she must be made to understand her likely fate if she could not bow to society's rules.

"The court is not a forgiving place," he managed in the end, searching for the right words to convince her. "Nor is our king likely to allow a woman the same independence as a man. You would have to leave court if you will not accept its rules, return to Yorkshire perhaps…"

"Never!"

"Lord Wolf must be your protector then."

"I have said no; I do not need a man's strength to keep me from harm." He heard the strain in her voice, and knew he was close to losing her. "Did you not hear me, sir? I thought we had reached an understanding on this matter. Must I now repeat myself?"

Hugh took three strides to reach her, swinging her to face him, his voice urgent as he stared down into her stubborn face. "For God's sake, Susannah, this is your life you are wagering against the king's favor. Do not be a fool. Your father was very wrong to allow you so much freedom that you failed to learn this lesson, hard though it may be for you to grasp now. There is no place at court—nor perhaps in the whole of England itself—for a young unmarried woman without title or money who refuses to live under the protection of a man."

He resisted the urge to kiss her, his gaze fixed on her pale, set expression. Was she even listening?

"I beg you to see some sense," he growled, wishing he could shake her. "You can have no idea of the forces that will be ranged against you should you choose openly to reject that rule. I would say nothing of your wishes, but you may not be so lucky if you choose to repeat these words elsewhere, and you should know that gossip at court has a way of outrunning its prey within hours. Not even Lord Wolf will be able to support you if your wild behavior finds displeasure in the king's eyes. And if you are brought down, he will be too, and your sister, Eloise, with him. Is that what you are seeking, Susannah? Disgrace and ruination for your whole family? Because that is what you will bring upon them if you speak like that before any other man."

Susannah closed her eyes for a long moment. Then she looked up at him, and he saw the hurt in her gaze, the feeling that he had betrayed her.

"Very well," she said stiffly. "I will make no decision yet about my future. But that does not mean I will marry you, sir. Nor anyone. But I shall keep my peace for now."

Hugh looked down at her soft mouth, and wished she could have said yes. That she would soon be his bride. For she was entirely too beddable to be left unmarried for long at court.

"Good," he said, and managed a smile.

He was free now. He had enjoyed her body, had offered her marriage, and now his duty was discharged. He should be happy. Satisfied, even. That was what he told himself, and tried very hard to believe it.

"Take me to my sister," Susannah whispered, not looking at him anymore. "I am tired and wish to see her."

His hands dropped from her shoulders. "Of course."

Susannah was exhausted by the time they reached the luxurious quarters where Lord Wolf and Eloise were lodged, dragging her feet on the cold stone flags of the interminable palace corridors. She had not lied to Hugh. She was indeed tired from the road, and had not eaten properly for days, having refused to eat at table with Hugh. She had feared he might make it too plain before the other men that he expected them to be married when they arrived in London, so had kept to herself as much as possible during their journey south.

Married! She felt sick at the thought.

To be married was not what she wanted, even if Hugh Beaufort knew how to make her shiver with delight. For once they were married he would no longer be her lover, but her master. And she had never yet met a married woman who was truly happy.

A strained look on his face, Hugh knocked at the door to her sister's quarters. Susannah heard Lord Wolf's deep familiar tones from within, calling, "Who's there?" and did not think she had ever been so happy to hear a man's voice.

She stood behind Hugh as he pushed the door open, then peered over his shoulder to see a tense Lord Wolf, dagger in his hand as though expecting trouble, and, rising from the table, her sister in a fine court gown, an incredulous smile on her face.

"Susannah!"

"Thank you, my l...
low, the skirts of b...
like birds' wing...
finery, with i...
knight's d...
acceptab...
lady...

THOUGH THE HIGH WALL...
the walk, the gardens at Greenwich...
and rightly so. Susannah had never seen so fine a disp...
color and fragrance, fruit trees trained against the warm stone walls in
the French style, herbs in ordered abundance in the formal gardens,
and early roses scenting the air everywhere with their fragrance, both
delicate and subtly powerful at the same time. The sweet riot of
scents in the queen's privy garden served to mask the less-pleasant
stench of the nearby river—though Susannah was well used to such
pungent odors after the farmyard that was her father's manor.

The court ladies wandered idly through the gardens, skirts rustling against the low hedges, ostensibly out for a walk in the scented
air but in truth accompanying Jane Seymour, the king's new favorite
and—it was whispered—the woman who would soon be the next royal
consort. Assuming, of course, that the king's chief advisor, Thomas
Cromwell, could make the charges against Queen Anne stick.

Though Thomas Cromwell, she had heard from Eloise, could
make mud stick to anything. Or anyone.

"Ah, so this is your younger sister, the girl fresh come from
Yorkshire," Jane Seymour had remarked when Susannah was intro-
duced to the queen's ladies by Eloise. The king's new favorite had
looked her up and down with undisguised curiosity, regarding her
with small bright eyes. No doubt there had been some rumors about
the strange circumstances surrounding Susannah's departure from
Yorkshire and her arrival at court. "Very pretty."

dy," Susannah had murmured, curtsying very
er gown—borrowed from Eloise—rippling out
on either side. It felt wrong to be wearing such
eweled velvets and rustling silks, when she was only a
ughter. But Eloise had assured her that it was perfectly
le for her to wear such materials now that her sister was a
and her brother-in-law high in the king's favor.

Now she was walking only a few feet behind Jane Seymour and
the king, trying not to trip, unaccustomed to her heavy skirts, and
careful not to catch the eye of any of the other ladies. For Eloise had
warned her that it was not a comfortable time to be at court, and to
look too directly at anyone might seem like a challenge.

"Mistress Tyrell!" a voice hailed her.

Susannah looked up with a ready smile on her lips. But it was
a courtier she did not recognize who had called her name, so she
glanced about for guidance from Eloise.

She had been surprised at the changes already apparent in her
older sister since returning to court, for Eloise looked haunted
and spoke nervously, always glancing about as though concerned
she might be overheard. Susannah had always thought her sister
too thin, but her slender neck was almost fragile these days.
Nonetheless, Eloise's dark, green-flecked eyes watched her new
husband with obvious attraction, so whatever was bothering her, it
was not loathing for the wealthy lord to whom she had been all but
sold by their father.

Her sister was speaking in a low voice to Lord Wolf, however,
their heads bent in conversation, and Susannah did not wish to
disturb them. She guessed something was amiss between the newly
married couple, a thought which disturbed her. Susannah had hoped
her sister would be content in her arranged marriage, but it seemed
even where there was some mutual attraction it was not easy to adjust
to being a man's chattel. Just as she had suspected.

The man was heavily built, dressed in black velvet, his hands thick with lavish rings that sparkled in the sunlight. He took her hand and kissed it, lingering over her skin. His swift glance upward made her skin crawl.

"You are every inch as beautiful as I had heard, mistress," the courtier murmured admiringly, then glanced at the king. "Have you been presented yet to His Majesty?"

She shook her head, smiling politely back at him. "Not yet, no. Forgive me if I offend you, sir, but I am new at court and do not know your name."

"My name? It is de Lacey. Sir Giles de Lacey."

She curtsied. "I am honored to make your acquaintance, Sir Giles. But who told you I was beautiful?"

"Wouldn't you like to know, my little jaybird?" Sir Giles smiled, and pinched her cheek in a way she found insulting. But since her sister was still turned away, there was little she could do but smile and hope to be rescued soon from this unmannerly gentleman.

At that moment, there was some noise ahead, and she hurried her pace, wondering if the man would leave her alone if she walked more quickly. But Sir Giles kept pace, watching her intently as they came to the large, flat stretch of lawn where several groups of courtiers were already engaged in games of bowls.

Sir Giles came alongside her again, murmuring in her ear, "So you are from the north?"

"Yorkshire," she agreed, glancing back at Eloise.

"Where the weather may be chilly, but the hospitality is hot to the touch!"

"Indeed, sir," she said vaguely, not really listening.

A few yards away, the king was teasing Jane Seymour in a jovial voice. They had stopped to play bowls together on the green, the tentative young woman frowning as she attempted to follow his instructions but failed to hit the jack. His Majesty was stout around the middle, with a reddish-brown beard, and he smiled more than Susannah had expected from a man whose cruelties toward his wives were well known. Whenever the king spoke, his courtiers listened with bent heads, not daring to meet his eyes, and his sharp gaze seemed to dismiss them as unimportant, constantly moving as though on the watch for enemies.

Susannah watched the couple uneasily, thinking of the queen locked up in the Tower of London while these two joked and played in the sunshine, perfectly at their liberty. But that was the price Queen Anne had paid for having married such a king and failing to keep him happy. With her newfound power must have come the very real fear that his attentions would soon turn elsewhere, and in this case it seemed he was not content simply to divorce his wife, as he had done with old Queen Katherine.

No, King Henry would have Anne's life for having disappointed him. And then marry Jane on the back of her execution.

Susannah shuddered.

"Are you cold, mistress?" Sir Giles asked at once, his tone solicitous. He slid an arm about her waist, drawing her clumsily against him, though she had not shown the knight any sign that she would welcome such an intimacy. "We can't have that."

Looking up, meaning to chastise this man for his insolence, Susannah realized with a shock that Hugh Beaufort was standing in the shade of a colonnade on the far side of the bowling green, watching them.

She felt a jolt as their eyes met, and for a moment she felt as though she could not breathe. There was a cold fury in his eyes, and an emotion she read as contempt.

Defiance flared inside her.

She turned to smile at the awful Sir Giles instead of pushing him away as she had planned. "I thank you, sir, but I am not cold. Merely…a little tired."

His leer made his thoughts plain. "Why, it sounds to me as though you need to lie down, my fair northern maid. That can be arranged, and discreetly too. My chambers are close by, but a few minutes' walk from the rose garden. The other ladies will not miss you, I am sure, if you were to slip away with me."

"No, sir, that would be most unfitting," she countered without heat, having met his kind before in Yorkshire. "As well you know."

A bird was singing in the blue sky above, silver-throated, reveling in its freedom. As the courtiers hushed, waiting for Jane's next fumbling throw, Susannah heard its song more clearly and looked up, squinting against the sun. It was a skylark, so high it was barely to be seen, just like the skylarks that played in spring and summer over the rough northern moors.

A wave of homesickness hit her, even though she had wanted to leave, had been desperate indeed to quit muddy old Yorkshire with its endless bad smells and unkempt farmers. Yet here she was, no better off than in Yorkshire, it seemed: a man on her arm she would rather shove in a dung heap than kiss, and Hugh glaring at her like she was planning to sleep with every blessed male in the king's court. Though even if she was, it would be no concern of his.

Sir Giles was still smiling, despite her rejection of his lewd offer. His arm was even tighter about her waist, indeed. She felt it creep up her fine gown as he spoke, brushing the underside of her breast. "You cannot blame a man for wishing to be alone with such a fetching young piece as yourself. Besides, there may be ways in which we can help each other, Mistress Tyrell."

"Indeed?"

"You are from the north," he said more deeply, close by her ear, and she knew it would look to Hugh—if he was still bothering to watch—as though Sir Giles was kissing her. "And so was I once. Not that I have been back in years, the roads are so dangerous and tiring beyond the midlands. But I still have friends there. Not so far north as your father's estate in Yorkshire perhaps, but about a day's ride south."

She caught some odd inflection in his voice and frowned, drawing back to look at him more closely. "Sir?"

"Indeed you may know one of my friends," he continued, his restless gaze slipping from her face to her breasts, making his interest in her plain as a pikestaff. Which he was himself, she thought. "A cousin of mine who lives near Doncaster. His name is Sir Francis Beverley."

"Sir…Sir Francis?" she stammered.

Her head swung and she looked directly to where Hugh had been standing. But the colonnade was empty.

"You know him?" Sir Giles asked. He was leering at her again. She had the distinct impression that he would soon force her to go with him to his chamber, whether she willed it or not.

To her relief, Susannah found herself freed from having to answer that horrific question. For her sister was suddenly by her side, one hand on her rich sleeve.

"Dearest," she said, drawing her away with a quick frown just as Sir Giles released her, "forgive me, but I am in need of you. We are bidden to our embroidery and our books, for the king rides out hunting soon and Jane Seymour swears she will not accompany him. So we are to keep her company in the queen's…" Eloise stumbled, catching herself, and flushed at her own dangerous mistake. "I mean, in the chambers reserved for ladies."

Susannah nodded, and turned to curtsy to the vile Sir Giles, but found him gone.

"Why did you let Sir Giles paw you like that?" Eloise demanded in a low voice, steering her down the shady colonnade and inside the palace. "He has a finger in every pie, that one."

"He nearly had his finger in my pie," Susannah muttered, then briefly told her sister what had happened to her after leaving their father's manor. She left out the night she had passed alone with Hugh in the forest, but admitted that Sir Francis Beverley had been wounded—perhaps badly—in a skirmish between the two men. "I hope Sir Francis was not badly hurt in their skirmish. I would hate to see Hugh suffer for my mistake. It was self-defense though, and Sir Francis did hold me prisoner several days, I'm sure meaning to rape me. Will Hugh be in trouble if he dies, do you think?"

"I don't know," Eloise admitted, but she looked troubled by this news. "Hugh mentioned some local trouble to Wolf when he returned from the north, but I fear we have not had the whole truth from him. Why in God's name did you not tell me of this business with Sir Francis Beverley as soon as you arrived at court? I have never heard his name before. But if he is indeed a knight, the king will need to be informed."

"The king?"

"Of course." Eloise had stopped outside a half-open door. She stood frowning, looking at nothing. "You swear Sir Francis did not rape you? You are still a virgin?"

Susannah hesitated. Then lied. "Yes."

"Then perhaps we should hold off from a formal confession just yet. His Majesty has more important things to think about, after all, and the wound Hugh gave Sir Francis may not be so very bad. I will seek guidance from my husband: he will know the law in this matter. But unless the man is dead, there may be no case to answer. He held you in his house against your will; Hugh took revenge on behalf of our father..." Her sister shrugged. "So honor is satisfied."

Within the sunlit chamber Susannah could hear the soft sounds of women laughing and chattering together, and guessed this was where she would be expected to sit and sew with the other women, and exchange gossip like all the rest.

Her heart sank at the thought of such restriction. Yet what could she do? There were none here who could understand her frustration at such womanly pursuits.

"Susannah," her sister said more softly, mistaking her expression, "there are men at court who would take advantage of your newness to this world. Some will be young and handsome, and most will seem more friendly than Sir Giles, yet have the same intentions. Nor do I advise you without good reason, for I have made errors myself on this score and was fortunate not to fall into scandal. So be on your guard, sister. Treat all men with due civility but never allow yourself to be alone with one. And if you cannot escape, pretend some hurt and cry out loud. Silence will only encourage a man whose mind is on rape."

Susannah thought of that small room where she had been imprisoned at the manor, waiting for Sir Francis to return, and shuddered. Crying out loud would have done her no good in such a place.

"Come," Eloise insisted, kissing her on the cheek, "let us go in smiling. You must not look so downcast, not after having put everyone out so dramatically in order to reach court. This trouble will soon blow over, you'll see. But stay away from Sir Giles. He may indeed have had word from his friend, and it would not do to encourage him into thinking he can ruin you with a word."

"I hope he cannot," Susannah agreed, but forced a smile on her lips.

She followed her sister inside the bright, airy chamber where the ladies were assembled, and made an awkward curtsy to the king's new favorite in Eloise's wake.

"Here, sit," Eloise muttered, then sat on her other side, indicating that she should start work.

She had been placed before an embroidery frame with a younger girl, maybe fourteen years of age, who seemed unable to stop giggling and pulling faces at her friend across the room. Biting her tongue against a reprimand, Susannah fumbled with the many colored silks while one of the other ladies entertained them by singing and playing the lute.

Glancing at Jane Seymour, Susannah tried to decide what had drawn the king to his new favorite. For Jane was no beauty. Her hair was too fair, her features were sharp, her mouth pinched, and although her waist was pleasingly narrow, she had none of the softer curves Susannah thought a man preferred in his bed. When the king, the most powerful man in the country, who could surely have any beauty he desired at the snap of his fingers, settled on such a very ordinary woman, there had to be some secret at work. But what?

"Ow!" she muttered, pricking her skin on the embroidery needle. She sucked at the blood, and saw several of the other ladies stare at her in disapproval. Resisting the urge to stick her tongue out at them, Susannah bent her head to the pattern, wishing her fingers were more nimble with a needle, as Eloise's seemed to be.

Someone scratched lightly at the door, then it opened. Everyone looked up. The lady playing the lute faltered, then fell silent.

A tall and slender woman stood on the threshold, surveying the assembled ladies, her flame-red hair contained in a fine gold net, indicating that she was unmarried. Her gown was deceptively simple, Susannah thought, for although it was made neither of silk nor velvet, nor adorned with jewels and lace as was the fashion, it caught the eye with its tight lines and low-cut bodice. This lady came forward, curtsying to Jane Seymour, yet seemed oddly hesitant, as though unsure whether she should be delivering her message privately instead.

"Mistress Seymour, forgive my intrusion, but your…your gown is ready to be fitted. The seamstresses await your pleasure." She looked down, her green eyes veiled. "Should I instruct them that you are occupied at present?"

Jane Seymour set aside her embroidery, stiff-backed and unsmiling. She seemed to disapprove of this messenger, her gaze resting on the woman's too-revealing bodice. "No, I shall come now. Margaret," she murmured, looking to one of the other ladies present, "and Eloise, will you both accompany me? I will need your help."

The red-haired woman stood aside, curtsying low as Mistress Seymour swept from the chamber, with the woman named Margaret hurrying after.

Eloise stood too and shook out her crumpled skirts, sighing.

"Wait, you...you would not leave me here?" Susannah asked in a low voice, catching her sister by the arm.

She did not like sounding plaintive, but she was unnerved by the idea of being left alone with these fussily dressed, prune-faced, straight-backed women. She was convinced they all knew she had run away from home, for not one of them had smiled at her yet.

"Mistress Seymour is being fitted for her coronation gown," Eloise whispered in her ear. "The queen is not even condemned, has not even been tried, and Jane must preen and make herself ready for the throne before the seat is even cold."

Her sister had spoken with uncharacteristic venom. But then, she had liked Queen Anne and been her lady since coming to court. It must have been very hard to see her arrested and imprisoned on such scandalous charges, and a new woman take her place at the king's side.

"Hurry, Eloise!" Margaret appeared in the doorway again to hiss at her, clearly flustered. "You will be missed."

"Supper, then dancing practice," Eloise told Susannah quickly. "One of the other girls will show you where."

Susannah stared, aghast. "Dancing practice?"

"Permission has been given for you to lodge at court until Father sends for you to return to Yorkshire. You will be expected to know the latest dances, Susannah. Do you?"

She shook her head.

"Then you must learn with the other newcomers." Eloise

straightened, shaking her head. "Do not look so whey-faced, little sister. I will see you at supper perhaps. If not, tomorrow. Has it been decided where you are to lodge tonight?"

"With the maids of honor."

"Good."

Then Eloise was gone. The redhead in the doorway had been waiting for her to pass, then turned to follow, but not before her curious, green-eyed gaze slipped from Eloise to Susannah. The woman hesitated, as though about to speak, then seemed to think better of it.

As the door closed behind them, Susannah returned to her increasingly haphazard embroidery. This should have been an idyllic time for her, she considered, frowning over the tangled silks. She was finally at court, and although the king was planning to execute his wife for treason, her sister had managed not to be implicated in that horror, and courtly life seemed to be rubbing along much as she had expected, on the surface at least.

Two things still bothered her though. One, Hugh's fury at seeing her in intimate conversation with another man. Did he think of her as his own property now that he had known her carnally? And two, what would Eloise say when she discovered that Susannah had been lying about her virginity?

Dancing practice turned out to be two and a half hours of dreary, repetitive twists, turns, and curtsies in a long and very drafty gallery overlooking the torchlit river. The only entertainment was the galliard, for its jumps, lifts, and touches seemed to her the height of intimacy—and yet it was permitted to dance like that before the whole court. But being the oldest among the girls learning the dances, for most gentlewomen came to court around the age of fourteen, Susannah found the whispers and antics of her companions tiresome, and was soon bored. She loved to dance, but this was more like pushing and shoving to music; one of the youngest girls eventually burst into tears and quit the gallery—to the jeers of the dancing master and his boy.

By the time they finished, the hour was late. Too late for anything but sleep. Her back ached, and her feet were swollen from hours of confinement in the tight, thin-soled dancing pumps Eloise had lent her after supper. Following the others back to the cramped quarters set aside for the maids of honor, those unmarried girls who waited upon the queen—when there was a queen to wait upon—she found herself quite unable to walk, and suspected a blister developing on her heel.

Halting, Susannah leaned against the wall to slip off her shoe, and massaged the sore ball and heel of her tortured foot through her stockings. As she had suspected, she could feel something soft and exquisitely painful through the rough material.

She sighed, closing her eyes. A blister would make life at court quite unbearable. So of course she had one.

She could not bear to squeeze her foot back into the dancing pump, so removed both shoes and carried them beneath her arm, limping in woolen stockings along the now dark corridor. The two candle bearers escorting the girls back to their chamber had long since vanished.

Pausing at the head of a broad staircase descending into shadow, Susannah heard voices whispering, but could not be sure if they were ahead or behind.

Were those the maids of honor she could hear? Or merely the wind through these high corridors? Perhaps it was the lapping of the River Thames against the quayside walls?

Now that she thought of it, she could not recall Eloise taking her this way after supper. There had been stairs, certainly, but none so grand as these. If only Greenwich Palace were not so vast.

Perhaps the stairs she sought were further along...

So she continued through the corridors, limping and halting at every new turn, and was soon thoroughly lost.

It was hard, in that strange whispering darkness, not to remember Sir Giles and how he had spoken to her that afternoon. His words had been intended as a threat, she was sure of it now. *Sleep with me or I will tell them everything.* Only she had no intention of sleeping with Sir Giles—or any man. So what would she do if he pursued that threat?

It was not as though she could expect Hugh Beaufort to come riding to her rescue again. He was as deep in this mire as she was. For Hugh had attacked a knight, and perhaps done him great harm, yet not informed the proper authorities on arrival at court. Nor had he disclosed how he spent the night alone in the forest with another knight's daughter—through no fault of his own, she reminded herself fiercely, as she would tell any man who dared ask.

Besides, Hugh was furious with her for talking privily with Sir Giles. She had seen it in his eyes. And he had not been at the feast that evening, for she had looked down the tables and caught no sign of him.

But then, neither had the king, though Mistress Seymour had been there, picking delicately at her food and trying to pretend she was unaware how many courtiers were staring at her.

Suddenly, she heard a scuffle of footsteps behind her, and the rumble of male voices. Light flickered on the walls, growing stronger.

Susannah stared about for some shadowy doorway to dive in, but there was nowhere to hide.

She stood there with her dancing shoes clutched to her chest, eyes wide, and tried to think of an excuse for not being demurely abed at that hour. Somehow, she suspected that "I lost my way" would not excuse her. At best, she would be condemned as slatternly and wayward for such behavior. At worst, they would think her a whore.

Harsh torchlight flared around the corner, dazzling her, the air thick with acrid smoke. Someone spoke sharply, demanding her name. A face loomed up out of the darkness, then a bearded mouth smiled.

It was King Henry.

Nine

"WHAT'S THIS? AS PRETTY a maid as ever I have seen…and still innocent, by the look of that face. Waiting for me, were you?" The king was drunk, she realized in dismay. His words were slurred, his bloodshot eyes unfocused. His smile broadened as he surveyed her from her dusty stockinged feet to her unbound hair. Turning from her to the men with him, he asked each in turn, "Did you send this girl to me? Come, which of you should I praise for this gift?"

"Not I, Your Majesty," they answered, staring over his shoulder at her. Some old, in somber black, others young men with jeweled dagger hilts, all surveyed her with curiosity, most leering, a few openly disapproving.

"I believe that's Wolf's new sister, Your Majesty," one of the younger men offered, winking at her. "You remember the one…"

"Wolf?" the king repeated, staring around at them, owl-faced. "Lord Wolf sends me his young sister to debauch? That cannot be. Where is his lordship?"

There was a strained silence. An older man bent discreetly to the king's ear, whispering.

"Yes, yes, and no doubt some woman should be sent for to escort the girl back to her chamber," the king interrupted impatiently, pushing him away. His gaze moved slowly over Susannah's figure, and she saw lust in his eyes. The king stroked his beard, licking his full lips as though she were some dainty morsel set before him at high table. "But there is some mystery here. Well, I shall speak with this girl myself. Don't fuss like an old woman, Cromwell, I am sick of your long face. Go now, leave be. There is no need to trouble Lady Wolf's sleep over this trifle."

King Henry seized Susannah by the elbow and steered her along the corridor, the others following at a discreet distance.

"No, indeed, Your Majesty, I can find my own way to…" she began, but the king made an angry noise under his breath.

"God's blood, would you defy your king?"

Susannah fell silent at that, unsure how to remonstrate with a drunken sovereign without risking her neck.

Within another few feet, they rounded a corner and there were the king's quarters, guarded and well-lit, the door standing open to reveal a series of chambers within which men moved, quietly preparing the royal apartments for the ceremony of the king's bedtime.

From the first moment she had recognized the king, Susannah had been frozen in fear. There was no hope now that she could escape censure, found wandering the palace after dark in stockinged feet, as though fresh come from some nobleman's bed.

Still she had thought it might be possible to make some excuse and slip away, to save Lord Wolf's reputation.

But now, being forced into his private apartments, past blank-faced guards with pikes standing to attention, Susannah realized the true gravity of her position. King Henry had mistaken her at first for a girl of low virtue. Yet now that he knew she was Lord Wolf's sister, she could see he was still minded to take her and make his apologies to Wolf afterward.

Through this lavish, high-ceilinged antechamber of gold and red was another set of rooms, more simply furnished but still clearly the king's. Servants straightened from their tasks, retreating to stand about the walls in silence as the king entered, and noblemen wandered in to stare at her without any discernible pity, no doubt entertained by her predicament.

Swaying, the king guided her to a broad-seated couch spread

with furs and velvet cushions, and indicated that she should sit, still looking her over with a lascivious stare that made his intentions clear.

"Fetch her wine," Henry muttered to no one in particular, and almost at once a jeweled gold flagon was placed in her hand, brimful of strong red wine that made her feel drunk just inhaling it.

Maybe a dozen pairs of male eyes surveyed her as Susannah stood in the center of this private chamber, wine in hand, refusing to sit even though her king had told her to.

"Y-Your Majesty," she said, curtsying with her head bowed, astonished by how calm she sounded when her heart was hammering so violently in her chest. "There has been a terrible mistake. I became lost after dancing practice and was seeking the room where I am to lodge with the other maids of honor tonight. I-I did not know how close I was to your chambers, Your Majesty, else I would never have dared…"

Ignoring her, the king snapped his fingers, barked, "Out!" and the chamber emptied at once, leaving them alone together.

She turned, staring in despair as the last man bowed out, and caught a sly look on the servant's face that filled her with horror.

The king threw himself onto the couch, and patted his lap. She tried not to stare at the bulging codpiece on show there, the finest black leather, shiny and tooled in gold.

"Come, girl, do not look at me with such big eyes. I shall not bite. Or not hard enough to mark you." Despite his words, he stared lustfully at her waist and bodice, not at her face. "Put down those shoes and sit on my knee."

"Your Majesty, I cannot!" she managed, shaking her head.

"You insist on refusing me, then?"

With any other man she would have spoken sharply. Told him she did, yes, and what of it? But this was her king. And he was not renowned for his fairness toward women. She floundered in a swamp of dangerous etiquette, unsure whether to risk displeasing him with a refusal or give in to his demands and be marked forever as the king's whore.

Many girls at court were clever and ambitious creatures, and would be deeply flattered and excited to be alone with King Henry. To sit on his knee—or lie in his bed—would be even better than a fleeting cuddle. But she had never found herself attracted to any man but Hugh Beaufort, and the thought of performing the same acts with Henry that she had enjoyed so much with Hugh made her sick at heart.

The memory of her night with Hugh made her back stiffen. Defiantly, she raised her chin and looked back at him.

"I must, Your Majesty," she admitted coldly, "yes. If you believe such an offer would be pleasing to me, then I can only beg your forgiveness and say I am not the girl you think me."

She waited, expecting a stormy response to that.

But to her surprise, the king did not call for his guards to have her dragged away to prison. Instead, he laughed.

"Little vixen!" He held out a hand to her, his thickset fingers bristling with large, gaudy rings that flashed in the firelight. "Come then, sit beside me. I swear by the royal seal, I shall not hurt you. What, still blushing as though I want your maidenhead? Surely you would not deny your king a few moments of your company?"

Susannah hesitated, then curtsied and took her place beside him on the fur-strewn couch. It was pleasingly comfortable, and the room was so warm, she had to admit to being a little weary. She dropped her dancing pumps to the floor, for it was too difficult to hold onto them and keep the wine in her cup from spilling.

"Here, let us share the wine. It can be our kissing cup."

Henry took the flagon and drank first, his sharp gaze on her face, then handed it back with a questioning look. Susannah drank too, though only a little, then gave him back the cup. The king drained it and set the flagon down on the floor, wiping his wet mouth with the back of his red velvet sleeve.

"So you are sister to Wolf's new bride." The king seemed more relaxed now that she had at least capitulated to his request to sit. "I know Eloise, for she has been about the court some years now. But what is your name, my northern maid?"

"Susannah Tyrell," she told him quietly.

"So you were lost out there, Susannah? In the dark?"

She nodded, unsure what to say, and tried to look anywhere but at his lap, where he had wanted her to sit. The silence between them felt awkward. He watched her broodingly, playing with his rings. Without thinking, she stretched down to rub one of her sore feet.

"What ails you now?" he asked, frowning.

"My…my feet, Your Majesty."

He grinned then. "Ah yes, dancing practice. Hence your lack of shoes. You dance well?"

"No, Your Majesty." She hesitated. "Though I do like to dance. There is no harm in it."

"Except to the feet."

She looked away shyly. "Yes, Your Majesty."

The king gestured to her impatiently. "Come, put your foot in my lap. I will take away the ache."

"Your Majesty?"

Henry flexed his fingers, then cracked his knuckles. "You must trust me. These are the hands of a healer," he murmured, watching her. "Come, mistress. Your foot in my lap. I insist upon it."

"But I…I should get to bed." Susannah cast her glance toward the closed door. Surely someone should have come by now? "Your men have sent for a lady to accompany me to my chamber?"

"Someone will come," he agreed lightly, "by and by. But such cruelty to your king. Must you refuse every request I make?"

She could smell the wine on his breath, he was so close. There were streaks of silver in his beard, and his cheeks were mottled. But he was the king. She thought of his queen, awaiting her trial, and felt sick.

Slowly, with a sense of horror, she raised her foot and let him take it onto his lap.

His smile disturbed her. He made some small noise at the back of his throat, then his fingers closed about her stockinged foot, squeezing.

"You should dance lightly," Henry murmured, "on your toes. Let the music guide you. Land too heavily and you will become sore." He rubbed her toes firmly, then stroked down the sensitive underside of her foot, smiling when she gasped. "Like that."

He was staring at her breasts, pressed tightly into her fine bodice. His fingers left her foot, stroking up past her ankle. She grew stiff and his leering smile widened, his eyes glittering as they met hers.

"I could be very generous," he said thickly, and his hand slipped higher up her leg, reaching her knee and the line of flesh where her stocking ended, held in place by a tied garter. "You would want for nothing, Susannah. And if there was a male child, you would be generously rewarded. And I would acknowledge him as my bastard, rest assured. Just as I have acknowledged young Fitzroy."

She stared, trying not to recoil in disgust, then suddenly remembered her sister's advice.

"Forgive me, Your Majesty, but I…I am hurt. Please stop."

His exploring hand stilled under her gown, and he peered at her, suspicious. "Hurt?"

"Yes," she agreed, and schooled herself to be firm with him. "I need female assistance. I am unwell."

His eyes narrowed, then he pushed further up her leg, undeterred by this ruse. "You seem well enough to me."

"But indeed I am not, Your Majesty," she insisted, then flushed with anger as his roving hand reached her thigh. "Ow! Ow, stop!"

At once the king removed his hand, glancing furiously at the door. His brows knit together in a dark frown. "Hush, girl, what are you about?"

"I told you, I am hurt. There is pain. You must…" She drew a sharp breath, meeting his eyes. Her foot was still in his lap, pressing against the smooth bulge of his codpiece. "You must release me at once, Your Majesty. So I may seek help, for I am not sure what ails me."

There was the briefest of knocks at the door, then a courtier abruptly entered the king's privy chamber without waiting for permission.

Frozen in horror, Susannah stared across at him, her eyes wide, putting shame aside and silently willing this intruder to help her. She recognized him from earlier, the older courtier dressed in somber black, a gold chain about his neck; his keen eyes assessed the situation at once, then he came forward and bowed, pretending to be embarrassed at having interrupted some intimate meeting.

"Forgive me, Your Majesty," he said blithely, looking unrepentant. "Some business has…erm…arisen."

"So late at night?" The king glared. "And have you not been told a thousand times to wait before entering my chamber, Cromwell? And a thousand and one times ignored my express order?"

Cromwell looked at him with undisguised hostility, then inclined his head. "Forgive me, Your Majesty," he repeated.

"Well, what is it?" the king demanded, bristling with fury now, still holding Susannah's stockinged foot on his lap.

Cromwell's gaze lingered on her. "It might be best to discuss this alone, Your Majesty. It is a delicate matter." He coughed. "The queen…"

The king's eyes closed briefly, then he almost pushed her away. "Go," he muttered, not looking at her. "Get out."

Susannah rose and curtsied low, murmuring "Your Majesty,"

softly under her breath, as though he had not just dismissed her like a common whore.

She stalked to the door, her head held high, and ignored Cromwell's contemptuous glance at her unshod feet.

Only as she passed the king's advisor did she belatedly recall that she had left Eloise's dancing shoes behind, lying on the floor beside the couch. But she refused to ruin the effect of her dignified exit by returning for the shoes, so she favored Master Cromwell with a cool nod and made her way unsteadily across the dimly lit antechamber, intent on gaining her freedom at last.

"Susannah, wait!"

She turned at the low command. Her stomach clenched when she saw who had called her name.

Behind her in the antechamber, leaning against a wall in the shadows, a boy at his side, was Hugh Beaufort. She could not read the expression on his face, but knew by his voice that he must have seen at least a little of what had been going on in the king's privy chamber.

Susannah raised her chin, looking back at him. Her cheeks became hot, but she refused to feel shame or humiliation. She had done what was necessary to survive an encounter she had neither sought out nor enjoyed. Let him judge her for it if he must.

Hugh handed his sheaf of papers to the pockmarked youth beside him, presumably his assistant, and muttered to the boy, without taking his eyes off her, "Give these to Master Cromwell when he returns, Jack. Make my apologies and tell him I was taken ill."

Hugh intended to speak with her.

Susannah picked up her skirts and hurried out of the antechamber. She did not quite run, but it was a little undignified.

She still had no idea which way to go, but she was not waiting around to be chided for wantonness by the king's clerk. Seeing Hugh

Beaufort had caused some odd breathlessness, more like a physical shock than attraction, and her throat felt raw, as though the air burned. The sooner she got away from him, the better.

—✺—

Waiting to be called forward with the latest ecclesiastical reports, the last person Hugh had expected to see in the king's lap was Susannah Tyrell. Yet there she had been, lying flushed and wide-eyed on a bed of furs, her foot in the king's lap, only a few feet from the door to his bedchamber. No doubt they would have soon adjourned there if they had not been interrupted.

He had stared past Cromwell at this desperate spectacle, and guessed in a flash why Susannah had refused to marry him. Why shackle herself to a lowly clerk when she could be the king's mistress?

And now she was trying to pretend she did not know him.

Fury rose in him, and he suddenly no longer cared what punishment he would face for failing to attend the king as Cromwell had requested. It had seemed an odd summons, dragged from his bed to present papers which could as easily have been laid before the king in the morning. Now he understood. Master Cromwell must have been aware that the king was interviewing a new candidate for his bed, and had decided to interrupt him. Such dark jests were only too customary for the king's advisor. There was also, perhaps, the less important matter of the girl's virtue to be considered.

But since it was already being whispered at court that Susannah Tyrell had lost her honor during her supposedly secret flight from her father's home, he doubted Cromwell would be as concerned for Susannah's virtue as he was for his own plans. To have set Queen Anne's fall in motion and shifted Mistress Seymour into position as her replacement, only to see his grand schemes crumble because Henry had tupped another maid and changed his mind…

No, Master Cromwell would not have been ecstatic about that.

Hugh caught up with Susannah along the dark corridor, his head still buzzing with that image of her in the king's lap.

"Stop running away from me, Susannah," he insisted, his voice hoarse. "What in God's name were you doing in the king's chamber?"

"What did it look like I was doing?" she retorted, whirling to face him.

He stared at her through the darkness, and there was a roaring in his ears. *She was not ashamed.* Something seemed to claw at his innards and he drew a pained breath, struggling against unwanted emotion.

God's death, did he have to find her so attractive? Her cheeks were finely stained with blood and she seemed overheated, her golden hair in disarray, her lip caught between her teeth. Her bodice was awry and she was not wearing any shoes, for she had left them behind in the king's privy chamber. He had seen them on the floor beside the couch, as though thrown there by a careless hand.

Susannah Tyrell looked—not surprisingly, he thought bitterly— like a woman who had just been caught in the act of lovemaking.

His fists clenched at the recollection of that intimate scene when Cromwell pushed open the door. Damn the king, was he so incontinent with lust he must tup every maid at his court? Though Susannah had not been struggling in his arms when he saw her, not crying, nor pushing the king away. They had been reclining together, like lovers: her foot had been in his lap.

Even now she looked defiant, even angry.

"You must forgive us," he said tautly, "if we interrupted your love play with His Majesty. Master Cromwell will only be with the king half an hour at most. You may soon return to finish your business."

Hugh did not see the slap coming, but he felt it. His ears rang and he rocked backward.

"How dare you, sirrah!" she hissed.

She pushed past him, leaving him with the delicate scent of lily of the valley, her golden hair swaying, and something in him snapped.

"Come back," he growled, and seized her by the sleeve.

Too hard.

The fine material ripped away at the shoulder where it had been but loosely attached to her bodice, leaving the sleeve hanging by its green laces, her pale skin exposed. She made a distressed noise under her breath, then fled away along the unlit corridor as though he planned to rape her.

Hugh stood a moment in the dark, his chest heaving, staring after her fleeing figure. He knew he should let her go—though she would soon be lost, heading in that direction. She was none of his, that was for certain. First promised to Sir William, now vying for the dangerous position of king's mistress, Susannah Tyrell was not a woman to be taken lightly.

Yet he had taken her in the forest, and enjoyed their night together more than any other he had spent with a woman. Now he hungered after her body in a way he had not thought possible. His cock stiffened to wood at the mere thought of her, he could not bring himself to eat, could not sleep, except to dream such lurid fantasies…

Witnessing Susannah on the arm of that courtier this afternoon, smiling and looking deep into his greedy eyes, Hugh had considered murder.

But the king?

That was a rival he could not hope to best, not even in secret, behind her lover's back. That way lay the scaffold.

She was not yet married though, he considered, his eyes narrowing. Nor was she any man's mistress. The king had been alone with her, that was all. He might be on the hunt, but that arrangement was not yet consummated. For a short while another man might stake his claim. What else could he hope for but a few nights of searing pleasure in her bed? Susannah had made it plain he did not attract her as a husband. Yet she had moaned beneath him in the forest. So there was one thing at least he could offer that she might find lacking in the king's bed, if whispers of Henry's increasing impotence were to be believed.

Hugh ran after her through the maze of palace corridors, calling her name softly, and found his prey at last in the shadows of a doorway, hiding from him.

She gasped, shaking her head. "No."

"Yes," he insisted, pushing her back against the closed door. It led to a chamber that was unused at night, so he had little fear of discovery as he took her face between his hands, stroking her cheeks. She moaned his name and Hugh smiled grimly, stroking his thumb across her mouth.

"Now, mistress," Hugh muttered, lowering his lips to hers, "I shall taste a little of what may soon be the king's property."

Their mouths met with a sudden shock. He felt a spark leap between them a second before, bright and sharp in the darkness, biting at his lip, then suddenly he was gasping as she was, drowning helpless in their kiss, his hands molding her face.

He had expected some resistance. A cry or struggle, some sign that she was not willing to be taken. Instead, Susannah gripped him by the shoulders, holding on as though she would fall without that support, and welcomed his tongue in her mouth. Not only welcomed, but joined with him in lust.

Her tongue played and slipped against his, darting in and out, echoing how they would make love if they were naked. And both wished to be naked and at sport, he had no more doubt of that. Their bodies pressed up hard against each other in the narrow doorway, striving to draw closer, to be so close indeed there was nothing between them, not even air.

She moaned against his mouth.

He released her face and cupped her breast instead, knowing her to be willing. Her nipple came erect through the thin silken fabric, tautening under his fingers. He smiled and dragged her bodice down. It came easily, loosened by the torn sleeve, and she made no demur. Her breast fell into his hand, soft and warm. Susannah moaned again, and he stroked his tongue deep into her mouth, deliberately reminding her of how they had kissed in the forest, how he had filled her.

Let her get such pleasure from the king, he thought. She could not, not if she lay with His Majesty one thousand nights. A bitter jealousy quickened in his heart and he fought against it, closing his eyes.

She was not his love. Susannah Tyrell might sleep with any man she chose; it was none of his business. For tonight she would be his lover though, and with that he must be content.

"Hugh," she whispered, stroking slowly down his back to his buttocks, encased in black hose. She cupped them firmly, dragging him into her hips. His leather codpiece was swollen out, his cock hard. It was clear from her murmur of pleasure that she could feel it.

Hugh dipped his head, dragging her nipple into his mouth. She cried out but did not stop him.

Her flesh tasted so sweet and fresh; he would never have surfeit of her body, never be satisfied with just one night in her bed, though he might lie to himself that he could.

He sucked hard, his hunger raw and demanding, almost intolerable now. It was late at night, most courtiers were asleep, but they were close to the king's apartments here and a guard might pass, or Cromwell on his way back to bed. Yet the needs of his body drove him on, unable to bring reason to bear on his desire to be inside her, to feel again the tight velvet sheath of her cunt.

For her not to be naked was wanton cruelty, he thought, and reached for her skirts.

"You want me?" he muttered, his mouth on her bare throat, feeling a need to mark her with kisses: his possession, his lover. "You want me, Susannah?"

For a terrible moment he thought she would refuse him, and his whole body tensed, steeling itself for another rejection.

Then her head tipped back, sending a rain of golden silk over and through his fingers, and he felt her exposed breasts rub seductively against his chest.

"Yes, Hugh. Take me."

"Here?"

"Yes," she gasped, then gave a little cry, as though unable to believe her own wantonness. "Here. *Now*."

Ten

Hugh Beaufort drew her skirts up to her waist, and seemed to delight in her wild moan. As well she might moan, Susannah thought, shocked by what they were doing. Yet she could not stop. It was compulsive, this need to be free of these trappings of courtly life, to have him suckle on her breasts and explore her body below the intricate folds of her gown. And the cool air was so glorious, why deny herself?

She was bared to him now, her gown held up, woolen stockings tied just above her knee, the rest exposed.

Hugh was gazing down at her. She guessed from the sudden catch of his breath that he could see enough, even in the heavy shadows of this doorway, to admire her pale nudity. She could not see his expression, for his back was to the light: one flaming torch at the far end of the corridor, stuck into a high sconce, setting the dark to flight.

He touched her, trailing his fingers up her leg to that yielding flesh between her thighs. There he paused, rubbing his fingers slowly along the damp notch in her flesh.

Susannah shivered with delight. Her cunt ached and moistened at the stroking of his finger, seeming to remember his touch from before.

His voice was unsteady. "You are mine tonight. Is that understood?"

"Yes."

He pushed one long finger inside, watching her response. "Good."

She stifled her instinctive cry, almost unable to bear the exquisite shock of his invasion, and arched her back, wanting—needing—more. A memory came to her of his mouth there, his tongue tasting her, playing her most tender flesh back and forth. Desire coiled inside her, twisting wildly, taking possession of every nerve in her body, the thread of her control soon wound so tight it would not take much for it to snap.

"More," she whispered.

Hugh pushed in deeper, two fingers this time, stroking her sensitive walls as he filled her, lingering on his withdrawal so that she sucked in her breath, trembling on tiptoe.

Then he bent, taking her mouth, his fingers still deep inside her. She moaned against his lips, wishing their kiss could go on forever, this give-and-take of desire, a sensual dance that left her breathless, yet knowing there was an even greater dance beyond it. A dance so intense she would forget her sore toes and her humiliation on the king's lap, and hear only the music in her head, the rhythms and cadence of love.

His fingers slipped wetly back and forth, in and out, pulling and rubbing against the tiny ball of flesh where her pleasure had its seat. His tongue stroked into her mouth at the same time, and the two between them, entering, withdrawing, thrusting, playing, brought her suddenly and swiftly to a point where her body could take no more.

She gripped his neck, digging her nails into his skin just above the plain shirt he wore, and sobbed, moving with him, then against him, rising and falling on his fingers.

"Hush, someone may come," he warned her hoarsely, glancing back along the empty corridor.

She bit her lip, containing her cries, then managed a shaky laugh as he slowly and carefully withdrew his fingers. "Yes, someone may indeed."

Hugh smiled fiercely, understanding the joke. His eyes met hers again, then dropped to her mouth. "I had hoped to take you to bed, Susannah. To make love to you at my leisure. But it seems this is where we must couple, right here in the king's corridor, or else give it up as lost. Perhaps it would be best to go our separate ways tonight…"

"No," she insisted, holding on to him. "Here!"

"Then we cannot tarry any longer but must take our pleasure swiftly. I will not be gentle."

"I do not want you to be gentle with me, Hugh. Not tonight or ever." She ran her tongue along her lower lip, and almost smiled to see his sharp green eyes catch on that movement, following it hungrily. "I was not made to be handled delicately like a glass vial, or kept on a high shelf where I might not be broken."

He gave a quick nod, jerking her close. "Then let us to it."

In truth, she did not mind if he was not gentle. Why should she, when she would not be gentle with him?

Hugh Beaufort felt the same greed as she did, but the same weaknesses too: they met as equals in this dance, both attracted but still unsure of the other, neither of them at a disadvantage. She had felt frightened when the king took her into his privy chamber, and helpless when Sir Francis had forced his attentions on her in a locked room. She had felt nothing but fury at Sir Giles and his vile pawing hands.

Yet with Hugh Beaufort, she felt only desire. And a strong suspicion that she needed to keep this man at arm's length, for such desire could be dangerous to her peace of mind.

But not tonight.

Tonight she would let Hugh near her again, into the circle of her being, so they could spend themselves in wanton lust.

Susannah cupped him between the legs, stroking the jutting codpiece, and felt his cock shift inside its black leather pouch, restless.

"Witch," he muttered.

"This is no spell I have cast upon you, Master Beaufort. It is lust, pure and simple." She smiled wickedly into his eyes, inviting him to use her. "Now enough of this love play. I wish to be ridden hard; let me be your mare. Will you mount me, sir?"

Speechless, Hugh growled his assent. He stepped closer, lifting her powerfully against the wall so their bodies were aligned, then fumbled to release his codpiece.

His cock sprang free, long and thickly rigid. It seemed bigger than she remembered, but then she had been lying down in the forest, under cover in the midst of a dark storm, and their love had been made by touch, not sight.

She ran both hands up and down his cock, squeezing and fondling, and was pleased when his head tipped back, a low groan issuing from his lips. She had so little knowledge of this art of love, yet seemed to understand his needs as though she felt them herself. And he felt hers, and assuaged them, as though they were two halves of the same body.

The head of his cock was wet. With his seed? She rubbed it round with her thumb pad, then brought her thumb to her mouth. He tasted delicious.

"Now," he grunted.

He parted her legs, holding them up and apart, and she helped him, eager to be mounted. His green eyes met hers as he positioned himself, his fat head stretching the slit, then drove inside her.

"Susannah," he gasped, stopping as soon as he had penetrated her, abruptly closing his eyes, perhaps gathering the lost threads of his control. "I cannot…"

She dragged her hands down his chest, wrenching his shirt and doublet open so she could touch bare skin. Then taste it, bending to lick at his nipple, her tongue merciless.

"That is…not…helping," he managed, his voice strained.

"Did you not order me to be your concubine?" she asked in a whisper, and sucked on his nipple, relishing the musky scent of his flesh. "I am serving you, Master Beaufort. You wish me to stop?"

"No!" He gave a strangled groan at his own weakness and began to thrust, holding her up against the wall. "Yes, I mean yes!"

She writhed against him, her movements deliberately slow and erotic. "Tell me what I should do to please you, sir."

"God's blood, do what you will!" Hugh's laugh was hoarse as she wrapped her legs about his hips, urging him on. "Be concubine or mare, I care not. Only let me love you."

Smiling, Susannah raised her head and kissed him on the mouth. Their tongues clashed hotly as he thrust, filling her perfectly, his strokes long and confident, reminding her why she preferred his company to that of any other man. But that did not mean she should accept his offer of marriage, she told herself sternly. For although it would be no hardship to marry such a man, what began well might yet turn sour.

Besides, Hugh had not repeated his invitation to wed. So perhaps it had been withdrawn. Perhaps he thought her the king's whore now.

Still, to have such joy in her bed…

"I want you to pleasure yourself." Hugh kissed her neck passionately, silencing her thoughts. His voice grew hoarse. "I know you must have touched yourself before. You are too wild to have lain chaste in bed every night with your arms by your sides. So touch yourself and show me."

Dazed with lust, Susannah slipped a hand down between her thighs and touched herself obediently. "Like this?"

"Yes," he muttered, watching as he thrust.

Susannah ran her tongue along her lips, breathing hard and pushing her hips wantonly toward him. She had lain abed many nights and performed this forbidden act alone, in sweet delicious silence, beneath her nightgown. She knew all too well what exquisite pleasures could be gained from her own wicked fingers, or the smooth, rounded head of a wooden peg pressed gently against her nether lips.

But to play her flesh with a man's cock riding there was quite another matter. Indeed, it was nothing short of heaven.

She felt swollen, on fire, as lewd a creature as ever whored for a man, and did not care if he saw it. Her blood ran hot, and her fingers slipped easily over the little thimble of flesh, making her lip quiver with sobs again, the bonfire ever hotter inside, burning her up.

His face was intent, shadowed, only the glitter of his eyes visible. "Let me see your pleasure," he ordered her.

She leaned back against the doorway, exposing herself more freely, hoping he could see the rapid movements of her fingers. Her heart galloped wildly, matching the turmoil in her blood. Each time he withdrew his cock, Susannah felt empty—desperately, heartrendingly empty, and craved the rhythmic thrusting back inside. And once Hugh pushed deep within her, she felt her body climb the steep mountain, always another few steps toward release.

"What do you want?" he demanded.

"Your cock."

"And?" he urged her.

She was panting, her body no longer her own to control. "Your seed," she whispered. "Fill me. I need it."

Hugh made a frustrated noise under his breath, tightening his grip on her body. His thrusts slowed and he kissed her almost violently, possessing her mouth. "I would, and gladly too," he told her, and she believed him, there was such power in his voice. "Yet I must not. It was madness enough the first time. We cannot risk a child."

She knew he was right. It had been madness when they lay together so completely in the forest, and would be again if he put his seed in her. She was unmarried, and her disgrace would be assured if he got her with child. Yet her body ached to feel his hot release inside her, and she had to battle that urge as she replied, closing her eyes, "Yes, I know, I know. Forgive me."

Could it ever feel this good with another man? Her wild imagination shifted in that instant to standing like this in a doorway with the king. Sickened, she shook the vision away. But she had her answer. No, it was not the act that made her blood race, but the man inside her.

As if in answer to her thoughts, Hugh lifted her hair and bit her on the neck—gently, but it was a gesture of possession nonetheless.

"There is not an inch of you my lips will not taste," he promised her darkly when she shivered.

That sounded like a threat.

"It is not the lips that concern me," she muttered, "but the teeth."

His smile nearly unraveled her. "You will learn to love both. To beg me for them."

"You would hurt me?"

"I would tame you, Susannah. You have been given your way too often and need to be corrected."

"And what was that correction for?"

"The king," he whispered in her ear, his breath warm on her throat. "One day you will have to tell me how you came to be so intimate with His Majesty. Tonight, our need comes first."

His mouth met hers again in a slow, strangling kiss, her very breath dragged into his body. Then he lifted his head in alarm, and she tensed, for both of them had heard male voices along the corridor. Though perhaps not coming their way, she hoped, staring up at him in horror.

With a harsh breath, Hugh began to thrust again, short hard thrusts that gave her no mercy. She knew it was madness not to leave. It could be anyone. It could be the king himself. Yet he could not stop until he had achieved his end, and she was caught helplessly in the same honeyed trap, her flesh tender and in need of completion, come what may.

"Take your pleasure, Susannah," he gasped. "I cannot hold back."

Her head was light, her blood roaring.

Swiftly, she rubbed herself again, shameless in her lust, and had to bite down on his shoulder as she arched into joy. It was as though her body had been waiting for a reason to explode into fire, and the merest touch of her fingers had lit its fuse.

"Yes!" Her cry was muffled against his body, blood pouring rich through her belly and cunt, her heart pounding, breath snatched away as she reached her peak. His cock shoved powerfully inside her, still hammering into her cunt even as it tightened around him.

His lips were drawn back, teeth bared, a grimace on his face as his own pleasure beckoned. Lost in ecstasy, her cunt squeezed his rigid organ like a fist, its long rippling waves compulsive, unstoppable.

"Christ Jesu!" Hugh cried out, shutting his eyes as though to hide the expression in them, then pumped inside her several times, hard and relentless, and abruptly withdrew, spending his lust on the floor, his groan echoing along the corridor. "Susannah…Susannah."

The men were almost upon them now, their footsteps loud through the flickering darkness.

Two courtiers she did not recognize, talking and laughing.

The men halted as they drew level with the doorway, and stood staring in shock, and then malicious amusement, as they realized what they had stumbled across.

A dirty little secret.

It had seemed to her earlier that everyone at court had a secret. Now this was hers. Could they have recognized her?

She hid her face in Hugh's doublet, breathing in his male aroma and the sharper, more acrid scent of seed, and prayed that they would move on without causing trouble.

But her prayer was unanswered.

"Hey there!" one of the men called out unsteadily. "What's this? Fucking a girl against the wall? Have you no shame, sir?"

The other laughed. "Aye, the whoreson has none. And no bed either, it would appear."

Drunk, both of them. *Go away*, she thought desperately.

"Give me leave, gentlemen, of your civility." Hugh was breathless, not looking at the men. His tone was light and self-deprecating, as though being discovered having sex in a corridor was nothing to be ashamed of. "I could not wait."

"He could not wait," the one repeated to the other, and both laughed this time.

"She must be good, this whore you do not wish us to see."

"Gentlemen, please!" Hugh's tone did not alter, but she saw his hand move to his dagger hilt in warning. "Let it drop, in the king's name."

The men fell silent at once, all laughter gone. When she peeked a moment later, the corridor was empty and there was no sign of them.

Susannah looked up at Hugh in a wondering way. She expected him to be curt with her, even offhand. But he merely smiled, brushing her cheek with an unsteady finger.

"Even the most vicious dog may be brought to heel by the sound of his master's whistle," he whispered.

For the second time, Hugh Beaufort had protected her, and thereby put himself in danger's way. If His Majesty should learn of this, she dreaded to imagine what Hugh's punishment would be for having used the king's name unlawfully.

—⁓—

"Ouch!"

"Hush, child," her sister told her, laughing at her panicked expression. "Sit still and stop fidgeting. I have done nothing yet, but if you move, it will mar all."

They were sitting in a corner of the maids' chamber where sunshine played across the floor in diamonds, filtered through the newly leaded glass in the windows.

The room was hot, and for comfort Susannah was still in her shift, having only recently risen from her bed. Before washing, she had coiled up her fair hair and secured it with a net, only then spying the faint marks on her neck where Hugh had kissed her.

Then Eloise had come in, looking for her, and there had been no time to let down her hair again.

Although most of the maids of honor had already gone about their duties, a few still remained, sitting on their beds to mend rips in their gowns or sew plain hoods. It was rumored that Mistress Seymour frowned upon too much finery, and since everyone knew she would soon be queen, more elaborate gowns were being stripped of their jewels or lace edging and made to look more simple.

Now her sister had said she would look well with an earring, and had produced an uncommonly thick and cruel-looking needle for the task, as though about to sew cowhide.

"Wait." Susannah frowned at the needle, rubbing at her ear lobe. "I…I may have changed my mind."

"Lily-livered coward!" Her sister took Susannah's ear in a firm grip, then thrust the needle through in a stinging flash. "There, it's done. Now you may wear an earring there. Only be sure and keep the hole open, else it will soon close up again." She hesitated. "Shall I do the other ear?"

"No, I thank you," Susannah said with a little gasp, her ear still smarting from its torture. "Just the one will suffice until I decide if I like it or not."

"Well, it is the fashion to wear a single earring," Eloise said doubtfully, "but among the gentlemen, rather than the ladies."

"Then I shall set a new fashion."

"Indeed." Frowning a little, her sister began to work a small earring into the hole she had made, a thin silver hoop with a single pearl. "I was told you were very late coming to your bed last night, Susannah. Now there are red blotches on your neck, which were surely not there when I saw you yesterday. Is there anything you need to tell me?"

"T-tell you?"

"You were seen in the king's company last night," Eloise murmured, glancing about to make sure they were not over-heard. When she saw the shock on Susannah's face, she shook her head. "For pity's sake, Susannah, do you have no discretion? Or did you believe such a scandalous thing could remain un-discovered? The court is already whispering that you have been marked as the king's new mistress, once he is safely married to Mistress Seymour."

"Oh dear Lord!"

Her sister looked at her directly. "Is it true? Have you been inti-mate with His Majesty?"

"No, no," Susannah exclaimed, then felt heat creep into her face and cursed silently, knowing her sister would take it for guilt. "That is…it is true that I was alone with the king for a short while last night. Though by accident, not by design. And he may have… rubbed my foot. But that was all, I swear it."

Her sister was pale. "So it is true. First this man in the north, Sir Francis, who would have bedded you given the chance. Now the king himself… Are you entirely without wits, girl?"

"I did not wish to be alone with the king, but did not know how to put him off," Susannah protested, her voice rising so that her sister had to hush her again.

She drew a shaky breath, hands in her lap, trying to control her temper. After all, she was hardly innocent of all misdemeanors, for immediately after leaving the king's company, she had coupled with Master Beaufort in the corridor, devoid of all shame.

"I did nothing amiss," she insisted, careful not to allow the other maids to hear her.

"And was it the same with Hugh Beaufort on the road to court?" Eloise whispered, her eyes narrowed on Susannah's face. "You did nothing amiss? For you were wild and out of sorts when he delivered you into our protection. And since then, I have barely seen you look at each other, the air between you is so strained."

"Are you finished there?"

Eloise sighed, shaking her head. "You must tell me sooner or later, Susannah. I am your sister and best placed to advise you if there is something wrong."

"Later then, not sooner." She knit her fingers together in her lap, sitting up straight. "My ear?"

"Your ear is very red. Perhaps I did not catch it right with the needle. Or caught it too well." She reached for a white napkin and dabbed at the ear with it. "We must watch it carefully though. I have heard of girls contracting fever after a pierced ear, and risking an inflammation of the brain."

Susannah stared.

"Oh, it will not be that serious, I am sure." Her sister finished her work, smiling in a somewhat mischievous manner, then stood back to judge the effect. "Yes, the single pearl works well with your hair bound in a net. Only your whole ear is turning scarlet now. I am a little concerned about it. Does the ear pain you?"

"It smarts."

"Perhaps one of the court physicians should look at it." Eloise pulled her up off the bed. "I shall help you dress, then take you to be examined. Come, you cannot stay in your shift all day like a woman whose work is in her bed. There are already rumors enough about you."

Master Elton, the physician, was a surprise to her. They found him in a tower room, surrounded by meticulously labeled specimens in jars, dozens of cloudy bottles and vials on the shelves, and old books heaped in leaning stacks on the floor. From his robes, Susannah could tell that Master Elton was a learned doctor, a little younger than Lord Wolf, perhaps a few years off thirty. He was tall, pleasingly broad in the chest and narrow at the hips like Hugh, with dark hair under the black velvet cap of the physician, and dark intelligent eyes. The man was built like a Norseman, she thought, watching from under her lashes as he set down his book and turned to examine her. Yet he had the gentlest hands, careful as any woman's.

The doctor removed her silver hoop earring, a lengthy procedure which pained her greatly, then tilted her head forward. His voice was pleasingly low. "If you could turn your head, Mistress Tyrell, I will examine your ear."

She obeyed, and felt his fingers touch her skin gingerly.

"How did this happen?"

Susannah glanced drily at Eloise. "My sister's handiwork. She would have me wear an earring whether my ear wanted it or not."

"I see." Master Elton released her neck and reached for a cloth to wipe his hands, smiling at them. "You will live. The ear is a little inflamed, but there is no lasting damage."

"No risk of brain fever?" Eloise asked, again shooting Susannah a mischievous look.

"It is true that brain fever may spring from even the smallest cut or graze. But such cases are rare and I have never known one myself." He smiled at Susannah, as though he had guessed that Eloise had been teasing her with such dark tales of misfortune. "Your sister concerns herself unduly, Mistress Tyrell."

Eloise gave the physician a quelling look, no doubt thinking the man impertinent, but merely remarked, "Well, I am glad for it," and shrugged. She seemed in better spirits than she had been for several days. Eloise and Wolf had argued recently, but Susannah guessed that they must have made up, for there was a glow about her sister this morning that she had never seen before. Unless Eloise was with child…

The thought made Susannah blench and stare blindly down at her feet. A child!

She had been so careless with Hugh the first time they lay together. Eloise had called her "wild" and so she had been, coupling with a man while she was still unmarried. And now she had performed the wicked deed again, and quite without shame, for she did not even blush to recall it. Yet how could such violent pleasures be wrong?

It seemed unfair that a man might sow his seed freely and escape censure so long as he was discreet, while a girl found to be too loose with her favors must be a whore and outcast.

Last night Hugh had ensured his seed did not enter her. But it was possible she was already with child and unaware of her impending disgrace. Her understanding of such matters was bare, mere whispers and laughter from the virgins she had known in Yorkshire, but she did know a woman might not realize her own condition for some months.

Her sister was impatient to be gone. She kept glancing at the door, her expression restless. "I must leave you to anoint my sister's ear with some smelly tincture or plaster, Master Elton, then send her back to her chamber for rest. I was due elsewhere half an hour ago, and dislike being late to my duties. Though if you would rather I remained—"

"Go, go, I do not need you," Susannah told her at once, waving her sister to the door.

In truth, she was keen for Eloise to leave; her sister had always been good at reading her expression, and would soon discover what lay between her and Hugh Beaufort if she kept pressing for the truth.

"Only if you are sure?"

"You heard Master Elton, and he is the doctor. My ear is a little red, that is all. There is nothing to be alarmed about."

After Eloise had left, Master Elton began to prepare a treatment for her ear, his movements deft and economical; he navigated the small physician's workshop with the grace of a dancer. The doctor was quiet in his speech and manners, barely raising his eyes to hers, yet there was an intensity about him that intrigued her.

"Has any ointment ever made you sick, Mistress Tyrell? Any herb ever caused your skin to itch?"

"None." She watched the physician work, thinking of Hugh; he too was a large man who knew how to be delicate with his hands. "But you must call me Susannah. I feel so old when I am called Mistress Tyrell. I am only eighteen, you know. It is no great age."

He smiled, looking at her assessingly. "You seem older."

"What is your Christian name, Master Elton?" she asked, knowing that she was flirting with him but having too much fun to stop.

He hesitated, then murmured, "Virgil."

"Virgil?"

He laughed. "Yes, it is a ridiculous name. But my father was a great Latin scholar and Virgil was his favorite Roman poet."

The door to his inner chamber creaked open a crack. The doctor did not seem to notice, still busy at his workbench with a pestle and mortar, but Susannah sat up, staring in amazement.

A woman was peeking out of his privy chamber, as though trying to see who was out there.

With a shock, she recognized the lady. It was the tall redhead who had come to tell Mistress Seymour her gown was ready for fitting. Was she a servant, perhaps, or a lesser lady of the court? No, she could not be a servant, for her clothes were too fine. No doubt the lady had some ailment and had come to the doctor for treatment, she thought. Yet how strange that he should have left her waiting in his privy chamber.

Was her ailment so dreadful she wished none to know of it? Or perhaps she was the doctor's wife, Susannah reasoned, studying her curiously. Though if that were the case, why would she be creeping about the doctor's quarters in such a furtive way?

Then Susannah took in the rumpled bed behind her, the woman slightly flushed, her mass of flame-red hair in disarray…

Was she the doctor's lover?

The redhead glanced in her direction and froze. She had slanting green eyes, quite exotic and unusual, with long dark lashes. Their eyes met, Susannah's questioning and surprised, the other's horrified.

Hurriedly the door was pulled shut again.

Master Elton must have caught the quiet click of the latch, for his head swung and he frowned. "What was that?"

Susannah did not wish to embarrass the man. She had taken a lover herself now, and knew the horror of discovery only too well.

"Nothing," she lied, smiling brightly. "That tincture smells awful. Is it ready yet?"

Eleven

"This place is a prison!"

Hugh slammed out of the clerks' chambers and made his way back to his own room, needing to be alone and unseen by the world, if only for the short space of an hour.

It was early evening and most courtiers had gone to the feast, the hall packed and rowdy tonight, the sounds of merriment echoing down the palace corridors. But he had little appetite for food, and none whatsoever for dancing and gossip.

He felt sick and ill at ease, his whole body rebelling against the hideous fever of queen-killing that had seized the court in recent days. For the very air was abuzz with the execution of those unfortunate men accused of adultery with the queen. Even now their gory, severed heads were being paraded on London Bridge as traitors against the king's divine person: crows would soon peck out their eyes, and sunshine would slowly blacken their grimacing faces as this terrible spring rolled into summer.

Whispers from those who had attended their hearings were confused. It was said the accused had denied all charges, or refused to confess. Only the court musician, Mark Smeaton, had confessed himself guilty of desiring the queen, yet that had not prevented the solemn pronouncement of the sentence of death on Smeaton, and his fellow accused, the courtiers William Brereton, Sir Henry Norris, Sir Francis Weston, and even Lord Rochford, the queen's brother. Others claimed there had been no proper trial, that the men were found guilty where they stood and taken straight out to the scaffold.

A few daring souls suggested the king was insane, that the hurt received during the joust in January had soured his spirit and turned his brain to madness.

Not all were horrified. Some were boldly ecstatic at the fall of Queen Anne and her favorites, and went about counting the days until she too should have her head taken off in public. Chief among them was Thomas Cromwell, the man of the hour, whom nobody dared criticize, for fear their own names would soon appear on the list it was rumored he kept on his desk, of persons suspected of treason.

Hugh could not voice his own suspicions aloud, but he had observed the king closely in recent days, and was inclined to believe the balance of his mind disturbed. How else could the king countenance the destruction of these innocent lives, and the death of his own queen?

Anne had been Henry's golden girl, once so highly favored, so beloved, the king had been seen groveling at her knees like a lapdog, begging for scraps.

Now Henry would see her kneel for the executioner.

This trial was cruel and unjust, Hugh thought. Yet none could stop the wheel of justice once it had been set in motion. None but the king.

He prayed that King Henry would be merciful; that he would issue a pardon for Anne Boleyn, and put her away quietly instead of executing her. Their marriage he had already dissolved, the king claiming—oh, the irony—that it was unlawful. Anne Boleyn could easily be kept in some remote place until her natural death.

But Hugh knew there was little hope of such an outcome. Following the execution of those accused of adultery with her, there could be no doubt that Anne's days on this earth were almost at an end.

Pushing into his darkened chamber, Hugh began to tear at his doublet, eager to be free of its restriction, and stopped dead.

Susannah lay on his unmade bed, nude in the firelight, propped up on one elbow, a golden curtain of hair falling across one breast and shoulder. Her blue eyes lifted innocently to his, and she smiled, the slow curve of her mouth lighting his blood with fever.

"Good evening, Master Beaufort."

"Susannah!"

Thinking swiftly, he shut the door to his chamber and barred it against his servant.

"Are you mad? Anyone might have walked in and seen you... like that." He faltered, his gaze drawn irresistibly to her naked body. Her breasts were so perfect they might almost have been the work of some Italian master, sculpted in white marble, but for the rosy blush to her nipples. He tried not to be distracted, for he knew how dangerous their situation was. "You should not be here. You will be missed."

"My sister thinks I am at rest, for I hurt myself earlier and—"

"You are hurt?"

"Only my ear." She smiled. "It proved nothing in the end, just a slight inflammation from the piercing. Master Elton gave me a tincture to apply twice a day."

Delicately, Susannah pulled back her hair to show him a silver hoop, adorned with a pearl that hung like a milky teardrop from her ear. The skin around the earring looked a little red.

"You like it?" she asked him softly.

His cock stiffened, and his breath constricted. He thought Susannah so seductive, lying there on his bed with her fair silken hair held up from her neck, a pearl shining in her ear, that he found it hard not to rip off his clothes at once and join her.

Hugh had seen no courtesan, however costly and experienced in the amorous arts, look as beautiful in the nude as she did tonight.

But "Yes," was all he could manage, in a voice that sounded far colder than he had intended. Though even that was the wrong thing to say. He should gather up her clothes and bustle her out of his chamber before they were discovered there. She would be punished severely if found in such wanton display, as would he for having taken her virginity: some grim cell in the Tower of London would no doubt serve as his resting place if her father could not be appeased for that loss.

God help him, he could not stop staring at her lush body, all soft curves and smooth skin, remembering how firmly her cunt had accommodated him, how tightly it could grip, squeezing his cock.

Lust was beginning to take him over, he realized, and could not entirely condemn himself for that obsession. If they were married, his desire would be considered natural. But as unmarried lovers, they must hide their sin from the world. Much as it irked him to do so.

If only Susannah would marry him.

She ran her gaze hungrily over his body. "Will you not come to bed, sir?"

His jaw tightened at the husky invitation in her voice, an offer that left him aching with frustration. "Willingly, madam," he agreed. "If you will change your mind and consent to be my bride."

She stared, and her voice grew defensive. "You know I will not, Hugh." She licked her lips, watching him. "All I can give you is consent to love."

"Consent to love?" he repeated.

Their gazes tangled, then she lowered her eyes, a wild look in her face. Not for the first time he wished he could read her thoughts, for the workings of her mind were a mystery to him.

Slowly, he considered what she had said, and came to a startling conclusion.

"What are you saying, Susannah?" His chest felt tight, as though the air itself had grown thick and cloying, and he was finding it hard to look at her. Yet he had to be sure. Hugh hesitated, struggling for the right question. "That you *love* me?"

She stiffened. "I did not say that!"

"Then what did you mean by 'consent to love'? That you wish to lie with me again, still unwed, yet will not take me as your husband?"

But Susannah lay stubborn and unyielding, looking up at him without answering. Her cheeks were flushed, and her hand crept down to cover the soft golden triangle of hair between her legs, as though she was suddenly ashamed of her nakedness before him.

"Will you not come to bed and forget these foolish questions?" Her eyes flashed. "For any other man, it would be enough to find me naked in their chamber."

He had proof of that enough. Temper made him unjust. "Aye, I have seen the other men buzzing about you. Wasps to the honeypot. They should take care they do not drown."

Her eyes widened. "The names of these admirers?"

"Sir Giles de Lacey, for one."

Heat filled her cheeks and he was suddenly ashamed. She was not his possession, to be questioned like a wife, called to account for the wanderings of her gaze. She had made that clear to him already.

Yet she did not deny it. "You do not understand."

"Then help me to."

"I do not think I shall," she said stiffly, and looked away. "You must learn to trust me, Hugh."

She was angry. And rightly so. He had offended her with his jealousy, fool that he was. Susannah Tyrell was a headstrong and passionate young woman. She neither loved him nor wished to marry him. But she knew what she wanted in bed and had a sexual appetite as strong as any man's. That her desire was for him, and not the king or another courtier, should please rather than disturb him.

Her naked body drew his gaze. Whenever he looked at her beauty, his blood sang and his cock ached to be inside her, to become part of her smooth-skinned maelstrom.

Nonetheless Hugh knew himself in turmoil. Each time they

made love, his need to make Susannah his bride grew more powerful. Yet she would have none of him. Indeed, even if they were wed, he doubted that he could ever control such a fiery bride. Or not without crushing her spirit.

"Still you stare and do not touch me," she whispered. "Does my body no longer please you, Master Beaufort?"

He knelt on the bed and took her hand, pressing it to his codpiece so she could feel his erection beneath.

"You feel that?" he asked huskily, and saw passion flare in her eyes at this proof of his arousal. "Your body could not please me more than it already does, Susannah. But this passion between us… It is too wild, too violent. I am not afraid to admit that I fear where it will lead us. For all I know, it will consume and destroy us if we continue to indulge our lust without the ties of marriage. King Henry's court is riddled enough with those who love where they should not, with debauched husbands and faithless wives. I would not add your innocence to its raging bonfire."

"Innocence?"

On impulse, Hugh leaned forward and kissed her on the mouth. She lifted her head and met his kiss eagerly, their tongues sliding against each other in heated play.

The longer they kissed, the more rigid his cock grew. It was soon too large for that restrictive space, and he longed to free it and take her.

"Yes, innocence," he muttered against her mouth. "And it is driving me mad."

Susannah murmured his name, rubbing her hand back and forth against his codpiece, teasing him in his agony. "Yet I am no virgin, sir."

"My doing."

"Yes, your doing," she agreed, smiling up at him.

His hand found her breast, smooth and warm and rounded like a dove's, and toyed with her tautening nipple.

"Forgive me, Susannah. It was wrong of me to lie with you when you were under my protection."

She arched beneath his caresses, moaning. She managed a soft throaty, "No need," then bit her lip as he played his thumb pad back and forth across her nipple. "I have no regrets on that score. It was a night I shall never forget."

"And last night?"

"Paradise." She was breathing hard, her eyes glittering as she watched him. "Your face when you came… I'll never forget that either."

He bent to take her mouth again and enjoyed the rapid beat of her heart under his fingertips, for he shared her arousal, remembering how urgently they had coupled in that doorway, unable to stop even when they were discovered there.

Hugh swore under his breath, his lust suddenly violent and dizzying. He had never intended to kiss her, nor touch her so intimately. To own the truth, he had intended to hand her a robe and wait outside while she dressed, guarding the door against intruders.

Yet here he was, taking possession of her mouth instead, one hand on her breast, his heart thudding against his ribs.

What was wrong with him?

This was insanity. To seduce her right here in the heart of the king's court, where everyone was watched, regardless of rank, and spy holes could be found even in the most private places. Lord Wolf had complained only a few days before that he was being spied upon in his chambers. But it was common knowledge that Henry had grown suspicious of everyone since Anne's arrest, even his most trusted friends and advisors.

He knew the penalties if they were caught, even if she seemed ignorant of them. How stringently he had avoided this kind of scandal before meeting Susannah, by keeping married women out of his rooms, having nothing to do with the queen's maids of honor, and visiting none but the most discreet courtesans for his pleasure and relief.

Yet suddenly he was breaking his own rules.

And it felt good.

"You may be no virgin, Susannah," he murmured, enjoying the taste of her skin as he kissed down her throat, "but you are innocence itself compared to many of the women who walk these halls."

"You think me shy and inexperienced, sir?"

He gave a hoarse bark of laughter. "No more so than Jezebel!"

"Jezebel?"

Was she offended again? He drew back to examine her expression. But she was smiling, her mischievous blue eyes veiled by her lashes.

"You think me forward to have come to your chamber like a whore and waited for you unclothed," she commented in a matter-of-fact voice, and did not wait for a reply. Deftly, she released his cock from the confines of his codpiece. He groaned as her hands closed about his eager, swollen length. "I am forward and headstrong, it is true. My father could not beat it out of me as a girl, though he tried a few times. Yet I am no whore. Merely a woman who knows what she wants."

"I cannot argue with that, mistress."

"Is that what I am now, Hugh?" she asked softly, running her tongue along her lower lip. Her gaze slipped like treacle from his face to his groin, dwelling on his cock as though imagining it inside her already. "Your mistress?"

"You would rather be my mistress than my wife?"

It was ludicrous to feel slighted by such a choice. He could not afford a wife, and to offend the king by marrying Susannah without her father's permission would be next to suicidal. For a woman to lower herself to the unprotected status of mistress was the perfect solution for a man who had no taste for marriage. So if Susannah had no objection, why should he?

Yet he was hurt and could not quite hide it, frowning. For it meant she thought of him only as a passing attraction. That one day she might move on to another lover. And he did not like the idea of that.

"Come here," she whispered, looking up at him where she lay, still propped on her elbow. "Let me show you."

Shifting, still on his knees on the bed, Hugh brought his lower body close to her face. His eyes closed on a wave of the most bone-melting pleasure he had ever felt as her mouth slid warmly down his cock.

Instinctively, he tangled his fingers in her long hair, jerking her into his groin. His eyes opened. He stared down at her golden head moving slowly and intently up and down on his cock, and his eyes narrowed, his breathing suddenly labored. She had performed this intimate deed in the forest, in their dark shelter, and he had almost spent in her mouth for the sheer pleasure of it. This time he had himself under better control. Yet still he was already there, teetering on the edge, knowing that at any moment he could lose himself and his seed in her throat.

As she resurfaced, her cheeks lightly flushed, lips wet, she gasped, "Is that what a wife does? Or a mistress?"

He could hardly speak. "I do not know. For I have neither."

"Then what am I?"

She closed her warm mouth around the head of his cock, sucking steadily until his vision blurred and he thought his body would burst like a firecracker.

"My lover," he told her hoarsely, then dragged her head back by the hair. Her throat stretched, pale and vulnerable, and he thought of the queen, awaiting her execution. The cruelty of it made him angry. "You are my lover. And I'm going to come soon. Not in your mouth though. I need to fuck you."

"Yes, sir," she whispered, and lay back on the bed without argument.

"Will you always be so submissive?"

"I doubt it."

Her honesty made him laugh, and her swift answering smile lit his soul with pleasure. For that tiny moment they understood each other perfectly.

He stared into her fierce blue eyes, and found himself grasping after something he did not understand, some thought or emotion so fleeting he had no time to study it before it was gone. It touched him deeply, nonetheless, and he knew it might return if he allowed it space in his heart. Never before had he experienced such a moment of intimacy with a woman, not even with the married beauty he had eagerly pursued as an awkward youth, thinking himself deep in love with her. Now he could barely remember her face.

Could this at last be a woman he might be able to love?

He had waited years to feel more than mere attraction for the opposite sex. And now must he find it in a dry place? Love where it could not blossom. Seed scattered on barren soil. Susannah was a woman whose very nature—fiery, independent, rebellious—rebuffed him. The irony was not lost on him.

But he could not explore that dilemma now. His need to come was stronger than any other consideration.

"Open for me," he commanded her, and felt a rush of power to see how swiftly she obeyed, her legs drawn up and parted for him.

Hugh wrenched off the rest of his clothing and positioned himself between her spread thighs, his breath hissing as she took his cock firmly in hand, guiding him in.

"I need you so much," he muttered, then pushed deep inside her with one thrust, sheathed instantly in moist heat, the hairs rising on the back of his neck. "Susannah!"

———

Her head thrown back, Susannah too cried out at his entry.

God, but she had felt so empty on waking that morning. Like a bird who needed to be fed his seed in order to survive. This need to be close, to lie skin to skin with Hugh Beaufort, was fast becoming a hunger she could not control. She was not in love with the king's clerk though. No, not love, a thousand times no to that madness. She would be his mistress, and perform those duties gladly, but never his wife. That way she could keep her distance. As his mistress, she could retain some form of self-government, not yield herself as every wife must do—mind, body and soul—into the hands of a man she hardly knew.

To be a man's mistress was fair trade. To be his wife mere slavery. Becoming a dutiful wife had been enough for her mother, of course, and for her sister, Eloise. But it would never be enough for her.

His hands slid beneath her buttocks, stroking and cupping her warm skin, making thought suddenly impossible—except for thoughts of lust. His green eyes clashed with hers and for that instant she was transfixed by his hungry stare, unable to look away, until his lashes swept down, dark and stubby, concealing his expression.

"Susannah," he repeated in a growl, and her greedy cunt responded to his voice in the most visceral way, clenching about him so that he groaned, head tipping back, his strong throat exposed.

What was he thinking? The same as her, no doubt. That he needed to lose himself in this pleasure, fucking until he was too exhausted to fuck any longer. The same mindless desire that seemed to flare up out of nowhere these days and consume her utterly.

She raised herself and ran her tongue lasciviously along his lower lip, sighing, "Hugh," before she kissed him.

He was so deeply embedded inside her, their naked bodies joined, flesh to flesh, that it felt totally natural to swing her legs about his hips, rub against his buttocks, draw him even deeper inside her. Now they were locked around each other on the narrow bed as though chained by tangling limbs, and it felt so good. It felt natural, she thought.

His tongue stroked inside her mouth, tasting and exploring her, making hot little sounds of lust under his breath.

She clasped the back of his fair head, running her fingers through the sleek strands, drawing him closer, opening her mouth for his tongue. No matter how close they came to each other, it never seemed close enough. As though she needed the clumsy mortal flesh they were both clad in to melt away into nothingness, leaving only their spirits mingling and floating together in the ether, irrevocably entwined one with the other.

Hugh gasped as he pulled back, seeming to feel something similar between them. "You are the most exciting woman I have ever taken to bed, Susannah. I could fuck you all night. Yes, and all day. And lose my position in the king's service, and my good name." He laughed huskily. "My wits too, the way this lust drives me."

He saw it in cruder physical terms than she did, Susannah realized, kissing down his neck as he spoke. But perhaps all men were the same when it came to sex. For them desire was a physical need, not a feeling which might stir the heart. Her father bedded his serving woman without sentiment, while Morag worshipped him. Her brother-in-law, Lord Wolf, seemed so cold with his wife, yet Eloise accepted his dominion without question. If she had stayed to marry Sir William, Susannah too might have ended up bound in servitude to a man whose only interest in his new wife lay between her legs.

She had hoped Hugh might feel more close to her as his mistress, more able to open his heart. But perhaps some men had no heart to open.

Kissing lower, her mouth closed around one dusky nipple hidden amid the thick, curling fair hairs on his chest. His breathing became unsteady, his heart racing beneath her cheek.

"Susannah," he managed, his voice strained.

This was power indeed. It made her damp and hot to know how much the simple touch of her mouth and tongue could unbalance him. She suckled, drawing on him even harder, her tongue playing his flesh until it tautened.

Hugh suddenly cursed, then slipped a hand under each knee, pressing her legs back and open. Now she was held wide open for him, and he took advantage, staring into her face as he thrust deep, grunting out his pleasure. His cock filled her again and again, sweetly sore, banging hard inside her to the limit of her body.

His eyes were wild and green, shining down at her.

"Take me," she urged him, feeling a little insane herself. "Use me, Hugh."

"I must not...come inside you."

He was right. Yet as though teasing Hugh as he struggled for control, urging him on to do precisely that, without even knowing why she would want such a dangerous thing, Susannah drew her nails down his damp spine to the firm round of his buttocks. There she slipped a tentative finger between his buttocks, massaging him there, and felt his whole body quiver against her, his thrusts slowing.

He swore under his breath. "For pity's sake, Susannah!"

Delicately, her finger stroked between his buttocks. She examined the idea of growing round-bellied with his child, and found it good. The disgrace of it meant little to her. Why should she not behave as she pleased with Hugh Beaufort? She must be free to take whatever pleasure she wanted and explain herself to no man. Otherwise her freedom was no freedom at all.

"I want you to fuck me as though we were man and wife, Hugh." She ground her hips against him. "Don't hold back this time. I don't care about the consequences."

"Temptress," he muttered, hiding his face in her throat.

Abruptly, he rolled over, taking her with him, his cock still deep inside her body. The world turned, blurring in the firelight. Then Susannah found herself kneeling astride him, breathless, staring down into his face, her hands resting on his flushed chest for support.

"You would be ruined if I got you with child," he said simply. "King Henry may sow his seed where he chooses, but he has no mercy for those who fall pregnant without a protector. This court is a dangerous place for a woman who ignores the rules."

"I know."

He frowned, as though struggling to understand her. "But you do not care?"

"I love to wager, to take a risk. Some women spend their whole lives trying to conceive. Maybe I shall be like that, and never have a child to grace my womb."

"But perhaps you are already with child."

"Perhaps," she agreed.

She leaned forward and slipped her tongue into his mouth. Hugh groaned, and they kissed feverishly, their bodies still locked together.

Slowly, disengaging her mouth from his, Susannah rocked gently on his cock, enjoying the powerful sensations as his flesh swelled and pulsed inside her.

"I like being on top," she told him, her gaze frankly admiring his naked maleness beneath her. "Now I am the man, and will control you."

He snorted. "You can try."

"Give me reins and a birch rod, I shall soon ride you to heaven, Hugh Beaufort," she promised him, and meant every word. Perched on top of his body, she could act the man, able to control how deep he thrust, when they should kiss, how long their fucking would last. "And hard too, so that you beg me for mercy."

"God forbid you ever sit astride me with a riding crop in your hand. I'd be striped red by the end of it."

She bent and kissed him again, more lovingly this time. "Oh, I would share the crop with you. So you might take your revenge after."

Though his chest heaved, he said nothing. But she felt his

cock twitch inside her and knew by his widening gaze that she had aroused him.

"Now shall we risk the odds?" she asked, smiling into his eyes as she sat back and ran a hand from his chest to the flat expanse of his belly. "Or play the safer game of pull and spill?"

He gasped. "You are a dangerous woman, Susannah Tyrell."

"One day, perhaps."

His hands clasped her by the hips; his green eyes closed with pleasure as she swiveled her hips, tempting him to thrust. "My hot, sweet wanton. May you never suffer for this wildness."

This wildness.

He meant her consenting to couple with him while still refusing to marry. Yet why should she marry just so they could couple? Pleasure could be achieved without that particular noose about either of their necks.

She licked her lips, her body tense with the same lascivious desire that gripped him. Marriage—respectable estate that it was—would surely spell an end to this wicked lust, these teasing exchanges that left her trembling and in heat. She could not imagine her sister and Lord Wolf behaving so lewdly in bed together, nor any other married couple she had known. So far this decision of hers—to refuse his offers of marriage—had gone unpunished. And she was glad of it, for she had a horror of traps and small places, and marriage was a trap with no hope of escape.

"What is your will, sir?" she whispered, and raised herself so far off his cock that his broad velvety head almost breeched her entrance, then slid back down until she was full of him again.

"To spill in you," he growled.

Again, she repeated her long moist slide up, then down again, right to the hilt, embedding him deep in her body.

"Then spill," she said throatily, daring him with her eyes to do it.

Hugh groaned, then snapped her to him and began to drive up into her body, holding her still while he claimed her. His thrusts were hard and possessive, giving no quarter to her soft flesh. Nor did she want any. She wanted this powerful desire, not dutiful acts of procreation and empty promises of fidelity. It made so much better sense, and left them both free to escape if desire ever died.

His body demanded and hers responded amply, eagerly, urging him on. She felt gripped by a sudden, intolerable urge to take his seed, to milk him of it, to let him fill her. Her breasts bounced to the swift rhythm of his thrusts, and his hand suddenly came up to seize one, cupping it mercilessly.

She rode him too, knees tight against his sides, leaning forward with a fierce smile on her face, a smile she could not seem to repress.

"Susannah," he said hoarsely, then thrust hard one last time and clamped her hips against him, groaning. She felt a hot rush and knew he had spilled his seed inside her.

At once she put down a hand to herself and rubbed hard, closing her eyes, gasping out her pleasure as she too came, his cock still pulsing inside her as she took her relief.

~

Later, she felt him stir and reach for his clothes, then wake her so she might dress by firelight. It was evening, and she was so drowsy she could barely stand, yet somehow Hugh wrapped her in a cloak, concealing her face under a deep hood, and led her through a maze of darkened corridors until she was back at the chamber reserved for the maids of honor.

"Sleep well," he said, his arm about her waist, looking into her face before he kissed her.

Hugh vanished into the shadows just as a patrol of yawning guards came past, pikes slung over their shoulders. The last two guards turned to stare after her with undisguised contempt as

Susannah slipped inside the warm, overcrowded chamber and crept stealthily through the other sleeping maids to her own mattress.

Let them stare, she thought carelessly.

Susannah lay in the darkness for a long while though, unable to sleep, her body sore and trembling from the unaccustomed fierceness of their lovemaking.

She had not been missed, it seemed. Yet for all her defiance, she was becoming a little afraid of this wild passion. Hugh was right about one thing; King Henry's court was a dangerous place to break the rules. She thought back over how willfully she had behaved since coming to court, how often she had flouted the rules, and wondered where it would all end.

In a lifetime of sinful undiscovered pleasure? Or a public whipping for her lack of chastity?

Twelve

BREAKFAST HAD BEEN LAID out for them on the cloth-covered trestle tables in one of the side rooms near the Great Hall, but few of the courtiers seemed hungry that morning. Some stood about in twos and threes, whispering amongst each other. Others were on their knees, praying silently. A few looked out of the window at the sunlit Thames, running swift and deep that mid-May morning, and seemed disinclined to talk.

Susannah drank some ale and picked in a desultory fashion at a dish of salted ham, not in the mood for a meal but knowing she might not get a chance to eat again until the evening.

"I hate this waiting." Eloise turned from her to Hugh Beaufort, who had chosen to take his breakfast with them that morning. "When will we know for sure, Master Beaufort?"

"Cannon will be fired from the Tower of London," he replied, equally quietly, then shook his head. "If we can hear the cannon fire from here, that is. It is quite a distance."

"The wind has dropped. We will hear it."

Susannah comforted her sister as a tear ran silently down her cheek. "Hush, Eloise," she murmured, stroking her shoulder, then glanced at Hugh over her sister's bent head. She felt so helpless, for she did not know what to say that would be of any help.

"Wolf did not wish to go this morning. To witness her execution. But the order came from the king himself. He had no choice." Eloise was struggling to speak, her words disjointed. "Anne was not a good wife, I know, nor popular with the people. But to lose her head… This is a wicked business."

Suddenly, one of the women at the window gave a strangled cry, and staggered, clutching at her friends. A few others gasped, crossing themselves as they realized the significance of the moment.

Others turned with strained faces, listening hard, Susannah and Eloise with them.

It was indeed a fine morning in Greenwich, gulls crying overhead and the tide lapping rhythmically against the river bank. But clear over these came the steady *boom-boom* of cannon being fired in the distance, its eerie sound floating down the river.

Hugh grew pale and crossed himself with a slow, deliberate gesture. "Anne Boleyn is dead," he muttered. His somber green gaze snagged on their faces. "Long live Queen Jane."

"Don't!" Eloise hid her face in her hands.

He had been speaking quietly so none of the others could hear him, but Susannah caught the bitterness in his voice. "They are to be married soon, did you know? They say the king will brook no further delays but must woo his new bride before Anne's body is even cold."

Eloise swallowed, ashen-faced and red-eyed. She turned away, looking agitated. Her hands were clasped together as though she were praying, her head bowed over them, fair hair neatly restrained under a French hood of black velvet.

"We must not speak of it," she whispered, shaking her head. "Of *her*. Never again. Anne is dead and it is over."

"It is over," Hugh agreed flatly.

"Yet so cruel a death…"

Sympathy in his face, Hugh unfolded a white linen handkerchief and handed it to Eloise, murmuring, "Death on the scaffold is always cruel, I fear. Though at least Anne was not burnt alive. The king would have been within his rights to order such a death, even for his queen, given that her adultery was treasonous. Her death by the sword would have been swift… She may not even have felt pain."

"You think not?"

"I think you should dry your tears, my lady." He looked troubled. "Lord Wolf will return from the Tower soon, and you must be strong for his sake. These are still dark times at court."

Eloise nodded, drying her wet face. "You are right, sir. I know it. Yet when I remember the early days, when I first came to court… It was such a happy place then. Before the baby, Princess Elizabeth, was born. There was never any doubt in anyone's mind that the king loved Anne, was besotted with her…"

"Hush, my lady, no more. It does you no good to dwell on these sad matters. Indeed it may do great harm."

Hugh led Susannah's sister quietly aside from the breakfast table, his arm linked tightly with hers, comforting her and murmuring advice in her ear.

Susannah looked about, suddenly uneasy. Some of the other courtiers were already glancing their way and whispering. No doubt Hugh was concerned that too much sorrow on Eloise's part would throw suspicion onto her, and onto Lord Wolf too. Everyone was so afraid, she thought angrily. Afraid to speak their minds, afraid to trust anyone, afraid to show any grief for the woman who had just been executed—who so recently had been their queen.

The rarefied surroundings of King Henry's court were nothing like how she had dreamed they would be as a girl: all silks and perfumes, dancing and laughter. If she had ever thought Yorkshire a dark and dismal place, she had known nothing of what was to come when she ran away to court.

Susannah gazed out upon the broad river, rolling misty white in the May sunlight, and could not imagine how it must have felt to kneel for the executioner on such a lovely spring morning, with the bustle of the noisy river within earshot. To make so cruel an end in the very midst of life, with warm sunshine on her face and all the birds singing.

Poor Queen Anne.

She had never known Anne Boleyn, but many had described the queen consort to her as beautiful and witty—and always laughing. Mistress Seymour was not fond of laughing, it was said, and Susannah had seen for herself that Jane was a plain woman, and rather painfully short on wit. Yet the king was to marry her.

And now there was no Anne to get in his way.

Hugh came back to her side, his face serious. "Your sister is unwell. She should return to her rooms. Will you accompany her?"

"Of course."

His eyes met hers. "Susannah…"

"Hugh?"

"Will you not reconsider my offer?" he asked abruptly, glancing about to be sure they were not overheard. "Any day now your father may write to demand your immediate return to Yorkshire, and after that it will be too late for me to state my interest."

She stared at him, more tempted to say yes than she dared admit. To accept his hand in marriage and spend every night in this man's bed, gloriously and unashamedly naked…

And yet it was foolish and impossible to dream of such an idyllic end to their affair. Even if she agreed, they would still have to fight to receive her father's permission, who wanted her for Sir William and no other man. And there was no surety they would be happy together even if their marriage were blessed by the king himself. For Hugh was a man like any other, and men often lost all desire for their wives once the first few years of marriage had passed. Her own father had soon left her mother's bed and turned to her nurse instead for his relief. Even King Henry had lost his desire for Anne Boleyn, though it was said his love for her had been a kind of madness that had torn England apart. It seemed there was no hope even for those most deeply and passionately in love.

It was too horrible to imagine herself as a staid and dutiful wife, seated before her embroidery frame or nursing her babies in some chilly room while her husband spent his nights elsewhere. No, her only true chance of happiness lay in remaining free of such ties. In being her own woman for as long as fate—and her hypocritical father—would allow it.

"I thank you for your kind consideration, sir, but I fear marriage would not suit me." Susannah dropped an ironic curtsy, looking up into his eyes in a forthright manner. The gown she had borrowed from her sister was a dark red velvet and very heavy, weighing her down. But it felt more courtly than any of the other gowns she had worn, and she liked the way his eyes seemed drawn to its rich fabric. Perhaps he would find it easier to think of her as his mistress when she was dressed so boldly, she reasoned. "Any more than it suited our late queen."

He grabbed her arm as she tried to turn away, whispering in her ear, "Do not put that particular sin on me. I am no Henry Tudor, to condemn you at my whim."

She shook off his hand and followed her sister into the corridor. It was quieter there, but not safer, for her sister had warned her there were eyes and ears everywhere at court. Eloise turned, frowning when she saw them arguing, but did not interfere.

Susannah kept her voice low, not wishing her sister to hear what they were discussing. "I am sure no man intends to loathe his wife when he marries her, Master Beaufort. Yet it happens often enough between a man and his wife that he falls out with her eventually."

"And sooner or later, your father will force you into Sir William's bed," Hugh growled, the light of frustration burning in his green eyes. "Do you not understand the way the world turns? You must face the truth, Susannah. Whatever declarations you make, however you present your case to your father, you cannot avoid marriage forever unless you intend to become a nun. You are a woman, and it is a woman's destiny to be married. No man would interfere with your father's right to marry you off to whomever he chooses, for you are his to dispose of as he pleases, under the law of England." He frowned. "Better to marry me than a man of your father's choosing, surely?"

"My father will find his path strewn with difficulties if he tries forcing me into a husband's arms against my will," Susannah promised him angrily, gathering her skirts to leave. "I will make him rue the day he was born."

"Stay a moment, Susannah." His voice was suddenly hoarse. "My offer still stands. Is there anything I can do to make you change your mind and accept me?"

She stared, unsure if he was serious or not.

Hugh laid a hand on her sleeve, almost crushing the tiny pearls sewn into the burgundy velvet. His voice deepened. "Susannah, I swear to you, I would always treat you well as my wife. You do not need to fear that marriage to me would be a trial or a penance. What we have done together is not right, and you know it. I must make redress by marrying you. You are no country squire's daughter now. You are sister to a lord, and a man who is my dear friend. What I have done dishonors Wolf as well as you."

Eloise came forward. "What's this?"

"Nothing," Susannah said quickly. "My business."

"You are a child," Eloise remarked dismissively. "Your business is mine to worry about, and my husband's. Sir," she said, turning to Hugh Beaufort, "please tell me what has occurred between yourself and my sister. Pray do not lie, for I have noticed many signs of intimacy between you two since your return to court, and have hoped myself mistaken. But now I must have an answer."

Hugh looked from Eloise to Susannah. His jaw tightened at the expression on Susannah's face. "Alas, I would speak more plainly if I could. However, I am not at liberty to satisfy your question. The answer is not mine to give, but your stubborn sister's. So you must forgive me, my lady."

With that terse reply, Hugh Beaufort bowed and strode away.

Eloise stared after him in dismay, then turned to her. A loose strand of golden hair had fallen down her cheek. She tugged on it absentmindedly, then sucked it into her mouth. "Oh, Susannah, what have you done?"

"I told you, it is my affair."

"That is no answer."

"It is all the answer you will get from me," Susannah told her haughtily.

"It is just as I feared when you came to court. You are foolish, and headstrong, and have no idea how dangerous a game it is you play. Though I had hoped…" Eloise sighed, her eyes sad as she looked down the corridor where Hugh had vanished. "Tell me the truth, Susannah. Have you been more intimate with Master Beaufort than is seemly?"

Susannah folded her arms, narrowing her eyes on the floor. "Ask all the questions you like. I shall not answer them. I shall say nothing more on the subject of Hugh Beaufort."

"You are so stubborn!"

"And you are not my mother!"

Eloise bit her lip angrily at that, folding her own arms. "Ass!"

"Nag!"

There was silence in the narrow corridor. Then Eloise began to laugh reluctantly, shaking her head. "Susannah, what am I to do with you? In all honesty, I would be more than glad to see you and Hugh married. It would not be a brilliant match, but Hugh is an ambitious man, you would never want for anything while he was in favor at court. But you must know our father would never allow him to marry you. You have chosen poorly if your affections have been engaged by a man you cannot hope to wed."

"I do not wish to wed Hugh Beaufort," Susannah replied, shrugging with a carelessness she no longer felt.

She was beginning to consider the whole thing a mess, and wished she had never left home, let alone seduced Master Beaufort in the forest that night. For now she could not seem to stop thinking of Hugh and the undeniable, dizzying pleasures his body brought her. Her life would run far easier without his smile and touch complicating everything.

"Nor any man," she added, seeing her sister's disbelief.

Eloise stared, her brows rising steeply. "Nor any man? But you must wed someone, Susannah."

"Why?"

"Because there is nothing else for you to do."

Susannah set her hands on her hips, drawing in a sharp breath. "Well, we shall see about that."

Her eyes clashed with her sister's for a long and difficult moment, then she turned her head, seeing a servant loitering silently in the shadows by the doorway. Alarm jumped in her heart, then she gathered herself, raising her voice.

"You there!" Susannah summoned the servant boldly. "Find a chess board and pieces, and have them conveyed to Lord Wolf's chambers."

"At once, mistress," the serving man replied, and bowed low before disappearing through one of the open doorways along the corridor.

Perhaps the man had heard nothing. And perhaps the moon was made of cheese.

Eloise was staring, her mouth frankly open. "You never cease to amaze me, Susannah. With all that has happened today, you want to sit down and *play games?*"

"You and I shall entertain ourselves while we wait for his lordship to return from…from the city. Perhaps we shall see his barge approach on the river." Susannah linked her arm in her sister's, pinning a stiff smile to her lips, though the Lord knew she felt little enough like smiling. "Come, let us walk back to your rooms."

The palace corridors were dark and narrow here, and she could not even bring herself to say the word "Tower" for fear it might be overheard. Greenwich Palace was a gilded prison, she thought bitterly, where you never knew who the guards were or what you might be punished for until it was too late.

"We used to play chess all the time as children," she reminded her sister lightly, "before you left for court and grew too aloof for such games. Do you not remember those days?"

Eloise managed a laugh. "Yes, of course. I had forgotten."

"You have a short memory."

Susannah looked at her sister, a little rueful now, for she regretted their argument. Over a man, too! Her body was still tingling from the way Hugh had stood so close, his hand on her arm, reminding her how intimately they had lain together. If she was not more careful, she would be half in love with Master Beaufort. And then all her plans for freedom and an independent life would be wrecked. For Hugh would enslave her more sweetly and readily than any old man, and she would not have the backbone to resist.

"Though I wish I had played chess more often since you left," Susannah added, lowering her voice. "Perhaps then I would have a better strategy for court life."

They walked slowly through the palace corridors, arm in arm, heads together and their heavy skirts rustling. As they climbed the stairs the scent of meat spits roasting with spices rose from the kitchens, mingled rather less pleasantly with the sweet-sour smell of the nearby river mud. The sun streamed in through open casements along the corridors, warming the palace. Several courtiers stopped to bow to Eloise, but she barely acknowledged them, flicking her painted fan back and forth as the heat of the morning increased.

"So the queen falls to the tower, and the king moves to a new square," Eloise whispered, not looking at her, but out across the rolling gray-green of the River Thames. "But what lies ahead for the pawns?"

Susannah shuddered. "Even a pawn may become a queen, if she learns to keep her head."

※

Later that evening, the door opened and Lord Wolf stood swaying on the threshold, cap in hand. His black hair was disheveled, his face drawn and exhausted. "Eloise?"

He must have witnessed Anne Boleyn's execution many hours ago, yet had not come back to his rooms at Greenwich, which suggested that he had been closeted with the king or his advisors. Either that or he had not felt able to face them. Certainly Wolf looked like hell, his eyes bloodshot, his doublet askew. And she noticed his limp seemed more pronounced than usual—an old injury, she had been told, received during battle as a young man.

Had he been drinking, she wondered?

"Wolf!" Eloise jumped up and hurried to her husband at once: the two embraced in silence, her arms lifting about his neck, his face buried against her pale throat.

It had been only a short while ago that they had been wed in Yorkshire, and although Susannah had thought their marriage doomed at first, it seemed the couple had found something to unite them here at court. Their desire for each other was burningly obvious, she thought, and averted her gaze. It made her body ache to be with Hugh, seeing the way they clung together.

Wolf disentangled himself with reluctance, glancing toward Susannah with a strained smile. "Good evening, Susannah." He limped forward to warm himself before the fire, and his glance swung drily about the room. "No Master Beaufort in tow tonight?"

Susannah struggled against the slow blush creeping up her face. Those sharp blue eyes saw more than she had realized.

"As you see, my lord."

"Don't tease the girl, Wolf," Eloise told him warningly, then stood on tiptoe, whispering something in his ear which Susannah could not catch.

His eyes narrowed as he listened, then he nodded. "I must remember to speak with Beaufort in the morning," he replied, but his gaze moved hungrily over his wife, and suddenly the chamber felt too warm and close, the fire too hot with crackling logs.

Setting aside her cup of wine, Susannah stood and shook out her crumpled velvet skirts. She had enjoyed keeping her sister company all day, but it was time to leave these two lovebirds alone.

"Pray forgive me, Eloise," she said, embracing her sister, "but I am fatigued after all our games of chess, and can barely keep my eyes open. No please, my lord, I need no escort. I can find my own way back to the maids' chamber, it is but a few corridors from here."

She went to the door, which Lord Wolf held courteously open for her, and dropped a curtsy to both, smiling up at them.

"I will see you tomorrow, sister. My lord."

Head bowed, she hurried away before Lord Wolf could change his mind and insist on escorting her back to the maids' chamber. It was dark between torches but she had little fear of molestation, not when every man in the palace was intent on keeping his head and avoiding the king's ire. There was a weasel-faced man leaning against the wall further down the corridor, who lifted his head at her approach and stared, but she ignored him. Some spy, she thought dismissively, set there to watch Wolf's chambers in case he had visitors who might incriminate him.

It was odd to realize how coolly she could accept such spies now, the constant observation of great ones at court, when on her arrival she had boggled to find men stationed at Wolf's door, or eyes watching from behind the arras, records kept of every conversation, however trivial, and daily reports made to Cromwell or King Henry, whoever had commissioned them. To speak unheard a courtier had to stay on the move, or walk in the palace gardens, or keep speech to the barest whisper.

Mercifully, she herself had never yet been followed, nor spied upon, for Susannah Tyrell was of little interest to the powerful at court. But that might change if she could not stay away from Hugh Beaufort, for he was much in the king's confidence these days and any woman he courted might end up hearing secrets she should not.

As Susannah rounded the next corner, her breath caught in her chest and she took a swift step backward, staring.

Hugh Beaufort, standing not ten feet away! And he was not alone, but engaged in conversation with a cloaked and hooded woman.

Hiding herself in the shadows, her skirts drawn in against the dusty wall, Susannah peered round at them. Her heart was suddenly beating fast, like a young girl in love. But it was only at the shock of seeing Hugh just as she had been thinking about him, she told herself.

Why in God's name was Hugh Beaufort wandering the palace so late at night? Perhaps he had spent the evening with Lord Wolf, and just left him at the door, for the two were firm friends. Yet if that was the case, why had Hugh not yet returned to his own chamber—and just who was this woman who seemed to be holding his attention so closely?

Hugh was talking softly to the woman, whose back was toward her. Their heads were close together, and for one moment it looked as though they were kissing.

Violent jealousy sparked inside her and she gasped, clapping a hand to her mouth.

How dared Hugh meet another woman secretly?

Yet why should Master Beaufort not meet—and bed—other women? Susannah felt angry with herself for being such a fool. They were not married, nor even betrothed. No oaths had been made, no promises exchanged between them. She was not even his mistress, but his secret lover. And an occasional lover at that. She had no right to confine him to her bed alone.

The thought left her cold at heart, and oddly disturbed. Her own freedom had always been precious to her, but Hugh's was another matter. She had not realized until that moment that she did not like the idea of Hugh Beaufort in another woman's bed.

Hugh put a hand on the woman's arm, and leaned close, whispering in her ear. Then he bowed and turned away, disappearing down the corridor as though returning to his room at last.

The woman stood and watched him go, unaware that she herself was being watched. Then she stepped to an oaken door set discreetly into an alcove and knocked. There was no answer. She waited an anxious moment, her foot tapping, glancing up and down the corridor as though afraid of being caught there, then pushed the door open a crack.

Whatever she saw within seemed to startle her, for the woman gave a sharp little cry, stepped backward, then hurried away in the same direction that Hugh had taken.

In the woman's haste, her hood fell back, revealing masses of red hair and a pale, expressive face. Susannah, darting out from the shadows in pursuit, recognized her at once as the woman she had seen hiding in Master Elton's private chamber. She decided to follow a little way at least, and see where this woman might lead her. If she could find out where she lodged, Susannah reasoned, she might be able to discover her identity.

Passing the doorway, Susannah saw the door was still open a crack.

Curious to know what had startled the other woman, she glanced into the chamber—and gasped.

The room was dark, except for one bright corner, which glittered with candlelight. Pushed up against one wall was a silk-covered daybed, strewn with cushions and surrounded by candles. On her hands and knees among the silken covers was a naked woman, fair hair tumbling almost to her waist, her smooth white backside toward the door. Her full breasts, hanging down, swung gently against the cushions. Behind her crouched a heavyset man, also unclothed, one foot on the floor, the other on the daybed. He was fucking the woman from behind, grunting as he labored hard.

Kneeling up on the daybed, still fully dressed with his back against the wall, was a gray-bearded man she did not recognize, though by his splendid jeweled doublet and chain she guessed him to be a nobleman. His codpiece was hanging open, partly unfastened, and his cock was deep in the woman's mouth. His hand gripped her hair as he thrust silently in and out, his face a mask of grimacing pleasure; the daybed creaked rhythmically as she served both men at once.

Susannah had never witnessed such a bold sexual performance before, and to her embarrassment she became instantly aroused. Her nipples stiffened against the restraint of her velvet bodice, and her core moistened and contracted, open to the air beneath her heavy skirts.

She had not meant to stand there more than a few seconds, yet found herself breathing more heavily, unable to move on. Her eyes were drawn to the pumping hips of the older man, his fingers tangling in the woman's fair hair as he used her mouth so freely. What must it feel like for the woman, she wondered, to be dominated with such complete male authority, entered by two men at one time?

Suddenly the nobleman glanced up and swore, catching Susannah's gaze upon them.

"A girl at the door!" he exclaimed hoarsely. "Quick, man. Who is it?"

His naked fellow looked round abruptly; there was something familiar about the way his dark head turned, but Susannah had already picked up her skirts and was running away down the corridor, her cheeks hot.

Oh good God. Had that been Sir Giles de Lacey?

She caught up with the cloaked woman just in time to see the whisk of her dark cloak entering one of the tower stairwells.

She peered inside and, to her dismay, found the winding stairs unlit. Nonetheless Susannah followed her prey up the steep drafty stairway at a brisk pace, glancing out of the narrow windows at every turn. It was a black night outside, the moon behind clouds and the air brilliantly still. Her skirts rustled against the stone, and she was sure her gasping breath must be loud enough for the guards to hear in the quadrangle below.

At the top Susannah emerged onto a narrow landing lit with one guttering torch, and shrank back at once in the shadows.

The mysterious redhead was there, only a few feet away.

It was too late to hide.

The cloaked woman looked round and stared, her eyes widening under the dark hood. "Who is that? Who are you?" Then she frowned, coming back. "Wait… You are Lady Wolf's young sister, are you not?"

Susannah felt ridiculous, still trying to melt into the shadows as though she could put the cat back into the bag. She straightened and stepped quickly forward, meeting the woman halfway along the landing. There seemed little point in remaining silent when she had already been discovered. Besides, she wanted to know why this woman had been talking to Hugh.

"Yes," she agreed, looking the redhead up and down. "My name is Susannah Tyrell. My father is Sir John Tyrell. And who are *you*?"

The woman studied Susannah in her turn, her gaze cool and assessing, then let her hood drop back to reveal her face. Her smile was wry. "Me? Oh, I am nobody."

She did not look like nobody. The woman's face was small-boned, with the kind of pointed chin that showed good breeding, her cheeks pale with a light smattering of freckles. Her cloudy mass of red hair was complemented by deep green eyes, not unlike

Hugh's, though hers were slanted, with long curved lashes. Her mouth was mobile, thinning to a straight line, then abruptly smiling, full and generous.

Susannah frowned, taken aback by the woman's directness and unsure how to continue. There was some secret here she did not understand, nor had time to uncover. Her instincts told her that this woman could be trusted. But her jealousy would not allow her to turn away.

"Do you have a name?" she demanded, then could not help adding, "And why were you so deep in conversation with Master Hugh Beaufort?"

"My name is Margerie." The woman hesitated, her thoughtful green eyes narrowed on Susannah's face. "But as for your other question, I am afraid that I am not at liberty to discuss that matter."

"Not at…*what*?"

"You must forgive me, Mistress Tyrell." Margerie dropped an ironic curtsy, then turned away. "I am late for my bed."

"Wait, I must know!"

Margerie stopped and glanced back over her shoulder, a sudden sympathy in her face. "He means something to you, this gentleman?"

Thrown off balance by the unexpected question, Susannah found herself taking a step backward, shaking her head.

Did he mean something to her? Hugh Beaufort? Of course not, she thought wildly. No more than she meant to him.

"Not particularly, no," she insisted, cursing herself for a fool. "I just wondered if he meant anything to you."

The woman's soft mocking laughter was no comfort to her. "Master Beaufort is a handsome gentleman, is he not? Those broad shoulders, that narrow waist…"

Susannah could only stare, furious and incoherent.

Their eyes met, and Margerie sighed, searching her face. "Forgive me, I did not mean to hurt you," she murmured, and stepped closer. "May I speak plainly?"

Margerie placed a hand gently on her arm, her voice dropping even lower as Susannah hesitated. "I have heard certain tales about you and His Majesty. No listen, I do not condemn you, for I know what it is to be in a man's power. And an offer from the King of England is not easily refused by any woman, let alone one who has left the safety of her father's protection as you have done. Oh, I can tell by your face that you think yourself free to do whatever you choose and live however you wish. But you must be careful, child. You are so very young."

"I am eighteen," Susannah said fiercely, her chin lifted. "That is hardly young."

Then she remembered telling the doctor that eighteen was "no great age," and her gaze faltered.

"So bold, such a firebrand." Margerie brushed her cheek with one trembling finger, her eyes shining in the torchlight. "When I was young, I made a terrible mistake over a man because I thought myself in love. It was only a moment's error, but it ruined my life. Do not, I beg you, take any more false steps that might lead you away from your good reputation. Or you may live to regret it, as I have done.

"Now please stop following me. I have given you my name, and will tell you nothing more." Margerie put up her hood and gazed at her coolly. "Good night, Mistress Tyrell."

Susannah met her eyes in disbelief. Her cheeks flamed with anger. But what else was there for her to do? Unless she wished to make a scene and risk alerting the palace guards, Susannah had no choice but to leave.

She turned away and began to descend the gloomy circular tower stairs, her head buzzing with frustration.

After three steps, she stopped and looked back, unable to believe what had just happened. Was she so witless as to be dismissed by this redhead, a woman who was surely no higher than her at court?

Without even thinking what she was doing, Susannah crept back up to the top of the stairs and peered out at the torchlit corridor.

From her hiding place, she watched as Margerie knocked once at another recessed chamber door, paused, then knocked again three times as though it was a secret signal.

After a moment, the door was opened for her and Margerie hurried inside, head down, her hood once more obscuring her face.

This time she did not come out.

Tiptoeing along the corridor, Susannah recognized the door as belonging to Master Elton, the doctor who had recently treated her. So she had been right—the two were lovers!

She stood before the closed door another moment, unsure what to do, and caught the sound of two voices inside: Margerie first, speaking urgently, then a man answering in a calmer voice, soothing her.

Master Elton, she was sure of it. And there was no hint of surprise in his voice, even though the hour must be past midnight now and the palace was quiet.

In God's name, were all the courtiers at it tonight? Perhaps the queen's execution had driven them all into each other's beds, desperate for some shred of physical comfort after the trials of the day.

She found the idea amusing at first. Then her mind began to churn with strange thoughts and feelings, jealousy being paramount among them. She knew Master Elton to be unmarried. Yet despite her warnings about lewd behavior, Margerie had risked her own reputation by visiting the doctor at night, immediately after speaking to Hugh Beaufort.

There could be another explanation for such behavior, of course. Dread coiled like a hard ball of twine in her stomach as she stood listening to their voices. What had Margerie said? *When I was young, I made a terrible mistake over a man. It was only a moment's error, but it ruined my life.* She shuddered. Margerie could be a courtesan, forced into such a life after losing her good reputation as a young woman.

And if so, was Hugh Beaufort one of her lovers?

Jealousy ate at her insides like a poison. Her chest was suddenly tight, her breathing ragged. She could stand to hear no more. Susannah turned away and groped her way back along the landing toward the entrance to the tower stairs. Yet she had not gone five paces when she heard rustling, and looked up in alarm to catch a glimpse of a sharp-jawed, whiskered man in black darting away down the stairs.

For a second, Susannah stood staring at the space where he had been hiding, her heart thundering in panic.

Then she remembered where she had seen him before. It was the same weasel-faced man she had passed near Lord Wolf's door, the one she had assumed was a spy set there to watch his lordship's comings and goings. Instead, the sneaky little creature must have left his post and followed her all the way along the corridor—no doubt also peeking in at those rude goings-on in the candlelit chamber— then up the tower stairs to Master Elton's door.

Perhaps, seeing her emerge from Lord Wolf's chambers, he had mistaken her for some person of interest, when in fact she was like Margerie. She was nobody. Nobody at all.

Laughter rose in her wildly, and she snorted, one hand clamped to her mouth. She had been so intent, watching Hugh flirting with Margerie, then the three lovers coupling feverishly—had that indeed been the unpleasant Sir Giles, taking the woman from behind?— that she had been unaware of the weasel-faced man watching *her*.

Susannah started down the winding stairs on a dangerous impulse, almost laughing, suddenly in pursuit of her pursuer, feeling her way clumsily in the darkness.

By the time she reached the bottom, the corridor was silent and empty. The spy had vanished. She peered up and down, recovering her breath, but saw no one. Perhaps she had been mistaken, and the man at the top of the stairs had been there quite innocently.

Yet all the way back to the maids' chamber, she felt uneasy, shoulders prickling, as though someone was still watching her. And it did not help that she kept remembering Hugh talking to Margerie in the corridor, their heads bent so intimately together. For a man who swore he wished to marry her, Hugh's gaze seemed oddly inclined to wander.

Well, God help him if he should offer for her hand again. For now she knew how easily Hugh Beaufort's head was turned by a pretty face, she would have none of him.

Thirteen

"MASTER BEAUFORT," THE KING exclaimed, crooking a jeweled finger to summon his clerk. "Present your report on the religious houses in the north. I am now at liberty to study it."

Hugh threaded his way forward through the throng of courtiers and clerks, dropped to one knee on the dais, and handed the papers to the king with his head bowed.

"My report is not quite concluded, Your Majesty, for which I humbly beg your forgiveness. It proved difficult to visit all the religious houses in the time allowed, for some of the larger properties are very complex in their financial dealings and took much of my attention."

Hugh hesitated, glancing up at the king and finding him absorbed by his report. He fell silent, waiting.

His gaze wandered further upward. Stars shone on the red silk hangings above the king's head, gathered together in rich folds, each pinned to the wooden frame with a perfectly carved rose, symbolizing the Tudor dynasty. Though without an heir to the throne of England, that dynasty might founder.

The king had his bastard, Henry Fitzroy, a sturdy enough youth. But every fool could see Henry wanted a son born between legitimate sheets. Small wonder the king was intent on fathering one by whichever queen could manage to produce a living boy to make him proud. Proud and complete.

. One of the wooden roses was cracked straight across. Hugh lowered his gaze to the king below.

"But if Your Majesty could spare me for a second visit to the north, I should be able to furnish your advisors with a more comprehensive report, including the majority of the smaller houses."

"Yes, yes…" King Henry agreed, not looking up from his narrow-eyed perusal of the documents. "Speak to Master Cromwell. He will make the necessary arrangements."

Suddenly the king slammed his fist down on the arm of his high-backed chair, crushing the papers in his other hand.

"God's death, but these figures speak for themselves!" he swore, a hard flush mounting in his cheeks. "These monks and priests and holy sisters are little better than leeches. They have been draining the lifeblood of England for centuries, damn them. And they think to sue for compensation? By the rood, they should be kicked out onto the roadside, every last one of them, men and women alike. Let them live in rags as vagabonds, and sleep in ditches when it rains. Let them see how the common people must dirty their hands with labor, and perhaps such hardships will bring them closer to God."

There was a hurried rumble of agreement from the watching courtiers, and an uneasy shuffling as many drew back from the dais. Few were willing to remain in reach of the king's lightning glance in such an uncertain humor.

Thomas Cromwell appeared, passing easily through the crowd, who fell back at the very whisper of his name, and climbed onto the dais with a weary smile.

Hugh rose and bowed to the king's advisor. Cromwell was the most powerful man in England at this moment, and deference was his due. Henry might rail at Cromwell furiously from time to time, but he still listened when Cromwell spoke, and frequently took the man's advice, which was more than could be said for any of his other councilors. And Cromwell was at least a subtle man. He did not strut about like many of the noblemen nor spend his time in corrupt and dangerous practices. Yet for the past few years, little had happened at

King Henry's court without Thomas Cromwell's knowledge—and tacit permission.

Robed in sober brown, a simple gold chain about his neck, Cromwell snapped his fingers and a cup of wine was brought forward.

"Your Majesty," he murmured.

Henry drank deep, then wiped his reddened lips on his sleeve. He was still shaking with temper. "By Christ!"

"It is being dealt with, Your Majesty."

"Not swiftly enough for my tastes."

Cromwell looked at Hugh, his brows raised. "Did they give you any trouble, these northern priests?"

"Not trouble, sir. But they had questions."

"And who can blame them? To find themselves suddenly homeless, unfed and unclothed after a lifetime of ease…" Cromwell spread his hands, his smile dry. "Your Majesty, all shall be undertaken as you have prescribed. But the timing may be a little awry, for we are talking about a great number of people who cannot easily be shifted from one place to…well, another. Now, there is the matter of your marriage to discuss. I am informed that the end of this month…"

"Not soon enough, by God!"

Cromwell waited a moment, inclining his head as though taking the king's outburst into consideration. "The end of this month," he continued smoothly, "will be propitious for a royal wedding, and is the soonest it can be achieved. Given the…erm…circumstances."

King Henry growled something coarse under his breath, then nodded to Hugh, dismissing him. He glared at Cromwell. "And meanwhile, I must be patient?"

"I fear so, Your Majesty."

Pushing through the crowd, relieved to have escaped his audience with the king so lightly, Hugh noticed the man he had seen with Susannah in the queen's privy garden a few days since. Sir Giles de Lacey, from an old French family like the Beauforts, one of those hangers-on in the royal train who had no clear purpose, yet always managed to be granted bouge of court, his place paid for each year out of the king's own coffers.

The courtier was looking directly at Hugh, his gaze unpleasant. There was a challenge in the older man's gaze that made it hard to look away, and Hugh found his hand dropping instinctively to his dagger hilt.

"Hold a moment there," Sir Giles insisted, stepping in his way. "I would speak with you."

Hugh met his stare, bristling at the arrogance in his tone. The knight outranked him, of course, but that did not mean he need be more than coldly civil.

"Sir?"

"You are Beaufort?"

"Master Beaufort, yes." With an effort, Hugh forced his fingers to unclench from the hilt of his dagger, for he was still in the king's presence, where such aggression could be considered a hanging offense. "You must forgive me, sir, but you have the advantage of me."

Sir Giles did not introduce himself, but looked back at him assessingly, as though perfectly aware that Hugh knew who he was.

Behind them, the king was still talking to Cromwell and his other advisors about the arrangements for his wedding to Mistress Seymour, the curt edge of sexual frustration in his voice. What Henry wanted was to bed his betrothed, but he would not take the risk of doing so before they were safely wed. So for the next ten days at least the court would have to bear his ill humor and bursts of temper.

Sir Giles lowered his voice, no doubt aware this would not be a good time to antagonize the king by speaking across him. "You were in the north country recently," he stated bluntly, "in the company of a certain lady, name of Tyrell, and were privy to her person, by all accounts."

Hugh was almost knocked off balance by the raw fury he felt. *Name of Tyrell*. The villain meant Susannah. *Privy to her person*. Sir Giles de Lacey might as well have shouted out in the Presence Chamber that Hugh had raped her.

He took a hasty step forward, his hand back on his dagger hilt. "What did you say?"

"Come, fellow, do not waste your breath on idle denials," Sir Giles said, watching him intently, "for I have heard enough of the story to guess the rest. Such a scandalous tale too. Now keep your countenance, man, unless you wish everyone in the room to know our business."

"Do not dare use that lady's name again," Hugh whispered, standing so close to the man that he could have strangled him just by reaching out, "or you will answer to me."

Sir Giles smiled coldly. "Your threats do not frighten me, Beaufort. You are a clerk, not a soldier. What would you do, man, beat me to death with your quill? I shall say as I find, and you will not stop me. Nonetheless, I am not a fool. The lady has a noble protector at this court, and I would not offend *him* by speaking too publicly of what I know."

He meant Lord Wolf. Sir Giles planned to take this matter to Wolf and reveal his affair with Susannah. A red tide shifted across his vision and Hugh knew he was burningly angry. Not only angry, but afraid for Susannah, whom he had seduced, and who should not be made to suffer for his untrammeled desires.

"You cannot speak of what you do not *know*!"

"Hush," Sir Giles said warningly, and both men stilled as the king's voice rose behind them, beating at Cromwell in a sudden welter of rage over some detail of his forthcoming wedding. It would not do to bring that wrath down on their own heads for causing a public disturbance. "Shall we step outside a moment?"

"Willingly," Hugh bit out.

They made their way through the crowd to the busy corridor outside the Presence Chamber, pressed with almost as many courtiers again, leaning against the walls or talking in groups. Sir Giles indicated the way, leading Hugh through that throng until they came to a quieter corridor. There he opened a door onto an empty chamber to one side of a small rose garden, where a fountain played merrily in the sunlight.

"Here we may talk more freely," Sir Giles murmured, and closed the door.

A second later Hugh was on him, his hands around the man's throat, tightening viciously, strangling him. "You dog," he said through his teeth, close up into his face. "Don't think for a moment that I will permit you to slur the good name of that lady with your vile insinuations. I would rather hang for your murder first."

Red-faced, tearing at the hands that choked him, Sir Giles finally managed to gasp, "*Pax!*" and Hugh released his grip so abruptly that the knight fell backward against the wall.

"You are mad, clerk!" Sir Giles exclaimed, rubbing his reddened throat and staring at Hugh as though he had never seen him properly before. "You must have lost your wits to attack me like that! I am a knight of the realm. Who are you?"

"I am the king's servant, and I would ask you not to forget it." Hugh straightened his doublet, gone awry during their struggle, then bent for his cap among the rushes. Dusting it off, he settled it back on his head and turned to face the man, still a little breathless. "Nor was I ever more serious in my life. Whatever you have to say about that lady will stay in this room, sir. Else you will suffer for it, knight or no."

"Very well." Sir Giles studied him angrily. "Since you will have it, I must tell you that my cousin is Sir Francis Beverley, whose manor lies near Doncaster. He was gravely injured in an attack that took place not long before you came to court in the company of

Mistress Tyrell. I had news this morning that he died of his injuries five days ago."

Hugh stood silent, his hands by his sides. A memory of their fight played out again in his mind: a confused skirmish between dark, tight-set tree trunks, his blade thrust into the knight's side, the horse terrified, running away into the storm, his master slumped across his neck.

He had thought the knight wounded, that was all. The blade had not bit deep enough to kill. But perhaps the wound had become infected, or else he was not attended until too late.

Now, by this account, Sir Francis was dead. And he, Hugh Beaufort, was his killer.

"My unfortunate cousin was long since widowed, so no wife mourns his passing. But his daughter, Ianthe, has been left penniless, for the Beverley estate is a poor one and has been failing for some years. I plan to write and advise Ianthe to seek compensation for his murder." Sir Giles paused, his lips twitching as though on the verge of a sneer, clearly pleased by the effect his words were having on Hugh. "From the king, if necessary."

Hugh shook himself from his stupor. This death meant trouble for him and for Susannah. And there would be more to come, for Sir Giles was not the kind of man to let such a chance slip by.

"What do you want?"

Sir Giles smiled as though he had won. His hand dropped from his throat and he sauntered to the window, looking out. "This is a pretty garden. I walked there with Mistress Tyrell not so long ago, and found her a most charming companion. But I believe you already know her charms…intimately." When Hugh drew breath, he held up a hand. "Pray don't attack me again, fellow. I merely state what everyone else at court will soon be thinking. When I tell the king the rest of my cousin's story, that is, and her shame is let out for all to see. Sir Francis, it seems, played host to Mistress Tyrell for several days—and nights—and all was set for a betrothal between them. Then you chanced along, with a pack of Lord Wolf's men, and tried to steal her away from the good knight."

"You lie!"

"Peace, I tell you." Sir Giles glared at him, drawing his dagger, the ornate handle flashing in the sunlight. "You see? Two may play at that game, sirrah. I shall not be taken by surprise as my cousin was, and stabbed before I even had a chance to draw."

"What? This is nonsense."

"I have my cousin Ianthe's sworn testimony on it. Aye, and her servants' too. Do you have witnesses to your fight with Sir Francis who can deny their story?"

"None but…" Hugh stopped short, only then seeing the trap laid before him.

"None but Mistress Tyrell?" Sir Giles prompted him softly. "Rumor has it you spent the night in the forest with Mistress Tyrell. Rumor has it she was not unwilling to share your bed that night, nor showed any anger or shame the next morning when you were discovered together by Lord Wolf's men. That you passed a pleasant night, in fact, in Cupid's bush, and left her all the sweeter for it."

Hugh said nothing, but his fists clenched and he had trouble breathing. Which of the men under Wolf's command had talked? He would tear the man's liver out and feed it to the dogs for this rank betrayal of his trust. And then he would come back and take this foulmouthed jackanapes apart.

"I see you are disconcerted by my tale, Master Beaufort." Sir Giles slid the dagger back into its sheath, the gesture intended as an insult. "Well, well. Perhaps now we can talk like gentlemen."

"I ask again, what do you want?" Hugh managed, his voice choked.

"Since you have made no declaration, I will assume you do not intend to marry Mistress Tyrell."

Hugh's face became like stone. He stared at Sir Giles. "That is no concern of yours."

"True, except that I have taken a fancy to the lady myself. And since it seems she holds her honor as naught, I would take it as a kindness if you could smooth the way for me with her." Sir Giles smiled unpleasantly. "I am a fair man though, Master Beaufort, and do not demand that you relinquish her bed altogether. I am willing to share. Indeed, if your mistress is as wild and willing as rumor has it, there would be plenty to go round."

Not to draw his dagger and plunge it into the villain's throat was the hardest thing he had ever done.

Hugh drew an unsteady breath. "And Lord Wolf?"

"Has he an interest there too? His wife's own sister?" Sir Giles looked troubled at last. "Lord Wolf keeps his women close and is not known for his love of sport. I would not wish to offend his lordship by sharing bedchamber spoils without his say-so."

By the rood, now the villain believed Wolf was bedding Susannah too. Bile rose in his throat. He knew Sir Giles to be debauched and known for his love of courtesans and orgies. But even so…

"I must speak to his lordship at once," he said grimly.

"Of course, of course." Sir Giles nodded, as though giving a servant permission to depart. "But I warn you, Beaufort, I can only be patient so long. I give you and his lordship a sennight to make your decision. If the lady has not come to me willingly by then, I shall feel duty-bound to inform the king that my cousin's death can be laid at your door, and that Susannah Tyrell is no honest virgin but a common whore, and a well-used one at that. I doubt that Lord Wolf would wish such shame on his bride's sister."

Hugh strode forward and seized him by the doublet, lifting the man up so his booted feet dangled. "You say one word against Mistress Tyrell and…"

Sir Giles spat, "How dare you, Beaufort? Let me go or I swear your mistress will never enter this court again, her reputation will be so trodden in the mire. If you think her faithful only to you, why not ask the lady where she was on the night of the queen's execution? For I can tell you now, she was not in her bed. Susannah Tyrell was with me and Lord Gifford, watching us at our sport with a married lady of the court whom I cannot name, but who was most accommodating."

"What?" Hugh released him, his hands suddenly numb.

"Oh yes, bold as any whore was your mistress. You may tell Susannah from me, I would have invited her to join us but she did not stay to see what I could offer."

"Get out!"

Sir Giles opened his mouth to speak again and staggered backward as Hugh punched him in the face. He knocked over a table, and lay crooked among the rushes, breathing hard.

"Get out before I break your jaw," Hugh told him, knowing that if the man stayed in that room a moment later, he would not be able to control his desire to murder him.

Scrambling to his feet, Sir Giles stared across at Hugh with narrowed eyes. There was blood on his mouth. "You will pay for this insult, Beaufort."

"I look forward to it, sir. Send me the bill." Hugh threw open the door. "Go."

Hugh stood alone in the chamber a few moments after Sir Giles had gone, his eyes shut tight, his fist curled against the back of the door. Outside the door he could hear the buzz of the court, the king's steward calling forward a petition to be heard, and struggled against the urge to be sick.

He opened his eyes. "No," he whispered hoarsely.

Susannah and Sir Giles at play with Lord Gifford and some other woman: the courtly sport of sharing a mistress, a practice he abhorred but which he knew went on behind closed doors. Two men sharing one willing woman. Or in this case, two of each sex enjoying each other carnally. The various possibilities left him breathing hard, staring at nothing, unable to prevent a low moan escaping as he considered them one by one, his unnatural imaginings put there by a few words from that vile creature, Sir Giles.

Blood roared in his ears. It could not be true. It was not true.

And he would prove it.

He found her in Lord Wolf's chambers, seated on a settle and reading through a sheath of Thomas Wyatt's poems that he himself had left with Eloise only a few days before, for he knew how her ladyship enjoyed poetry.

"Oh!" Clearly startled by his sudden arrival, Susannah put aside the poems and smoothed out the skirts of her gown. She sounded oddly nervous. Was that guilt in her voice? he wondered. His fists clenched and he had to make an effort to smile, for he was no doubt looking rather grim. "I am afraid my sister is not here at present, sir. Nor his lordship."

"No matter." Hugh turned and nodded to the plump, curly-haired maid who had appeared at his knock, a face he remembered from their first journey up to Yorkshire. "You may go. I wish to speak with Mistress Tyrell privately."

Susannah glanced at the maid, who seemed reluctant to leave them alone together. "Go on, Mary. My sister will not mind."

Alone with her at last, he found to his irritation that he could not find the words to broach the subject. *Have you played at country pleasures with Sir Giles de Lacey and Lord Gifford?* It was simply not a question he felt able to ask. So he stood, arms folded, and looked down at her in silence instead.

She had never looked lovelier, her golden hair simply dressed in a net of pearls, her dark green silk bodice cut low enough to show the full swell of her breasts but with a lace trim that discreetly hid her nipples. When Queen Anne was still alive, the gown might have been a bright red or yellow silk, with a hint of nipple visible. But already gowns were more muted, bodices and waists less provocatively cut, for Mistress Seymour was rumored to prefer dark colors, and disliked too much flesh on overt display.

"Sir?"

He could not bear it a second longer. Something broke in him at the sound of that one word. "Susannah," he said huskily, then knelt before her. He took her hand and raised it to his lips. His eyes closed. The scent of her flesh was intoxicating. "Susannah."

It sounded as though she were smiling, her voice a little puzzled. "Hugh?"

Visions of her with other men filled his mind and he beat them away, furious at himself, angry enough to flay the skin from his own back. This was his problem, not hers. She would never… Not like that. He knew Susannah better than any other man alive, and he trusted her. He had taken her innocence. By God, she was still innocent, even now. There was nothing in her that would find interest in such lascivious sport.

And yet there was doubt in him, and it would not easily be laid to rest. Doubt that such a gorgeous woman would want to spend the rest of her days with a clerk, a servant of the crown, when she could have a wealthy gentleman or even a nobleman in her bed.

He had to ask. His stomach clenched with a sick fear, his heart unnaturally loud in his ears.

She would hate him for it. But he had to ask.

"Have you ever lain with another man?" Eyes still closed, head bowed over her hand, Hugh listened to the silence, which seemed to drag on forever. He drew a deep unsteady breath. "Susannah? Have you ever… God's blood, why can I not ask this? Have you ever made love with any man but me?"

When the silence continued, he opened his eyes and looked up into her face. Her half-smile was frozen on her lips, her eyes full of hurt. Pain burned through him, searing his heart, his mind, and it was all he could do to speak again.

"Have you?"

She withdrew her hand from his. Her voice was cold, chilling him. "You know I have not."

Hugh rocked back, staring at her, nodding. He could barely speak, his voice choked. "Sir Giles de Lacey."

"That toad. What of him?"

"He said…" Hugh struggled against the pain, grimacing. Why could he not simply say what was on his mind? "That you and he… Tell me true, where were you on the day Anne Boleyn died? Who were you with that night?"

She was looking shocked now. "My sister. I was with Eloise."

"All night?"

"No, I left her around midnight, when Lord Wolf came back from…" Her voice faltered and a blush crept into her cheeks. "I left them together and walked back to the maids' chamber."

"Alone?"

She nodded.

"Then why is your face hot?" He brushed her cheek with one finger, pain whipping through him, scorching away his defenses. "Susannah?"

"Oh God!"

She was trying to hide her face in her hands, her whole body shaking. He dragged her up off the settle, his arms about her waist. "Talk to me," he growled in her ear, and was horrified to find tears in his eyes. Did she mean so much to him? What was this madness? His voice grew hoarse. "Tell me the truth, for pity's sake. Give me the worst of it."

Susannah threw back her head then, and to his confusion Hugh saw that she was not weeping as he had thought, but laughing.

"Susannah?"

"You fool," she whispered, her eyes alight with laughter—anger too, he thought warily—then brought her mouth slowly to his. "You think I would give *this* to just any man?"

A hot spark leaped from her lips, igniting the desire he had been suppressing since he walked in and saw her. Now it roared in his head, his lust for her consuming him like a bonfire on which they both burned, dazed by the heat and helpless to resist.

He kissed her as hungrily, as though they had been parted for a thousand years, his hands pressing her back, dragging her against him so she could feel his arousal. He did not bother to hide his need to dominate her, his tongue parting her lips and thrusting roughly into her mouth, possessing her with total will.

"I could not bear to think of you with another man," he managed breathlessly, then kissed her slender throat. The desire he felt was dizzying, he could no longer control it. "Marry me."

She pulled back, staring. "What?"

"I do not care about the consequences. Let us be married here at court. Secretly, if needs must." He kissed her again, hotly, and cupped her breast, wishing they were alone in his chamber so he could tip her back onto his bed and make love to her as she deserved. "You are mine. You hear that? Mine!"

She cupped his face and kissed him back. "I hear you," she murmured, and stroked a loose strand of hair away from his eyes.

"I will not share you with another man, and I cannot take the risk of leaving you free any longer. The thought that you might be suddenly married off to Sir William Hanney is driving me insane."

He ran his thumb along her lower lip, parting her unbearably soft lips, then dipped his head and licked along where his thumb had been. She shivered in his arms and he closed his eyes, kissing her deeply. To experience this desire forever, to be her husband and wake with her in his bed each day, to watch her bear his children and grow old with him, suddenly seemed to him the most perfect thing on earth.

"Marry me, Susannah. Today, tonight, tomorrow if you must. But soon, for the love of God." He laughed huskily. "Before I run wild with this need for you."

But she did not answer, and when he looked at her, Susannah was frowning, though the flush of desire was in her face too.

"Speak your mind," he said simply.

"How has this sudden storm blown up, Hugh?" she asked, her serious blue eyes intent on his face. "It seems to have come out of nowhere. This business with Sir Giles de Lacey… He has spoken to you, but said what? That I lay with him?"

Hugh shrugged, angry with himself for giving the knight's testimony even a second's credence. Her innocence shone out of her, and he had known it as soon as he heard the sordid tale. "With him, yes, and with another man. That you gave your innocence to Sir Francis in that house. That you have been willing to share yourself with more than one man." He saw a brief flash in her eyes. "What is it?"

"I saw him with a woman by accident, when passing an open doorway. Him and another man. Older, a nobleman. They were…" She bit her lip, still frowning. "Sharing the woman."

Everything became clear to him. "He told me that story, no doubt hoping to make me believe you and he had been intimate."

"And now?"

"I never believed it." He stroked her cheek, thankful that his instincts about her had proved trustworthy. "But his lies worry me; I cannot deny it. You are unprotected against scavengers like him while you are unmarried. Within a sennight, Sir Giles plans to take some unpleasant tale to the king about you and Sir Francis. It seems the man was his cousin, and news has come that he…he is dead."

Susannah grew pale. "Dead?"

"Yes, it would seem my thrust did for him, though I had not thought it a mortal wound." Hugh held Susannah in his arms, torn up by guilt. He had seen the look on her face and wished to reassure her, but knew it would not be easy when he could not even reassure himself. "There is no need for you to concern yourself with this business. I will go to Lord Wolf this afternoon, tell him everything, and together we will decide what is to be done. Then you and I will be married, and it will be too late for Sir Giles to ruin your reputation at court."

"Lord Wolf?" She looked almost horrified and pushed him away, her expression distracted. "No, no. I will not permit it. You would have to tell Wolf and Eloise about… About what we did together in the forest. What we have done since then."

"So what?"

"I do not wish my sister to know. Nor his lordship."

He could not understand her anger, reaching for her again. He found himself strangely drawn to her body, smoothing her tense shoulders with his hands, hoping to soften her mood.

"Susannah, there is no blame for you in this. I seduced you. We were alone together in the forest all night and my lust could not be contained. Men will understand, and not seek to make you feel less than you are for it. Your father will not be able to stop it, not once he knows we have lain together. And once we are wed…"

"But I do not wish to marry you!"

Her shout made Hugh recoil. The blood drained from his face as the words echoed stupidly in his mind and he struggled to understand them. For a moment he wondered if he had imagined her shout, the room was so silent now.

Susannah was staring at him, breathing hard, as though she had surprised even herself with the vehemence of her declaration.

"Hugh, I c-cannot marry you," she stammered. "And you did not seduce me. I seduced you." Her smile was strained. "How easily you have forgotten what passed between us. Perhaps there are other women whose charms you have forgotten since lying with me."

"What?"

But she shook her head at his exclamation, continuing doggedly, "Now you and Lord Wolf will decide my future, it seems. Because one man has died, and another is bent on some paltry revenge, I must be married where I do not love."

She swallowed, meeting his eyes directly, seemingly oblivious to the agony she had inflicted. It was a pain that was preventing him from being able to do anything but stand and stare, his arms useless by his sides when he would have given his life's blood to embrace her.

There was a red spot burning in the center of each cheek, as though Susannah were ashamed. Yet Hugh knew she was not a woman to feel shame. Or to admit it, at least. Was it anger, then?

"Well, I shall not do it," she muttered. "No. This is my body and my consent, and I do not give it. Not even to you, Hugh Beaufort. *Especially* not to you."

"But why?"

She faltered, and shook her head, turning away. He had so rarely seen her uncertain that he frowned, listening closely. "Because… Because there is no need for you to sacrifice yourself for me. You will not always be a clerk, Hugh. You have the makings of a great man at this court. And one day you will wake up and wish you had a wife to bring you pride, not one you had to marry under her father's whip."

Fury surged through him as he understood her thinking. "That is no reason! To marry you would be no sacrifice, and it is the right thing to do." He added, exasperated, "You bring me pride now, for God's sake."

"Did it make you proud to hear Sir Giles spill his poison in your ear? To suspect, even for a second, that I might have lain with such a man?"

He stared, unable to speak, his hands clenching into fists.

"The truth, at last." Her smile hurt him. "I will speak with Sir Giles. He will not take that vile tale any further. Nor his fancies about

Sir Francis. He plans to tell the king you killed his cousin, I take it, and that we spent the night together? How does he know that?"

"One of Wolf's men," he said tightly, his gaze dropping to the floor. For she was right. He had suspected her. He had not trusted her fully. Only a brief flinch, a sudden fear that the tale might be true, but it had been enough to betray him to her. "Someone talked."

"How tiresome."

"If you refuse my offer of marriage this time, Susannah, I shall not come after you again," Hugh warned her unsteadily.

There was a cold anger within him that craved release, clawing at his chest so that he could not breathe. It was not aimed at her, though she was the one who stood before him. He held onto his anger and dared not let it out, not where she could witness his weakness. He thought of the sneering Sir Giles and wanted to snap his neck. If that man laid so much as a finger on her...

He finished, "It must be marriage now, or nothing."

"Good," she countered, "for I should not like this thing between us to become predictable."

He raised his brows incredulously. "Predictable? This?"

She stared at him, then fumbled at her belt. Her hand dipped into her purse, and she drew out the ruby ring he had given her after their night in the forest. "You must take this back. I cannot keep it."

His jaw hardened. "No."

"Take it, sir."

"I would rather eat it."

Susannah thrust the ring back into her purse and swept to the door. Her straight gaze met his, glancing back, and Hugh saw anger and hurt there to match his own. And could do nothing to assuage it.

He did not understand her. Had something happened to spur Susannah on to this new clash of wills between them? His eyes narrowed on her face. Perhaps there was nothing to understand but willfulness and spirit. A wild horse that would not be broken to bridle.

A flame that would leap from thatch to thatch, burning everything in its path.

"Sir Francis dead," she said, no longer looking at him but at the ground, her hand on the door. "That is a blow indeed. But his death was not your fault. He kept me prisoner; he insisted on that fight. And a marriage between us would not bring him back to life; it would only make us both miserable. I would not be free to live the way I choose, and you would not be free to…pursue other interests."

"I have no other interests," he insisted, frowning. "Susannah, what is this about? Of what am I accused?"

Her lips tightened. Still she did not look at him. "There are things here that can be mended though. Mended or muddled through. I shall talk to Sir Giles."

"He wants you," Hugh said hoarsely.

"Then he will have to want and not be satisfied," Susannah replied sharply, and shrugged. "He will not be alone in that, at least."

Fourteen

SUSANNAH TURNED TO LOOK in the glass held up by Mary, but could no longer recognize herself. The heavy silver skirts of her gown contrasted with the narrow waist from which a thin chain dangled, and the tight bodice which could not quite contain her breasts. Her hair had been left to swing free down her back, a golden curtain adorned by a few silk flowers. Her face was partially hidden by a mask, black with silver edging, which she wore tied on, and hoped it would stay in place during the evening's festivities. The masque was to be in honor of King Henry's impending nuptials, only a few days away now. The court had been ordered to celebrate his wedding to Jane Seymour, and now every night was filled with frenzied dancing and drinking, with private chambers set aside for courtiers whose tastes ran to wilder pleasures, and day parties on the river, where barges hung with silk and filled with musicians floated up and down past Greenwich Palace, entertaining the nobles.

"You look lovely, child, and quite mysterious in that mask," Eloise remarked, passing her a dish of sweetmeats, which Susannah politely refused. "Oh, take one, please. If you will take neither bread nor meat, you should take sweetmeats at least. You have eaten nothing today. And what you ate yesterday and the day before would not sustain a bird. It is not like you to refuse food." Her sharp eyes surveyed Susannah's face. "You are pale. I do not like it."

"I have been unwell, that is all. The air at Greenwich does not suit me."

"I thought it suited you better than the air in Yorkshire,"

Eloise said, raising her eyebrows. "Is that not why you ran away from home?"

"That is too long ago. I cannot remember."

Lord Wolf, who had wandered in a few moments earlier in search of his wife, turned to look at Susannah. His sharp blue eyes studied her dispassionately. "Perhaps you will be pleased then to hear that your father has written to beg your release from court. I have not yet replied. But if you are willing to return home…"

Pain struck at her heart, an icicle thrust deep into her chest. Susannah managed an airy smile nonetheless. "Court life wearies me. I should like to see Yorkshire again."

Her sister looked up astonished from directing her maid how to pin her hair, ready for her smart new silk hood. "What's this? You swore you would never return home."

At least life at home would be uncomplicated, Susannah thought wearily. She did not voice that cowardly thought, but shrugged. "Well, perhaps that was before the queen's execution."

Silence descended on the small bedchamber, and she looked up warily, suddenly realizing that she had said something dangerous.

"That will do, Mary," Eloise said calmly, dismissing her wide-eyed maid.

When the door had closed behind her, Eloise turned and stared at Susannah. "Are you trying to get us arrested? You must not mention Anne Boleyn. And in front of Mary too. She will take this tale straight to the servants' hall, you know."

"Forgive me," she muttered.

Wolf was leaning against the bed post, staring at her, too. "I think you had best explain yourself, Susannah. Is this abrupt change in your humor due to Hugh Beaufort?"

She looked from Wolf to her sister, unsure what to say. Had Eloise been secretly discussing her and Hugh?

Eloise made a face. "I told Wolf what happened when you left our father's house, and he agrees with me that no one can call Hugh Beaufort to account for defending your honor. Any man would have done the same."

"Sir Francis is dead. Does that change matters?"

Something flickered in Wolf's face. He was a hard man to read, she thought, but she did at least think him loyal to her and Eloise. "It may do. He died of his injuries from the fight with Hugh, I take it?"

Briefly she outlined what Hugh had told her, but again left out the passionate night she had spent with him in the forest. If she could leave court quietly and take this trouble far away from him, she might yet save the king's clerk from an accusation of murder and rape.

For that was what the courtiers would whisper when the story came out, and she knew it. That Hugh had raped an innocent virgin that night, then refused to marry her. Even if they married, the story would still besmirch his reputation and his career at the king's court would be ruined.

"I have not yet had a chance to have private speech with Sir Giles, but perhaps a chance will arise at the masque tonight. For he has threatened to go to the king with what he knows if...if I will not lie with him."

Lord Wolf straightened, his eyes fierce. "Cur!"

"You will never lie with him!" Eloise exclaimed furiously. "The villain should be horsewhipped."

"He *will* be horsewhipped," Wolf promised his wife through clenched teeth, his expression grim. "And worse."

"No, no!" Susannah felt like stamping her foot. She glared at them both, knowing herself to be under their control as an unmarried woman and hating how helpless it made her feel. "You will ruin everything with this show of temper. If you attack Sir Giles, he will go to the king with this tale, and spread it about the court that I was in Sir Francis's bed some two or three nights before Hugh came to find me. Then no man will touch me, except to mark me as a whore."

Wolf's face had darkened with anger while he listened. He glanced swiftly at his wife, who had opened her mouth to speak. "Wait, Susannah speaks the truth. She would be ruined if such a story were known widely. There have been whispers already about her, it would be believed with little proof."

"I agree, my lord." Eloise nodded, looking frightened. "But my sister cannot lie with Sir Giles to keep it quiet. To give her virginity to such a man… It cannot be countenanced. And it would break, not save, her reputation. It must not be done."

Susannah drew breath unsteadily. "Of course I shall not go to bed with Sir Giles. But I must somehow persuade him to act the gentleman and stay silent. Even if that means speaking sweetly and flattering the toad where he does not deserve it."

Wolf laughed harshly. "You will not succeed. Nor should you try."

"My lord." She went to him, meeting his cold blue gaze directly. "Please trust me, and allow me to play this game my own way. If I do not succeed, then you may take up the matter yourself. Only do not treat me like a child, for I am not one."

He looked at her in silence a moment, searching her face. "Did Sir Francis rape you?"

"No, my lord," she said truthfully.

"Then you have nothing to fear."

"Except rumor."

Wolf smiled drily. "You learn court ways fast. Yes, rumor may kill a man—or woman—overnight. And though they have tried to keep the worst of it from my ears, there have been whispers about you. That you have been wondrously free with your favors and your body. That you are no virgin, but have lain with the king, and with Lord Gifford, and sundry other knights and squires."

Susannah gasped. "Untrue!" she choked, furious to the point of tears, and also ashamed, for she had indeed been free with her body where Hugh was concerned. "All untrue!"

"I know it. And the fact that you have not been sent away from court indicates how little substance there is to such idle and vicious gossip. At any other time, the accusation would have been investigated and the rumors dismissed as nonsense. But with the queen lately dead, and the king in such ill humor…" Wolf shrugged, but she could see how angry he was. For such slurs against her chastity must soil his family name too. "Nonetheless, you are right. We should play this quietly first, and see how things fall out with Sir Giles. There is no harm in persuasion where brute force will almost certainly fail."

"And what does Master Beaufort say to your plans? Does he allow you to take his part in this?" Eloise demanded, her face flushed.

Wolf's head swung back and his gaze sharpened on Susannah's face. "Is there indeed something between you and Master Beaufort? I have wondered, and asked him myself, only to be denied. But I have eyes. If you two have been intimate, you should declare it now."

She felt oddly menaced and took a step backward. If she admitted the truth, the long friendship between Wolf and Hugh would surely be at an end. Her tongue stumbled over the lie, and she felt sure the sharp-eyed Lord Wolf must guess her guilt. "I…I am fond of Master Beaufort, my lord. We have not always agreed on every point, but he has been a good friend to me. That is all. And no, sister. Hugh is most unwilling for me to speak to Sir Giles. But I have assured him it is the only way."

But if he guessed that she was lying, he showed no sign of it. Instead Wolf took up his wife's cloak and set it about Eloise's shoulders, for the hour was late and they were expected at the masque. "Well, I have heard Hugh Beaufort say he would never take a bride who was not mild and obedient, so I am not surprised to hear you do not agree. For though you are not quite wild, sister, you are not quite tame either." He smiled drily, then settled his own mask over his eyes. "Once this thing is settled, you will return to Yorkshire?"

Again her heart contracted painfully. Return to Yorkshire? The place would be like death to her. But at least there she could be sure Hugh's reputation would not be tarnished by his proposal to her. And why should he want her anyway, if what Wolf said was true? She must be the furthest from a mild, obedient bride that he could imagine.

"Yes, my lord," she managed, fiddling with her mask so she would not have to meet his gaze. "It would be for the best if I removed myself from court, don't you agree? That will allow the gossips to talk about somebody else for a change."

"I hope you have not forgotten that your father is still resolved on a marriage between you and his friend Sir William Hanney. He mentioned it in his letter to me. By all accounts, the old man is most anxious to wed you with all speed, presumably before you can run away again."

She stared, but said nothing. What could she say?

"So if you go home to Yorkshire, that is what you will face." Wolf paused, frowning. "You are sure a marriage between you and Hugh Beaufort might not suit you better, Susannah? The two of you have seemed very close since your arrival at court, and I could intercede for you to the king if your father's permission is not given. His Majesty does occasionally take pity on such cases."

She would marry no one if she had her way, Susannah thought. Not without love. But Lord Wolf would not understand. Her sister's union with Wolf had been arranged by their father, yet their marriage did not seem as much of a prison as Eloise had at first feared. So they might believe a loveless marriage would work as well for her. But they would be wrong.

"Marry a clerk, my lord?" she replied lightly, and shook out her skirts as they moved to the door. "No, that would not suit me at all."

—◊◊◊—

She looked everywhere for Hugh at the masque, aching to see him again, and at last caught a glimpse of him through the flickering candlelight. Standing at the refreshments table, he was conversing with a young woman in a red mask, himself masked in black and silver, a dazzling stranger, though she would have known him anywhere.

Hugh was not wearing his clerk's robes, which had confused her at first, but a shirt and black doublet with silver thread, his powerful thighs encased in black hose. She had forgotten how tall he was until he turned to greet Lord Wolf, and she saw the two men were about the same height, their easy smiles reminding her how much Hugh stood to lose if their friendship was broken.

He looked more like a nobleman tonight than a clerk, she thought, and stared hungrily across the bright chamber at him. She had lied to Wolf. She would marry Hugh if he were a lowly tradesman. If he were a beggar, even. She would lie with him unmarried in any rough state, and know herself in utter bliss, if only they were both in love.

But they were not in love.

Though if by some miracle love blossomed between them, she thought uneasily, marriage would not necessarily be the answer. For Susannah knew how high his courtly ambition reached, and how besmirched her own reputation was becoming. Margerie had hinted as much when she warned her not to take any more "false steps."

Wolf seemed unaware of the extent of her shame, but she was teetering on the edge of absolute disgrace. If she fell, as Anne Boleyn had so lately fallen, and was marked out as unchaste and a wanton, Hugh could no more marry her than he could marry the Whore of Babylon. Not if he saw himself as the king's chief clerk in years to come.

Could she stand by and watch Hugh's chance of greatness destroyed, simply to assuage her own selfish need for him?

Eloise touched her arm. She too was watching Hugh and Wolf converse, her eyes cautious. "You told Wolf that you and Hugh were friends," she murmured. "But Master Beaufort has offended you in some way, has he not? When you came to court in his company, I thought…"

Her sister hesitated, glancing from her to Hugh. "Well, I see now that the breach between you was this terrible business with Sir Francis. But it should have healed by now. Does Hugh hold you in contempt for having been that brute's prisoner and forced to spend time under his roof? I thought Master Beaufort a fair-minded gentleman, but if he blames you for that, he will fall in my estimation."

"He does not blame me," Susannah said huskily.

"Then what is it that makes you so stiff with him? I have seen you together; you are more like enemies than friends." Eloise was frowning. "He was gallant, was he not, to fight Sir Francis on your behalf? Hugh Beaufort is strong, but he has not been trained as a soldier, as my husband has. He risked his life by defending you."

"I know it."

"Well, it is your choice." Eloise gave up, shaking her head. "But I confess, I do not understand why you dislike him so much. I have always found Hugh Beaufort to be good company, and a true and honest gentleman. He writes poetry, did you know that?"

Susannah stared. "No, he has never mentioned it."

"Then perhaps you should ask him about it." Her sister looked round, her mouth breaking into a smile as she saw Hugh and Wolf approaching. Her voice dropped to a whisper. "This may be your last chance to put all right between you, Susannah. Before you go home to Yorkshire." Gathering her skirts, the masked Eloise dipped into a coquettish curtsy as her husband appeared at her elbow. "My lord… and Master Beaufort, if that is indeed you below the mask. I trust you are in good health, sir."

Susannah curtsied to the two men, lowering her gaze past Hugh's strong thighs to the silver buckles on his shoes. She had not expected them to come across the room so soon, and had been caught off guard, suddenly unsure what to do or say. Her mouth turned dry, her heart began to thunder in her chest, the roar of blood in her ears deafening her.

As she rose, lifting her eyes to Hugh's face, she felt a terrible shock run through her. For instead of the easy-mannered gentleman she knew, this man was a cold stranger. Masked, his mouth unsmiling, he looked down at her with glittering green eyes.

"Lady Wolf, Mistress Tyrell. Thank you, I am quite well."

Hugh bowed to each of them in turn. When he straightened, looking directly at her, Susannah saw that his fists were clenched by his sides, his whole body rigid. But with anger or disgust?

They had parted on such bad terms, with her insisting she would speak to Sir Giles alone. Perhaps he thought her capable of sleeping with the knight to avoid his sordid tale reaching the king's ears. Perhaps he even thought she had already done so, though in truth she had not even seen Sir Giles yet to speak with him.

Her throat burned, her eyes suddenly damp with unshed tears behind her mask. If Hugh thought her so low a creature, after all they had been through together, after she had given him her body and lain with him in unadulterated pleasure, then she hated him. She hated him!

But the worst was yet to come.

Hugh Beaufort held out a hand, still unsmiling. "You know the galliard, Mistress Tyrell?" The musicians had begun to play behind them, and courtiers were already leading their chosen ladies out to dance. "Would you do me the honor of dancing it with me?"

Dance with him? And the galliard, so intimate a dance that she had found it quite shocking when the dancing master showed her and the other girls how to perform it.

Eloise was staring at her. Wolf stood at his wife's shoulder, masked and grim. It was like one of her childhood nightmares where she was disgraced and found wanting in front of everyone, only she was not asleep. For a moment the whole court seemed to be waiting on her reply, the vast echoing chamber oddly still, all the masked figures turned in their direction, only the music continuing unabated.

"I thank you, sir, yes."

Susannah put her hand in his and allowed Hugh Beaufort to lead her out to where the other dancers were waiting. Without a word he spun her to face him, bowed while she curtsied, and the dance began.

"Have you spoken with Sir Giles?" Hugh asked.

Stepping lightly around him, she tried to keep herself from reddening. Damn him. "No."

"But you will."

"I have said so." She let a little of her anger spill over, trembling in her voice. "It is no concern of yours, sir."

"You have made that plain, madam." He was angry too, but speaking quietly, for they were not alone in the dance. "And yet it is my concern. I would take this burden from your shoulders. It is not fit for a woman to bear such a load alone. I would carry it for you."

"It is not a heavy burden. Leave well alone."

Susannah turned and leaped high, and Hugh caught her in the air, his hands firm on her waist, pulling her into him as he drew her down to the floor.

For a few breathless seconds they swung there, chest to chest, face to face, intimately close. It was like making love in public. She felt a sticky warmth between her legs, and knew herself still eager for his touch, that if Hugh Beaufort should lay her down on the floor right here in front of the court, she would not only permit it, but enjoy his seduction.

His brilliant green stare met hers through the eyeholes of the mask. "Susannah," he said in a hoarse whisper, his words meant for her alone. "For God's sake, do not be tempted to speak with Sir Giles alone. It is too dangerous. The man cannot be trusted. He will seduce you in return for his silence—and still ruin you."

The music tugged at them both. He released her, but reluctantly, and they turned apart, threading a path through the other couples.

His words stung her like a whip. She blinked, but could see nothing, her eyes welling with tears behind her mask, the vast candlelit chamber and its dancers blurring to a silvery lake.

It was exactly as she had thought. Hugh did not trust her. He thought her a fool and a wanton.

She bumped into another dancer and recoiled, apologizing for her clumsiness. Someone swore, shoving at her. Her mask slipped and she struggled to replace it, banging into somebody's elbow. A woman beside her sniggered, murmuring, "Country slut," under her breath. So Margerie had not been exaggerating when she said her reputation was already at risk.

Susannah whirled, furious now, only to find herself lost in a circle of sneering, astonished faces.

Then Hugh's hand was on her arm, pulling her aside and out of the dance. "Come," he ordered her when she resisted, his voice terse. "Or I shall put you over my knee again."

Her face burnt with bitter rage. This is how it would be if they married, she told herself. Hugh Beaufort would be her master then, and chastise her at his will. She remembered how he had spanked her in the forest, his hand falling hard, and her enforced surrender, the hot ache between her legs. To be legally bound to him, subject to such a man's will…

He pushed open a door. Suddenly there was cool air on her face and the night sky was dark above. She could smell the early roses and the first buds of sweet jasmine all around them, a cluster of night stocks, their heady scents thick, drugging her senses.

"This way," he muttered in her ear, leading her swiftly down a sandy path and round a corner, then whirled her about to face him.

His hands came down hard on her hips, drawing her near just as he had done when they were dancing. The music had started again, close by their hiding place, and she found herself swaying as though still in the dance, remembering each step they had taken around each other, how their hands had brushed, his eyes watching her intently.

"Master Beaufort," she began, flushed and breathless, but his finger pressed down across her lips.

"Hold your tongue for once, Susannah," he whispered, staring down at her. "We cannot be discovered in this place."

"Where are we?" she whispered back, frowning.

"The queen's privy gardens."

Slowly, Hugh dragged his finger down her lips, her chin and throat, to the shadowy cleft at the top of her bodice, covered so discreetly with lace.

"I told myself that I should let you go," he muttered hoarsely. "That you did not want me. That it was over."

"It *is* over," she told him, taunting herself with the sting of hurting him. Cruel to be kind, she reminded herself, staring into his green eyes. He would thank her for this one day. For marriage to her would surely ruin him. That had been plain from the way the other courtiers treated her during the dance. Her name was already in the mire.

She surprised herself with her sudden desire to keep him free of scandal. But perhaps this was how it felt to care for someone more than one cared for oneself.

He studied her intently. "Only problem is, I don't think it is."

Her skin prickled with awareness. He was so close she could hear his breathing catch in his throat, see the faint flush in his face that told her he was aroused.

"How can you be so sure?" she whispered daringly.

Hugh made a rough noise under his breath, then pushed her backward, pinning her against the stone wall. Unable to move, she watched as his masked head lowered to hers, blocking out the stars.

"Because of this…"

His mouth slanted down, taking hers with a force that shook her to the core. She gripped his broad shoulders, opening to him willingly, urging him on. The danger they were in, the forbidden place, the possibility of discovery by the king's guards…none of it meant anything to her. Her body had taken over her mind, blocking everything else out, and she was lost in the desire she had been holding back for so long.

His tongue thrust possessively into her mouth, and she moaned, arching beneath him. Then his hands found her breasts, dragging down her bodice, letting her flesh spill out. She gasped against his mouth, shocked by the feel of the air, her sudden vulnerability.

"Hugh… No!"

But he did not stop. His thumbs rolled over her nipples, bringing them erect in an instant. Then he pinched one of her nipples quite deliberately, and Susannah hissed, rubbing herself against him in an age-old movement, impossible to suppress.

"That's it," he muttered in her ear, then kissed down her throat. "Show me what you want, slave."

Fifteen

SLAVE!

Heat coursed through her at his deliberate word, "slave," leaving her core so moist, her legs trembling, that it was all she could not to fall to her knees before him.

So nothing had changed between them, she thought desperately. Was that still what she was to him? His concubine, willing to yield herself to him without question, without the slightest control over what he might do to her?

God's blood, she must be losing her good wits to let any man touch her like this, use her, treat her so carelessly.

"Bastard," she managed, her heart juddering, and was rewarded with a throaty laugh.

She tried to slap him, but Hugh seized her hands and bore them down mercilessly to her sides, pinning her against the wall with the weight of his body. He was physically her superior and he was letting her know it without compunction. He smiled at her, letting her see that all she had succeeded in doing was knocking his cap to the ground. Then his mouth took hers again, and she felt herself grow hot and slick with longing, her neck driven back under the relentless plunder of his tongue, unable to challenge his mastery over her.

"You are mine," he told her starkly, gazing down at her helpless body as though on his own territory.

He raised his hand to her mask and stripped it away, studying her face. With his still in place, Susannah felt more exposed than ever, as though he could see right through to the heart of her.

"We may never be married," he whispered harshly, and leaned forward, his breath hot on her throat. "We may never lie together again as lovers. You may belong to another man. But you will always be mine, Susannah Tyrell, and I want you to know that. To be sure of it with every fiber of your being, as though my name were stamped across your breast."

Saying that, he released her hands, then cupped her bare breasts. His fair head bent. He sucked one nipple into his mouth, almost cruel in the pitiless way he was taking her, possessing her, arousing her. She cried out, equally desperate for more, for harder, for crueler.

"Let me…" She was incoherent, her hands shaking. Not content with being his passive slave any longer, she reached down and curved her hand over the aggressive thrust of his codpiece. "Please."

He helped her silently with the fastenings, but she heard his breath quicken and knew he wanted this as much as her. Then he was free and in her hands. She ran her fingers up and down the rigid column of his cock, worshipping it, hungry for his strong male flesh inside her. His cock twitched and he groaned under his breath. She squeezed him between her palms, then rubbed her thumb across the broad sloping head, eager to feel the moisture there, the sign that he was ready to be inside her.

Sure enough, her thumb smeared across a tiny bead of seed, and she made a little sound, unable to stop herself. As though starving, she raised her thumb to her mouth and sucked hard, drawing his release onto her tongue, reveling in its sharp taste. Then she licked her palm, all the way up and down, and took his cock in hand again, fisting him.

He swore an oath, and his head tilted back, the veins standing out on his throat. "*Susannah*."

She wondered if he had taken so much pleasure from the other women he had bedded, and remembered Margerie, the redhead she had seen him so intimate with, late at night, the two of them in conversation, his hand on her arm. Margerie had then gone straight to Master Elton's chamber. Was she Hugh's mistress that he shared with the doctor? Or perhaps he did not know of her other lovers…

Need welled inside her, dark and unhappy, and she dropped to her knees before him, not caring if she soiled her silver gown. He gripped her hair, knowing at once what she intended, and not trying to stop her.

"Yes," he growled, staring down.

Cupping his buttocks in the smooth black hose, she slowly drew his cock inside her mouth, letting his length fill her until it knocked against the back of her throat.

Gagging, she pulled back, admiring the thick glistening shaft as it emerged from between her lips, a thing of beauty and power. Then she sucked on him again, licking around his broad head, drawing his darkly veined cock back inside, not caring how greedy it made her look.

His breath hissed out, then Hugh pressed her back against the wall, holding her head still while he thrust urgently into her mouth. He made no sound, but his fingers tangled in her hair, driving deep again and again, his whole body intent on reaching orgasm.

He was not gentle, nor would she have welcomed gentleness. There was something inside both of them that needed this hot, angry lust, this using of each other's bodies, blind and deaf to reason, the only thought in their heads the intense driving need for completion and release.

Was this what Hugh wanted though? A submissive slave in his bed, an obedient, unquestioning wife at his side? She could never be such a woman, though it thrilled her to allow him dominion over her when they were intimate together. But in her head she was still fierce and free, however he made her perform, and was content only to submit for her own pleasure, not his. *A firebrand*, Margerie had called her. Well, and so she was. But burning for his touch.

Lord Wolf's words echoed in her mind too. *For though you are not quite wild, you are not quite tame either.*

No, she was not the perfect bride for him. She never would be. And this lust, though violent now, would fade in time.

Hurting at the knowledge that this would be the last time they could be together, the last time her body would know his, Susannah looked up and saw Hugh watching her intently from behind his mask. She did not think she had ever seen him look so wild, so out of control.

Their eyes locked and he gave a muffled groan, as though that sudden contact between them was unbearable, too intimate to be borne, then he thrust deep. She closed her mouth about him, sucking hard as his cock swelled and pulsed, discharging seed into her throat in a hot rush.

"Jesu!"

His gasped blasphemy told her everything she needed to know about his state of mind. This was not done by choice, this furious lovemaking, any more than she obeyed by choice. It was done through sheer necessity, both of them in the powerful grip of a desire neither could entirely control.

She kept sucking after he had spent everything, refusing to let him withdraw, and Hugh permitted it, stroking her hair, watching her with a strange expression.

"Stand up, Susannah," he ordered her after a short while, his voice still ragged, almost accusing. "I'm not done with you."

She struggled to obey, keeping her gaze on his face, climbing him unsteadily like a ladder, resting her hands on his powerful thighs, his flat belly, the broad expanse of his chest, still heaving under her fingers from the intensity of his climax. She remembered him riding her in bed, and the way she had swung herself over, straddling him, how his face had changed as she rode him instead, acting the man and enjoying it.

The music continued in the great chamber behind them, floating out on the quiet night air, the somber beat of the tabor speeding up, like the racing beat of her heart, as another galliard was danced. Then she heard the hautboys join in, and the pipes, lilting high above. Her hips swayed instinctively and she took a light step forward as Hugh stepped back, watching her, his straight mouth almost smiling.

He lifted her hand to his lips, pressed his mouth hot to her palm, then turned her slowly in the dance, leaning close.

"Hugh," she whispered, meeting his gaze, her own desire still urgent, hunting for release.

"Yes, my sweet wanton?"

She shook back her hair, not caring that the pearl net was tangled, nor that her brow was damp with perspiration. "I need..."

His hands dropped to her waist and he lifted her, stepped swiftly back against the wall. "Yes?" he demanded, pushing against her. "What do you need?"

"To be pleasured."

His eyes were laughing behind the mask, she was sure of it. "A bold slave indeed, to expect such a gift from your master."

But his hands were already dragging her skirts to her waist, confident of her acquiescence. Her thighs parted quite naturally for him, her flesh eager to receive him, her core slick with yearning.

His fingers found her and pushed inside, stroking and tugging until she was lost in desire. It was as though he knew exactly how to touch her, how light, how strong, how much she burned for his fingers. He watched her face as she writhed against him, helplessly gasping out her pleasure, and said nothing, gave no indication of his feelings.

Susannah urged him on with sobbing little sounds of greed, and did not care if her behavior was wanton, or if he thought her a whore. She was beyond all thoughts and considerations, except one: the need to feel Hugh Beaufort inside her again.

"Yes," she hissed, feeling his length, already risen to hardness again, nudging at the entrance to her body. His broad head pushed her secret lips apart; their eyes locked together as he entered her. She grunted as Hugh plunged deep inside. "Christ, yes!"

He drove in hard, as though he was desperate, as though he had not already come, and his hands gripped her buttocks as he thrust. Holding her up against the wall, the thick head of his cock pushed repeatedly inside her, battering her until she thought she would die from being filled, and emptied, and filled again.

She had missed him inside her, she realized, and knew a sudden bittersweet agony as she looked ahead to the months and years she must spend without this pleasure, without him.

She slid her hands up his chest, then wrapped her legs about his hips, moaning with joy as Hugh shifted to fill her more completely, growling, "Susannah," in her ear.

His heart was hammering under her hands, racing and rolling, the pace of his fucking swift, relentless. They were so good together now, the desperate lunges of their first coupling a distant memory. And her body rejoiced in the way he challenged her, testing him right back, provoking him to take her to new heights. He was stretching her now, pushing hard; it was almost painful to take him.

Yet she loved this, she thought dizzily. She loved him.

She loved him.

Oh great God in heaven, she thought, staring at his masked face, the perspiration on his brow, his parted lips, the dark stubble on his chin. She had thought this lust, pure and simple. The desire of one body for another. But she loved him. That was why she could not bear to see him hurt by his association with her, why she could not allow Hugh to throw his career away by allying himself with a woman whose fragile reputation might at any moment shatter.

How to tell him that she loved him though? And what could it change between them if she did, if Hugh knew what she felt?

Nothing, she realized in despair, it would change nothing. Except to make the pain of their inevitable parting even more unbearable, if that were possible. Hugh Beaufort could not marry such a wanton and keep his position at court; sooner or later the stories would get out, or her wildness would be exposed by some terrible misdeed, and then she would be ruined, and her husband along with her.

But this…

They could have this moment, at least. This pleasure. This final glorious union.

Her body tensed, clenching against his. The long, deep strokes of his fucking took her higher and higher into ecstasy, her senses almost leaving her when she climaxed, sharply and with exquisite intensity, every atom of her being shattering on an invisible wall of pleasure. She flattened out shaking hands against his chest, then screwed them helplessly into fists, crushing his black and silver doublet between her fingers, her mouth open on a hissing cry, wrenching at the air.

"Yes, yes, yes!" she gasped, loving him.

He was panting too. "This is madness. I will get you with child. We should not…"

Then his head tipped back, and Hugh groaned out her name, his voice tortured, almost unfamiliar. The rapid strokes of his cock slowed. Abruptly he jerked hard and deep inside her, his chest heaving with effort, and she felt the hot wet rush of his seed.

She would never feel that sensation again, she told herself, dazed now that it was over, unable to explain how it had started, how one kiss had led to this moment.

They hung there against the wall of the palace for an age, breathing hard, trembling and drenched in perspiration, but warm in each other's arms, sated. She rested her damp forehead against his chest, and heard him sigh, his powerful body supporting hers, seemingly effortlessly. It was as though neither of them wished to move and break the spell, for then cold reality would pour back in and they would have to look at each other with new eyes, knowing this was the last time. The last time they would belong to each other, the last time their bodies would be joined in this intimate dance of love.

Then she stirred, hearing voices on the other side of the garden wall, and pushed at his chest.

"Hugh," she whispered. "We cannot stay here."

He grunted his assent, then slowly withdrew from her sex. She felt the absence of him at once, as though her life had suddenly become an empty room. Misery swamped her as he slowly tidied his clothing, his head bent, and she felt him close off from her, a distant look about his face as he straightened, running a hand through his short fair hair.

"Shall we go back inside? We can say you were unwell and needed air. Though they will not believe us, of course."

Hugh bent and retrieved his cap and her mask, handing her the latter without comment. Seemingly intent on brushing dirt from his cap, he did not look at her again. It was all she could do not to grab at his doublet and swear that she would marry him, that she accepted his offer.

But she was learning to be more ladylike, to push her feelings down and smile when she felt like screaming.

To lie.

He held out his sleeve and Susannah placed her hand on it lightly, aware of the muscular strength beneath her fingers, a strength that had held her against the wall while he took his pleasure.

The night had grown still and the moon had sailed out from behind the clouds, shining down on them with a pale luminous glow that lit the high walls of the palace and made even the red roses look white. To her relief, the voices she had heard were slowly moving away from them, no doubt guards on patrol who had not noticed them in the shadows.

Still masked, Hugh's eyes met hers, an intense green, then looked away abruptly. "Do you still plan to see Sir Giles? To speak with him alone?"

She nodded, though it gave her little joy to think of that interview.

His voice grew terse. "Wolf told me tonight that your father has written to request your return to Yorkshire. And you did not put up any objection."

She closed her eyes briefly, then reopened them, forcing herself to smile. There was a trick to it, lying. She just had to work out what it was, which would take patience.

"I wanted to find out what life was like at court. I know now, and will not miss it. Besides, the king will have a new queen again soon, and Mistress Seymour is unlikely to give me a place among her maids of honor. It seems like a good time to go home."

"Mistress Seymour dislikes you that much?"

"No, but when she is told that I am a whore, and no maid," she said simply, "she will dismiss me from court."

His face stiffened. "That can be remedied."

"By marrying you?"

"Precisely."

"Of course, not all unmarried ladies who take lovers at court are caught and punished for it," she mused, then wished she had not. His head had turned and he was staring at her.

"What do you mean?"

"Nothing." She shuddered, then forced herself to say what was pressing so violently against her heart. "Hugh, I saw you with a lady on the night of the queen's execution. It was late, and your conversation looked…intimate."

He was frowning. "Do you mean Mistress Croft?"

"If her name is Margerie, then yes. She has red hair."

"Her name is Margerie, and I did speak with her that night, it is true." He sounded awkward and off balance, as though caught out in a lie. "She came to speak to me about Lord Wolf. That is, she used to be his… Forgive me, I cannot speak of it."

Susannah smiled, though it hurt. "It is a secret then."

"It is not my secret, but…" He drew a sharp breath, his arm suddenly stiff beneath her hand. "Drop it, would you?"

Grief twisted inside her at his harsh tone. She stumbled over her own feet and would have fallen if he had not dragged her up.

"If you return home to Yorkshire," he told her bluntly, "your father will marry you off to that old bastard Hanney before you have time to unpack."

"He can try," she managed with a gasp, fighting to keep the hurt and betrayal out of her face.

Margerie Croft.

He had slept with that woman, or come close to it, she was sure of it. Why else the denials and secrecy, the awkward way he had turned her questions aside? Why else had Margerie smiled and laughed, describing him so lustfully as handsome? *Those broad shoulders, that narrow waist…*

"But I fear my father will find me as hard to persuade to marriage as you have," she continued, pushing her chin up. "I shall no doubt end an old maid. Well, a spinster. For I am no longer a maid, am I?"

They had reached the discreet side door back into the palace.

Beyond it she could hear the music beginning again after a period of silence, and a great rumble of voices as the crowd milled about. Had Wolf and Eloise missed her, she wondered? But of course they must have done. Perhaps they thought her closeted with Sir Giles.

Heat filled her cheeks at the nauseating thought of what she might yet have to face from that quarter. Sir Giles triumphing over her, putting his vile paws on her body, and that insolent smiling look when he realized she had come to win him over, to make some kind of deal…

"Susannah," Hugh began hoarsely, but she interrupted him.

"Please don't," she told him, forcing a smile, then shook off his hand before entering the palace alone. If Hugh Beaufort thought her abrasive and willful, so much the better. At least he would not find her malleable. "You're spoiling the moonlight."

⁂

Susannah had screwed up her courage to face Sir Giles and somehow persuade him, though she was not sure of the best argument for this, to stay silent about the events surrounding Sir Francis's death. But in the event she did not see Sir Giles that night, and it was not until after King Henry's wedding to Jane Seymour that she had a chance to speak with him.

There was a rich feast held at court, and afterward dancing, and it was as they were on their knees for the king and his new bride to enter the hall that she saw him. Sir Giles was looking straight at her from across the crowded chamber, his eyes narrowed on her face.

Eloise was kneeling by her side, her sister's head bent as she waited for her lord, but Susannah said nothing to her. What was there to say?

Her heart began to race. She decided not to be a coward and wait for him to approach her, but to face the villain directly.

The king passed by with Queen Jane on his arm. The new royal consort had chosen a dazzling gown of blue and silver for this first official feast, and walked in silence, her eyes dutifully downcast, the very picture of newly wedded obedience. Susannah looked up at her covertly and wondered how long the new queen would last before she was accused of some crime. But of course such thoughts could never be voiced, even to oneself.

She rose and slipped discreetly away from Eloise, crossing Sir Giles's path as he followed in the wake of the king's train.

"Sir," she murmured, and met his eyes as she curtsied, repressing her shudder of disgust. "I would speak with you, if I may."

Sir Giles stopped and raised his brows, then glanced about at the thronging crowd of courtiers. "Here?"

"Privately."

His creeping smile nearly made her flee in horror. It was only the thought of the damage this man could do to Hugh Beaufort that kept her standing there.

He indicated a way through the crowd. "There is a quieter chamber through there, not much used during these occasions. We should be able to speak more privily there."

She followed him at a distance, hoping no one would notice them slipping through the crowd together, and soon found herself in a small over-warm chamber lit only by torches. There were no seats, so she stood by the unlit fireplace, and Sir Giles came to her at once, lifting her hand to his lips.

"Madam," he said, pressing his wet mouth to the back of her hand and holding it there rather longer than necessary. "I had almost given up hope."

"Master Beaufort has told me what you said," she began quickly, without wasting any time, for the longer she was alone with this creature the more likely it was they would be discovered together. "He says you plan to go to the king with some fantastical tale of my exploits with your unfortunate cousin Sir Francis."

"Who is now dead," Sir Giles agreed, as though wishing to make sure she understood the full weight of her situation. He then added piously, "God rest his soul. Yes, that is indeed what I intend to do. Unless…"

She waited impatiently but he did not finish. "Unless?"

"Unless you consent to please me in ways I think you will under-stand only too well." Sir Giles was still holding her hand. He took it, his oily gaze locked with hers, and placed it very deliberately on the obscene bulge of his codpiece. "What do you say to that, madam?"

She did not draw her hand away, though it nauseated her to remain motionless. She wanted to frighten him if she could. "Let me understand you aright, sir. You wish to marry me?"

He released her hand as though she had stung him. "No, madam," he replied waspishly, "I most certainly do not. I saw you peeking in at our sport that night, lascivious wench that you are, when you should have been abed with the other maids. Marry a whore whose body belongs to any man who whistles for it? I would rather sleep in a bed of nettles."

"Then what?"

"I would fuck you," he said bluntly, looking her up and down. "Take my pleasure with you. Maybe more than once. We shall see how you please me the first time. For I shall not lie with you twice if I begin to itch after we have lain together."

"Begin to itch?" she repeated blankly, then stared. "You mean the pox? You think I have the pox?"

He shrugged, a look of distaste on his face. "They say the king has had you, and every fool knows the king must have the pox. For His Majesty has lain with enough whores in his time. Ergo, if a man lies with you, he might as well lie with the king and catch the pox. Though if on closer inspection I find you unfit for tupping, your pretty mouth will suffice to please me. If you take my meaning."

Susannah felt sick.

"Now don't make that face and pretend to be offended. I am hard for you, madam. You have already done half the business. If we go away to my chamber, you can perform the other half and we shall both be satisfied. Nor will the king need to hear that my late cousin broke your maidenhead on his cock, or that he later met his end on Master Beaufort's sword." Sir Giles came closer, then cupped her breast as though weighing it. "My cousin's family do not know by whose hand Sir Francis died. Nor shall they, if you consent to pleasure me."

She could not bear it a second longer. "Oh, go to hell. You can tell the king whatever you like, I'll have none of you!"

Her hand flashed up and caught him hard across the face. He fell back with a cry, rubbing his cheek.

"Are you mad?" Sir Giles gasped. His face contorted with temper, and he seized her by the nape of her neck, forcing her down to her knees. "I'll teach you to strike me, you whore!"

Susannah struggled, choking and flailing out at him. Then suddenly her assailant was gone, and she was staring at a tangle of limbs where Sir Giles was rolling on the rushes with Hugh Beaufort. She got shakily back to her feet in time to see Hugh's fist collide with Sir Giles's jaw. He raised it for another blow.

"Hugh, no!" she exclaimed, fearing for his position at court if Hugh was found brawling in the palace like this.

Hugh glanced round at her, his face taut with anger, his eyes an icy green. "Get back in the hall," he said in a clipped voice. "Leave him to me."

But Sir Giles found the strength from somewhere to shove Hugh away and scrambled to his feet. The knight crouched there a moment, panting wildly, his cap gone, his thinning hair flopped forward over his forehead. Then he straightened his crumpled doublet and staggered back toward the half-open door into the Great Hall, where the sound of dancing and festivities were drowning out the sounds of their struggle.

"I shall inform the king of this attack," Sir Giles warned Hugh in a breathless voice, then shot a look of seething contempt at Susannah, "and that your whore dared strike me. Rest assured, clerk, I shall not remain silent about your unprovoked murder of my cousin."

"Good," Hugh said tightly, his hand on his dagger hilt. "I want the world to know what manner of man Sir Francis was, and will gladly face any punishment the king chooses."

Sir Giles stared, his face twitching, then he left the room, leaving the doors wide open so they could be seen by the courtiers beyond, some of whom turned to stare.

Susannah closed her eyes and counted to five. It was a trick she had used as a child when something had gone horribly wrong, to keep herself from crying. Then she went to Hugh, who seemed to be in a daze.

There was a trickle of blood on his clenched fist. "Are you hurt?" she asked, laying a hand on his arm.

"It's nothing. A scratch."

"You should not have done that." She swallowed. "He will avenge himself on you now."

Hugh nodded, then looked at her, his face stony. "You let that dog touch you, hurt you. I would have killed him, and been hanged for it too, except I feared how it might look for you."

"I don't care what happens to me. Only you." She closed her eyes. "Yet I lost my temper with him, all the same. He offered to roll me in the hay, then suggested I had the pox. I told him to go to hell, and swore that I would not sleep with him."

He gave a hoarse bark of laughter. "Then we are as bad as each other at such delicate negotiations."

"I fear so."

Hugh took her face in his hands and kissed her on the lips. "Marry me, Susannah. What is there to lose now?"

She drew back, shaking her head. "Hugh, they can see us from the hall!"

"I do not care."

"Well, I do. Forgive me…"

She left him, too unsure of her feelings to remain, and hurried into the hall, pushing between the courtiers in an effort to leave Hugh behind and find her sister. There were tears of rage and despair in her eyes, for she knew this must be the end. Sir Giles would take his tale of murder and debauchery to the king at the earliest opportunity, and beyond that catastrophe she could not imagine. But she knew they must not be seen together, for the more people suspected of their intimacy, the nearer Hugh would come to ruination. And all because of her.

Hugh caught up with her and grabbed her arm, ignoring the startled faces around them. "Susannah, stop."

She looked at him impatiently, her vision blurred with tears. "Hugh, no man will blame you for what you have done. You did what any gentleman would, faced with a villain. But they will blame me for my wantonness, and my blame will become yours if we marry. No, you know that I am right." Her voice dropped to a whisper. "This court, *this king*, will not suffer a whore to go unpunished. What further proof of that do you need than the events of this past month?"

He was staring, his face very pale.

"You should hold yourself aloof from me, Master Beaufort," she told him, and could not meet his eyes, for the pain was too much. "At least until this business is forgotten. Perhaps one day it will be."

There was some commotion behind her. She looked round and there was Eloise, her face over-flushed, her lower lip red as though she had been biting it. "We are going." She took Susannah's arm and began to drag her away from Hugh. "Now, if you please."

"What?" Susannah asked, frowning.

"I can't stay."

But before Eloise could elaborate, there was Thomas Cromwell himself standing behind them, his expression cool and watchful.

Both of them curtsied low, in deference to the great man's influence at court these days, but it seemed the king's chief advisor was in no mood for civilities. He neither bowed nor smiled, merely asked where Lord Wolf could be found.

Eloise drew herself up stiffly, gazing past Cromwell with a terse expression. "He is behind you, sir."

Susannah thought she had never seen Wolf so conflicted, his blue eyes sharp with anger. But he bowed politely to Cromwell and listened to what he had to say without looking away, although it was clear he had been coming to speak to Eloise.

Had the two had some kind of quarrel?

"The very man I need," Cromwell said smoothly. "My lord, His Majesty has sent me to order you north. Word has reached the king tonight that an uprising has taken place along the northeast coast. His Majesty requires you to gather your men and put down this revolt before it spreads further south."

Oh sweet Jesu, Susannah thought, looking from Wolf to Eloise. Wolf had been called away to fight. What if he never came back? She did not know if her sister would survive such a blow. For she felt certain Eloise had formed a love attachment for her husband since their arranged marriage, even if the two of them still fought like two cats in a sack.

Wolf was frowning. "At once?"

"Naturally."

There was a sharp flick to that word, and Wolf seemed to pick up on it, inclining his head respectfully. "I am at His Majesty's command."

"I am glad to hear it. His Majesty will speak with you in one hour in his privy chamber."

When Cromwell had gone, Susannah turned discreetly away from Lord Wolf and her sister, for she had seen the storm brewing in Eloise's eyes during that brief conversation. While the couple spoke in low voices, she looked across at Hugh Beaufort, still watching her with the strangest expression on his face. She lowered her gaze to the ground, and let the pain consume her. Marriage! As if such a thing were even possible…

Master Beaufort was a fool if he thought his life could continue unchanged if they wed. To be married to a known wanton would mark Hugh out as a laughing stock at court. Men would whisper "Cuckold" behind his back, just as the women had whispered "Slut" while she danced among them. Sir Giles would not be silenced now, not without a miracle. Soon the king would know, and Lord Wolf would know, and her father would know, and the whole court would know her shame.

Not that she felt ashamed. She looked about at their smirking faces and suddenly wanted to yell at the top of her voice, *Yes, I lay with Hugh Beaufort, and I loved every minute!*

But she could not. Such things were not done at court.

Lord Wolf had finished his conversation with Eloise, and limped past her to speak with Master Beaufort. Her eyes widened as she overheard some of what was being said.

"Would you escort my wife and her sister home to Yorkshire?" Wolf was asking in a low voice. "I am to see the king tonight and take my orders from His Majesty. When I accept them, I also intend to ask his permission for Eloise to leave court. If the king grants it, she can leave immediately. But I cannot allow her to travel unprotected."

Susannah heard Hugh agree, the two men clasping hands, and she turned away, her heart juddering with pain. She wondered how she had so offended God that she would be forced to travel yet again in the company of Master Beaufort, the last man in the world she needed to see right now, her body aching for his, as the dry earth aches for rain.

Then she caught Eloise's eye, saw her sister's pale face and tortured shake of the head, as though she too would deny the king's orders, and knew she was not the only one suffering here.

"Oh, Eloise," she murmured, and reached for her sister's hand; she squeezed it reassuringly.

She lifted her chin, refusing to look at Hugh again for fear of revealing her anguish. So she was leaving court after all. It was over, all over, and in the end, the decision had been taken out of her hands. Nor was it such a terrible thing. Sir Giles could do his worst and she would be several hundred miles away in the north. But at least this time she would have a task to occupy her mind—and body—on the long journey: that of keeping her frantic sister comforted in Wolf's absence.

Sixteen

Early autumn 1536, Yorkshire

HAVING RIDDEN TO THE brow of the hill, with one accord they reined in and gazed down silently on the manor farm estate. Hugh sat comfortably astride his chestnut gelding, one fist resting on his hip, the other holding the reins slack, for his mount had been ridden hard these past few days and was happy to stand awhile, cropping the grasses. Beside him sat Wolf, on his favorite black stallion, leaning forward in the saddle, his eyes narrowed as he stared up at the cloudless sky.

"I tried every argument to prevent Susannah from having to marry old Hanney," his lordship murmured, glancing his way. "But Sir John is a stubborn man. He would not listen to me."

"I thank you for trying anyway, my lord."

Smoke was rising gently from the ancient, cracked chimneys of the big house, the other buildings softened by the early autumn sunshine, some of them ramshackle, others newly built, their red bricks gleaming. Now that they were sitting still, the loud cackle of geese could be heard from below, and the barking of a dog, and closer to hand, the herding whistle of a shepherd or his boy somewhere behind them on the hill.

This place was a long way from London, Hugh thought. He remembered a long, hot afternoon that spring when he had escorted Susannah Tyrell back to Wolf Hall, only a few miles from this very spot, and how her hair had gleamed in the sunshine, her bared shoulder tempting him as she rode just ahead, smiling back at him.

His groin stiffened and he tried to ignore the relentless pangs of desire. Yet how could he? Lust had been eating him alive for weeks now, driving him mad with hunger. He could no longer sleep at night but lay either wakeful and feverish, or dreamed of Susannah, his body stiff with desire for a woman who was no doubt peacefully asleep hundreds of miles away.

"You are my friend, Hugh. And always will be." Wolf shrugged. "I am glad though that I was able to be of service to you in that other matter."

Hugh smiled humorlessly. "Sir Giles and his tale of woe?"

"I have stopped his mouth for now with veiled threats and the promise of advancement when I finally return to court. But Sir Giles will not hold his peace forever. Not when there is compensation to be had for his cousin's untimely demise." Wolf let his horse move forward to tear at a rich clump of grass. He looked curiously at Hugh. "Eloise tells me you and Susannah had some understanding at court. You have come here with the intention of asking for her hand, I assume?"

"Demanding it, more like," Hugh said starkly. "And not for the first time."

"I wish you well with that. Susannah is still promised to Sir William as far as I am aware, and she can be as stubborn as her father. She has come to visit Eloise frequently since you left for court, and has never mentioned you. If I did not know better, Hugh, I would think her quite resigned to this arranged marriage with Sir William. Yet when we speak of you, Susannah is clearly affected by the mention of your name, though she tries to hide it."

Hugh heard the question behind Wolf's statement and ignored it. He had never spoken to anyone of that night in the forest with Susannah, and whatever she might have said to her sister, he would not be the one to break her confidence. But it gave him some hope to know that Susannah had not forgotten him after he had been summoned back to court.

"How is your wife?" Hugh asked instead, turning the subject. "I was sorry to miss Eloise when I rose this morning."

"Yes, you must forgive her for that. Welcoming you with wine and feasting last night may have proved too much for her delicate condition, so that she could not leave her bed for breakfast." Wolf grinned, suddenly at his ease. "It is strange, knowing I shall soon be a father. I have promised Eloise I will lead a more sedate life. But, alas, I am still the king's servant and must fight on his command if the need arises."

"I hope it will be a boy, my lord," Hugh said, smiling back at him, "for you will make a good father to a son."

"And to a daughter, if that is what God sends us. I will be thankful if my child is born healthy, whatever its sex."

"Amen to that." Hugh kicked his horse to a walk. "Shall we go down?"

"And brave the Gorgon?"

It was Hugh's turn to grin. "Ah, Susannah is not so fearful when you get to know her, my lord."

Raising his eyebrows at that, Wolf walked his horse beside Hugh's in the sunshine, leaning back in the saddle as the slope steepened. "Indeed? Now that *is* interesting. I require details."

"To say more," Hugh pointed out, laughing, "would be most unchivalrous of me."

"Spoilsport."

Hugh enjoyed this easy banter between them. He had missed his friend when he had to return to court without him during the summer. But he too was the king's servant and must go where ordered. Now he had come north on the king's business again, and made this stop at Wolf Hall with the intention of not paying court to

Susannah. Not after the way she had dismissed him in the summer, saying she had no need of a husband and would be content never to lie with a man again.

That rejection had hurt.

But desire was a hard mistress to ignore, and he had not yet given up hope of being able to persuade Susannah to marry him.

He would offer once more, he told himself.

Once more at least. And after that, find some other woman to assuage his needs. Though God knows, he had found no other woman desirable since Susannah.

He frowned as Wolf winced, his friend shifting uneasily in the saddle. He had been wounded and almost died in that skirmish against the northern rebels, but being Wolf, had insisted on getting back in the saddle as soon as the physician had allowed him to rise from his sickbed. Now Wolf seemed returned to full health. But perhaps that was an illusion.

"Your wound still troubles you, my lord?"

"On the contrary it has healed well and gives me little trouble these days. But sometimes I move a certain way and the scar pulls." Wolf shrugged, his expression turning stoical. He looked away, down at the farmhouse, his voice softening. "It is rather like love. You think the pain is done, and then it comes back and stabs at you again, reminds you where the steel entered. Perhaps I will never be entirely healed."

Hugh said nothing for a while, thinking while he guided his horse carefully through a small muddy rivulet, which widened gradually into a stream at the bottom of the hill. The water ran deep there, and the horses picked their way carefully through the rushing ford. They were nearly at the manor gates now, which stood open and undefended, one leaning drunkenly against a tumbledown wall. It seemed that Sir John was in need of refilling his coffers so he could repair his estate. Perhaps Sir William Hanney had offered some discreet remuneration in return for Susannah's hand in marriage, for with a profligate father like Sir John, she would marry with no dowry but her body.

His jaw tightened.

If he could not have Susannah Tyrell, he was determined that no other man would bed her. Not while he was still alive. No, she would have to live her days out as a holy sister if she refused him again.

Though it would be hard to gainsay her father, whose power over his daughter's body was absolute. The thought made him furious.

"She thought me in love with some other woman at court, you know," he muttered, drawing rein at the gates and staring in past the chickens and young pigs running wild.

Wolf grinned at him. "What, some other young beauty who caught your eye?"

"Mistress Croft."

His friend stilled, very straight in the saddle. "Margerie?"

Hugh looked at him, annoyed with himself for forgetting that Wolf had once been enamored of Mistress Croft.

"Forgive me, I wasn't thinking. There was never anything between us. But Susannah came across us once, and mistook what she saw. It was the day of Queen Anne's execution. That evening, if you recall, you bade me carry a message of thanks to Mistress Croft for her friend Kate Langley, for you were being watched and dared not risk it yourself." He shrugged. "Susannah saw me with Margerie, and thought we were lovers."

"I do recall that night, yes." Wolf seemed to brood, staring ahead in the sunshine. "I once thought Margerie my enemy. Yet she was the one who came up with a plan to save my wife from the king's bed. If it had not been for Kate Langley's performance that night, persuading the king we were in love and that my wife was frigid, Henry would have bedded Eloise and got her with child— and thought nothing of it. Some noblemen might think themselves fortunate to be granted a chance to raise a king's bastard as their own, Hugh. But I could not stomach the thought of Eloise suffering his lecherous rape." His voice grew cold with contempt. "*Droit de seigneur.* The French nobles may have left England to the English, but their traditions remain…"

He glanced sharply at Hugh, his blue eyes narrowed on his face. "You did not know the whole story at the time. I trust you will keep it to yourself now?"

"You do not need to ask, my lord."

"Of course not." Wolf frowned. "Forgive me, friend. These are such unsettled times, one forgets who can be trusted…and who cannot."

Hugh smiled. "There is nothing to forgive." He turned his horse in a wide circle, for the beast was restless. Just as he was. Restless to discover the truth, to ask the question burning on his lips. "It is time. Will you come in with me, my lord?"

"I thank you, no. Watching lovebirds at play was never my idea of amusement, and besides, I have a wife at home who will be missing me." Wolf turned his beast back toward the hill they had just descended. "No doubt I will see you on your return. I wish you good luck in your endeavor, Hugh."

Hugh watched Lord Wolf go, then kicked his horse forward into the manor farmyard. Now that he was alone, his heart began to race uncomfortably, his fists clenched on the reins, despite his attempt to relax them.

He had smiled in front of Wolf, and spoken confidently of courting Susannah. But in truth, he was nervous as hell.

Ever since leaving court, he had been thinking of this moment, imagining Susannah's face when she saw him again, how she might have softened toward him since their bitter parting in the summer. Misjudging her mood was turning into a repeated mistake on his part. One day in the summer, walking with her in Wolf's apple orchards,

Hugh had thought her open to another offer of marriage—and had foolishly asked for her hand.

He could still recall the flash in her eyes as she cast him down, reminding him that she wished to be free of all such ties. That marriage would be a living hell to her. "Even if you are roasting there with me!" she had exclaimed, and thrown down his ruby ring. "Take it back; you must take it back!"

But he had refused. That ring had been his gift to her. She could not throw it back at him, for no promise had been attached to it.

A woman was standing in the backyard by the kitchen door, staring at him, shielding her eyes against the sun. "Master Beaufort, is it not?" she called, frowning.

He dismounted and walked forward, holding his horse. He recognized her as one of the house servants, a voluptuous woman in early middle age, hair tumbled out of her cap, a smudge on her cheek, yet clearly once an attractive woman.

Her clear eyes assessed him, then she spun scoldingly on the gawky young girl at her side, folding lengths of soiled linen into a barrel to be washed. "Not like that, Bess! Here, leave that and take the master's shirts for rubbing." She turned to him again. "Can I help you, sir?"

"I am here to see Mistress Tyrell." He saw the look in her eyes change, and cursed under his breath. Had she been warned to refuse admittance to any visitors asking for Susannah? "I must speak with her at once on a matter of some urgency. Will you fetch her?"

The serving woman gestured vaguely across the motley assortment of farm buildings. "She will be somewhere here. Avoiding her chores as always." She glanced back at the house, then hesitated. "But I must take you to the master first. Sir John does not allow his daughter to see visitors alone."

So he had been right.

"I must see Mistress Tyrell at once, and in private," Hugh insisted, then met the woman's eyes. "Please, madam."

She blew out her cheeks, then shrugged. "Very well," she muttered. "Your visit can do no more harm than has already been done to the girl, and may do her some good. Let me see if I can find her." She turned away into the mouth of a darkened alley that ran between sunlit farm buildings, looking back at him, a challenge in her eyes. "Follow me, then."

Hugh found the woman's high-handed tone unsettling, for surely she was only a servant of the house. Yet he too was a servant, he reminded himself drily, even if it was to a king. And she did appear to guard her mistress's welfare zealously; for that, he could not fault her.

Tying his horse to a post, Hugh followed her into the shadows, letting his hand fall unobtrusively to the hilt of his dagger. For he had not failed to notice the burly farm laborers turning to look as he rode in, their stares narrowed and unfriendly, some armed with pitchforks and axes, others with sturdy-looking hoes.

He was on enemy territory here.

―――

It was cool inside the threshing barn, and he stepped inside thankfully, for the autumn sunshine was unseasonably hot. Susannah came forward at the sound of her name, her hair and simple gown in disarray, her wide blue gaze fixed on Hugh. The serving woman spoke sharply to Susannah, but he was too busy staring at his mistress, drinking in her beauty and the sensual sway of her hips, to hear much of what was being said.

How had he gone so long without seeing her? It was an urgent physical need, this desire to touch her, love her, to become one with her.

Had her mouth always been bow-shaped?

He stared, unable to stop himself from imagining his tongue running along those soft lips, as her tongue was doing now, then plunging between to taste her, tempting Susannah into carnal pleasure.

Suddenly they were alone, staring at each other across the dark soil floor of the barn; his heart crashed into the silence, and then restarted with a painful jerk.

"I know we did not part on pleasant terms," he managed awkwardly, taking a few steps toward her, cap in hand, struggling to remember the speech he had so carefully prepared.

Only she would not allow him to finish, of course, but had to interrupt shrewishly. "Pleasant? I should think not!"

"Susannah, for pity's sake!" he exclaimed, and at once abandoned his admittedly futile attempt to woo her with subtlety and compliments.

Frustration tore at him as Hugh finally understood how Susannah had not changed, could never change, would always and forever be this stubborn piece of gorgeous womanhood that he wanted to press against him.

That was the only time they were in harmony, it seemed to him. When they were naked and gasping together in some honeyed stewpot of a bed. As he wished they were now…

"I have made my apologies for what happened," he began again, his heart clenched like a fist as he stared back at her. To have come all this way only to be dismissed like a schoolboy… "Hear me out, at least."

He meant only to reassure her, his hand outstretched, but she snapped, "Don't touch me!" and ran away, disappearing into the shadows of the barn, shouting back at him.

Not so easily dismissed, Hugh trod swiftly after his mistress while she continued ranting, and stood just within reach of her delectable body. His cock grew hard, remembering how hot and tight she was, a furnace of desire, and the sheer pleasure of lying with her, his face nestled between her breasts. Her voice lashed at him. Still he restrained himself from making more than the simplest replies to her accusations, not willing to argue with her again.

God, but she was beautiful.

A silence fell between them, then suddenly his desire snapped and he pulled Susannah toward him, desperate for her mouth, her kiss.

She did not fight him but yielded at once, holding onto his shoulders as he tasted her soft lips, licking into her mouth, sliding inside, their kiss long and heated.

"Hugh," she moaned, and he cupped her breasts, rolling her nipples between his fingers under the coarse fabric of her country gown, his lust unquenchable.

"Yes," he muttered, though he was not sure if she heard him, then lifted her in his arms and carried her into the darkness at the back of the threshing barn. There were a few empty stalls set aside there for horses, but private enough for his purpose. There he laid her gently on a deep, soft bed of straw, and lay down beside her, kissing and stroking her. But his restraint could not last, and he rolled on top of her, so aroused he was soon lost to all reason, caressing her slender body while she whispered, "Not here, not here!"

"You want this as much as I do. God's blood, woman, I have been driven half out of my wits these past weeks." He lifted her gown, finding her ready for him, wet and hot. "Refuse my offer of marriage if you will, Susannah, but I cannot hold back any longer. I must touch you again."

He slipped one finger into her cunt, and she gasped, her hips jerking toward him. "You want this too," he reminded her, and slipped his tongue into her mouth just as he pushed a second finger inside her. Her body was so snug it seemed to draw him in. His cock ached to be inside her again, to work hard and know that sweet wild moment of release. He pushed another finger inside, stretching her tightness, then pressed his thumb against that delicate little nub of flesh that always made her gasp. Her back arched and she urged him on with throaty little sounds that made it clear she was still his. His to enjoy. His to possess. But not his to marry, it would seem.

Impatient to enter her, unable to control his hunger, Hugh withdrew his fingers and tugged at her bodice instead. The coarse material gave easily, and her breasts spilled out, firm and enticing.

"Beautiful," he muttered.

Then he stroked and suckled on her breasts, bringing her dusky-pink nipples to a peak so that Susannah was soon writhing beneath him, moaning, "Yes, take me."

He wanted to fuck her. Could barely think with his cock so hard and swollen, still restrained in his leather codpiece. But he wanted her to come too, to feel the same exquisite pleasure her body gave him. So he knelt between her legs, pushed her skirts to her waist, and buried his mouth in the sweet hot flesh between her thighs. God, he needed to be inside her. His tongue worked furiously, drinking in her juices, licking up and down the silken heat of her core, sucking hard on her nub until she stiffened, crying his name incoherently, then plunging his tongue deep inside her, fucking her with it, making her want him.

"Please," she was gasping, her thighs wide for him. "I need to… Please don't stop."

Then he heard it.

A man's voice, calling, "Susannah!" somewhere outside in the farmyard. Her father, hunting for her among the outbuildings. He would look inside the threshing barn at any moment, would find his daughter on her back in the straw, and between her spread thighs…

Hugh wrenched himself away from her, panting and furious. Susannah was staring up at him, wide-eyed, confused, gorgeously naked and ready for him. But there was no time to explain. No time to recover his breath or think what was to be done.

He grabbed at her arm, helping her swiftly to her feet so that her crumpled skirts fell down, decorous again, hiding her wet desire.

"Susannah?" Her father called again, demanding that she come to him. He was close by, his voice echoing about the barn, its door left half-open, sunlight spilling in…

"Go to him," he told her urgently. "I will remain here. No one need know…"

Then her father was standing in the doorway to the barn, staring at them. He yelled at Susannah, and she tried to explain, to find a suitable lie to hide what they had been doing, but her father was no fool.

"Get behind me, girl!" Sir John ordered her, berating her when she did not move, and finally Susannah stumbled toward him, looking back at Hugh, an expression of shame and despair on her face that made him so furious he wanted to knock the old man down.

He struggled to unclench his fists. This was her father. With any other man, he would have settled this with a fight. But he could not attack Susannah's father, a man more than twice his age, and clearly frail despite the rage in his lashing voice.

"Now, Master Beaufort, what is the meaning of this?" Sir John demanded, launching into a tirade that ended with the old man insisting he would send for his sword and run Hugh through with it.

Hugh tried to listen attentively, to accept his reprimand from her father in silence. But all he could see was Susannah behind him, fear in her face. Not fear for herself, nor even for him, Hugh realized. No, Susannah was afraid for her father. God's blood, did she think him capable of killing an old man?

"What do you have to say for yourself?" her father demanded, his face flushed and choleric.

Hugh switched his attention back to her father. "I intend to marry your daughter, sir. I wish to make Susannah my bride as soon as may be, if you will consent to the banns being read in church."

"You can wish all you like, boy," her father growled. "I will not give my consent. Not to such as you."

"Father," Susannah whispered hesitantly, clutching at her father's sleeve, her face burning as though ashamed of how discourteously her father had addressed him, "you forget, Master Beaufort is the king's clerk, and much respected at court. He has the king's ear."

"I do not care if he has the king in his pocket. Silence, girl. This is none of your concern." Sir John straightened, staring at Hugh. The jerk of his head was a deliberate insult. "Be off with you. And do not come back or I shall have you whipped from my land like a beggar."

Hugh did not move, his feet planted wide.

In a second, he considered a range of possible responses to Sir John's rude dismissal. He considered pushing the knight aside and seizing Susannah, carrying her off on his horse like a spoil of war. He considered drawing his dagger, having it out with Sir John once and for all. Then he considered the look in her eyes, and how she would never forgive him for humiliating or hurting her father.

She had fled from Sir John's demands, had admitted to hating the cruel restraints of his authority, knew he would almost certainly force her into a marriage she did not want: and yet Tyrell was still her father.

As if reading the turmoil of his thoughts, Susannah stepped out from behind her father and met his eyes. A message flashed between them. *Please don't.* Then the beautiful mouth he had so recently been kissing opened to deny the passion between them, and he listened in stunned silence as Susannah lowered herself to beg, to send him away, to finish it forever.

"Hugh, please," she told him, "my answer must be the same as my father's." She stared at him achingly. "It is over."

※

The next dawn was a chilly one. It seemed autumn had finally set in and banished summer for good. Hugh rose barefoot from his bed, threw open the shutters and stared out over a misty landscape, the rough slopes and valleys of Wolf's large estate still dark enough to be partly night, only the distant hills turning milky with the first light of day. His jaw tightened as he remembered the events of the day before, and his hand clenched on the sill. He had left the manor farm under the hostile glare of Sir John's men, and ridden hard back to Wolf Hall, only to regret his decision as soon as he dismounted.

He should have gone straight back to claim her.

Only Wolf had stopped him, a warning hand on his shoulder. "Wait until morning, my friend. You are in a fury, and no man acts wisely in temper. Dine with us tonight. Give us the pleasure of your company and we will talk this thing over. Tomorrow will be soon enough to claim your bride. If that is what you intend."

It was what he intended. She was his perfect woman. Not demure and obedient, nothing like the wife he had once envisaged as gracing his bed and table. No, she was a wildcat, all claws when caged, yet marvelously sensual and bold when given her head, a free spirit whose plans never seemed to include him.

He was in love with her.

He had realized that, painfully and unequivocally, as he rode away from her father's house through the beautiful sunlit fields of northern England and saw the rest of his life as a desert, a barren landscape without her.

He should never have left her there. God knows what her father had done after his departure, he thought. Locked Susannah up in her room, he had no doubt. Beaten her, perhaps. He swore under his breath. If Sir John had taken a switch to Susannah, he would punch him in the face, even if he was her father.

The man was a coward and a brute. He deserved no respect because he had none for his daughter.

He called for the servant to bring water, then dressed hurriedly by the cold dawn light. He had laid out his clothes the night before, knowing what he wished to wear for this visit to Sir John: his black and silver doublet, the one he had worn at the masque, and his best hose, his finest leather boots, and a cloak to keep out the autumn chill. He hesitated over the dagger, then sheathed it at his belt. He could not travel abroad without a weapon, so he must trust himself not to draw on his prospective father-in-law, whatever the provocation.

Before leaving, he took a small, rolled-up paper from his despatch bag and secreted it in his doublet.

A stupid thing, in truth. A poem he had written for Susannah. Nothing like Thomas Wyatt's elegant verse. Yet he had spent much of the early hours toiling over it, and knew no other way to express himself to the lady, for his body always seemed to do the talking once they were together—and it was time his heart made itself known to her as well.

Wolf and his lady were still abed when he descended to the echoing hall, for it was still early. Not wishing to disturb their sleep, he called for his horse and waited in the cold dawn outside, looking up at the sky as it flushed slowly from the east.

He and Wolf had discussed at length last night how he might proceed, what arguments he could put forward to make his marriage proposal sweeter to both parties. Yet he had formulated no plan this time, had no speech prepared. All he knew was that he intended to insist on marriage to Susannah, and if Sir John would not accept his suit, then he would bloody well take her away with him and install Susannah at Wolf Hall with her sister until such time as he could respectably marry her.

Though quite how he would manage this feat of abduction with a dozen hostile men servants and laborers blocking his path out of the manor, he was not sure. Nor how he would persuade a choleric gentleman so fervently against his suit yesterday to accept it today.

But he must try, Hugh thought desperately, swinging up into the saddle when the horse was at last led out to him. Or he might as well go hang himself, for he would have no peace with Susannah wed to another man.

He took the same route he had ridden with Wolf the day before, and forded the stream in the same place. But today the manor farm stood silent and empty. No laborers were in the yard raking through muck and straw, no small children scattered grain for the chickens, and where the barrel had been set out for washing day, the ground stood empty, the damp black earth churned up as though by many hooves.

As he sat frowning at this mess of hoof prints, a woman in an apron and coarse gown came to the kitchen door and stared out at him. It was the servant he had talked with yesterday, the woman who had allowed him time alone with Susannah.

Hugh gathered the reins in his hand, looking about for a less muddy spot to dismount. "Good morrow," he said pleasantly enough, though his nerves were stretched thin. "I have come to speak with Sir John Tyrell. Is he at home?"

"No, sir, he is not."

He stopped where he was, looking at her more carefully. The serving woman's face was streaked as though with tears, and her hair looked even more bedraggled than yesterday, her plain cap askew. Fear spiked through him as he looked about himself, considering the empty farmyard, the muddied ground confused with hoof prints, and the woman grieving.

"What is your name, mistress?" he asked.

"Morag," she said simply, not giving herself any title.

"What happened here, Morag?" He pointed at the hoof prints with his riding crop. "These look fresh."

"Mistress Susannah ran away in the night," she told him, confirming his fears. "Packed some clothes, stole a horse. By the time I

found her bed had not been slept in, she was long gone. John was…"
She caught herself and gave a little shake of her head, as though
tripping over a lie, then blushed when his eyes narrowed on her face.
"The master was furious. He gathered all the men, sent some on foot
with sticks to beat the hedgerows, others on horseback or carts to
search the fields and roads north and south. They are all out looking
for her, Master Beaufort. But they will not find her." She managed a
wan smile. "Not my Susannah. For she does not want to be found,
you see?"

He nodded grimly. "I do indeed. What a mess this has become.
I should never have left her yesterday… Do you know where your
mistress is bound?"

"No, sir. But far away from Yorkshire." She hesitated, looking
at him, then added daringly, "I should not tell you this, but Sir John
wrote to Sir William Hanney last night. To set a date for their nuptials. So Susannah knows what awaits her if she is brought back."

Hugh closed his eyes and counted to ten, waiting until he was
calm again before reopening them. He could only imagine what state
of mind she must be in, like a wild bird caged again after a brief
period of flight, and knowing it would be forever.

"Thank you, Morag," he said, slowly turning his horse around.
"I make no promises, but I will find Susannah if I can. I have an idea
where she may be headed."

"If you do find her, do not bring her home, sir," Morag called
after him. "There is nothing here for her any more but unhappiness."

He raised his hand in a salute, then galloped away from the
manor, urging his horse south. His throat was tight, and he felt like
throttling someone, seized by unspeakable terror for the woman he
loved. Yet he stayed stone-faced, staring ahead as the horse thun-
dered along the lane, passing men with sticks and dogs, uncaring
what they thought of his mad ride. He did not dare allow himself
to think too hard about the future, the damage that might already

have been done, for fear he would weaken and break down into tears himself.

He had left Susannah in the care of her father, and thought her safe there, at least for a short while. Now she was gone, and must have slept out of doors last night in some chilly wood, or ridden through the dark, wretched and alone, desperate to get as far away from home as possible.

His face grew grim. Susannah was impulsive, headstrong and willful, her passions too violent to be contained or denied for long. To be facing a life of servitude to an old man, or the alternative of years of fleeing from town to town, living under an assumed name, working at whatever trade she could find just to stay alive, must feel like the end to her. He thought of her at court, beautiful and sensual in her velvets and silks, and knew she would not wish to eke out such an ignominious existence. Rather death, than such a life.

He only prayed he was not too late.

Seventeen

IT HAD BEEN THE worst night of her life, and soon it would be light again: a faint glimmer threaded its way through the branches. Susannah had buried her head in her cloak an hour ago, hearing the first birds begin to sing in the misty branches above her. But now she could ignore it no longer. Her eyes flickered open on another dawn she did not want to face. Another day of misery and despair, her heart sunk so deep in the mire she had forgotten how to smile, how to laugh, how to feel happy. Her life was broken and she was broken with it. There could be no going back this time, no reprieve. And he would never come looking for her, not after she had sent him away like that, let her father humiliate him in front of her. Once she might have hoped…

But hope was too far away now, a tiny light on a dark horizon, a star blinking out before she could fix on it.

Susannah rolled over onto her back, covering her eyes with her sleeve, and struggled against tears. She hated weeping. What good would it do to grieve for her lost happiness, for those vanished days at court when she and Hugh had fought, and made love, and met each other's eyes across the hall during feasts and dancing?

The forest was cold, and she had shivered through the early hours, even wearing men's clothing and wrapped in her cloak. She did not want to be miserable, but it was impossible not to keep counting her losses. She could not dwell on Hugh Beaufort, for the pain was too great. But she would miss her old nurse, Morag, despite knowing that she was her father's lover, a secret she had not yet forgiven her father for keeping. She would miss her dear sister, Eloise, whose unborn baby she would never meet. She would even miss Wolf, for all the coldness of his noble stare, for now she knew his lordship to be good company, not so aloof as she had thought at first.

It felt like death, losing her family forever. Yet she could not have stayed another night under her father's roof.

"I have held Sir William off long enough," he had shouted at her after Hugh left, his face red with temper, "out of sympathy for your *innocence*. But it is high time I gave you to him, for you are no longer the child I remember."

Marry Sir William, a man as old as her father and whom she barely knew, knowing her only purpose was to bear him an heir?

Not while I have breath in my body, she had sworn fiercely to herself.

That night, after the household was abed, she had crept out in the dark, stealing a horse and making her way south. Unerringly, she had chosen the same route she had taken the last time she had run away. Traveling faster this time though, hardly stopping to rest more than an hour at a time, driven as though in fear for her life, she had cajoled her exhausted horse into the forest and searched about in the twilight, finally stumbling across the exact spot where Hugh had built their little shelter.

Most of the branches and twigs had tumbled down, but some were still in place. Tethering her weary horse to a tree, she had knelt in the gloom and threaded the narrow branches back together, then dragged ferns across the top and inside, making a dryish place to spend the night.

It had seemed like the right idea when she fled the manor, making for this forest, this special place where the two of them had made love for the first time. Here she could think, consider what to do next, how to live out her life without a male protector.

But she was alone this time, and the forest proved damp and chilly, a grim place without Hugh to put his arms about her.

With no way to light a fire, she had spent the evening shuddering with cold, hidden inside the shelter with her arms wrapped about her knees. She had taken out the ruby ring he had given, hoping to gain some strength by his gift, but could not see it in the dark. Then exhaustion had taken her, and she had curled up in the dark, alert to every menacing crack and rustle in the forest, now waking, now dreaming, never quite asleep.

Now it was day, and as she stirred, feeling wretched and desolate, she became aware of a noise outside the shelter. The sound of hooves, slowly but unmistakably picking out a path between the trees, crunching over twigs and dried leaves.

Her breath caught in her throat, and a cold terror seized her. Her heart was suddenly pounding. Had her father found her?

Susannah clambered up, pressing her face to the scratchy branches, and peered out into misty dawn light. She was not afraid of being beaten for running away, for that pain was only fleeting. But she knew now, deep in her heart, that she would do anything to avoid marriage to Sir William Hanney. *Anything.* She would not go home.

Then she saw who the rider was, and her heart almost burst in her chest. It was like a dream, as though she were still asleep, and he had come to rescue her, so perfectly solid and handsome and dependable that it could not be real.

She stared, blinking. It was him. *It was him!*

Smashing her way out of the makeshift shelter, leaves and fern in her hair, her men's clothes muddied and unkempt, Susannah ran toward him, sobbing, "Hugh! Hugh!"

The most intense emotion flashed across Hugh's face as he saw her. There had been a drawn look before, pale and haggard, his green gaze hunting intently through the trees. But at the sight of her running, he froze, his eyes closing briefly, and she saw his mouth move silently, as though in prayer. Then he dragged on the reins, sliding out of the saddle and to the leafy floor in the same movement.

"Susannah!"

His arms had opened wide for her, but he still reeled under the impact, laughing hoarsely as she flung herself at him. Then he was lifting her off her feet, swinging her round in a circle, her hair flying, and she knew that he was real. Master Beaufort had come for her. And she was a fool.

"Are you going to spank me?" she asked.

"Not this time."

Hugh met her eyes, and a shock ran through her, for she could see the same turbulent emotions in his gaze that were in her own heart. He cupped her cheek, then bent and kissed her, his tongue stroking deep and tender in her mouth, reminding her what lay in store.

"This time I'm just glad to see you alive."

~~~

It was strange, riding back to Greenwich Palace at Hugh's side, seeing the familiar towers rise up above the trees and knowing that her sister and Wolf would not be there to greet her. This time she was in truth Hugh's mistress, and had finally agreed to accept his protection. Indeed, she had welcomed it. For that long night in the forest had taught her a sharp truth: that to be a woman and alone in this cold world, without family, without friends, without any way to feed and clothe herself, was not wondrous, as she had once believed, but terrifying. And while she did not expect him to repeat his offer of marriage—for why should he, when he had been rejected so often?—she was at least hopeful that Hugh would treat her well, and not abandon her once he had taken his fill of her body.

He glanced at her as they rode through the narrow archway of the palace gate. "Scared?"

"A little."

"Yet you have done this before."

"That was only for a short while. Now I must pass as a boy for several days." She stared at him. "And what if I need to use the privy?"

His laughter only slightly reassured her. "You will not be at court long enough to be discovered, I promise it. Tonight you will sleep in my chamber. I will tell the steward you are my page, and that you are ill and cannot perform your duties. Tomorrow I will seek out Master Langley, who supervises the clerks, and beg a few days away from court. He is sure to agree, for he will not have been expecting my return yet. Then we can ride into Kent, where my aunt will look after you until I can free myself from my court duties. She is a good woman; she will not turn you away."

"I thank you, for you know I may never go home again." She was frowning though. "You will be...safe at court?"

"Safe?"

Her eyes flashed. "I am thinking of a certain redhead."

"You mean Margerie Croft?" This time his laughter was incredulous. "Sweetest Susannah, I have told you, she means nothing to me. I have only ever spoken to her at Wolf's request. Besides, you may rest easy while we are apart. I believe that lady's affections lie elsewhere."

Sweetest Susannah.

Yes, she liked that. Trying to hide her smile, she thought back. "With the doctor, you mean? Master Elton?"

"Perhaps." He shrugged. "I saw them together once in the Great Hall at Greenwich. They were just talking. But the way I would talk to you, not how a doctor talks to those who need his advice. I would not be surprised to hear Master Elton had taken her as his mistress.

Though he will face some trouble there, for Margerie Croft does not have an easy reputation."

They were entering the inner courtyard. Susannah nodded, ridiculously pleased that she would not have to fight off that beautiful red-haired woman, then lowered her head in horror as one of the grooms turned, staring as they rode in together.

"What if I am recognized?" she whispered.

"Keep that cap on, pull up your collar, and all will be well. Speak to no one, remember. Or if you must speak, try to sound gruff, scratch your arse before replying, and perhaps spit on the floor too." Hugh jumped down from the saddle, grinning at her outraged expression. "That should persuade most doubters that you are no lady."

Hugh came round to her, holding his horse's reins. "Can you get down without my help?"

"I am not entirely helpless," she hissed, then saw the humor in his eyes and bit her lip, struggling to suppress her smile in front of the watching grooms. "Damn you."

He was mocking her. This was a new Hugh she was not accustomed to seeing, charming and easy-mannered, his eyes lighting her in a way she had never noticed before, a tender look in his face at times, as though he saw her as more than just a mistress.

She could not hope for a settled future though, not after everything that had happened between them. And the life of a mistress seemed preferable to that of a wife, free from all the usual rules and restrictions. Indeed, if his intense and passionate lovemaking over the past few nights was what she had to look forward to, she would not lack for much as Hugh Beaufort's mistress.

"I trust you will not be forever damning me when you are my wife," Hugh murmured, his eyes still smiling, and turned to unfasten his saddlebag. Turning back, he glanced up and met her eyes. His smile slowly faded as he saw her stricken look. "What is the matter?"

"I did not think…" She could not say the words.

He stared. Slowly, comprehension dawned in his eyes. "You did not think I intended to marry you?"

She nodded.

Hugh looked stunned. "What are you saying? That you were willing to ride back to court with me as my mistress? Openly and despite the danger?"

Struggling to breathe, Susannah gathered the reins clumsily in one hand, ready to dismount. She was not a natural horsewoman, unlike her sister, who might have been born on a horse. "Yes," she muttered. Then added defiantly, "What of it?"

He made a noise under his breath. "You are a brave woman."

"Me?"

He did not know her that well if he could think that. She was not brave. Far from it. If only he knew, she thought, and suppressed wild laughter. She had told him "No" so many times, and thought herself free of such womanly ambitions. Yet now she felt turned upside down by the simple revelation that Hugh Beaufort still wished to marry her, that marriage to her was not merely a question of honor to him but of abiding desire.

Did he mean it? She was suddenly a little shaky.

"Here, let me help you," Hugh insisted, reaching for her, but she shook her head fiercely.

"Who knows if we are being watched? What man ever helped his page dismount?"

She enjoyed wearing men's clothing, for it gave her freedom to move in a way that felt more natural than the constant decorum required in a gown. But right now she felt awkward under his narrowed stare, knowing how the tight hose displayed her behind and thighs, more rounded than any boy's.

She dropped to the ground, weary after so many days on the road, and still dazed from the knowledge that he wanted her for his bride, despite her wantonness, her lack of decorum.

And turned, coming face to face with Thomas Cromwell.

"Mistress Tyrell," Master Cromwell said calmly, and inclined his head while she stood gasping, shocked that they had been discovered so easily. How had he known of their arrival? Then he looked at Hugh, and his voice grew chilly. "Master Beaufort. You travel slowly, sir. Your arrival has been expected since yesterday morning, when Sir John Tyrell came to court with news of his daughter's abduction."

She stared, shocked. "My father?"

Hugh's face hardened. Furious, he glanced at her, then back at Thomas Cromwell. There were suddenly men all around them in the courtyard, some armed, ensuring there could be no escape.

"It was no abduction, sir."

"That remains to be seen. Even if there was no abduction, and she left Yorkshire with you willingly, you are still guilty of seducing an unmarried gentlewoman. If you would accompany me, I will see that Mistress Tyrell is taken to the maids' chamber until such time as your fate has been decided."

"His fate?" Susannah repeated, frightened at last.

"And your own, Mistress Tyrell."

Hugh's eyes narrowed as Thomas Cromwell summoned two of the queen's ladies from the doorway behind them. Then he looked at her, and she saw the darkness in his face, and knew it for her own. Her heart clenched in anguish. How was it possible that they could be dragged apart just at the very moment when they had come together at last?

"Forgive me, Susannah," Hugh muttered, ignoring the others, and drew off his riding gloves, holding out a hand to her. "I brought this on you. But I have always wanted you for my wife, not my mistress. My heart has never moved from that fixed intention, and never will, even unto death. I love you. You must believe me."

Susannah's eyes widened as she looked upon his face. "You... love me?"

But before she could take his hand, the two women slipped between them in a rustle of heavy-skirted gowns, flanking her like guards. She recognized them vaguely as particular favorites of the new queen. Their looks were contemptuous, their expressions coldly disapproving, and she knew herself despised.

They thought her a whore. Well, it was not the first time she had seen that look in another woman's eyes. There would be worse ahead for her. And for Hugh, now that they had been caught together.

No doubt her father would be pleased now. He had ruined her. But if he hoped by this to gain his revenge, and her obedience at last, he would find himself thwarted. For she would never return to his house. Never.

Hugh turned to Cromwell, almost begging. She hated to hear that placatory tone in his voice. "Sir, Mistress Tyrell must not be held to account for my lust. I alone am to blame for her seduction. I should be punished, not her."

"Hugh, no," Susannah told him, frantic to stop him taking the blame, but already she was being pulled away.

At the narrow courtyard door into the palace, she struggled free of the women and looked back. Hugh had been surrounded. She saw the flash of metal as a pike was lowered, threatening him. Someone called out an order, and Cromwell bent his head, speaking quietly with the captain of the guard.

"Mistress Tyrell," one of the women said sharply, grabbing at her arm, but she shook off her hand, angry now.

He was the man she loved. And he loved her too. Why should they not be together?

Then she heard a shout, someone calling for the rivermen. Where were they taking him? On the Thames?

Oh my God, she thought, and stumbled blindly, nearly falling as one of the women pushed her toward the palace. They were taking Hugh Beaufort to the Tower of London.

Hands behind his back, Hugh stared down at the river through the narrow slit of his window. Ten days had passed since his arrest. Ten days in this sere and barren time of year, with yellowing leaves on the trees and drafts that struck chill into his bones at night. No word had come yet of how long he would be incarcerated here. But he had heard from other prisoners that some men imprisoned here for the seduction of unmarried women of gentle birth had spent years, rather than months, in this grim place.

The irony was not lost on him. He had hoped to save Susannah from marriage to an old man, yet he himself might be an old man by the time he was released.

The wind blew back his hair, chill and damp with rain. Hugh narrowed his eyes on the gray-flecked river. He had seen the barge swing slowly in to the landing steps ten minutes ago, but the river wall hid the occupants from view.

More prisoners for the Tower?

He had not given up hope of a visit from Susannah, or a letter to let him know how she fared, though he knew the likelihood was remote.

He had been assured several times that Mistress Tyrell was not being kept at the Tower, though she had been heavily "chastised" at court and was now under the strict supervision of the queen's ladies. His eyes closed on a wave of guilt and desolation; he was tormented by the thought of what her chastisement might have entailed. All because he could not keep his lustful thoughts to himself, nor his hands off her body.

Susannah would have been lucky to escape a whipping. Pain swamped him, and he bent his head against the stone window, feeling cold darts of rain strike his cheek. And he had not been there to stop it, to comfort and hold her. Nor had she written. Perhaps she was angry with him for having seduced her.

Presently, he heard voices and footsteps in the corridor, then the sound of keys jangling.

Had the river barge brought him a visitor?

Hugh turned at once, breathing hard, and shoved a hand through his disheveled hair to rake it down. His heart was racing, and he had to force himself to be calm.

It could not be her. How could it be her?

And he did not want Susannah in this foul cell anyway, with the stench of river mud and rotting straw underfoot. This was no place for a lady. Better for her to stay at court and try to regain some royal favor if she could, make her fate less precarious.

He thought of Queen Anne, imprisoned in rather more spacious quarters but still within the Tower, and felt his nails dig into his palms. Her slender neck had met the blade's edge not far from this spot. Life was so cruel and short. Why should he and Susannah not try to snatch a little happiness before their deaths?

The door to his cell was unlocked, the steward stood back respectfully, then a cloaked man ducked his head and entered.

It was Lord Wolf.

"Friend…" Hugh could barely speak, he was so overcome to see someone he trusted at last. "How goes the world, my lord?"

"More slowly without you." They clasped hands, and Wolf gripped him hard. "You are pale, Hugh. Are they feeding you properly here? Meat and bread?"

"I am well, thank you. It is cold, that is all. The window here is open to the air, as you see."

Wolf nodded, glancing about the cell, not meeting his eyes. "I shall have a thick country jacket sent up from court for you, and more blankets. Those look a little threadbare." He made a face at the stinking straw, scuffing it with his toe. "I've slept in better stables than this on the march. At least you had on stout riding boots at your arrest. Court shoes would rot in here during the winter."

Hugh felt a chill run through him. "Am I to understand that my stay here will be a long one, my lord? I have had no word."

"I am here to escort you back to court for questioning, after which the matter of your sentence will be decided by Thomas Cromwell, who has taken a keen interest in this matter." Wolf met his eyes at last, and Hugh saw a pitying expression on his face. "Forgive me for being the bearer of such bad tidings. There is no help for it, Sir John is livid and will have recompense for what he is insisting was his daughter's seduction. That other problem has come up again too… Sir Giles is refusing to hold his peace any longer, and has petitioned the king himself for your execution for his cousin's murder. I did what I could, but he will not be persuaded." Wolf clapped a hand on his shoulder. "And I thought you would prefer to see a friendly face before your trial."

"I do," Hugh agreed huskily. He felt sick though, his voice raw with it. "These are heavy charges against me indeed. I will be lucky to escape with my life."

"You are in danger, yes. But you still have friends at court, Hugh. You must not despair."

Hugh searched Wolf's face. "Thank you, my lord. I do not deserve your friendship, not after my behavior with your wife's sister."

"She is a beauty, Hugh, and a headstrong woman, by God. No man blames you. But there are always consequences. As the king himself knows. Which may weigh in your favor."

Hugh looked away, desperately glad he had not destroyed his friendship with Wolf but unable to say more than a hoarse, "Thank you," again. He knew though that he would be a prisoner of the Tower for many months, possibly even years…assuming he was not sentenced to hang for Sir Francis's murder.

Catching sight of the papers lying on his mattress, he bundled them up and handed them to Wolf. "Will you do me a favor, my lord, and see these delivered to Mistress Tyrell?" He frowned. "If I have permission to write to her, that is?"

"Of course you may write to her. I will send them to her by courier this very day. Susannah was sent back to Yorkshire a few days ago, not to return without the queen's permission, under pain of imprisonment. I am afraid she was whipped for her part in this, but I saw to it that she was properly cared for after her punishment. Her father has disowned her, unfeeling bastard that he is, but my wife will happily take her in." Wolf smiled, clearly trying to reassure him. "Susannah will be well treated under my roof. Indeed, Eloise will be glad of another woman in the house when her confinement begins."

Hugh closed his eyes. "Your wife is a good woman, my lord."

"Better get your cloak now," Wolf told him, not unkindly. "There is a chill wind on the river."

Hugh nodded abruptly, and reached for his cloak and cap. "So be it. I saw the barge arrive. We are to go by river to Greenwich Palace for my trial, I take it?"

"Whitehall." Wolf drew his cloak about him, and shook the straw from his boots. "The court has moved."

———

A crash brought Susannah to her feet, staring. Alarmed, she threw aside the richly embroidered christening gown she had been painstakingly sewing all morning, her eyes burning over the tiny stitches required, and hurried through to her sister's bedchamber.

Eloise was on her hands and knees in a slanted patch of wintry sunshine, peering under the bed. Beside her on the floor was a heaped assortment of old wooden chests, chamber pots, soiled clothing, and bric-a-brac. She looked up with a guilty start when Susannah entered, a dusty smudge on her cheek, her hair hanging down from her wifely cap.

"Oh," Eloise managed, and waved her hand to clear the air of dust, its thick motes spiraling in the rays of winter sunshine. "Forgive me. Did I disturb you?"

"Eloise, what on earth are you doing?"

"Cleaning out under the bed now that the New Year is almost upon us," her sister said in a matter-of-fact way, then sat back with a frown of pain, rubbing her back. Her huge belly protruded, big with child, and she ran a hand over its smooth curve too. "This was Wolf's mother's chamber. He said she kept a box of rattles and rag toys in here somewhere, from when he was a baby. I thought perhaps it might be under the bed, but all I found were these." Eloise picked up a rusty iron implement, shaped rather like a ladle, and examined it with raised eyebrows. "I wonder what this is for?"

"I don't know, but you should not be crawling about in the dust in your condition. Leave this mess to the servants and come sit with me." Susannah smiled, trying to cajole her into taking more care of herself. "I have almost finished his christening gown. Do you wish to see it?"

"*His?*" Eloise shook her head, laughing. "I will see it when it is finished, I thank you. It is unlucky before. But why are you so sure this baby will be a boy?"

"You are carrying low, and you have not suffered much from sickness," Susannah pointed out, helping her sister carefully to her feet. "Everyone knows that means it is a boy."

Eloise suddenly grimaced, clutching her belly.

"What is it?" Susannah stared, unsure what to do. She had not thought her sister's confinement due for another month, and knew it could be dangerous if a baby arrived too soon. "Is...is the baby coming early? Should I send one of the servants for the midwife?"

"No, no, the pain is passing." Her sister let out a long breath and sat down heavily on the edge of her bed, still rubbing her belly, rocking back and forth as though to comfort herself. "It comes and goes. Oh Susannah, some days I am so scared. I don't know how I will get through this."

Susannah closed her eyes briefly, then sat down beside her sister and took her hand. This fear was something she could understand. "I know it's hard but you must trust your instincts. Listen to your body, Eloise. It knows what it needs, and what it doesn't need. Animals give birth alone, and take no help either from God or each other. You will have me, and the midwife, and even Wolf has promised that he will be on hand if you need…I don't know, your back rubbed, perhaps?" They both laughed at the thought of stern Lord Wolf rubbing her back. "Though I think he would rather wait downstairs to hear the news when the day comes."

"He is a man. It is not his place to attend me in my confinement," Eloise said bravely enough, but it was clear she was still worried. "You truly believe my body will know what to do?"

"A woman's body is a miraculous thing," Susannah said softly, and placed a tentative hand on her sister's vast belly. "It will know."

"That is all very well for you to say, but you are not with child."

Susannah sat very still, staring at the golden motes of dust still dancing and spiraling in the air. She said nothing, but her heart was racing and she felt a little sick. She needed to protect Hugh against further punishment. But it was a secret she had carried too long, and she was relieved that the impossible deception was over and she could finally lay that burden down.

Catching her stillness, Eloise frowned and glanced at her averted face. "Susannah?"

Her gaze flashed to her sister's own waist, hidden by a thick gown and woolen country shawl. "Do you not tell me that you too…? Oh please, God. Not out of wedlock."

Rising from the bed, Susannah turned, red-faced, and lifted the shawl to display the unfastened back of her gown, where the skirt would no longer fit to the bodice and had to be laced more loosely.

"I do not know how many months," she whispered, aware that one of the servants might overhear, "but I too shall be a mother by this summer, God willing. Pray forgive me, Eloise. I know my disgrace has been a sore trial to you, and that I have brought enough shame on the family already. But I love Hugh Beaufort, and I am glad to be bringing his child into the world."

"Oh, my sweet sister." Eloise stood clumsily and embraced her, holding Susannah tight in her arms, or as tight as her huge belly would allow. "I keep thinking of you as a child. But indeed you have grown to be a woman this past year, and should be Master Beaufort's bride. I will write to Queen Jane today and let her know this news."

"No…you cannot…no!" Susannah stared, shaking her head, incoherent with horror at the prospect of this new shame.

"Nonsense, of course the queen must be told." Eloise kissed her, then pushed her away, suddenly flushed and yawning. "I am so sleepy now. I must rest for an hour or two. And you should rest too." She smiled, patting Susannah's hand. "Shall we lie down together and give our poor bodies a well-earned sleep?"

Susannah managed a shaky smile. "No, thank you. I have a…a letter to write."

"To Master Beaufort, in the Tower? Does he know of the child?"

"Not yet."

"You should tell him. It is time."

Susannah nodded, her throat thick with unshed tears, and struggled to conceal her pain, turning away from her sister with her arms wrapped tight about herself, the shawl pulled across her breasts.

"Yes, it is time. We may never be together, but Hugh should know that he will soon be a father. Even if it must be to a bastard child." She drew a sharp breath, hurrying to the door. "I fear the news will bring him little cheer though."

"The Tower is a cruel and lonely place in the winter," Eloise called after her. "Especially for those who have been given no hope of release. It will bring him comfort, I can promise you that."

When she had penned her letter to Hugh and given it to her sister's steward, knowing it would soon be on its way south, Susannah returned to her sewing. She smoothed out the rich christening robe on her lap. Her hand stole to the hard mound of her belly, which in recent weeks had begun to rise up and make itself known, much to her dismay. Now at last she would not have to conceal herself when dressing, and wear bulky clothes and shawls to distract her sister's gaze.

She had not suffered much sickness either. Could it be a boy?

She held her belly tight and closed her eyes, imagining how a boy would grow to look like Hugh Beaufort, with green eyes and thick fair hair, and a smile so charming that he would soon have every woman wrapped around his finger.

Momentarily setting aside her nephew's—or niece's—christening robe, Susannah unfastened her belt pouch and took out the ring and paper that she kept there. She read through the poem he had sent her, smiling mistily at the last lines.

I love thee now more true, rebelliously,
Than ever I did love when I was free.

Then she slipped the ruby ring onto her finger. She had begged Lord Wolf to have it altered, and he had agreed, so now the ring sat glinting, a perfect fit.

She would never now be Mistress Beaufort. By the king's own decree, Hugh had been imprisoned in the Tower indefinitely, for seducing a maiden of gentle birth and not reporting a fight in which he had killed a knight of the realm, even though that death had grudgingly been deemed self-defense, thanks to the testimony of several of Wolf's men who had witnessed Sir Francis snatch her and ride away into the forest.

Once she would have been horrified to think of herself as any man's wife; it would have seemed a betrayal of all her childhood dreams. Now though she longed to see Hugh again; and not just see him but kiss him, lie with him, be joined to him as his wife. Not as his possession, but his lover and companion—and his eager concubine too, satisfying their mutual desire. For he had said he loved her, and Susannah knew she loved him.

Only it could never happen now. Or not in the flesh.

"So long as I wear your ring," she whispered, taking up the letter he had sent her, "I shall be your wife in spirit, Hugh. Even if not in name."

There at the bottom of his poem, in a neatly penned postscript, were the words, *Consider the ring a promise, as well as a gift. Your betrothed, Hugh Beaufort.*

⁓

New Year passed quietly enough, the weather turned bitter, and the ground grew hard and cold. Susannah wrote again to Hugh in the Tower. But no reply came. She fretted over his silence for a few weeks, then decided to put it from her mind. It was strange, but being with child seemed to have conferred on her a kind of serenity that took the place of her old impulsiveness. She began to wear Eloise's old gowns, specially made for an increasing belly, and walked out whenever the weather was dry, enjoying the crisp air on her cheeks.

Yorkshire was a white, frozen landscape in January and February, ice cracking underfoot as she walked and all the spiders' webs and hedgerows laced with frost in the early mornings. Susannah found a new joy in walking now that riding was forbidden her, and often she would walk alone, and hum and talk to her unborn child in the womb, hoping it could hear her voice and be comforted.

Eloise's baby was born in the small hours of a moonless night, so that the midwife took a while arriving. Susannah found herself murmuring advice to her panting sister while the women servants scurried about, bringing bowls of steaming water for cleansing, and binding cloths to keep Eloise still during her pains. At last the midwife arrived, and ten minutes later the child was born.

While her sister slept, pale and exhausted, Susannah carried her baby nephew to the door for Wolf, who had spent the night pacing the upper landing, tight-lipped with horror at his wife's screams, to admire.

"You have a son, my lord," she murmured, drawing back the cloths so he could see the babe's face. "A healthy boy."

"God be praised." Wolf touched his son's cheek with a gentle finger. His blue eyes raised to hers. "I pray you will know this happiness too, Susannah."

Following the usual rule, her sister was confined to her chamber until the lying-in time was over, and Susannah found herself alone more frequently, reading Hugh's poem over and over, or staring out at the frosty hills and meadows from her bedchamber window. Her belly was growing round now, and she found herself easily tired, sleeping in the afternoons as her sister had done.

It was hard, facing her pregnancy alone, knowing Hugh was several hundred miles away in London, confined to a cell at the Tower, where she was not permitted to visit him. But she had to be strong for her child's sake. She watched in wonder as Eloise nursed her baby son with love and attention, only rarely permitting the wet nurse to perform that duty for her. Was that not the true meaning and purpose of motherhood, she pondered? To be strong and love her child, however stony the ground they must walk together?

One day, sleeping fitfully on her bed in the late afternoon, Susannah heard the door creak open and sat up, blinking. She had closed the shutters and the room was dark.

"Who's there?"

There was a dark bulk in the doorway. It came toward her while she stared, still half asleep. The bed dipped, then suddenly a man was bending over her, his mouth brushing her lips.

"It is your husband-to-be."

Her heart jerked in sudden, violent joy. "Hugh!"

It was like a dream.

She struggled up, throwing her arms about his neck, kissing him back without trying to conceal her passion. Her lips met his, and their tongues stroked deeply against each other, each of them soon gasping, making little noises of need against each other's mouths.

"Oh, Hugh, how is this possible? I thought I would never see you again."

His arms came around her curved belly, lifting her toward him, and he kissed her throat, laughing under his breath. "I thought the same, my love."

"What... What did you call me?"

Hugh drew back, looking down into her face in the darkness. "My love," he said deeply.

She cupped his face with both hands, stroking his cheek. "I never thought to hear you say those words again either. When you did not write again, I thought...I thought you must be angry. That you did not want a child born out of wedlock."

"Nor do I," he agreed.

Heat flooded her face and she fell back on the pillows, staring at him, a terrible desolation in her heart. "You... You do not want a child?"

"Out of wedlock," he repeated.

She stared, only slowly understanding his words. "So we are to be married after all, is that what you mean? I can hardly believe it possible. But the king... How are you here, Hugh? Have you been pardoned for my seduction?"

Hugh rose and opened the shutters, then came slowly back to the bed. He lifted her hand, where the ruby ring still gleamed, and kissed it. Just the feel of his warm lips on her skin aroused her.

"I did not write because I did not wish to raise your hopes of a wedding between us. But it seems Queen Jane spoke to the king on our behalf, my love. Repeatedly." His eyes met hers. "King Henry took some persuading, but eventually I was released and sent north to marry my pregnant bride before she could disgrace her family any further. Not that I consider our child a disgrace. I would welcome him or her even born out of wedlock. But since the king has seen fit to offer me new employment..."

"New employment? Hugh, that is wonderful news."

Hugh smiled, then bent his head to kiss her intently. For a while the room was silent as they explored each other's bodies with lips and hands. She began to feel almost lost in their hot endless kisses, her mouth tingling with pleasure. But there was so much joy to remember, and so much pain to forget, it could not be achieved in a short time, she thought dizzily.

"I am to offer my assistance in the dismantling of monasteries in the north," he murmured at last, stroking an exploratory finger under her skirt while she shivered and arched against him. "The work could take a year or two to be completed, it seems, during which time I am to remain in Yorkshire. Afterward I must return to court to present my report. At which time I may bring my wife and child south with me if I am content to pay for their lodging." He smiled, and ran his tongue along her lower lip in a decadent promise. "Which I most certainly am. For I do not think I could live without this."

Daringly, he teased her thighs apart, and slid a finger inside her core.

She was hot and slick with longing for him, and moaned, raising herself for more. "Oh yes please, Hugh. It's been so long."

He leaned forward, kissing her mouth while he pushed another two fingers inside, stroking in and out of her flesh.

"My love," he muttered hotly against her mouth, "I would like nothing more than to spear you with my cock, and do precisely what I have been dreaming about for the past few months in that godforsaken cell at the Tower, which is to mount and ride my betrothed until I burst." His thumb pressed against her nub, rubbing languorously until Susannah groaned and writhed against him, her head thick with lust. "But is it safe? With the baby?"

"I don't know. I think so. I… Oh God, I hope so." She clutched at his shoulders as sudden hot pleasure snatched her breath away and she climaxed, shuddering hard against his fingers. "Hugh, I love you! I love you!"

He grinned down at her, then unfastened his codpiece, shifting between her thighs. "I love you too, my gorgeous, hotheaded, wanton darling."

"Not here," she whispered, though her mouth was already dry at the sight of his thick, heavy cock, remembering the pleasure he could give her with it. "What if someone comes in?"

"I asked Wolf to see we are not disturbed for the next hour," he told her, then kissed her so hungrily she thought she would faint. "I want to remind myself why I was—and still am—willing to die for you."

"I know why," she said shyly. "I've read your poem so often now I could recite it in my sleep."

Hugh slid inside her with a gasp, and both lay still for a moment as he gritted his teeth and clearly fought the urge to come. "No poetry, my love. I beg you. At least, not while…I'm inside you."

She shifted, taking him deeper, and clasped her legs about his hips, seeing how easy it was after all to accommodate him on top while her belly was so round.

"You may have to let me ride on top again soon," she pointed out with a sudden gasp, then moaned as he began to thrust. "If you can bear…to let…your wife ride you."

His laughter was muffled against her throat. "I fear you have done little else but ride me since I first met you, Susannah. But never fear. I am a lucky man. For I have discovered how great the pleasure is in bedding a headstrong woman." He turned his head to kiss her. "Bedding—and wedding."

*Keep reading for an excerpt from the third book in
the Lust in the Tudor Court series*

Rose Bride

Greenwich Palace, Spring 1536

THE KING'S ATTENDANTS MEANT to rape her. And no man at the court of Henry Tudor would dare call them to account for it. For she had offended the king himself, and this was to be her punishment.

As soon as King Henry had drunkenly bellowed, "Out of my sight, vixen!" Margerie had picked up her skirts and run from the Royal Presence.

She had foolishly refused to lie with the king, disgusted by his reeking breath in her face, and her first thought was of escape. If she could only reach the safety of the women's quarters and conceal herself there...

But his men had followed, swift as hounds on her scent, cornering her in one of the royal antechambers. She counted five attackers, fury in their eyes, with a sixth lurking a few feet away, perhaps less eager than the others for a rape.

She did not waste her breath on pleas for mercy. There was little hope of reasoning with them. Nor would a single gentleman among them step forward to save her. The place was hushed, the hour late. Even if she screamed, none would come running. For these were the king's privy quarters, and it was the king's own gentlemen who had come after her.

The king's gentlemen!

Contempt lit her eyes as she glared round at the ring of leering, drunken faces, smelled the wine on their breath, and could not help seeing how one lewd youth had already unfastened his hose in readiness.

"Fie, sirs!" she exclaimed. "Have you no shame, six men to attack one woman?"

"Perhaps you should have considered the consequences before you insulted His Majesty," one of the older noblemen growled.

"I did not mean to insult the king." Her face grew hot with shame. "His Majesty tried to… That is, the king wanted me to… I may be flame-haired but I am no whore, my lord."

But the lord stepped closer, his look threatening. "A whore is precisely what you are, Margerie Croft, and not because of your red hair." He pointed to the floor. "Now lie down for us, Mistress Croft, or we shall drag you down."

She pressed herself against the wall, suddenly terrified. The vast tapestry behind her swayed precariously, the torchlight dazzling her as she searched for some way of escape.

Dear God, do not let them take me by force.

Sir Christopher, who had pursued her in the past to be his mistress, reached out to stroke her cheek, his own voice slurred with drink like the king's. She shrank from his touch.

"Before you lament this punishment, Margerie, remember you have no one to blame but yourself. You refused the king tonight. And for that insult, you must be chastised."

"It was a misunderstanding, that is all," she told him. "His Majesty thinks me a harlot because of my…my error with Lord Wolf. But that was years ago when I was but a girl. I am a respectable woman now."

"And an ungrateful one. Was it not at the king's pleasure that you were allowed to return after your disgrace?" Sir Christopher clicked his tongue disapprovingly. "Yet you will not grant His Majesty a little pleasure in return."

She shivered, knowing nothing she could say would sway these men from their purpose. They were king's men, and this secret punishment was to be meted out to her on his behalf so His Majesty's honor might be satisfied.

"Look how she stares, how she pants… Those green eyes bright as a cat's. Oh, she is wanton indeed," one of the younger ones whispered over the nobleman's shoulder, his hand cupping a swollen groin. "Hold her down for me. I want to go first, teach her a lesson."

"Now, Marcus," drawled the older man, turning to clap him on the shoulder, "have a little patience, boy. There is plenty to go 'round."

A slender man in a handsome gold-and-silver doublet, still youthful enough to have no beard, stirred at the back of their group. He was the only one frowning with distaste. "Sirs, I must protest. A rape is no good sport. Let us leave this ugly business, gentlemen. The lady is not willing."

"She'll be willing for a shilling!" one cried out in a jest, and several laughed, gazing hotly at her breasts where they spilled over her bodice.

Sir Christopher turned to the young man, his expression venomous. "What is your objection, Lord Munro? The king bade us use this wench as we would, did he not?"

The young lord muttered, "She should be taught to respect the king's bidding. But not in such a way that the court will be enraged."

"Margerie Croft is no virgin," the older man told him impatiently. "All our pricks together will break nothing but her pride. If such sport is not to your taste, Munro, leave us to our man's work and go find some young stag for your bed."

They all turned then, hooting and mocking the young lord, who slunk away into the darkness with a sullen look. While they were busy laughing at the youth, Margerie picked up her skirts and ran out of the antechamber into an unfamiliar side corridor.

"Ho there, the whore has slipped her leash!" one of them exclaimed.

A shout went up and the men pursued her, laughing and whooping drunkenly, pouring out of the antechamber after her like hounds on the trail of a fox.

Her heart was thumping. She had to get away from them. But the corridor was dimly lit and narrow, and she did not know the way. She glanced back and did not see that the ground was about to slope abruptly upward. Tripping over her own feet, Margerie fell heavily to her knees on the stone floor. She hissed, wincing. The men were almost upon her. Her head swung, searching for some way of escape. There was a darkened doorway to her left, its door partially open.

She clambered through the narrow doorway on hands and knees, hampered by her gown. She could see nothing in the darkness, but the floor was dusty and she knocked over a stack of empty wooden crates in her hurry.

"Oh, sweet Lord, I beg of you, no," Margerie cried in horror as the king's men found her again.

They pushed into the chamber, surrounding her with lusty delight.

"But this place is perfect for a rape," one said, holding his flaming torch aloft to reveal some kind of storeroom. "We will not be disturbed here. Shut the door, let us be about it."

She was dragged unceremoniously to her knees, her arms pulled tight behind her back. One of the younger men tumbled the velvet hood from her head so that her mass of red hair burst out, unrestrained.

"By Christ, she's a beauty!" he exclaimed thickly.

Then Sir Christopher was there again, towering above her. He dragged her head back cruelly, and Margerie found herself blinded by the flaming torch held above their heads. She stared up at avid, jeering faces, on her knees in the center of a tight-pressed ring of male bodies, some unlaced, their stiff members jutting toward her.

"Pray let me go," she moaned, but Sir Christopher pressed a heavy hand over her mouth, silencing her. She felt sick and dizzy. She could smell sweat and horses, his leather glove, the acrid stink of unwashed flesh. There would be no escape from this rape, she realized, and began to tremble.

Suddenly a door creaked open behind them. She could not see the man, but heard a male voice, deep and quiet.

"My lords? May I be of some assistance?"

There was a sudden silence among them. Sir Christopher's hand lifted from her mouth, shifting to his sword hilt instead. Her other attackers fell back, a few glancing at each other over her head, abashed. Nonetheless they did not seem deterred by his presence, only a little embarrassed at having been caught.

"Who are you, sirrah?" the boy demanded arrogantly, his hand falling to his dagger.

"I am Master Elton, court physician," the man replied calmly. "I treated you recently, my lord Shelby, if you recall."

The boy flushed hard. But his hand dropped away from his dagger. "Oh yes, I remember. Well, go about your business, man. This is no affair of yours."

Her heart sank. She had hoped to be saved by this newcomer. But he was no great lord as she had at first thought, only a doctor. He could not stop this pack of rutting dogs.

But to her surprise, Master Elton did not leave. "What have you there, my lords?" he asked, almost idly. "Some dangerous beast you have cornered, perhaps?"

He came forward. His physician's robe did nothing to disguise the long, lean grace of this man's body, his roped belt accentuating narrow hips beneath a muscular chest. Court physician or not, he did not seem afraid of the company and their cruel purpose. He came toward her without hesitation, stepping between the nobles as though oblivious to any threat they might pose.

"A woman?"

Sir Christopher swore under his breath. "Leave us. This is the king's business we are about."

The doctor ignored him. His eyebrows rose as he studied her face, then he glanced about at them. "His Majesty ordered you to attack this defenseless female?"

Nobody replied. His hand reached for hers, and they did not stop him.

"Madam?"

Dazed by this unexpected change in her fortune, Margerie did not stop to think. She looked up at him gratefully, setting her hand in his. She came to her feet in response to his pull, then tried to draw back her hand.

His fingers tightened on hers, refusing to let go.

Her startled gaze shot to his face. She found herself staring into dark eyes that met hers intently. There was a shadow in his face that called to her, as though this man understood hurt and despair for he had known them himself. His hair was dark too, curled at his temples, thick locks falling almost to his shoulders.

Master Elton spoke as though they were alone together, his voice deep and rich, stirring her in some unfathomable way. "I must lock up the storage room," he told her, "but then I beg you will permit me to escort you back to your chamber. The hour is late and a lady should not be wandering the palace corridors unaccompanied."

There was a growl of dissent from the watching nobles. Yet to her astonishment none of them challenged the doctor's right to remove her. Margerie gazed round at them. At any moment she feared to be seized again, and this upstart doctor be dismissed with the threat of a whipping.

Slowly she groped after the truth, though it seemed impossible.

These lords were wary of him. Yet how was it that a mere physician could have power over men as influential and highborn as these?

Master Elton was still holding her hand, his strong fingers locked intimately with hers. When she did not reply, he raised his eyebrows, watching her with those dark, intelligent eyes that seemed to know precisely what she was thinking—and feeling.

She found her courage again, and with it her voice. "I…I thank you, sir."

"My lords, I must beg your pardon for interrupting your sport," he said, turning to her attackers. "But this lady seems uncomfortable in your company."

Master Elton drew her out from their silent circle, a look of irony on his face. He bowed to Sir Christopher as the knight shifted to block his way.

"You look well, Sir Christopher. I am glad."

Sir Christopher's mouth tightened, as though that soft emphasis had conveyed some special meaning to him. He glared at the doctor sourly. They were about the same height and build, she realized, though the knight was perhaps a shade taller. For a moment the atmosphere was tense in the narrow space, and she feared for her savior.

Then the knight shrugged and stepped aside, letting them pass.

"You may go on your way, physician, and take this creature with you," Sir Christopher said. His gaze flicked over her with contempt. "No man wants soiled goods anyway. Not even for sport."

Without another word, the physician led her away into the small gloomy chamber from which he had emerged, taking a moment to bar the door behind him in case the king's men changed their minds.

She looked about the room. There was a high table crowded with bottles and physicians' instruments, and a small leather-bound volume lying open beside a candle as though he had been reading before he was disturbed. A doctor's workshop, Margerie thought, glancing at more bottles arranged in a shadowy alcove. She found herself breathing more easily, for she had only narrowly escaped harm.

Glancing at the open page of the book, she saw it was not a doctor's journal with a list of medicaments, as she had at first assumed.

It was poetry. In Latin.

Master Elton turned from the door and fixed her with a hard look. His casual air had dropped away. "Do you have a death wish, madam?"

Margerie flushed angrily. "I beg your pardon?"

The physician looked her up and down assessingly, taking in every detail of her flushed cheeks and unbound mass of red hair, then the fine silk gown, her thin-soled leather pumps showing beneath. The bodice sat tight about her breasts, for she had been a girl and narrower in the chest when she last wore it at court, and she saw his gaze linger on the creamy flesh there.

No doubt he was wondering if she was a courtesan. Perhaps even considering if he could afford her services on a physician's wage. She was used to such unpleasant conversations. But for some reason the thought of this man propositioning her left a bitter taste in her mouth.

"I do not recall seeing you at court before," he commented, "so I must assume your foolishness tonight was the result of inexperience rather than a wanton desire to be ravished by those courtiers."

Her lips tightened at this insult. She wanted to speak her mind, tell him exactly what she thought of his misinterpretation of tonight's events. But she kept silent. This man had just saved her from what would undeniably have been a rape.

He raised dark eyebrows at her silence. "Will you give me your name?"

"Margerie Croft."

His eyes narrowed on her face, suddenly fixed and intent.

Heat entered her cheeks as she realized her name was known to him. She ought not to be surprised. Everyone at court knew of Margerie Croft, the infamous whore who had taken young Wolf to her bed, then run off to France with another nobleman, an infirm youth who had died without marrying her, leaving Margerie to earn enough for her passage back to England—as a whore, it was whispered by some.

Her eyes met his in sudden anger. Yes, her history was infamous, she thought fiercely. But she was no whore. And never had been one. She had never spoken of those days to anyone, allowing the world to slander her as they wished rather than lower herself to some paltry self-defense. She had her pride.

"Mistress Croft," he said softly, "my name is Master Elton. Do you have any idea how dangerous it was to allow yourself to be alone with those men?"

"You think I *allowed* that to happen, Master Elton? I was summoned by King Henry tonight so he could…" She faltered, seeing the look in his eyes. Caution entered her tone as she finished lamely, "So he could speak with me."

"I see." But his voice had grown cold. She could guess what he was thinking. "And afterward?"

"Afterward," she repeated, shuddering as she remembered what had followed her abortive interview with His Majesty, "they cornered me in one of the royal antechambers. I tried to escape, but they were determined to…"

"Make your better acquaintance?" he suggested.

"Punish me." Margerie lifted her gaze to his, meeting it unflinchingly. "I had displeased the king, you see. So they had little fear of reprisals, whatever they might choose to do to me."

"You seem curiously unmoved by that prospect."

"Merely resigned to my fate. Men rape women. It is the way of the world."

Something flickered in that level stare. Contempt? Her temper rose. "Sir?"

Turning to a nearby shelf, the doctor began·to pack away a row of thin-necked bottles into a cloth bag, checking each stopper and label as he did so, his movements careful and precise.

"No doubt you find me impertinent, mistress?"

She could not deny it.

"Forgive me." He glanced over his shoulder at her, his smile thin. "But your story is, you must admit, a little incredible. What was your crime tonight against His Majesty?"

"That is my business."

"Do you remain silent for your own sake or mine? I assure you that I have no intention of becoming embroiled in this affair. But you must know the king's ways, as all the world does. Perhaps if you had taken some respectable female companion with you to His Majesty…"

She glared at him, nettled by the suggestion that she was to blame, and he shrugged, continuing to pack away his bottles.

"I gave you my name, sir," she pointed out. "I am Margerie Croft. Or are you alone at this court in not knowing my reputation?"

"I know your reputation, mistress."

Margerie raised her brows in a delicate question as he turned to face her, but the doctor did not elaborate. His stare moved instead from her face to her breasts, small but made more prominent by the tight silk bodice, then her narrow waist and hips, for her height had kept her figure girlishly slender since childhood.

She felt the touch of his gaze on her body as a physical thing, as though he had stroked her with a long cool finger, and her pulse raced, suddenly wild. Her cheeks began to burn. "You dare to judge me, sir?"

"I have said nothing, madam."

"Your eyes speak for you."

Master Elton came close, still gazing on her body as though imagining how she would look naked. That look made her tremble.

"Do they?"

His voice was curt. She had the impression of tremendous energy held in check, his whole being focused on her in the most disconcerting way. He could not be much older than her, perhaps eight and twenty years of age. Certainly Master Elton was not past thirty. Yet he had the poise and authority of a much older man.

"You are indeed a beautiful woman," Master Elton agreed. "Your form stirs a man to lust, and I am a man like any other. But I am not convinced that men must always act upon their desires, especially when restraint would prove the better course. Man's control over his baser instincts is what separates him from the beasts."

"I thought it was our ability to think that makes us superior to the animal kingdom."

"Oh, not superior." There was a drawl in his voice now, his mouth twisting as the dark gaze lifted to her face. "I cannot allow those men who would have raped you to be superior to a beast in any way."

She was taken aback by his casual insolence toward such powerful men. "They were afraid of you, I think," she said impulsively. "Why?"

He raised his eyebrows. "I saw no fear in them. I am but a doctor. Why should the king's men fear me?"

"I do not know, sir. That is why I asked."

Her height meant they stood as equals, gazing into each other's eyes without speaking. She recalled how her body had responded to the touch of his hand, her heart racing as though in fear for her life, and wondered at it.

Since her girlhood she had been left unmoved by the lustful looks and caresses of men who wished to bed her, and had eventually come to consider herself frigid, a creature without passion. Indeed,

Lord Wolf—then an untitled youth—had written as much to her after she fled their illicit night together, blaming her for not responding to his lovemaking.

You must have ice water in your veins, Margerie Croft, not to have been moved by the heat of my desire.

She had not received that letter for several years, until she had returned from France to her grandfather's home. Even now though, she felt again the shame that had risen in her at Wolf's insults.

To be passionless, to be cold at heart… These were crimes against a woman's nature, and she knew it. Yet the merest touch of Master Elton's hand had left her shocked and unsettled. How was this doctor so different from the other men who had tried to seduce her?

She shivered, her gaze dropping.

It was painful to meet those intelligent eyes and guess what Master Elton must be thinking. Her infamous seduction all those years ago meant she was too well known as a wanton for him to hold any other view of her character. And if she continued to look so boldly at this man, he would think she wished to warm his bed tonight, instead of the king's.

"You asked to escort me back to my chamber," she said coolly. "Will you hold to that promise, sir?"

"I have to take these medicaments back to my rooms. I will walk with you to your chamber first."

"Are these not your quarters?"

"No, I lodge in one of the towers. The physicians only use this room when we are summoned to attend His Majesty, as we were earlier tonight."

That surprised her. "You attended the king tonight?"

"Yes."

"For what purpose?"

"I cannot discuss it with you, mistress. I am bound by a sacred oath to keep such matters secret." Master Elton closed his book of Latin poetry, marking the page with a strip of black silk, and placed it in the cloth bag with his medicaments. Then he took up his bag, and gestured her to the door. "It's late, and the courtiers who attacked you should have gone by now. Shall we go?"

She hesitated, studying her rescuer in a moment of indecision. His features were a shade too strong to be classically attractive, his nose aquiline, his mouth straight and unrelenting, like the hard jut of his chin. His dark hair curled under the physician's cap, not cut short like most courtiers' but long enough to brush his broad shoulders. She thought it gave him a very European look, dangerously unconventional. His eyes were impenetrably dark too, deep-set and heavy-lidded, watching her with a hint of the same restless interest she felt for him.

She ought not to find such a man pleasing to look upon. Yet she could not seem to stop staring… There was a sensuality about him that made her heart beat faster, her body aware of his in a way she had never been with any man before. Indeed, she could not help wondering what it would feel like to lie beneath that lean body, to have his mouth on hers, to accept him into her body as she had once accepted Wolf.

A night in Master Elton's bed would be very different from those abortive hours she had spent with Wolf. For she had taken Wolf to her bed on the orders of her mother, whose obsession with her advancement at court had known no limits, and not because she felt any desire for the nobleman.

With Master Elton though, it would be hard to say no if the doctor wished to take his pleasure with her. And this time she would have no virginity to lose.

"Yes," she managed, belatedly realizing that he was still waiting for her response. "Forgive me."

"Mistress Croft, you have done nothing that needs to be forgiven," Master Elton murmured, a faint smile on his lips as he bent to blow out the candle. "The same may not be true for the rest of us, however."

Her breath caught as the room was plunged into smoking, velvety darkness. And she was glad he could not see her face. For his smile had sent a jolt of heat to her belly and thighs, her whole body suddenly alight with desire.

The darkness brought illumination. He wanted her. And she wanted him. That was what she was feeling.

Lust.

Groping her way into the torchlit corridor afterward, Margerie did not dare look at him again, caught in the grip of some sexual urge so strong she was left breathless and trembling, shocked by the visceral nature of her response.

Don't show him how you feel, she told herself sternly. He was a man, and she was alone with him. Had she no sense of self-preservation whatsoever?

———

That night, lying in bed in the dark, cramped quarters she shared with the other women of the royal wardrobe, Margerie felt again that sweet, languorous heat burning in her body and secretly wished she had taken advantage of the darkness.

She could have lived up to her reputation for once, grasped the doctor's shoulders and pressed her mouth wantonly against his. Something told her Master Elton would not have pushed her away.

About the Author

Elizabeth Moss was born into a literary family in Essex, and currently lives in the southwest of England with her husband and young family. She also writes commercial fiction as Victoria Lamb and Beth Good. For more information about her, visit her blog at www.elizabethmossfiction.com.